Everyone's basking in Rachel [barcode: KT-491-558]

'Transporting'
SUNDAY TIMES

'Intoxicating. I loved this book!'
SANTA MONTEFIORE

'Should be on everyone's summer reading list'
CLARE MACKINTOSH

'Hugely enjoyable escapism.
I enjoyed it ENORMOUSLY'
MARIAN KEYES

'Glamorous and beautifully written'
DAILY MAIL

'Filled with excitement and danger'
STYLIST

'An atmospheric page-turner'
DAILY MIRROR

'Deliciously intoxicating'
HEAT

'Thrilling, captivating'
DAILY EXPRESS
★★★★★

www.penguin.co.uk

'An exquisite tale of love and dark secrets'
LISA JEWELL

'Hidden secrets, dazzling sunshine. This book is a total joy'
LUCY DAWSON

'Will have you yearning for a gin fizz'
KATE RIORDAN

'Rhys writes like an exotic dream'
LIZ NUGENT

'Completely compelling and atmospheric'
JANE FALLON

'A natural successor to Patricia Highsmith'
SARRA MANNING

'A world of glamour, uncertainty and intrigue. It's a gem'
COLETTE MCBETH

'A glorious mix of old-school glamour and a labyrinthine plot full of class war, politics and sexual tension'
VERONICA HENRY

'Sumptuous'
AMANDA JENNINGS

Rachel Rhys is the pen-name of the much-loved psychological suspense author Tammy Cohen. Her first novel as Rachel Rhys was the acclaimed, bestselling *Dangerous Crossing*, a Richard and Judy pick, followed by the bestselling *A Fatal Inheritance*. Her atmospheric new novel is set in the exotic city of Havana on the cusp of revolution, where a young Englishwoman finds scandal, romance and adventure. Rachel Rhys lives in London with her family. You can chat with her here:

www.tammycohen.co.uk
Facebook: MsTamarCohen
Twitter: @MsTamarCohen
Instagram: tammycohenwriter

Also by Rachel Rhys

Dangerous Crossing
A Fatal Inheritance

Island of Secrets

Rachel Rhys

BLACK SWAN

TRANSWORLD PUBLISHERS
61–63 Uxbridge Road, London W5 5SA
www.penguin.co.uk

Transworld is part of the Penguin Random House group of companies
whose addresses can be found at global.penguinrandomhouse.com

First published in Great Britain in 2020 by Black Swan
an imprint of Transworld Publishers

A CIP catalogue record for this book
is available from the British Library.

ISBN
9781784164898

Typeset in 11.52/14.41pt Adobe Garamond by Jouve (UK), Milton Keynes.
Printed and bound in Great Britain by Clays Ltd, Elcograf S.p.A.

Penguin Random House is committed to a sustainable
future for our business, our readers and our planet. This book
is made from Forest Stewardship Council® certified paper.

1 3 5 7 9 10 8 6 4 2

For Roma 'Still Got It' Cartwright

'I prefer drawing to talking. Drawing is faster, and leaves less room for lies.'

– Charles-Édouard Jeanneret-Gris,
aka. Le Corbusier

'Havana has been a fascinating city, quite the most vicious I have ever been in.'

– Graham Greene, letter 1954

Do you believe in God, Cyp? I'm quite certain that you don't as you don't believe in much of anything. But if you do, even just a little bit, please pray for me. I am so very far from home.

– Aunt Sap

Prologue

IT WAS A still, soupy morning, the day Antonio Manuel fished Jean Summers's body out of the water.

He shouldn't even have been there. That's what he'd tell people that day and for the rest of his life, whenever he was called upon to tell the story – which he would be a lot.

He ought to have been at home in bed, running his hand along the curve of his wife's hip under her filmy Saturday-night nightdress, on the only day of the week when he got to lie in past 6.30 a.m. But then Theresa had started on about needing more honesty in their relationship, which she had been doing ever since the crazy woman next door started up a Women's Book Group, which was just an excuse, if you asked him, for them all to drink mint juleps and bitch about their husbands.

No, not *honesty*. What did she call it? *Authenticity*. That was it.

She started up again about *authenticity* until he'd about had enough. 'I work my guts out all week, and then I gotta come home and work some more, trying to figure out what it is you want me to say. I love you. We're happy, or happy enough, ain't that so? So what is there to talk about?'

In the end he'd got into a funk and slammed out of the bedroom, thumping down the stairs to make good and sure she'd got the message of how little he appreciated being harangued like that in his own home. He banged the front door extra hard to further emphasise the unfairness of it all.

If Antonio had known then how many photos would be taken of him that day, or how widely they'd be circulated, or for how many years into the future, he might well have gone back upstairs and chosen his clothes more carefully. As it was, he had on the old pair of shorts he wore around the house because he could tie them so the waistband was good and loose and didn't dig into his burgeoning stomach, and a T-shirt with a tear under the arm that Theresa kept threatening to burn.

Where else could he go at six forty-five on a Sunday morning other than down to the jetty at the end of the track, on either side of which was clumped the sleepy town of Port Jethro, Texas, and make his way to where his old boat was tied to the second post from the end?

Half an hour later, he'd stopped the motor and was sitting back in his boat with his line trailing in the tranquil water. He was still feeling aggrieved, but the urgency of his anger had dissipated. He'd fixed the basket on Theresa's bicycle just the week before, without her even mentioning that it had a great big hole in it. If that wasn't *authentic*, he'd like to know what was.

So absorbed was he in his thoughts, he wasn't looking at the water, and it wasn't until his line snagged and the rod bowed dangerously that he realised there was anything amiss.

4

Afterwards, people would ask him whether he knew straight away it was a body. They always craned just that little bit forward when he got to this part, not wanting to miss a thing, and after a while Antonio no longer got that dry-mouthed, shaky feeling when he talked about it.

Even so, no matter how old he got (and he lived to see his fifth great-grandchild born) and no matter how many private sorrows and tragedies (and there were many), the image of Jean's corpse floating in the sea, yellow hair streaming, in a green dress with the skirt rucked up around her thighs, remained seared across his memory.

The sea does things to a body. By the time Antonio had managed to reel in the corpse close enough to tie it to the boat using the cord from his own shorts looped loosely around a swollen wrist, he had just about got his own stomach under control after twice being sick (over the other side of the boat, out of respect). But still he felt hollow and weak, as if he'd just sobered up from the worst hangover of his life.

He knew who she was, of course. Everyone in these parts knew about Jean Summers going missing off Hugh Hardman's yacht just a few miles away. Everyone had their own theories. About the Hardman family. About what happened that night. The papers had been full of nothing else for days, just endless photographs of Jean taken from her films or from magazines. That dazzling smile, those exaggerated curves, the sequinned gowns, the white fur stoles, the diamonds, the fairy-tale house built just for her.

There would be times in the future when Antonio would regret having found the body, when he'd wish that just for a day or two, an hour even, he could be known for something else he'd done.

But now he felt descending upon him a great weight of responsibility. To do right by this woman. To bring her safely home. Which is why he made sure before setting off that her dress was pulled down, that her head was safely protected from banging against the wooden hull of the boat, the foam gently wiped from her mouth with the hem of his shirt. No matter who she had been in life, in death she became his most precious cargo.

Only when he was satisfied that she was comfortable did he slowly turn his boat and set a course back for the jetty, carving a straight, dignified path through the smooth, cloudy water, man and woman side by side, keeping each other company as the day ripened around them, while on the shore the people of Port Jethro awoke and made their Sunday-morning pancakes and coffee and sucked in their teeth when they saw the state of the weather outside, the thick heat of it, and life went on.

1

SHE CLAMPS HER thighs together. Shifts her legs fractionally to the side. Can they see up her skirt? It is tight enough that it ought to move with her body – it certainly makes walking awkward enough, forcing her to take small, hobbling steps like a Japanese geisha – but she is just so high up here on this damned stool. Her own foolish fault for thinking there would be something glamorous about working in an architectural company, not realising that every time she was called out of the typing pool to take dictation or, as now, keep a record of the draftsmen's morning meeting, she'd be perched up here on public display. With that sea of men staring at her, pale moon faces growing out of grey suits like a field of tall mushrooms, eyes darting behind horn-rimmed spectacles. So many of them with poor eyesight.

'That'll do for now, Miss Bailey.'

Mr Sturrock has elegant hands like a pianist and most of the girls in the typing pool are soft on him. But Iris doesn't like his smell. Sweet and cloying, as if he has washed every inch of himself in perfumed soap. As if he is hiding something.

For a moment after she is dismissed she remains on her stool, trying to work out the logistics of her dismount. Eventually she wriggles off, a movement made more difficult by the elastic roll-on girdle she wears beneath her clothes, and walks to the door, cheeks burning, clutching her notebook to her chest and only too conscious of the eyes on her back – well, all right, on her bottom. *Click clack.* How she hates the sound her heels make on the polished parquet floor in the uncomfortable blue shoes that crush her toes together so that when she takes them off in the evening they are folded one over the other like a litter of sleeping puppies. She looks at the shoes the draftsmen wear, leather brogues with wide, flat soles – and imagines walking around in them, planting one foot solidly in front of the other, standing firm on the ground. How would that change a person's confidence and sense of place in the world?

Back in the typing pool, she resumes her seat. She is in the third row, second desk from the end. As she passes behind Joyce's desk, her friend twists her head around and Iris makes a face, rolling her eyes.

'Is there something the matter, Miss Bailey?'

Oh, isn't it just typical of her rotten luck that the Wicked Witch of the North should happen to look up right at that very moment?

'No, Mrs Latham. Sorry. Just had something in my eye.'

The older woman glares at Iris from her desk at the front of the room where she oversees the girls in the typing pool and flaps her hand, motioning for Iris to take her seat. And now her card will be marked *again*. It is all too tedious for words.

Iris thinks about the old art-school gang – Shirley, Violet, Eric, Jack – and imagines them giggling together in the back row of a lecture on the French Impressionists, or else standing behind easels, mixing up colours on their palettes to capture the exact shade of green of the apples in the bowl on the tablecloth. The injustice of being stuck here while they carry on without her makes her want to scream. 'I can't believe your parents could be so cruel,' Violet had said. 'You're the most talented of the lot of us. I don't even want to go on if you're not here.' And yet she had gone on, Iris couldn't help noticing, and seemed to be doing perfectly well, thank you very much.

The keys of the typewriters around her clatter as Iris violently winds a fresh piece of paper into her own machine and begins typing up the morning's notes from the squiggles of shorthand on her pad.

Measurements and dimensions and materials and regulations. Before Iris took the job, she'd imagined offices buzzing with creativity, dashing young men with pencils tucked behind their ears bent over drawings of sleek villas, all glass and cedarwood, or ultra-modern office blocks soaring into the sky. This is the 1950s, a new golden age of architecture, they are always being told. There is Goldfinger with his concrete tower, and the Royal Festival Hall, still controversial six years after opening, and over in France, Le Corbusier's uncompromising modernist blocks. But at Underwood & Sturrock, there are only notes about thermal insulation and drainage systems.

What she wouldn't give to be back at Hornsey School of Arts, sitting in her little corner by the radiator with the sun streaming in and a sketchpad in front of her. The pencil between her fingers just thrumming with all the worlds it contains in its sharpened lead.

Clack, clack, clack go Iris's fingers over the keys. Those months at secretarial college have trained her well. Next to her, Pamela stops abruptly. Leans forward to study the page currently looped around the rollers of her typewriter. Sighs. Reaches for the circular typewriter eraser. Now she will have to take the page out and erase the mistake on each of the four copies underneath it, painstakingly layered with carbon paper, then feed the stack back in and try to realign the paper to exactly the right position. It's never completely accurate. Mrs Latham looks up and frowns. Her hair is set so firmly that when she moves her head all her tight, mean curls move as one, solid as a helmet.

Iris needs to go to the toilet, but the clock above the door informs her it will not be her lavatory slot for another forty-five minutes. Her thoughts drift back to the ball last weekend, remembering how her fingers flew across the sketch paper as if of their own accord. The host's pink cheeks when he slipped her an extra five shillings at the end of the evening: 'You were the hit of the night'. That rush she'd had, feeling like, for once, she was doing what she was meant to do.

At 2.45 p.m. Mrs Latham calls Iris to approach her desk. 'Mr Underwood needs a letter doing urgently. He asked for the new girl. He might wish to ask you a few questions about yourself, but you will keep your answers brief, Miss Bailey. You are not paid to chat.'

When Iris enters Mr Underwood's office, he doesn't look up from the letter he is reading. She hovers behind his desk. Finally he raises his head, looking annoyed. 'Well, don't just stand there, for goodness' sake.'

He dictates a reply to the letter on the desk, which is curt and, actually, if you asked Iris's opinion, which of course no one ever would, bordering on rude. Still, the act of getting it on to paper seems to mollify him and after Iris has put her pen down he is in more expansive humour.

'Have you settled in, Miss Bailey?'

'Oh yes. Thank you.'

Mr Underwood is older than Mr Sturrock. Mid-forties, Iris guesses, with a square, pink face. On his desk there's a framed photograph of a blonde woman in a felt hat with her arms around two blonde children.

'And you draw, I understand.'

'Pardon?'

Iris is too surprised to moderate her tone and it comes out much louder than she'd intended. Mr Underwood smiles. 'Don't look so shocked, I haven't been spying on you. I was at the centenary party at your secretarial college. We have strong links with them, as I'm sure you know – they have sent us many excellent typists over the years. Mrs Latham herself was one of them.'

This is news to Iris.

'I was exceedingly disappointed not to get one of your portraits, but then you were so inundated with requests.'

'Yes,' says Iris faintly. 'People did seem to quite like it.'

The truth was, she had been mobbed. It had seemed like such a ridiculous idea at first, when she was summoned in June to see the principal of Bradfield Park Secretarial College: 'Finally, we have found a use for your endless scribblings.' On every other occasion she'd sat in the principal's office there had been, displayed on the desk in front of her, a selection of sketches that she'd made in various classrooms and meeting rooms when she ought to have been practising shorthand or typing columns of numbers or whatever other task she'd actually been set. Half the time she hadn't even been aware she was doing it but had found her eyes snagged on the way so and so was bent over their work, or such and such was leaning back with their pen between their teeth, and had been surprised to look down a few moments later and find a fully formed likeness there on the page. But now the desk was clear and here was the principal, for once smiling, and inviting her to be one of the star turns at the College's upcoming centenary party, circulating amongst guests, dashing off portraits to hand out as party favours.

'Tell me, Miss Bailey,' says Mr Underwood, 'did you have any official training for that, or are you one of those self-taught geniuses? Those Picasso types?'

Iris swallows the urge to detail to her boss the great Spanish artist's rigorous formal training in classical art from the age of thirteen.

'I did a year's foundation course at art school.' But my parents wouldn't let me stay on to do a degree. Iris doesn't say it. Realises it would carry little weight.

Now Mr Underwood wants to know if she's still drawing, as if it were a fad rather than something that flows through one's veins like blood. Then she realises he means for money.

'I did sketch at a few weddings over the summer. And that led to some engagements at private parties. Last weekend, Rupert Cunningham, the writer, held a masked ball at his country estate in Wiltshire and asked me to draw there.'

'Well, you know I admire that immensely,' says Mr Underwood, by now fully warmed up and clearly judging her to have been allowed quite enough time now to talk about herself. 'It's so important for a woman to have an interest. I am always suggesting my wife take up something. Tennis or bridge. This is 1957, not the Victorian era. The way I see it, marriage should be an equal partnership. If a man goes out to work, the woman ought also to have something she does for herself out of the house, even just a small thing, so she has something to talk to him about at the end of the day. Like your drawing.'

Iris can't decide whether it's the reduction of her art to a little hobby or the implied criticism of the blonde, felt-hatted Mrs Underwood that makes her feel more deflated. Either way, she is relieved when a sharp knock at the door saves her from having to reply.

Mr Sturrock comes striding in, bringing with him his over-sweet smell. He walks past Iris with a curt nod and hands his partner a folded piece of paper. 'Here's that report you wanted to see. The urgent one.' He nods again on his way out.

Mr Underwood opens the paper and chuckles.

'An eight,' he says, smiling at her as if it ought to mean something.

'An eight?' Iris repeats.

'Oh, don't look so worried, Miss Bailey. It's only a bit of fun. We do it with all the new girls. A bit of a tally around the office and come up with a score. Of course, I don't always share the results with the young ladies concerned, for obvious reasons, but an eight is nothing to be ashamed of.' He catches her eye and, misconstruing her expression, adds, 'And if you smiled a little more, I expect you'd be a nine.'

Outrage fizzes in the pit of Iris's stomach, though whether

13

this is down to the fact of being judged in this way or of only getting an eight she cannot say.

'I expect you have a young man,' Mr Underwood goes on, fixing her with his bloodshot eyes. 'A pretty girl like you.'

'Yes, there is someone.'

Iris tries to ignore the way her heart grows heavy at the thought of Peter.

After work, she and Joyce treat themselves to a coffee at the Moka Bar on Frith Street. 'You know, the worst thing about it was, I actually thanked him,' says Iris, leaning on the Formica counter. She doesn't tell Joyce that a little, shameful part of her had felt proud of that eight and had leapt at that nine, dangled in front of her like a carrot.

'It's happened to a few of the other girls,' says Joyce. 'Not to me, though.'

Iris takes a sip of her lukewarm cappuccino so she doesn't need to meet Joyce's eyes, because the thing that stands between them – which is also the thing neither of them would ever say – is that Joyce, with her round, homely face and her pink cat's-eye glasses and her solid figure will not score highly with the men in the office, despite the fact that she is kind and smart and has read all the Russian classics, even *War and Peace*.

The day has left Iris with a bad taste in her mouth, and she travels home to Hemel Hempstead in a fug of dissatisfaction and pipe smoke, courtesy of the man sitting opposite her in the train carriage. Walking home from the station, her sense of being at odds with the world only increases. Is this really to be her future? *Clack-clacking* away at Underwood &

Sturrock until she gets married. And then what? A life like her mother's? Washing on Monday, pillowcases and stockings draped over clothes horses and the whole house smelling of damp and soap powder; shopping every day, the same shops in the same order – baker's, greengrocer's, butcher's – then back home to cook dinner, ready in time for her husband when he comes home from work.

Iris lives with her parents in a semi-detached house in a tree-lined street where the air is thick with inertia. When she steps through the door of number fifty-one, there is a sense of claustrophobia, as if the house is shrinking around her bones, and her nostrils fill with the smell of roasting fat. Even though meat rationing finished – finally – three years ago, supplies are still a long way from what they were, so one is supposed to be happy with joints the size of cricket balls, all fat and gristle.

'Is that you, Iris darling?' her mother calls from the kitchen.

Hanging up her scarf, Iris makes a face at the coat-stand, trying to judge by her tone what state her mother is in. She's always worse later in the day, when there's a thick pane of glass separating her from the world.

'There's a letter for you there,' her mother adds.

Iris glances at the table by the front door on which her mother has neatly stacked the day's post, ready for her father's return.

For a second, Iris holds the envelope in her hand, savouring the weight of the thick, luxurious paper, before turning it over and sliding a fingernail under the flap. The letter is folded into three, and after she has opened it up, Iris scans the typewritten text impatiently, not really taking in what is being said, aware only of a building conviction that her life is about to change. The word *Havana* leaps out at her, followed by the word *wedding*, but her eyes are drawn to the bottom of the page.

Nell Hardman, reads the exuberantly looped violet signature. And underneath it in brackets *(please pretty please say you will!)*.

2

IT HITS HER the second she exits the plane. A solid wall of damp heat that sticks Iris's clothes to her skin.

Rancho-Boyeros airport is a long, low-slung building and Iris is thrilled by the sight of palm trees shimmering through a heat haze in the distance as she crosses the tarmac. Already the regimented line of oaks and elms that border the little park she crosses on her way to Hemel Hempstead station seems like a long-distant dream. She had left London the day before – or the one before that. It is all such a blur. There was that first flight to Amsterdam, before the longer one to Montreal, her heart thundering in her chest like a runaway horse as the plane tilted up from the runway. While the impossibly glamorous air hostesses patrolled the aisles, topping up glasses of wine and Scotch and lighting cigarettes, Iris had wrestled with remorse for her impatience when saying goodbye to her parents and Peter, excitement at leaving leading her to skate over the way her mother's left hand, tiny in its white glove, fluttered at her throat, even while her right clutched tight to the handbag Iris knew would contain the little bottle of Equanil she never went anywhere without, and how the groove in the centre of her father's forehead, down which, when she was younger, he would let her roll a shilling, appeared horribly pronounced in the sickly light of the airport terminal. Peter had pulled her roughly aside. 'Say you'll always be my girl,' he'd whispered. 'Let go, that hurts,' she'd said, trying to pull away, but Peter's fingers were digging into the soft skin of her inner wrist. 'Not until I hear you say it.' His face had darkened and, though Iris tried to tell herself it was romantic that he felt so strongly, she found his intensity unnerving. 'I'll always be your girl,' she'd repeated woodenly.

MISS IRIS

The sign is held by a young man wearing a smart cap and a dark uniform, though when Iris gets closer she notices that his shoes, for all they are polished to a dazzling shine, are worn at the heel. He straightens when she approaches, his eyes sliding down and up her like a slow-moving elevator. But when he speaks, he is deferential enough.

'Miss Iris?' *Meeseerees.* 'I am Raúl. You come with me.'

The car is black, with a rounded bonnet that rises up like the hump of a whale. Despite her crumpled green dress and her hair, which is already wilting in the heat, making a mockery of the sleepless night she endured before leaving England with sixteen small, tight rollers jabbing into her skull, Iris is conscious of Raúl's unabashedly appreciative gaze as he holds the door open. As she settles herself into the back seat, there is a moment when anxiety about being here on her own, so far from home, gets the better of her and she wonders if this might be the last time she is seen alive, even catches the eye of a passing schoolgirl in the hope she might imprint her face on the girl's memory.

On the move, Iris starts to unwind her window, but Raúl waggles his finger, pointing to a control on the walnut dashboard. And soon, blissfully cool air is blowing through the car. It is Iris's first experience of air conditioning and instantly she loves it, as the sweat dries on her skin and actual goosebumps rise up on her arms. She stares through the window. The city begins almost as the airport ends, the roads wider than back home, teeming with giant cars like the one she is in right now but in bright jewel colours – blue and red and green and orange. Here are gleaming, palm-shaded pathways in between the lanes of traffic, along which smartly dressed women push prams out of the harsh glare of the sun, and a railway running parallel to the road. There are grand stone buildings with flights of steps leading to pil-lared porticos, and in the distance tall buildings and cranes strung across the horizon. True, she spots a couple of matted-haired men dressed in little more than rags, with that telltale blank stare of the hopeless poor, and once she glimpses, off down a side street pitted with potholes and running with muddy water, a jumble of what look like crude timber shacks. But mostly her impression is of a smart metropolis with its own heartbeat, worlds away from the one she has left behind.

How has she arrived here? It seems obvious to her now, in her exhausted state, that a mistake has been made. This is not, as her father has been at pains to point out, what people like them do. Now, when she tries to think of how she met Nell Hardman, it seems so unlikely, as if she must have dreamt it.

*

She'd been booked for a party at the last minute, having had the stroke of genius to print some business cards and distribute them at a previous event. All she had was an address in Knightsbridge and a name, Mr Draper, and the theme of the party: knights and nymphs. Posh girls glee-fully dispensed with their corsets in order to swathe themselves in the sheerest of materials, artfully wrapped to emphasise bosoms and waists, leaving creamy shoulders exposed. Arthur Draper was the son of a financier, a fey young man just down from Cambridge wearing a foppish interpretation of a knight's costume, all voluminous bell sleeves and thigh-high boots. He fancied himself some sort of theatre impresario, though as far as Iris could gather, he was merely using Daddy's money to fund some sort of comedy act featuring his university chums.

All night they had come, the gay young things of the upper classes, loudly eschewing convention while at the same time covertly sizing up each other's status, the girls with their extravagantly curled hair and English-rose faces, the boys with their freckles and trust funds. One inter-changeable with the next, until . . .

'Christ, you're sickeningly good, aren't you? The only thing I know how to draw is a cheque.'

The accent was American. Southern, Iris guessed. Whirl-ing around, she found herself staring directly into a pronounced cleavage attached to a young woman slightly older than herself with dyed platinum-blonde hair and dar-ing flame-red lips which opened when she smiled to reveal an astonishing amount of healthy pink gum. She, too, was wearing a length of material arranged around the curves of her body, but unlike the other nymphs, whose makeshift gowns trailed romantically on the floor, this one stopped at the top of her thighs, showing off her strong, tanned legs and the towering red-and-white shoes that made her unnaturally tall.

'I'm Nell,' said the woman, who had been leaning over Iris's shoulder to admire her sketch of a Surrey debutante. 'Nell Hardman. I'm in England on vacation, staying with an old friend of Pop's.'

Iris smiled. 'No relation of the famous Hugh Hardman, I assume?'

She'd meant it as a joke, not really expecting this woman to claim any connection to the notorious director whose film-star wife had died mysteriously during a cruise on the family yacht some years before. But Nell had nodded and held out her hands, palms up, in supplication.

'Daughter – but please don't judge me. Mama was Pop's first wife. Childhood sweetheart. 'Course, she was straight outta the door once Jean Summers came along. Oh, don't look so downcast. She got over it a long time ago, and now Mama and Pops are quite disgustingly friendly. In fact, they cooked up this trip for me between them. They said it was so I could pick up some culture, but that's just Mama code for bagging myself an aristocratic husband, preferably a duke.'

'And how have you got on?'

Nell made a face. 'Number of aristocratic beaux: zero. I think your men are a little afraid of me.'

Iris thought that was probably true, though she didn't say so.

'And your women think I'm a whore.'

Nell emitted a sound from the back of her throat that was more bark than laugh.

'I've been watching you all night. I'm *obsessed* with you. You have this way of talking to people, getting them to relax their guard and then – *bam!* – you swoop in for the picture. It's really quite something.'

'I wouldn't exactly say . . .'

'You would be such a hit in the States. Oh my word. I am not going to *rest* until I find a way of bringing you over.'

There had been something about Nell that struck a chord with Iris, a sense that, in different circumstances, they might even be friends. And then had come the letter with the violet signature. Nell's father was getting married again – Iris had thrilled at the sophistication of that insouciant *again*, as if marriages were as predictable in their comings and goings as seasons. It was to be a no-expenses-spared wedding at the Havana mansion belonging to his great friend, the businessman Bruce Bonini. Nell had *pounced* on the chance of getting Iris to come out – and when the bride's family had heard about the portraitist she'd met in England who was the very latest thing at society functions, that had quite sealed the deal. In the hallway of her parents' house, one arm out of her coat, Iris had read the letter again and again. That name, Hugh Hardman, so familiar from a thousand newspaper headlines, jumping out at her in that narrow space with its heavy, bevelled glass mirror hanging from the picture rail reflecting back her shocked face.

In the back of the car, Iris stifles a yawn. Despite her exhaustion and her misgivings, she finds her soul stirred by the brilliance of the sky, which is the kind of blue you see only on picture postcards, that unreal, Technicolor blue. Once again, the sheer unlikeliness of her surroundings hits her.

She is not in her narrow, lumpy childhood bed in Hemel Hempstead. She is not taking dictation or listening to Peter detailing the concept behind his latest *piece*, which is the word he uses for the numerous abstract canvases he's been producing in recent months. Instead, here are enormous black birds circling overhead, their wings vast and fluted against the sky, and men with skin darker than their boot polish cleaning shoes on street corners. Here is sun reflecting off the polished stone path in the centre of the highway and a horse pulling a cart in which an old woman in a hat sits holding a caged bird. Here is a world in which nothing is familiar and everything is yet to be discovered. Up ahead, the tall buildings have grown bigger and grander as they've drawn closer and the streets teem with people and vehicles. Music floats down from balconies and through the windows of bars, left open to the air. The rhythm of it is different to what she is used to. Fast and unpredictable. The car passes a street vendor selling tomatoes and bananas and . . . can those be fresh pineapples? Iris gazes in wonder.

She tries to imagine what Peter would make of it all but cannot picture him here. It's hard now to remember how impossibly flattered she'd been when he'd first singled her out – two years ahead and easily the most handsome boy in college – and how she'd loved to walk out of lectures to find him waiting for her, with his hair quiffed in the front and a cigarette behind his ear. And if Peter dominated their conversations – well, that was only natural; after all, he was older and more knowledgeable. They discussed their dreams for the future. Well, mostly Peter's dreams, really. He was going to get a studio that he could sleep in also and make a new kind of art to reflect what he called the growing disaffection of post-war youth. Iris could just imagine it. Peter with his own place and she with hers, the two of them meeting in the evenings to compare the work they'd done during the day. The future was exhilarating, and her parents' initial disapproval only added an extra frisson of excitement. Though they hadn't yet met him, the fact that Peter was doing a three-year art degree was enough in itself to convince them of his unsuitability as a boyfriend.

But after a few months the doubts had crept in. Peter had a way of talking over her when they were in company or, when alone, waiting until she finished speaking and then launching into something so completely unrelated to what she'd said it was clear he hadn't been listening at all. And though he played lip service to the cause of female emancipation, often holding court in the cafeteria, espousing his progressive theories about equality for everyone – women, coloureds, Jews – in private he was put out when Iris made plans without consulting him, regaling her with reasons why her choice of action was entirely the wrong thing. If she told him she was going out with Violet or Shirley or, God forbid, Jack and Eric, he would come up with a last-minute proposition of his own and sulk if she refused to change her plans.

She'd made the momentous decision early on that she would let Peter have sex with her – that's how the girls all referred to it, as if it was something one had done to one. In this she had been guided by Shirley, who had asked her how she would feel if she died tomorrow without having 'done it' and then marched her off to the Marie Stopes clinic, where Iris borrowed Shirley's ring and pretended to be married then emerged some time later with a fearsome-looking rubber thing in a case. This, apparently, was a Dutch cap, which instantly put Iris in mind of a bonnet – not terribly good for getting one in a passionate mood. She'd thought Peter would be delighted, but instead he'd seemed quite taken aback when she shyly told him that she was ready to go all the way. One moment he'd been kissing her on his parents' narrow bed while they were visiting his grandmother in Sidcup for the day, hands roaming insistently; the next it was as if someone had taken a pin and let all the ardour out. They had done what they set out to do – or at least she assumed they had, it had certainly been sore enough – but there had seemed very little enjoyment in it. Peter had lain stiffly on top of her, making small, jerky movements, his head rigid, staring ahead of him as if unable to tear his eyes from the silver-framed photograph of his parents' wedding, his mother in a white cloche hat, which, Iris couldn't help thinking, ought to have been somewhat offputting. Then all of a sudden he'd made a sound – the first one since the whole thing started – that was like he'd been thumped in the back in order to forcibly eject something from his windpipe. And it was over. 'You'll enjoy it more the next time,' he'd assured her afterwards. But the two subsequent occasions had followed the same rather underwhelming pattern, though she'd pretended to like it so as not to hurt his feelings.

Then, when she finally gave in to her parents' nagging and brought Peter home to meet them, she had seen a side of him that threw her completely. For a start, he'd arrived on the doorstep wearing a suit instead of his usual leather jacket and baggy tweeds, with his hair flattened and combed. Iris hardly recognised him. Though his features were the same as they always had been, he appeared plain. Not handsome at all. Then he'd done everything he could to toady up to Iris's parents. Laughing at all her dad's jokes, never missing an opportunity to call him 'sir'. And when her mum, her eyes tellingly glassy, had asked him about his plans for the future, he'd talked animatedly about getting a job in an advertising firm, going into an office every day to design ways to help sell soap powder and denture cream.

When she'd brought it up the next day in college, he'd acted wounded. 'I thought you'd be pleased I made an effort with your parents,' he'd said. 'I told them what they wanted to hear. Anyway, you should have more patience with your mother after everything she's been through.'

Iris had ended up apologising, as she always seemed to be doing, and thanking him. But now she'd seen how convincing he was at acting conventional, she couldn't rid herself of the suspicion that perhaps that's who he really was.

Still, at art school he cut the same dashing figure as ever and her friends kept telling her how lucky she was and, like most young people still finding their way, Iris placed rather more faith in her friends' opinions than in her own. Plus, she reminded herself now, it was largely down to Peter that she made it to Cuba at all.

Her parents had been implacable in their opposition to the trip. First, they'd tried reasoning – it was too far, too dangerous, too much of an unknown quantity. If she took holiday leave from work so soon after starting, she would lose her job. Peter could hardly be expected to put up with her going off who knows where with who knows whom. The reasoning had soon given way to stark warnings. She would be kidnapped, sold, married off against her will.

Finally had come the threats. If she accepted this absurd, dangerous offer, going back on the very generous agreement they'd made that she could have her year at art school as long as she then settled into secretarial work, she could expect no more support from them.

'This just isn't what people like us do,' her father had said. 'People like us don't hop on aeroplanes to Havana or hobnob with film directors and Hollywood actresses.' And it was that more than anything, the lumping in of Iris with her parents, the expectation that she would want the life they had, that had hardened her resolve to seize this chance with both hands.

This impasse had stretched on for five long days until Peter, of all people, had stepped in to breach the divide. It had happened when he came for tea.

'I hope you're here to talk some sense into her,' her mother had said, furtively untying her apron and bundling it into a drawer in the kitchen and fumbling in her handbag for another Equanil.

Her father shook Peter's hand. 'Always a pleasure to see you, young man.'

Iris didn't know what was wrong with her. She ought to have been happy to see how well her parents got on with her boyfriend, but instead she felt on edge. While Peter drank Scotch with Iris's father in the front room and opined solemnly on the performance of the newish prime minister Macmillan, Iris once again broached the subject of Havana with her mother. They were standing side by side in the kitchen, preparing a light supper of poached salmon and boiled potatoes.

'No.' Her mother held up her hand in a cease-and-desist

gesture. 'I will not hear any more. Your father and I have told you how we feel about this. You are nearly twenty-one years old. It's time you realised life isn't about doing what you want all the time. It's about duty and sacrifice. When I think of what my brother and sister would have given to have what you have – a good job, someone decent to step out with. A secure future.'

Iris knows she has lost the argument whenever her mother brings up her two older siblings, who died in the Great War, one at the Front, the other just a few months later from Spanish influenza in the outbreak of 1918. Iris's mother, the youngest by a long way and doted on by the other two, had almost overnight become an only child to parents who were half eviscerated from grief. Who could have imagined that, twenty years later, history would repeat itself so cruelly?

Over dinner Iris tried again. 'I just feel,' she said, as the piece of salmon she had speared on the end of her fork slowly flaked off on to the plate, 'that this is the kind of opportunity that comes along once in a lifetime and I ought to grasp it with both hands. And Peter agrees with me.'

Three pairs of eyes swivelled toward Peter. 'Well, I wouldn't go so far as agree,' said Peter slowly. 'It seems a dashed long way, and we have no idea what kind of people they are.' He caught Iris's eye and paused. 'However, Iris wants to go, and I think it's important she has this opportunity. A woman ought to have an adventure or two before she settles down.'

A stillness came over the table then, Iris's mother frozen in the act of raising a glass of water to her lips using both her hands, one steadying the other. Her father coughed just once, as if discreetly dislodging something from his throat.

Iris's mouth felt horribly dry and she had an urge to say something – anything – to change the subject, but before she could speak Peter turned to her, and she knew from the expression on his face that she did not want to hear whatever he was about to say.

'What I think is, Iris should go for this jaunt if her heart is set on it and have her little bit of excitement, get it out of her system. And then, when she gets back, we can start saving for the wedding.'

3

Raúl gestures over to the right, where the streets grow narrower and busier, the skyline jagged with steel skyscrapers and cranes. 'That way centre Havana,' he says, and makes a face that seems to indicate it is beneath her interest. But they are not going that way; instead they branch to the left, where the houses become increasingly imposing and further apart, separated by high walls and luscious green foliage. They pass a couple of residences that look official, with flags outside hanging limp in the humid air. Government buildings or foreign embassies, Iris supposes.

Raúl points to a road off to the right and says something in Spanish, curling his hand up and down in an imitation of a wave. Iris catches a fleeting glimpse of the sea through the gap between two large hotels.

They pull off the main road and through a set of gates towards an impressive, colonial-looking house painted in a rich clotted-cream colour with a wide central turret and high, arched windows with slatted shutters and wrought-iron balconies. It is surrounded by vegetation – tall, slender palms, and shrubs with large, shiny, emerald-green leaves. It is a splendid building, grand and built to impress, but still there is something about those blank, shuttered windows that catches in Iris's throat.

A hard-faced man, in a dark suit in spite of the heat, steps out to shut the gates as they pass. Iris gives him a smile from the back seat but he looks right through her.

When Raúl comes around to hold the door open, Iris finds she doesn't want to leave the car. Something of her uncertainty must show in her face because Raúl's expression seems to soften as she finally climbs out, and he winks at her in a way that seems to speak more of solidarity than lasciviousness.

Iris follows Raúl around the side of the house, past yet another unfamiliar tree bearing clusters of oval-shaped leaves, amongst which hang huge, shiny green pears with leathery skin of a kind Iris has never seen. He gestures for her to wait.

Alone, Iris becomes acutely aware of all sorts of new sounds – the raucous birds in the branches of the strange tree, a crackling sound – it must surely be an insect – coming from a low bush, a wireless playing music from an open window high above, some sort of warbling love song.

The door opens and a familiar figure bursts forth. Cut-off blue jeans so tight they could be sewn on, purple-and-white gingham shirt knotted under a voluminous bust. Pillar-box-red lips.

Iris doesn't think she has ever been so happy to see anyone in her life as she is now to see Nell Hardman.

'You came! I was so worried you wouldn't. Mama said no English girl would be crazy enough to travel halfway across the world on the invitation of someone they met once at a

31

party. But I said, "Mama, Iris Bailey is different." And I was right.'

As Iris pulls away from Nell's welcoming embrace there comes a realignment. Things which just moments before seemed alien and suspect now appear exotic and intriguing.

'Let's go get you settled into your room so you can change your clothes,' says Nell, linking her arm through Iris's. Iris looks down at her wrinkled green linen dress, which had seemed so sophisticated when she put it on in her Hemel Hempstead bedroom.

'Is it always this hot?' she asks. Nell glances at the sky as if she has only now noticed the heat pressing down on them like a hot flannel.

'Oh, don't you worry. The rain will come any second, and then you'll be crying out for the sun to come back.'

Iris is led around to the back of the house, where there is a covered terrace with heavy-looking furniture – armchairs and a sofa with padded cushions and wrought-iron bases and a circular table with a glass top. The floor gleams with pale marble tiles and the seating area is mapped out by white pillars which hold up a flat white roof.

They follow a path that leads across a lawn. To the left, a swimming pool presents a glass-still surface to the sultry air. Beyond it is the high green fence of a tennis court, its net resolutely unfluttered by any breeze. There are wooden sun-loungers arranged around the pool, and a couple of sun umbrellas.

On one of the loungers reclines a young woman wearing white wide-leg trousers, her hair wrapped in a white scarf. She raises her dark glasses as they pass. Iris waves, and the woman moves her hand at the wrist, as if lifting her entire arm would require too much effort.

'Lana,' says Nell, rolling her eyes. 'The bride.'

Iris would have liked to say more, but they are already moving on, under a canopy of trees, and her attention is caught by something else.

'I've never seen pears like that,' says Iris, pointing to the shiny, dark green fruits she'd noticed earlier.

Nell throws back her blonde head and laughs.

'You never ate an avocado, Iris?'

Avocado. Of course.

'And those' – Nell points to a tall tree that wears its huge, flat leaves like a grass skirt around its trunk, where Iris now notices clumps of green fruits – 'are bananas. Please tell me you've eaten a banana, Iris.'

Iris makes a wry face, although the truth is she was nearly nine years old before she had her first taste, when Prime Minister Attlee declared National Banana Day in 1946 and each child in the country was given a piece of the exotic fruit that had almost entirely disappeared from the shelves during the war.

They arrive at a two-storey white building, modest in comparison to the house behind them, with its own small, vine-covered terrace boasting a round, glass-topped table and four chairs. The leaves on the vine are dense and green, and there is a heady, sweet smell like coconut coming from some yellow flowers near the ground. Two of those enormous black birds circle above them. 'Vultures,' Nell tells her, and bursts out laughing when she sees Iris's face. 'Don't look so alarmed, Iris. They're everywhere here.'

They enter a narrow hallway with a high ceiling. 'Straight ahead there's a little kitchen,' Nell points out. 'And this is the sitting room.' She leads the way into a squarish room. Once Iris's eyes have grown accustomed to the dim light seeping through the shuttered windows, she sees two wooden armchairs facing a narrow sofa across an elegant low table covered with a white lace cloth. The floor is patterned with tiles of green, brown and cream.

'Bruce hasn't set his interior designer loose on the guest house yet,' says Nell. 'Our host,' she says, responding to Iris's unasked question. 'Though I expect he will any day. Watch he doesn't marble you in your sleep. He's so enraptured with the stuff.'

'Who exactly are the Boninis anyway?'

'Bruce is Pop's best friend. Our two families go back for ever. And Barbara is his wife. You'll meet them both soon enough, only, Iris . . .'

For the first time in their short acquaintance Nell's expression appears serious. Without her brilliant smile, Iris sees to her surprise that Nell might actually be quite ordinary looking underneath all the expert make-up. Plain, even.

'. . . Be careful around Bruce, okay?'

Careful?

'Oh hell, no need to look so alarmed, Iris. I didn't mean anything by that. Bruce is my brother Eddie's godfather. He's practically family. I only meant . . . No – nothing. Forget it.'

Iris finds herself struggling to keep up.

'Lord, listen to me prattling on when you're worn slap out,' says Nell, seeing her confusion. 'Let's get you to bed before you pass out. A coupla hours' rest and you'll be good as new.'

They go back into the dark hallway. After Nell flicks on the light, they climb the steep staircase, Iris's feet feeling as if they are encased in stone after her epic journey. They emerge on to a long corridor with an arched recess opposite the staircase in which hangs, in pride of place, an oil painting featuring a graphically wounded Christ. Four tall doorways lead off the passageway. Nell stops outside the last one.

'Here's your room. See, it has its own key, so there's no need to worry about the Americans. Though, frankly, I wouldn't turn my nose up at that kind of worry.'

What Americans? What worry? Iris wants to know, but already she is eyeing the bed longingly, with its canopy of mosquito net and the wooden ceiling fan sending down a delicious draught that flutters the edges of the pillowcase. To her surprise, she sees her suitcase is already here.

Nell says something about coming to call for her later and closes the door. Iris lifts up the corner of the mosquito net and crawls under it without even taking off her dress. She closes her eyes and within minutes she is drifting off to sleep and has stopped worrying about who she might be sharing the house with and what she is doing in this hot sauna of a country with exotic fruits growing right outside her window and why, when they passed the bride by the pool, she appeared to be crying.

Dear Uncle Cyp

Thank you for the beautiful flowers, though I do have to tell you they ended up in the garbage can and for that you can blame Hugh. He would keep asking who'd sent them and then something got into me – you know how it does – and I refused to tell him just on the principle of it. I don't want Hugh to know about you. He'd go all out to seduce you, and knowing you, you'd put up no resistance and I'd be left out in the cold. Anyways, he got so mad he picked up the whole thing, vase and all, and dumped it all in the trash.

Then there was a scene. Well, you can imagine.

Faye appeared – I've told you how she lurks – and naturally she took Hugh's side right away. Said I was enough to drive anyone to distraction. Lord knows she must have learned that one from her grandmother. And then Lana has to come and try to single-handedly bring about world peace, flitting from one to the other and back again until we were all spinning. And then Hugh apologises, but in a way that makes it obvious he's only doing it as a favour to the girls, which of course they lap up like he's a goddam ice-cream float. Which makes me the bad guy. Again.

Honest to God, Cyp. Next time, send hard liquor and be done with it.

Love, Aunt Sap

4

TWO DISTINCT NOISES:

Rain
Men

As she comes fully around, she refines those first impressions:

Harder rain than she has ever heard in her life
American men

Iris fumbles her way out of the mosquito net and pads across the tiled floor. Her window, like all the others she has seen, is firmly shuttered, and the room is pitch black, but there is a crack of light running along the bottom, which she aims for.

She finds the latch and opens up the wooden shutters, expecting it to be dark outside, but instead there's a slate-grey sky visible through the solid sheet of rain – so much rain there is water bouncing off the windowsill and running off the flat banana leaves in rivulets.

The rain drowns out every sound, particularly after Iris

leans out of the window to turn her face upwards, her soaked skin feeling cool for the first time since she arrived in Cuba. For a moment she forgets those male voices and is startled when, having ducked her head back inside and shaken out her dripping hair, she hears a bark of deep laughter coming through the floor. She stops still then creeps softly to her door.

Two men, talking in the sitting room below.

'Should we go listen at the door for bluebottles?' the higher-pitched voice says.

'Better to just stand beneath the window and sniff,' replies the second.

This is when she realises she is sharing this guest house with two American men she has never met. She recalls Nell's remark about the lock on her door and her fingers fold around the large brass key.

There is a small bathroom attached to her bedroom, with a high ceiling where the green paint is peeling, and a basin and toilet, and a tiny shower cubicle tucked into the corner. At some point during her sleep she was sufficiently awake to take off her green dress, which lies at the foot of the bed like a pile of wilted leaves. Now she wears just her white slip. When she looks at her reflection in the small round mirror over the sink, her dark hair hangs down in rat's tails around her face. She imagines her mother's frustration that all the effort with those hard little rollers should be ruined for the sake of a few short seconds of gratification.

Iris does the best she can washing herself in the shower with a block of brown soap. The water is lukewarm at best, but now that the rain has stopped suddenly, as if someone had turned off a tap, the temperature is already rising again and she doesn't mind the tepidity. Still, she feels disoriented.

Can it really be possible that she has slept only for an hour or two?

Opening her case, she frowns, realising how woefully inappropriate for the Cuban climate are the clothes she has brought. She selects a pair of snug-fitting navy-blue trousers that zip up the side and skim the ankle which her mother had declared indecent, and a sleeveless white blouse, and slips her bare feet into her single pair of open-toed sandals. Also white. Are they too garish? She turns her pale foot this way and that.

There is nothing to be done about her hair, which will dry now as it pleases, neither curly nor straight but some in-between state that serves no useful purpose at all.

The corridor outside her room is in darkness until Iris locates the light switch. The walls here are the same pale green as her bathroom and dotted with gold-framed paintings, mostly depicting saints and religious themes. There is a lot of blood.

The men's voices sound more muffled from up here. Perhaps they've gone outside now that the rain has stopped. Iris feels self-conscious as she makes her way down the steps. Who are these Americans? What will she even say to them? If they are friends of the family, why aren't they in the main house?

Outside the sitting room, she hesitates, but when she ventures in she finds it empty, only the double doors open to the outside. The men are, as she'd thought, out on the terrace. By now, Iris has recognised that she is shockingly hungry. Should she perhaps go in search of a kitchen or pantry before introducing herself to these Americans? Already this is how she thinks of them. *These Americans.* Intruders into the space she had thought hers.

No. She will get this over with. This is why she is here, after all, to do a job. She is justified in being here.

With this in mind, she strides across the room, through the double doors and out into the blinding sunshine. The first thing she notices is the sky beyond the vine-dappled terrace, now deep cobalt blue, as if the rain had never happened. Then she notices a man sitting in the cane armchair directly in front of her, so small his feet dangle just above the ground. By contrast, his head seems enormous, as if borrowed from a much larger man. High, domed forehead, looming above neat, dainty features, thinning brown hair receding away from his face like a low tide, even though she judges he cannot be much more than thirty. Pale, intelligent eyes staring at her intently from behind round tortoiseshell spectacles.

'Our resident artist, I presume?' says the little man, without getting up. 'Joe and I were wondering whether you might actually be dead.'

So engrossed has she been in the oddness of the man's looks that she hasn't noticed the second man leaning against the trunk of the vine, almost entirely obscured from view, thanks to a fug of cigar smoke that surrounds him.

When it becomes obvious that the cloud of smoke is not going to speak, Iris feels compelled to say something herself.

'The light here is terrific, isn't it? I mean, it must be getting on for evening now, and yet the sun is so bright. I've never seen anything like it.'

There is a noise from behind the screen of smoke, but Iris concentrates on the little man in the chair, observing how, when he smiles, his peculiar features are transformed into something quite beatific and radiant.

'Yes, there is a quality to it that is quite extraordinary,' he agrees.

40

'You will be wanting to paint the sunset, I imagine,' says the second man, who is gradually taking shape through the smoke. 'Perhaps you should fetch your paints now, so you don't miss it.'

There is a burning in her chest and face. Iris knows she is being mocked. It wasn't she who claimed herself to be an artist. She knows she is just an amateur sketcher with only a foundation year at art school to her name.

But now the little man has leapt to his feet – and really, why did he bother when he is practically the same height as when he was seated? – and is stepping forward with his hand outstretched. That smile, up close, is so disarming that Iris feels her irritation evaporating into the heat of the day.

'I've been unforgivably rude. Please let me introduce myself. I'm Eugene Stringer. I'll be covering the wedding for *Life* magazine, and Joe here is the snapper.'

Iris shoots an alarmed glance at the second man, who is now revealed to be as tall as the other man is short, with wavy dark hair worn longer than she is used to and a strong, straight nose, flattened slightly at the end, as if it has set badly after being broken. His mouth is full and, quite honestly, wasted on a man, set above a determinedly square chin, and his brown eyes gaze impassively out at her from a lightly suntanned face.

'Joe Garston,' he says, raising a hand. 'Photographer.'

Did he emphasise the last word deliberately, realising she had no idea what a snapper was?

'By the way, I wouldn't set too much store on that.' He indicates the brass key, which is still in Iris's hand. 'It's more for show than anything else. The same key opens all the rooms around here. But don't worry. You're perfectly safe with us.'

His smile is like a challenge and Iris decides to ignore him and address her remarks to the more amiable Eugene.

'Can you tell me any more about the wedding? I mean, I know Mr Hardman directs films and I know, obviously, that his last wife died.' Then she adds, 'Tragically,' for good measure.

Iris judges it best not to bring up the rumours that have dogged Hugh Hardman since his wife, Jean Summers, then the highest-grossing actress of her day, disappeared off the couple's yacht in the Gulf of Mexico, the body being found six days later by a local fisherman. The inquest had found no evidence of foul play, but that hadn't stopped people speculating. 'Is the new bride an actress too?' As soon as the question is out of her mouth, the picture comes back to her of the woman crying by the swimming pool. How strange that she had forgotten her up until now.

A look passes between the two men.

'Tell me, Iris, how much have you been told about Lana Mickelson?' Eugene asks her.

Goodness, how big his eyes look behind those glasses.

Iris searches her memory, but there is nothing. All her attention has been on the famous groom. 'Not a lot, really.'

Another infuriating look is exchanged, before Eugene leans so far forward with that large head of his that Iris worries gravity will topple him.

'Well,' he begins. But whatever he was about to say is drowned out by a familiar voice that reverberates in the hot air and seems to set the leaves of the vine fluttering.

'Here you are. Thank Christ for that. I thought we might have killed you off already, before we've even got started.'

Iris is surprised to see that Nell has changed. Now she wears a very short diaphanous black beach-style cover-up with an ostrich-feather trim which hangs open to reveal a red two-piece swimming costume – bikini, Iris knows she must get used to calling it – that leaves very little to the imagination. She senses Joe Garston's attention shifting to the new arrival.

With Nell here, Iris can no longer ignore her hollow stomach, which has begun to emit low growls.

'Is it dinnertime?' she asks brightly, and cannot understand why her companions smirk. Only when she looks again at the sky and notices how the sun seems higher than the last time she looked does the truth dawn.

'What's the time?' she asks faintly.

'Just after nine,' says Joe, glancing at his watch. 'In the morning.'

Nell steps towards Iris and takes her arm.

'Now don't you worry, after I flew home from England I slept for a week. Come with me, let's get you some food before you really do drop dead from starvation. There's so little of you to start with, goddam bitch.'

She steers a shocked Iris back towards the path down which she came. As they pass under the low-hanging banana leaves that hide the main house from view, Iris hears a peal of male laughter erupt behind her and is grateful for the few remaining drops of rain that drip from the branches overhead to cool the fire in her cheeks.

Approached from the back, the main house is even grander than Iris remembers. Above the ground floor with its towering arched doorways and wrap-around terrace, two rows of French windows lead out on to balustraded balconies, the whole thing overhung by a mansard roof whose black tiles sparkle in the sun.

Nell is telling Iris more about her American housemates. 'Joe Garston – isn't he a stone-cold fox? – made his name after the war ended when he was still very young. He was posted to Germany with the army. Legend has it he won a camera in a poker game and started photographing everything he saw. You know – ruined buildings, starving kids, people fighting over a loaf of bread, that sorta thing. Then he was in the Middle East. And Korea.'

'And now he takes photographs of society weddings?' Iris doesn't mean it to sound mocking, but something about the tall American's arrogance has got under her skin. 'He must find that rather dull.'

Nell smiles. 'Or maybe he got tired of photographing death and now prefers to celebrate life? Anyways, I think there might have been some sort of trouble out there in Korea. Something went wrong, that's what he hinted to Pop when he booked him. So now he sticks to weddings. Which is lucky for us.'

They are walking past the now-deserted swimming pool, and Iris looks at it longingly. Already all trace of the rain she woke up to has been burned away by the blazing heat.

'And the other man?' she asks. 'Eugene, is it?'

'Oh, he's a bona fide genius, didn't you know? He has written for all the big newspapers and magazines – *Harper's Bazaar, Tatler*. He was one of those prodigy types. Wrote a novel that won every award going, and a play on Broadway, though that was a few years ago now, and I think his star might be on the wane at this point in time. Can't think why else he agreed to come. I just hope . . .' Nell stops suddenly.

'You hope . . . ?' Iris says, alarmed by the shadow that has fallen across Nell's face.

'I just hope he is here to cover the wedding and not to go digging up dirt about Jean's death. That's all anyone seems interested in still. Jeepers, it's so dull. And now they've opened the whole thing up again . . . Oh hell. I'm not supposed to talk about that.'

'About what?'

Nell looks at her ruefully. 'This is your fault, Iris Bailey, for worming secrets out of me – how do you do that? The fact is, the police have reopened the investigation into Jean's death. As if there hasn't already been enough misery.'

'But why?'

Nell shrugs, ruffling the ostrich-feather trim on her beach cover-up.

'New evidence, or so they say. Sounds to me like they might finally have got to Jimmy Palicki. He was the steward who talked straight to my chest and went AWOL as soon as we reached dry land.' For a moment she looks as if she is about to say more, then she stops herself. 'Let's not talk about all that, or I'll be fixing my first Martini right now, before breakfast. And then Christ only knows what family skeletons I'll be spilling by lunchtime.'

They have reached the house and Iris follows Nell's swishing posterior through the side door. She wants to ask Nell more about Jean and this intriguing new evidence, but she doesn't dare, lest she, too, be accused of dirt-digging.

As they enter a high corridor she can hear sounds coming from the first door to the right – pots being scraped and water pouring from a tap, a woman shouting in Spanish.

'The kitchen,' says Nell unnecessarily. 'We're heading to

the dining room. Most of the clan will be at breakfast, so you can get all the introductions over with in one go. Oh, and Isabella will be there, she's the best wedding planner in the whole wide world, don't you know. Well, so she says. Lana's grandmother, Meredith, booked her. She's the most frightful snob. Only the best for our Lana.'

They have entered a hallway with marble flooring – so this is what Nell meant about being marbled – and a grand staircase that rises up from one mid-point then branches into two, each wing held up by Grecian-style pillars. A crystal chandelier dominates the hallway, so colossal that Iris feels nervous passing underneath it. There is a marble fireplace, with scrolled edges upon which sits a large, polished wood clock. It is simultaneously the most opulent and the least welcoming house Iris has ever set foot in.

'And Meredith is Lana's grandmother, not her mother?' Iris asks as they approach a door leading off the hallway.

Nell gives her an odd look, as if she wants to say something, but already the door is opening and they are stepping inside a dining room, at the centre of which is a long oval table heaped with platters of boiled eggs and pancakes and thinly sliced ham, and bowls of bananas and other fruits that are unlike any fruits Iris has seen, with glistening flesh of yellow and pink, and around which sits a great number of people who all stop what they are doing to stare.

'I bring you Iris, famous portrait painter, newly arrived from England,' announces Nell, to Iris's intense embarrassment.

Instantly there is a blur of colour from one end of the table and a large woman with a shock of white hair piled high on her head, wearing a dress with a pattern of tropical birds and a huge smile, swoops down on them.

'I am Isabella Cavalcante, organiser of fabulous weddings all over the world. And you are so ridiculously pretty I think I will have to kill you.' *Keel* you, is how she pronounces it. 'Let me tell you, when this Nell informs me that in England there exists such a thing as a wedding artist, I say I must have her. *Breeng* her to me.'

Isabella introduces Iris to the others at the table.

'Do not even try to remember all the names, or your head will explode, and it is far too beautiful for *dat*. Mr Hardman himself isn't here yet. He is finishing work on a new movie in California, but he arrives this evening, together with our host, Mr Bonini. But the beautiful bride, Lana, she is here. And later today we put you to work drawing her. The picture will be a wedding gift to Mr Hardman. And after you will also draw Mr Hardman for his wife. Is that not *romanteec*?'

Iris is pleased. The party portraits, dashed off in a flurry of lines and shadings, have an immediacy that she loves, but they can't compare to a piece – there she goes using Peter's pompous term – where she has had the opportunity to arrange the sitter as she chooses, according to light and background, and the time to study them properly and tease out their defining essence, the thing that makes them who they are.

Lana Mickelson looks poised and self-contained this morning. A world away from the tear-stained woman Iris glimpsed by the pool the day before. Up close, Iris is taken aback to see how very young the bride-to-be is. Not even twenty, she would guess. Iris has no idea how old Hugh Hardman is, has never even seen a photograph, but he is old enough to have adult children. She looks again at Lana's soft, rounded cheeks, with that telltale pink glow of youth, and her wide grey-blue eyes and the wisps of blonde baby hair that still curl around her hairline, and she feels a stirring of unease.

Glancing quickly away, she finds herself gazing into another pair of eyes, the exact blue of the swimming pool they passed on the way here. The eyes are set in a handsome, squarish face framed by curling fair hair and they are fixed on Iris in undisguised appreciation.

'I'll sit for you any day,' says the blue-eyed man, who turns out to be Nell's brother, Eddie. 'And if you absolutely insist, I will even take all my clothes off, in the interests of artistic expression, of course.'

'Goodness gracious, Eddie, do you want to scare the poor girl away when she's only just gotten here?' says a plump-faced woman in a yellow dress with little puffed sleeves and a sweetheart neckline that shows off the little silver cross around her neck. She gives Iris a warm smile. 'Don't mind my son. He has the manners of a peasant. I'm Connie, by the way. Connie Hardman.' Iris's eyes widen. So this is Nell's mother? Iris comes from a world in which divorce is something shameful, so the presence of Hugh's first wife here at his wedding to his third strikes her as nothing less than astonishing.

Next to Connie, an older woman, heavily made up, with skin stretched tight as canvas over a tiny face dwarfed by an excessive hairdo – jet black and towering, and lacquered to within an inch of its life – stares at Iris and flicks her silver cigarette holder so that the ash falls directly into the remains of a boiled egg on her plate. Iris's stomach groans. 'Nell has told us all about you.' The woman's voice is refined but raspy. 'We want to know all about the famous people you've drawn in England. Have you done the Queen?'

To Iris's consternation, she appears to be quite serious.

'Oh, now, Meredith.' Connie again. 'Naturally, she won't have drawn the Queen. There are all sorts of rules and etiquette about things like that. There'll be bodyguards and courtiers and goodness knows what else to contend with.'

'But you have drawn some minor royals?'

'Don't worry, Meredith, Iris has the best pedigree,' says Nell, coming to Iris's rescue.

Though the conversation appears to be good-natured, there is something odd in the atmosphere, a steel wire of tension vibrating silently behind the quips and the chatter. Next to Iris, Isabella makes a noise in her throat that is so discreet it might not have been a noise at all, but it has the effect of focusing all the attention in the room on her. Iris wonders if she'll be invited to eat with them. There is an empty chair at the far end of the table, next to a very thin, sallow-looking young girl, not more than seventeen. The girl's lips bear the ghostly trace of a smile, though her eyes, enormous in her sunken face, are expressionless. Iris doesn't relish the idea of sitting with all these strangers, but those bread rolls in the basket look so good.

'Now you've said hello, you can go to eat,' says Isabella. 'My *Gad*, you must be ready to eat your own arm.'

It's a timely reminder that, despite Nell's arm still linked through hers, Iris is not a guest here. She is staff.

As she turns to leave, the fine hairs prickle on the back of her neck as she feels the sallow girl following her progress with her huge, fathomless eyes.

5

'NOT TOO UNCOMFORTABLE, I hope?'

They are sitting out on the terrace. To be precise, Iris is sitting, half obscured by her easel, while Lana Mickelson reclines on a rattan chaise longue, her face resting on her arm, which is hooked over the back of the chaise, her expression pensive.

'No, it's fine. Thank you.'

Polite, but not effusive. Not unfriendly, but not warm either.

Iris's pencil makes lines on the canvas, capturing the curve of Lana's calf and the fall of her skirt, the way her bare feet dig into the padding of the cushion. Moving almost without her being aware of it, her fingers create the contrast between the slant of sunlight across the girl's chest and the black shadow underneath, the pitted texture of the plaster wall behind. Before she started art school, Iris had drawn what she believed she could see – an eye with an identifiable eye shape, a uniformly ridged lip. Only slowly had she learned to draw what was actually there – an assortment of lines and shapes and shadows and contours that slowly built up to reveal a living, breathing human being. But that was only a part of it. A portraitist must also be a student of human nature, learning to look for all the ways in which a person will reveal his or her self – a tightness around the mouth, a pink bloom on the chest – all the clues that lead one into the life at the centre of the sketch. But in the case of Lana Mickelson, she cannot find a way of unlocking her subject's expression. She cannot find a way in.

'Will it be a big wedding?'

It's the least objectionable thing Iris can think of to say. If she can only get the girl to loosen up a little, drop her guard.

Lana shrugs. 'Big enough,' she says. 'I would have preferred it to be just the two of us, but Bruce – Mr Bonini – wants a big show. I think there are some business associates he is trying to impress.'

Iris examines her face for signs of resentment, but it is impassive, as ever. She dredges her mind for something else to say and is about to ask how Lana met Hugh but bites the question back when it occurs to her that the most likely explanation, considering the gap in their ages, is that Hardman was Lana's boss.

'And the bridal shower?' she asks, having learned from Nell that this will be another of her official engagements, not that Iris has the first idea what a bridal shower entails. In Hemel Hempstead, weddings tend to be quiet, one-day affairs – the ceremony followed by a modest reception, and a honeymoon, if one is lucky. 'That at least will be more intimate, I imagine. You'll have your friends. Will your mother be there?'

The effect upon Lana's features is one of a shop shutter coming down.

'I'm afraid my friends are hundreds of miles away and my mother is dead.'

Iris could kick herself. She'd been trying to break down barriers, and instead she might as well have erected a brick wall. Why does she never think before she speaks? Why must she always act on impulse? She remembers Miss Barker, the deputy headmistress at her school, saying, 'When the first thought comes into your head, Iris, hold it there until you're quite certain there isn't a far better-judged second or even third thought following close behind.'

'Oh, I am so sorry.'

'Meredith, my grandmother, brought me up, and my sister, Faye, too. You met her at breakfast.' Iris remembers the sallow-faced young girl. 'What I mean is she brought us up in her own fashion. My father hasn't been on the scene since before Faye was born.'

'Well, at least you will have some family here.'

A flash of something briefly animates Lana's face then is gone before Iris has a chance to analyse it.

'I do envy you having a sister,' Iris blunders on, still trying to forge the intimacy a successful portrait demands.

'Yes. Although it can be a responsibility, too. Are you an only child?'

'Yes. Well, no, not exactly. I did have an older sister, Wendy, but she died when I was very young. Measles.' Iris doesn't usually like to talk about Wendy, but she hopes that by opening up to Lana she might persuade the girl to drop her guard. 'I don't really remember her, so it hasn't affected me so much, but my mother has never quite recovered.' She doesn't mention the bottle of pills in the back of the bathroom cabinet or the one her mother carries in her handbag so that she sometimes rattles when she walks, or the small window of opportunity in the day when she seems animated to the point of euphoria so that if one asks her something, she is almost certain to agree, followed by the vast chunks of lost time where it is as if she is trapped behind thick ice, impossible to access.

For a few moments Iris works on in an awkward silence broken only by the scratching of her pencil on the paper. Lana emerges from the page in her sleeveless dress with the wide belt and the full skirt that hangs over the chaise longue, practically brushing the gleaming floor, her bare toes contrasting with the dainty white gloves that cover her hands. Here is her hair, pinned into a pleat at the back in the French style, all except the few feathery wisps around the temples that are so beastly to paint.

Noises come from inside the double doors that lead into the house. A door shutting. A low hum of conversation, amplified by the silence out on the terrace. The hum grows louder, more agitated, and now a woman's voice hisses: 'It's all right for you. I'm the one who's gonna get it in the neck when they see that bottle.'

Lana, who has shown no sign of listening, gets unhurriedly to her feet and closes the terrace doors.

'Sorry,' she says as she resumes her position.

'Oh, heavens, don't worry at all. I know what families are like.'

Iris gets back to her drawing, determined not to say anything more. Whatever is going on inside the house, it is none of her business. She is here only to work. Dutifully, she continues, her pencil tracing the long stretch of Lana's throat.

'Do you have a boyfriend, Iris?'

It's not a subject Iris particularly wants to discuss, but any chink in Lana's veneer must be taken advantage of. 'Yes, fiancé, actually.' The word sounds ridiculous with that French accent on the end.

Now, finally, she has Lana's attention. 'Tell me about him. How did he propose? Was it romantic?'

Iris remembers that scene around her parents' table when Peter had said that thing about her having a last adventure before she settled down. How he'd sulked when she berated him for it afterwards.

'I was trying to do you a favour to get your parents to agree to you going,' he had said. 'And it worked, didn't it? Fat lot of thanks I get, I must say.' Peter often did this. Made her feel like she was the one in the wrong, even when it jolly well wasn't her who told her parents their only child was getting married.

'But now they're going to be expecting a wedding. It's pretty low of me to make one up just so I can have their blessing to scarper to Cuba, when my mother has been dreaming of nothing but that one day since I was born.' She didn't much care for the way Peter was looking at her. They were standing under a lamp post just a few doors along from Iris's house where they could say goodbye out of sight of her parents' windows, and Peter's eyes – which she'd once thought the spit of James Dean's, whose early death two years previously had been Iris's first real experience of grief – were glassy in the dim light.

'Bloody hell, Iris. Are you being deliberately dim? There *will* be a wedding. I'm asking you to marry me.'

'Well, you needn't sound so cross about it.'

Surprise had put her on the defensive and they glared at each other for a moment before Peter softened and reached out to pull her in towards him. 'I'm sorry,' he said. 'It's probably not the most romantic proposal. To tell you the truth, it's a bit sooner than I'd have liked. But we love each other, don't we? So we'd have got married eventually. And, this way, it gets your parents off your back. So what do you say? Please say yes.' Crushed to his chest, she nodded, and only later did it occur to her that not being able to think of a good reason not to do something wasn't at all the same thing as wanting to do it.

'Oh, he's an art student,' she tells Lana. 'Very handsome. And yes, it was frightfully romantic.'

But still the connection between subject and artist does not come. Everything else in the portrait is perfect – the folds of the skirt; even those blasted baby hairs – but the face itself eludes her. Iris faithfully follows the lines and the shadings that she sees. Lana is not classically beautiful. Her face is just a little too wide, her forehead too high. But there is something compelling about the combination of youthful softness – the way her features seem almost blurred at the edges, the hint of down on her cheeks – and her unnatural stillness and poise. Yet though Iris notices all these things, there is a disconnect that happens between her pencil and the paper so that what emerges on to the page seems lifeless and flat.

Portraits have always been this way with her – that need to establish an accord with the subject, to draw out their truths in order to truly capture them. 'Anyone can draw a likeness,' her favourite tutor at Hornsey had said, 'but drawing a life, that's something else.'

*

Making her way back to the guest house after the sitting is over, Iris feels deflated. The picture is accomplished enough. Only anyone who knew Lana well would realise that the core of her, the *Lananess* of her, was missing, but that is scant consolation. The next sitting will be better, she determines. Yet still Iris finds it hard to raise her spirits. She has been so looking forward to coming to Havana, but a strange atmosphere clings to this wedding so that there is an edge of chill in the air, even in this infernal heat, and the muscle in the corner of her jaw is permanently clenched.

Iris is vaguely aware that one of the wooden loungers around the swimming pool is occupied, but she keeps her head down, reminded since breakfast of her status as help. She will do her job and remain as unobtrusive as possible until it is time to fly back home. And then what? Peter's face comes into her mind and she quickly slams the shutters down.

'Iris! What in God's name is the matter? You look like you have the weight of the world on those petite shoulders of yours.'

There's something about Nell, springing up from the lounger, that lifts Iris's spirits despite herself. By rights, she should have nothing in common with this cheerful young woman from a background so entirely unlike her own, and yet there is an affinity there that transcends their differences and makes her feel less alone.

'I've just done a decidedly lacklustre drawing of the bride.'

'That's because Lana does not like to give any of herself away. I should think she's a bit like those primitive tribes – you know the ones I mean – who believe that if you take a photograph of them, you're stealing their soul.'

Iris smiles. It is all but impossible not to, when Nell

herself is so friendly and agreeable, though, truth be told, Iris doesn't quite know where to put her eyes. There is so very much of Nell on show, that is the thing. Her very full bosom is hardly contained by the narrow band of the red bikini top, and everywhere Iris looks there are hips and thighs and curves. Nell loops her arm through Iris's.

'Anyways, I shouldn't worry one little bit. You're already a hit with my family. Eddie hasn't stopped talking about you.'

Iris feels her cheeks blazing. *Grow up*, she tells herself sternly. For goodness' sake, she is engaged now – how unlikely that still sounds, as if it is something that happened while she was sleeping. She ought to be able to receive a compliment without blushing like a schoolgirl. She changes the subject.

'I'm to draw at the bridal shower tomorrow,' she says. 'Do you have any idea who will be there or what we will be doing?'

Nell rolls her eyes. 'We're having afternoon tea at the Tropicana club at Vedado, which is not so far from here, in the boondocks of Havana. It'll be you and Isabella, and Lana, obviously, and Meredith, me and Mama, and Faye, who you saw at breakfast, only don't sit too close to her, in case a careless exhalation blows her clear away. Oh, and our hostess, Barbara Bonini, who you won't have met, on account of she sleeps in a coffin during daylight hours. That's a joke, Iris, please don't look so alarmed. And assorted other wives of men Bruce is trying to impress.'

'Well, that all sounds very jolly,' says Iris, although it doesn't at all. 'I must say I do think it's nice the way all of you from Mr Hardman's first family are so supportive of him marrying again.'

Nell's normally animated face goes very still and she presses her lips together in a way Iris doesn't much like.

'What I mean is, I know Lana's mother is dead, and she clearly doesn't have much family, so I'm sure she appreciates you all being here, and . . .'

'There's something I probably should have mentioned before.'

Iris stands stock still.

'The thing is, and there's no easy way to say it . . . Oh, Iris, please don't be mad. If I'd told you the truth, you might not have come, and I so wanted you to come.'

'What truth?'

'Oh boy, here goes nothing. Well, the fact is, Iris, we *are* Lana's family.'

Iris frowns. 'Well, of course, you'll all be related after the wedding.'

'Not after the wedding. Now. We are Lana's family now.'

Only after Iris continues looking completely befuddled does Nell spell it out, and it is the first time Iris has seen doubt in her new friend's face, a nervousness that makes her appear all at once like someone older, and drabber.

'Lana's mother was Jean Summers, Pop's second wife. Lana is his stepdaughter.'

6

'I HAD NO IDEA,' Iris says, the words muffled, on account of her head being in her hands.

It all makes sense now. That strange, charged atmosphere at breakfast, Lana's flash of animation when Iris had mentioned her family. Had she thought she was making fun of her?

'What kind of magazines do you read over there in England? Clearly, they're nowhere near trashy enough. And why do you think they're getting married on this island in the middle of nowhere? Do you really think the great Hugh Hardman would give up a chance to be centre stage at some showbiz wedding in Hollywood if he could help it?'

They are on the terrace of the guest house, under the spreading vine. From a china cup by her elbow comes the smell of the coffee Eugene Stringer has just brought her. Iris senses the journalist hovering by the chair in which she has been sunk ever since returning from her encounter with Nell Hardman, as if he wishes to comfort her but is unsure how. To her right is the stack of papers he was reading through when she interrupted him, a pen neatly placed on the top like a paperweight, even though there is no chance of the pages blowing away in this still heat.

'How is it even legal?' she asks, looking up finally. 'She's his stepdaughter. Surely there's a law against it?'

Eugene takes off his spectacles and cleans them with the hem of his linen shirt. Without them, he seems much younger, and oddly vulnerable, with that rounded head of his, like a baby's.

'No law broken – well, not beyond the laws of good taste. Lana and her sister, Faye, were already ten and seven by the time Hardman left Connie for Jean. And their mother died not even five years later, which is when they were packed off to live with sweet ol' Grandma Meredith. And even during those years Hardman was married to Jean, they were either away working separately or else running out on each other over some argument or other. So I guess you could argue Hugh and Lana didn't exactly have time to build a father–daughter relationship.'

'Even so.' Iris is not to be placated. 'He is so much older than her. What can she see in him, beyond a search for a father figure to depend on? And what can he see in her, beyond a younger version of her dead mother?'

For a moment Eugene looks lost in thought, then he puts on his glasses again and starts leafing through the papers, which Iris now sees are Xeroxed newspaper cuttings.

'Let's see. That party on the yacht where Jean disappeared was to celebrate Hugh's forty-fifth birthday. So now he'll be getting on for fifty, while Lana is nearly twenty.'

'But that's horrible.' Iris didn't mean to say this out loud; it just burst out of her.

Eugene's smile is short-lived. 'It's a big gap for sure, but not impossible. Hugh is still a fine-looking man. The heart makes its own allowances. Plus, this way, he gets Manderley back, which I'm sure hasn't escaped his attention.'

'Manderley? Is it a dog?'

Eugene giggles. 'It's a house, Princess. You don't mind if I call you Princess, do you? I'm so terribly in love with Princess Margaret, and you remind me of her with your dark hair and those big eyes of yours and that divine way of talking. Manderley is the ranch Hardman bought Jean as a wedding present. In the Nevada desert – I'm amazed you haven't heard about it. Does England not have newspapers? *Life* magazine declared it "the Most Beautiful House in the World" in 1949. He bought it on the proceeds of *A Different Dawn* and had it totally re-styled for him and Jean to live in. Poured his blood and soul into it. Then, come her death, he finds she's left the whole shebang to Lana in her will.'

'But why . . . ?'

'Oh, honey, who knows? But let's just say Hughie's yacht was not a happy ship when Jean departed it.'

Iris's curiosity has been piqued, but it's clear Eugene isn't about to say more and, besides, she can't stop replaying in her head that moment she'd told Lana Mickelson how nice it was that she had family here at her wedding. She doesn't see how she will ever recover from the sheer mortification of it.

'What I don't understand,' she says now to Eugene, 'is why they invited you to cover the wedding? What I mean is, someone with your reputation is going to attract a lot of attention. Surely they'd want to keep something like this quiet?'

'They didn't exactly ask me, Princess. I wanted to come. Are you kidding? Dead film stars, family scandals – what self-respecting writer could resist?'

There is something brittle in his tone that makes her wonder what it is he isn't saying. She remembers Nell's comment about how he hadn't had a literary success in years. Perhaps it is financial necessity that has brought him here. She wonders if it feels like a humiliation.

'I suppose the surroundings don't hurt either,' she says, trying to assuage his feelings.

'Sweetie, I burn in the sun and I can't swim a stroke and, frankly, most people are dull enough when they have work to talk about but unendurable when they're at leisure.'

Iris blinks at him. She has never heard anyone talk quite the way Eugene Stringer does, with that soft, melodic voice that is so much like music that one doesn't immediately notice when he's saying something rude and it's only afterwards that one thinks to oneself, *Oh*, but by then he has moved on to something else so smoothly one wonders if perhaps one misunderstood.

'But that still doesn't explain why they agreed,' she says, returning to the mystery of Eugene's presence here.

Eugene smiles, and Iris is struck by the sudden sweetness of his face. Such a queer fellow. One minute so odd-looking and the next so endearing.

'What do you know about Hugh Hardman, Iris?' His voice is low, and he leans towards her so that it doesn't carry.

'Not a huge amount.' Iris is uncomfortably aware that this is almost a mirror of their conversation this morning about Lana Mickelson and is embarrassed by her own unforgivable lack of curiosity. She had been so anxious to leave

England and so caught up in this fairy-tale opportunity that had fallen into her lap she hadn't even thought about the real people behind the famous names. 'That is to say, I know that he has won lots of awards and things, so he's obviously very good at, you know, directing. But I also know he falls out with people a good deal. There was that film, wasn't there, the one he shot in Africa, where two leading actresses walked out in the middle of shooting?'

'Well, to be fair, only one of them walked. Pamela Lemoine got dysentery, and I'm fairly sure she had to be carried out on a stretcher. But yes, he is . . . controversial. By all accounts, he is one of those men who can't conceive of a world outside of themselves. I think that's why he agreed to me coming here. Vanity.'

'And he doesn't care what the world thinks about him?'

'Not a bit. Just as long as they *are* thinking about him. Don't forget, he's very used to scandal. There are plenty who think he gave Jean a helping hand overboard, which is probably why the police have reopened the case.'

'I thought that was supposed to be a secret.'

Eugene dips his head so he can look at her over the top of his spectacles.

'There are no secrets in showbiz, Princess.'

Iris wants to ask him whether Nell's fears are grounded and he is here just to write about the case, rather than the wedding, but she doesn't dare and, anyway, she supposes the stack of newspaper cuttings answers that question. 'May I?' she asks, picking off the top sheet. 'Jean Summers Feared Dead', screams the headline. Underneath is a short newspaper article from the *LA Times*, dated 25 September 1952.

Concerns are growing for the safety of film star Jean Summers, 39, who disappeared overnight from a yacht in the Gulf of Mexico. The actress and her husband, film director Hugh Hardman, were celebrating his forty-fifth birthday with extended family and friends on board Mr Hardman's yacht, the *SallyAnn*. The alarm was raised by the vessel's captain, Dwight Wilson, after Miss Summers' cabin was found empty early this morning and a search of the boat revealed no trace of the Academy Award-winning star. The yacht set off from Cancún on Thursday morning on what was to have been a five-day cruise. According to a police spokesman, at this moment, the *A Different Dawn* actress is still being treated as a missing person, but hopes are fading the longer the search continues.

Iris shudders. There's something appalling about reading something with the advantage of hindsight, knowing how a situation turns out while lacking the power to change the outcome. Disquieted, she riffles through the rest of the stack and pulls out another cutting. This one, dated 22 October 1952, is headed, unimaginatively: 'Jean Summers Inquest'.

Jean Summers fell from her husband's yacht while under the influence of alcohol and other substances, a Texan coroner declared today. Mr Henry Washington said the actress's blood contained 14 per cent alcohol, which is over the legal limit for driving. It also contained traces of chloroquine, an anti-malarial medication which can cause blurred vision and confusion. Miss Summers had been filming abroad prior to joining her husband, the film director Hugh Hardman, and other family and friends, to celebrate Mr Hardman's forty-fifth birthday. Mr Washington said the combination of the alcohol and the medication would have made the actress woozy and disoriented, and if she'd come up on deck to take some air she might have leaned too far over the edge and pitched overboard, striking her head on the way down. Though the body had been in the water some time, there was evidence of surface bruising to the arms and head, some of which had been sustained prior to entry into the water, but there was, said Mr Washington, no evidence of any struggle or foul play. Therefore, he ruled her death accidental. No one from the Hardman family was available for comment.

Iris replaces the cutting on the pile. She leafs through the others without much appetite. 'Party Death of Film Star Jean'; 'Jean Summers Mystery Death' – the headlines are depressingly similar, all the reports carrying a photograph of the actress, mostly wearing very little, against a backdrop of the sea or Hugh's boat.

'And have you come up with any theories yet?' She is trying to sound worldly, as if she talks about death and possible murder all the time.

Eugene arches an eyebrow so that it soars like a gull into the sky of his vast forehead.

'Honey, it's *always* the husband, don't you know that? Everybody knows that the *SallyAnn* – did you know that's what the boat is called? He named it after her role in *The Understudy*. Don't you think that's adorable? – was a floating tinderbox. Don't believe what you see in the magazines – all those photographs of Hugh and Jean with their arms around each other. Love's young dream. Let me tell you, by the time they set sail, those two couldn't stand the sight of each other. Hugh believed she was being unfaithful and it was driving him just about crazy, trying to find proof, and she was taunting him with it in that way she had. Plus, of course, the two of them drank like fish. And it didn't help that the whole extended happy family, plus the Boninis, were on board to celebrate Daddy's forty-fifth. Mind you, from what I hear, every one of them had a reason for wanting Jean dead. You know Nell worked as her assistant? I don't suppose Jean made her life easy. My, but that woman had a talent for upset.'

Eugene doesn't bother to hide his admiration. Affection, even.

'Do you feel . . . *compromised*, having to write about these things?' Iris ventures.

Well, you'd think she'd made the funniest joke ever, the way that man laughed.

'Princess, I've been compromised so many times it's practically my default position.'

Seeing her expression, he curbs his giggles. 'The fact is, I'm finding it hard to care too much about the rich, famous Hardmans when Cuba itself is so deliciously exciting.'

'How do you mean?'

'The *rebels*, Princess. Don't tell me you haven't heard of them. The Castro brothers, who are just about the most handsome men you ever saw, and the Argentine, with his big, brown eyes. All of them holed up in the mountains on the east side of the island, growing beards and wrestling in the mud, and sleeping outside and cooking over open fires and waiting for the glorious revolution to take hold.'

'Revolution?'

Eugene's eyes are huge behind his glasses.

'Gracious, they really don't have newspapers in England, do they? People here have had enough of President Batista and his buddies selling off Havana to us Yanks so we can cram it full of casinos and brothels, and letting us run all the most lucrative sugar and tobacco plantations on the island and pocketing the proceeds while the country starves. There have been protest movements and insurgencies for years. Any minute now, the whole thing is going to go up like a box of firecrackers. You know, that's what I oughta be writing about, not who wore what diamond tiara to Hugh Hardman's third wedding.'

'So why don't you go and find them? These rebels?'

Eugene looks surprised. And then sad.

'They wouldn't talk to me, Princess. They'd want a serious writer. And that ain't me. Hell, I don't think I even want it to be me. There's altogether too much seriousness in the world as it is. Only . . .' He pauses to take off his glasses and give them an unnecessary wipe. 'Only I would, just once, like to do something that leaves a mark. I would like to make a difference.' He puts his spectacles back on and grins at her. 'Isn't it ironic that here I am, longing for a little gravitas, and there's Garston, trying to convince himself he's perfectly happy to swap bombs for bouquets. Say, wouldn't it be a gas if all of us here are pretending to be something we're not?'

On the way up to her room, Iris is pensive, only now realising just how much there is lurking under the surface of this wedding. Pushing open her door, she stops, staring at the envelope on the floor. Standard white of the kind that pour out of company mailing rooms every single day. Her name is typed neatly on the front.

Someone must have come along and pushed it under her

door. Surely it would have been easier to come and find her? After all, she has been out there on the terrace in full view for the last two or three hours.

She tears open the flap, extracting a single piece of paper that has been neatly folded into quarters. When she opens it up and reads the two short lines of type, she gasps.

> don't trust nell
> she kills people

7

An hour after finding the note, Iris is still on edge. It isn't just the message, so starkly printed in black, that word 'kills' jumping clear off the page, it's also the realisation of just how far she is from home and how little notion she has of who she can trust. Her first instinct is to tell someone – anyone – but when she goes through the candidates she finds the only person she really wants to tell is Nell herself. And she can't help doubting the wisdom of that. The note is clearly someone trying to make trouble and, if she shows it to Nell, who knows what ructions might ensue, with Iris right there at the heart of them.

Out on the guest-house terrace, she fans herself with a banana leaf Joe Garston has presented her with. 'It was just lying on the ground,' he said, handing it to her as if it were of no consequence to him whether she took it or not. But when Iris peers through the gathering gloom to where the vegetation grows, separating the guest house from the main house grounds, the green leaves are all firmly attached to the branches, with no detritus underneath. To her surprise, the vine overhead seems to have come to life now evening is here, small white flowers opening and releasing a powerful scent that hangs in the air tangible as mist.

'Night-blooming jasmine,' says Joe when she enquires. 'The flowers only come out after dark.'

Iris takes a deep breath in, savouring the sweet, rich aroma, which gets into her head, turning her thoughts deliciously languid and sluggish, and rolling the exotic-sounding name around her tongue. Joe himself is in a restless mood, smoking a cigarette as intently as if it were of itself an artistic endeavour, like painting a picture or writing a poem. She finds his presence unsettling. He is loitering, as if he wants her company, yet when she tries to talk to him about his years of war photography, he shuts her down instantly. 'I'm done with all that,' he says with a dismissive wave of his hand. 'What fool would go haring off to hostile godforsaken countries no one has ever heard of to be shot at every day for months on end to take photographs he might not even be able to sell, when he could be paid handsomely to swan around a Caribbean island snapping beautiful women in beautiful clothes?'

Joe Garston lacks Eugene's lightness of being, so that rather than coming across as amusing or sardonic, as he probably intends, his words sound bitter and harsh. Still, for all Iris tries to corral her impressions into a low opinion of him, she keeps coming up against the physical facts: the surprisingly long, thick eyelashes; the way his smile reveals long teeth on either side of his mouth that give him a wolfish air; the deep burnt brown of the skin on his forearms, speaking of years of exposure to harsh climates; the smooth hollow where his neck meets his collarbone. All these things mean that Iris finds herself pulled towards him, even while her brain is listing his many deficiencies. Arrogance. Defeat-ism. Rudeness.

Her thoughts are interrupted by a distant rumbling, which gets louder and louder, until . . . 'I am dying. No, really, do not expect me to talk to you, because I am a dead woman. A corpse. Look.'

Isabella, the wedding planner, sinks down on to one of the chairs with her head thrown back, arms and legs use-lessly trailing. She has changed into a silk trouser suit festooned with red poppies that, to Iris's untrained eye, resembles a pair of exotic pyjamas.

'The heat in this damned place is making me crazy,' she says, addressing her remarks to the vine overhead. 'My brain has shrivelled' – *SHREEveld* – 'to the size of a wal-nut. And everyone is asking things – "Isabella, can you do this, can you do that?" – as though I am an octopus with enough arms to do eight different things all at the same time.'

Isabella's arrival summons Eugene from his room, and she sits back up, inspecting the three of them in turn, with the same benign appraisal as Iris's ceramics tutor used to survey her pupils' latest pots.

'So, my darlings. I am like the postman. I have come with invitations. Mr Hardman has now arrived with Mr Bonini, and Mrs Bonini is asking that you join them for cocktails. She is a great admirer of yours, Mr Stringer. She says you are a genius.' *Jinyus.* 'So I ask if she has read your book and she says no, but this is a fact that everyone just *knows*.'

'I'm flattered,' says Eugene, looking entirely unmoved.

'And you're sure we're all invited?' asks Iris.

'Oh yes. All. In fact, Edward Hardman insisted that I tell you this personally.'

Iris holds the banana-leaf fan up to her face in case she is blushing.

Twenty minutes later, they are following the poppies on Isabella's back along the pathway through the little grove of banana and avocado trees and past the swimming pool. The sun is lower in the sky now, but the heat is no less sticky and the powder-blue crêpe dress that Iris has changed into is already clinging to her skin, the elastic girdle encasing her like a tight, giant bandage under her clothes. A loud giggle followed by a soft *thuck-thuck* gets her attention, and she follows the sound to the distant tennis court, where a man and a woman – she cannot see their faces – are playing, both in tennis whites. The woman reaches up on her toes, and Iris can see that it is Lana, her blonde hair burnished by the last of the evening sun. She serves gracefully and there is the gentle whir of the ball through the hot air, and then, 'Out!' calls the man from the other end. Lana shrieks and runs towards the net and vaults cleanly over, her white skirt flying up around her like the silk of a parachute. The man, who is Eddie Hardman, falls to his knees in mock surrender, and she leans over him with her racquet raised as if to strike him, half shouting and half laughing: 'I won. Submit!'

The covered terrace of the main house, where, earlier, Iris had attempted to capture the essence of Lana Mickelson, now looks to be densely populated, with figures standing and sitting and lounging. Did one of these shadowy figures type that note and slip it under her door? Iris drives the thought from her head. There is music playing, a soft saxophone accompanied by a piano and snare drum, and a low buzz of conversation.

Iris hoped they might slip into the throng unnoticed, but Isabella has other plans.

'Darlings, I bring to you our genius creatives.' Her voice bounces off the smooth, white render of the terrace ceiling.

The conversation stills, the music too loud, and all the faces are turned towards them like dogs catching a scent on the air. Next to her, an unsmiling Joe Garston mutters something under his breath that she doesn't catch, while Isabella propels Eugene towards a redhead who inhabits her wrought-iron armchair like a throne and holds out a limp hand to him, as if she expects him to either kiss it or bless it.

'Barbara Bonini. Charmed,' she says, her heavy-lidded eyes sliding over the reporter's unusual form, that body hardly bigger than a child's on which the head teeters. Her gaze alights on Joe Garston and she sits up a little straighter, her hand reaching up to pat the back of her auburn hair, which is coiffed and sprayed into submission. She asks Eugene if he is working on a new book but seems not the slightest bit interested in his answer. Instead, her eyes keep darting back to the photographer, like a lizard flicking out its tongue.

By the time it is Iris's turn to be introduced, it is as if their hostess has exhausted her store of pleasantries, and she can hardly summon the energy to raise her eyes to Iris's face, so they come to rest around the point where the crêpe dress dips in a half-hearted V over Iris's flattish bosom.

But there is no time to wonder if she should feel slighted because Isabella has her by the arm and is pulling her towards two middle-aged men standing at the back, detached from the rest of the group, smoking cigars the width of Iris's arm. One of the men is short and slight with delicate, feminine features and a small mouth ill suited to the girth of the cigar. The other towers over him, broad-shouldered and tanned, with a handsome, craggy face in which his eyes glint like chips of broken blue glass resting in the sand. But she is not looking at his face. Instead, her attention is drawn to the top of his head, on which sits a tall, cowboy-style hat of a kind Iris has only ever seen at the pictures. He removes the hat to reveal a full head of leonine hair, which he shakes back extravagantly and runs his long fingers through.

'We're honoured you came all this way, Miss Bailey,' he says, in a voice that sounds like water bubbling down a deep well, or that first clap of thunder that makes you jump up from whatever you're doing and rush to the window.

When Hugh Hardman smiles at her it is as if he means to convey that it is she who is conferring a favour upon them, rather than the other way round. His blue eyes never leave her face and she has the oddest feeling of being fixed in place by them like a butterfly on a pin.

'I must confess I'm a little afraid of you. I'm told you have a way of getting under your subject's skin so the real person appears on the paper, no matter how well we might try to hide ourselves.'

'Well . . . I . . .'

'The thought excites me, but it's also terrifying. That's a lot of power you have in those tiny hands.' Before she knows what is happening, he has captured one of the aforementioned hands and is displaying it upon one of his own vast, outstretched palms like a prized cut of meat on a platter. And all the time his eyes are on her and she cannot look away, much though she wants to. Her skin prickles with cold and she knows without looking that it has come up in goosebumps.

Abruptly, Hugh drops her hand and turns to his companion, and Iris feels a curious sense of abandonment.

'Bruce, meet Miss Bailey. She's come to draw our souls out of us. Literally.'

Bruce Bonini makes a slight adjustment, angling his face towards Iris, even while his body remains facing forwards. He really does have the daintiest features for an older man: the fine, pointed nose; the perfectly shaped brows. When he turns to her she smells his cologne, a pungent mixture of leather and spices that crawls into her nostrils. 'Welcome.' He puts out a hand to shake hers, and she is surprised at how limp and cool his hand feels, and when she looks into his flat, dark eyes they seem to absorb the light and reflect nothing back.

'Oh!' Her heart jolts within her chest as from the corner of her eye she sees a pale blur approaching through the air and she instinctively puts her hands up to protect her face.

'It's only a moth, Miss Bailey,' says Bruce as the enormous creature, four times the size of any moth Iris has seen at home, settles on the glass shade of a lamp set on a low table to Iris's left. Now the shock has worn off, she can see it is a lovely thing, chalky white with a delicate green pattern. 'May I?' Iris steps back to allow Bruce to lean forward and carefully pinch the fragile creature's folded wings between his thumb and forefinger before walking with it to the edge of the terrace.

Nell appears by her shoulder and Iris jumps, thinking of that folded paper back in her room. *don't trust nell*. Luckily, her new friend's attention is fully on Joe Garston. 'Don't you think he's the dreamiest man you ever saw? I could eat him up with a sundae spoon.'

Iris is handed a drink with green leaves floating in it that she is informed is called a Mojito, although she has to have it spelled out for her three times. She positions herself awkwardly behind Meredith and Connie, who are perched side by side on a cushioned sofa.

The record playing inside the house finishes, and in the crackling silence that follows, as the needle skitters around the edge of the vinyl, there comes the noise of running footsteps and breathless laughter, and Eddie and Lana approach from the direction of the tennis court. Eddie is first, but Lana pulls on his shirt to slow him down. Looking up, they seem to become aware of the gathering on the terrace for the first time. Lana's arms drop to her sides and to Iris it seems as if her shoulders slope towards the ground. They walk the rest of the way as if conscious of being watched, stiffly and with a distance between them.

'Greetings,' says Eddie, breaking into a smile as he catches sight of Iris. He flings down his racquet and sinks on to the floor facing her, leaning back against Nell's knees.

'Ew, get off! You're all sweaty.'

nell kills people

Iris is struck by how comfortable Eddie is in himself. With his golden hair and his even features and easy manners.

As Lana walks past Hugh they kiss lightly on the lips, which makes Iris feel so peculiar she has to look at the floor, where Eddie Hardman's fingers are splayed out, the nails neatly cut. To her left, young Faye Mickelson is curled up on a chair with her legs folded under her and a shawl around her narrow shoulders, despite the heat. She, too, has watched the kiss between her sister and her fiancé. Unlike Iris, she doesn't look away, and when Iris next glances over the girl is still gazing at Hugh Hardman, as if he is the only food her near-starved body craves.

Iris doesn't realise quite how strong the cocktails are until they return to the guest house and she twice has to put her hand out to grab hold of a branch or the trunk of a tree, glad she is at the back of the little group and hoping the darkness masks her unsteadiness.

'Nightcap, Princess?' asks Eugene, who has been leading the way with a torch, and even though Iris is quite sure she has had enough she finds herself reluctant to go back to her room, knowing that at some point in the day someone crept up to her door and slid underneath it a note, the sole intention of which must have been to scare her.

Moments later, she is sitting at the terrace table breathing in the intoxicating smell of the jasmine and sipping something that on first taste burns the back of her throat but which improves with each subsequent encounter, until she is quite disappointed to find her glass empty. 'Just one more can't hurt,' she responds when Joe returns from the kitchen with the bottle.

It is at some point during this second glassful that, despite her doubts, Iris finds herself telling her housemates, these two practical strangers, about the strange note that was slid under her door. It is something to do with the combination of the alcohol and the way the dark night is amplifying her nervousness at the thought of returning to her room.

'What do you mean? What kind of note?' It's no surprise

that a photographer and a journalist should require the physical evidence, so now she must make her way upstairs to produce it, after which it is pored over and handled, until its corners start to fur and the impact of the words begins to diminish.

'I'd be able to tell immediately what typewriter had been used,' says Iris, unable to resist showing off. There are precious few advantages from her year at secretarial school, so she can be forgiven for making the most of this one. 'Machines are like people: each has its own little quirks. For example, look at the letter e.' Eugene picks up the torch and the two men peer at the unfolded paper. 'See how there's fractionally bigger spacing between it and the preceding letter? And the letter n. If you look really carefully, you'll be able to tell it's just slightly lower than all the other letters.'

'So, if you found the typewriter, you'd know who sent the note?' asks Eugene. 'Or if you discovered the machine this was typed on was in the Boninis' house, you'd at least know that whoever typed it has been here and it's not someone passing on a message sent from outside?'

Iris stops nodding when she sees how he is looking at her, and his meaning becomes clear.

'Well, yes, but if you think I'm going to go searching . . .'

'Of course you're not,' snaps Joe. 'Bruce Bonini is not the kind of man to welcome someone snooping around his house.'

He is only being sensible, Iris supposes, but there is something about the photographer's assumption of authority that makes her want to do the exact opposite of what he is telling her.

Excusing herself, complaining of a headache, Iris goes to

her room and turns the key in the door. Despite what she now knows about the keys all being the same, it is only when she hears the clicking of the lock that she lets herself finally relax. To her surprise, her temple is indeed throbbing. And despite her marathon sleep the previous night, she is bone tired, every muscle and nerve and sinew of her aching from the constant effort of interacting with strangers in a place that is so utterly unfamiliar.

Lying in bed, she gazes up through the gauze of the mosquito net to where the blades of the fan circle overhead as images of the day scroll through her weary, alcohol-soaked mind. From the corner of her eye, she can see where the anonymous letter, neatly folded back into its envelope, sits on top of her chest of drawers.

But when at last she succumbs to a hot, clammy, restless kind of sleep, it is not Nell who haunts her dreams but the image of Bruce Bonini, on the edge of the terrace, holding the giant moth up towards the starry Havana sky as if to release it, then methodically rubbing its wings and thorax between his thumb and forefinger until it was dust.

Dear Uncle Cyp

I'm back in LA. Only for a week while they try to dry out Errol enough to reshoot his big scene. God, it's good to eat decent food again. First thing I did off the plane was head to Philippe's for a French Dip. Heaven.

Well, you'll be glad to know, I did it. There. Aren't you proud of me? The lawyer had one of those faces like he was weaned on a pickle. Every time he said 'your husband', he looked at me over the top of his glasses like he was reminding me I was married, like I might have forgotten. At the end I said, 'I pay you because you went to Law School, not because you went to Moral Judgement School.' He was all flustered then. Said, 'I don't know what you mean, Mrs Hardman.' And I said, 'There you go again.' I'd already told him to call me Miss Summers. I've no wish to share a name with Frau Connie. Bad enough we share a husband. For now.

Manderley was a gift, so that counts as my property, and all the money I earned before I met Hugh. I haven't a clue how much that was, darling, but I know it was enough to make the bank manager break out the good bourbon whenever I stopped by. And the other things that came before Hugh – the house in Beverly Hills and that ghastly Manhattan apartment with all that dark wood which I wish to God I'd never let that realtor talk me into. Why didn't you stop me?

Such a bore, but if there's to be a divorce, and I'm not saying there is, so don't start spreading that around or it'll come back to bite you in the ass, Mel says I have to start separating off the finances from now. And what's the use in paying Mel 15 per cent if I'm not going to listen to him?

So now, if anything happens to me, Lana gets the lot. Apart from Manderley, which is held in trust until she marries. Not that she'd have any idea what to spend any of it on. Cookies, probably. I know I'm a bitch and heading straight to hell, but would it kill her to have just a little more self-control? 'There's a pretty girl in there, among all that padding,' I said to her the other day, and you know what she said? 'At least the padding means the pretty girl is comfortable.' All straight-faced, you know? I had to admit it was pretty funny, though I did see her staring at herself long and hard in the mirror later on, so maybe it hit home. I put in some provision for Faye, too, in the will, even though the God's honest truth is the girl really isn't all there. She still follows me around the house like a shadow. And I know for a fact she goes through my things when I'm not around. Christ knows I love my daughters, but sometimes when I drive away from the house I feel a weight lifting clear off my heart and my soul dancing a fucking jig.

Now, don't you worry about Hugh. The way to handle my husband is to remember he's just a giant baby who can't conceive of a world outside of himself. All it takes to keep him happy is to pat him on the head and tell him how wonderful he is the whole time. It's when folk start treating him like an actual grown-up that the trouble starts. Do you know, last year, he refused to go to a party because Manny Farber was on the guest list, on account of how Farber used that word 'cruddy' in a review of *A Different Dawn* – you might know it as *A Different Yawn*? So Farber was uninvited. Let it never be said that the great Hugh Hardman doesn't know how to nurse a grudge!

But as long as it's all going his way and the studios keep sending him eighteen-year-old starlets to break in and telling him he's the greatest thing since apple pie, he's perfectly content. And meantime, I get to do some breaking in of my own . . .

And if that doesn't bring you racing westwards at a rate of knots, I don't know my Cyp.

Love, Aunt Sap

8

BY THE FOLLOWING morning, Iris is finding it hard to remember her misgivings of the night before. The heady smell of the night-blooming jasmine lingers, even though the flowers have closed in the light of the sun. Facing her is a wall entirely masked by a dense mass of luscious greenery – tall, thick green stalks which sprout graceful fernlike leaves, tendrils of bright pink buds, a low bush with large, waxy leaves and sprigs of red flowers – while to the left those exotic trees, with their cargo of green bananas and avocados, screen the main house from view.

She and Eugene and Joe are out on the terrace of the guest house eating some orange-fleshed fruit, which turns out to be mango, which Eugene sourced from the main kitchen. Taking another bite, Iris decides she has never tasted anything more delicious in her life, and doesn't even mind that the juice is trickling down her chin and on to her lap. It is one of those moments where it seems to her quite impossible that the world could be big enough to hold both this terrace bursting with new smells and colours and tastes, and her parents' dark, narrow hallway in Hemel Hempstead with its low ceiling and the dado rail that separates the mustard paint above from the drab floral wallpaper reaching to the skirting board below.

'What kind of business is he in, Bruce Bonini?' she asks, trying to dab the juice with her finger. 'I mean, he is obviously jolly successful, whatever it is. This isn't even his only house, is it? Don't they live most of the year in California, or somewhere like that?'

She is infuriatingly aware again of having said something unintentionally amusing.

'Bruce Bonini and his friend Meyer Lansky and a few other fine gentlemen who you might meet at the wedding between them run most of the gaming joints in Havana,' says Joe, glancing in the direction of the main house as if to make sure they can't be overheard. Iris finds herself mesmerised by his mouth, the sheen of mango juice on his full lips. For one mad moment she lets herself imagine what it might be like to lick it off, before guilt about Peter snaps that window shut. 'They also do the same thing in America, but with a hundred times the bureaucracy and a thousand times the risk of being banged up in jail for the rest of their lives.'

'Laws and taxes being such a drag,' Eugene says, rolling his eyes. Iris remembers their conversation about the rebels in the mountains, growing their beards and waiting for the chance to seize back control.

'Havana is a playground for Bruce and his buddies,' Joe continues. 'President Batista lets them do what they want as long as they give him his cut. Prostitution, narcotics. They bring their ill-gotten gains from their operations in America and use it to build their shiny hotels and casinos, and Batista reaps the rewards. It's like an endless circle of dirty money.'

'You should hear the stories about him.' If Eugene's eyes got any bigger, there surely would not be room for them on his face.

'Batista?'

'No, Bruce. They say he snipped off a man's tongue once with a pair of kitchen scissors, when he found out he had informed on him to the FBI.'

'That's a myth, though,' says Joe, seeing Iris's reaction. 'He would have got a minion to snip it off for him.'

Iris stares at them with her mouth open, the mango all but forgotten. This must be a joke. She thinks of the man she met the night before out on the terrace of the main house with his fussy little mouth, and his wife with her red hair set like a helmet. Thinks of his delicate fingers pulverising the moth in her dream. But no, it's too absurd.

'So you're saying our host is an American mobster.' She smiles, waiting for them to smile back in return.

Two sets of eyes regard her steadily.

Afterwards, she tries to make sense of it. Could Bruce Bonini really be who they say he is? And if so, how is it Hugh Hardman and he are such great friends? She thinks about the film director, remembering how the sheer force of his attention had left her immobilised on the terrace, as if the rest of the world was falling away and there was only him and her and this new reality that contained them both.

Only now does it occur to her that perhaps they are both dangerous, Bruce and Hugh, each in his own way.

*

By the time Iris arrives at her second sitting with Lana she has quashed her worries and decided once and for all that Eugene and Joe were joking, or at least exaggerating. Such things belong in films. This is real life and, in real life, she has a job to do. She is determined that today's sitting will be better than the last. Today she will get underneath the smooth skin of her subject and bring her finally to life.

But Lana is as slippery as ever. Cool and unflustered, even when Iris reminds her that she was wearing a completely different outfit the day before and would she mind going to change because, otherwise, they will have to start over again.

Iris wishes she could find something to unlock the Lana she saw yesterday on the tennis court, hair flying, racquet raised in triumph, laughing with her stepbrother. But all her attempts at conversation are cut short. It is as if they are on that very same tennis court, she and Lana, and every time Iris plays a shot there is Lana, standing impassive at the net to block it. The weather? *Oh, you get used to it.* The wedding preparations? *I mostly do what I'm told.* Their hosts? *The Boninis have been so generous.*

Only once is her answer anything other than predictable, when Iris asks whether she minds the wedding being here on this island so far from everyone she knows. 'Actually it was me who suggested it. I like to keep things quiet.'

It's not even as if Iris is given any option to talk about herself in order to further the conversation along. Lana seems almost insultingly incurious about where Iris has come from, or how she ended up here, or how she feels being away from home for the first time. Eventually, confidence boosted by being part hidden behind her easel, Iris jumps right in.

'My mother's nerves will be shredded, wondering what's happening to me. She was so worried about me coming.'

Reclining on the chaise, Lana does not immediately react and Iris feels the stirrings of despair. While, on the canvas, she has brought to life the folds in Lana's skirt, the exact texture of the rattan, the shadow her cheek throws across the arm it rests on, the girl's face refuses to animate itself. Everything is there, just as it appears: the thick lashes, darker than one might expect; the wide, shallow structure of her face; the soft, unfinished curve of her cheek. In most respects, it is a very pleasing picture. And yet, when Iris steps back from it, she sees just another young woman who could be any young woman. She does not see Lana.

'It must be nice, though, to have people worry about you,' her subject finally responds.

Too late, Iris remembers the dead mother, Jean Summers, with her radiant smile, her fresh, blonde beauty. The sexy but sweet girl next door, the bombshell wife. Those had been the roles Jean was famous for. White lace dresses emphasising a waist so tiny a man could put his hands around it and have them meet at the fingertips.

'I'm sorry,' she says. 'That was insensitive.'

To her surprise, Lana laughs.

'Oh, please, don't concern yourself. Even when she was alive, Mommy wasn't really the worrying type.'

Iris is not sure how to respond. In her experience, worrying is sort of what mothers are for. Not that there seems to be much point to it. Her own mother worries equally about everything, from whether her latest haircut is too severe, to the nuclear threat, to whether the devilled eggs she served to the Richmonds the previous weekend might have been a mistake, so there is no hierarchy of fear, just a constant high-pitched hum of tension running through her life.

How would she have been if Wendy had lived? Iris rarely allows her mind to go here, where lies a knot of white-hot pain which, if she were to start to unpick it, might never stop unravelling. Who would her mother be if she was still the mother to two daughters, if she didn't need a pill to get up in the morning? Would there be any need for the incessant worrying, the reliance on her myriad household chores as a structure to get her through her life, so that if something goes awry, like last week, when the greengrocer was closed for a family funeral, or when an unexpected rain means the sheets that were very nearly dry now can't be put back on the beds, or a visitor delays the cooking so there's no time to prepare coronation chicken and something has to be rustled using spam from a tin, it's as if the world has stopped turning. 'I have unusually sensitive nerves,' her mother once said and after that Iris imagined that her mother's nerves were missing an outer layer, the raw insides exposed to the elements.

One time during a long argument about going to art college, when Iris had declared, 'It's the only thing I really love,' her mother had looked at her with an expression that bordered on venomous. 'No one gets what they love, Iris. It's about time you learned that. Save yourself a lot of heartache.'

How different might her parents' relationship have been if Iris's seven-year-old sister hadn't died during the measles epidemic of 1941? They are content enough on the whole, she supposes. There are few arguments. Raised voices rarely ruffle the thick air of the house, but there is something in the way her parents move around each other, never quite coming together, like racing cars around a track, that makes a hole open up in Iris's heart.

Thinking about her mother now, here on this terrace in this city so far away from home, Iris has a sudden longing to see her, to try again to build some bridges with her. Her chest constricts when she thinks about all the different ways she and her mother have failed each other.

'You're lucky. Of course, I only knew your mother from her films, but she seemed like she'd be great fun.'

A cloud floats across the shallow planes of Lana's face but is gone before Iris's pencil registers it was even there.

'She could be, yes. Sometimes we'd have these little parties, just on our own, where we'd dress up in her best clothes and jewels and furs and drink pretend champagne out of crystal glasses, or she'd wake me while it was still dark and we'd drive to the beach to watch the sun rise. But that was when I was younger, before she ran out of steam. The thing about Mommy was that she had children the way other women have, I don't know, shoulder massages, or dance lessons. Without thinking about the long term. It was something she thought might be amusing, and when it turned out not to be, at least not all the time, she was surprised to find she was stuck with it. After that happened, we kinda reversed roles.'

'How do you mean?'

'I started looking after her instead of the other way around. She was what you'd call highly strung.'

'But I'm sure she loved you both enormously.'

Iris is wishing she had never started this conversation. She is out of her depth here. Lana hasn't moved, the perfect model. Yet Iris senses the turbulence beneath that placid surface. If only she could find the crack that would let this true self out.

'Have you met Faye yet?'

Iris recalls the girl she saw right here just the night before, the long, pale bones of her arms pushing through her skin, the huge eyes fixed on her sister's fiancé.

'Not properly. That is to say . . .'

'My sister is all the example you need of what my mother's kind of love can do.'

Iris is still thinking about Lana's cryptic comment a few minutes later when she goes indoors in search of the lavatory, making her way to the vast marbled lobby with its crystal chandelier. The stairs sweep up on either side, and behind them is a short corridor that leads into another, far less grand lobby, where Lana has assured her she will find a guest cloakroom. It was such a strange thing to say but the girl had clammed up again immediately afterwards, refusing to be drawn further and now Iris's head throbs with questions.

The back lobby is darker than the main lobby, illuminated only by dim wall lights. There are three doors leading off it, one of which does indeed lead to a large cloakroom, with a black-and-white chequered floor. As Iris washes her hands, she hears noises outside – a door creaking, followed by footsteps tracking across the marble floor. Emerging into the lobby, she notices the next door along, which had been closed, is now ajar. Through the narrow gap she can see the room is a study with a polished walnut desk and, pushed towards the back of the desk, a typewriter under a canvas cover.

Of course she won't go in. It would be unforgivable if she was discovered.

And yet.

Iris remembers the ugly black type of that anonymous letter. Now that the shock of it has passed, she finds herself increasingly irate. Nell has been nothing but kind to her since the moment they met, and along comes a coward hiding behind a keyboard to settle some sort of private grudge – and drag her – Iris – into it. The urge to take a closer look at the typewriter is overwhelming. She puts out a foot and gently nudges the door open with her toe.

The study is Bruce's. Iris is sure of that immediately. Even from the doorway it has that masculine smell of leather and cigar smoke. She steps tentatively into the room, modest in size, but with those high ceilings that are everywhere. The floor is polished parquet, with a large rug. The walls are lined with wood panelling. It is as if a designer has taken a photograph of a study in an old-fashioned English country house and recreated it exactly in this tropical outpost.

The desk has a burgundy leather inlay and three neat shelves at the back, one for envelopes, one for blank paper and the other for writing paper with Bruce's name and address embossed at the top and – could that really be? – a coat of arms. The typewriter itself, once she removes the cover, is a smart-looking Smith-Corona, smaller than the machines they use in the typing pool, dark grey with green keys. At first she is surprised to think that Bruce Bonini, this supposed mobster, might know how to use such a thing. Then it occurs to her that he probably employs a secretary to come in here and type up his correspondence, perhaps sitting at this very desk. The thought that this is not after all a private space, but somewhere a typist, perhaps a girl just like herself, might come to work, makes her feel a little calmer.

Despite her boasts to Eugene and Joe, it is impossible for Iris to tell just by looking at it whether this is the machine on which the anonymous note was written. She picks up a sheet of blank paper from the stack in the tray at the back of the desk and feeds it into the typewriter, relieved at the smooth, silent motion of the well-oiled roller. Of course, she won't actually press the keys, she tells herself. That would be foolhardy. She goes to the doorway, as if to leave. Peers out. The hall is empty. The air undisturbed. It would take her just a few seconds.

She turns back into the room. Heart hammering, she quickly types out, 'The quick brown fox jumps over the lazy dog.' It's the most famous pangram of them all, the one every novice typist starts out on. The clattering keys sound deafening in the otherwise silent house. Then she snatches the paper off the roller and slams shut the typewriter lid before heading once more to the door, sagging with relief when she sees the hallway still empty, no sign of Bruce or his men coming to find out what the noise is or Lana wondering what's taking so long.

She is readying herself to step outside when she hears footsteps approaching from the main lobby. For an agonising moment she is rooted to the spot as panic mushrooms inside her. *Whoever it is will be going upstairs. They won't come this way.* As the footsteps grow louder, she darts back inside the room and crouches down behind the desk, where she is hidden by the three under-desk drawers. *They will go into the cloakroom*, she tells herself, *then I can leave.*

But the footsteps don't go past the slightly open door; instead, they proceed directly into the study. Huddled on the floor with her arms wrapped around her knees, Iris feels the pounding of her heart in her thighs and her shins. Only now does it occur to her that the door being left ajar might indicate a temporary absence, someone popping out to pass on a message or pick up something they'd forgotten.

From her hiding place, she watches a man's shiny black shoes cross in front of the desk. Has he seen her? Her mouth is dry as dust, but she dare not swallow. Just as she convinces herself it is all over and she must stand up and explain herself, there comes a clicking sound, followed by the low rumble of a drawer being pulled along its runners and the clink of metal on metal. The shoes turn and walk away down to the other end of the room, the sound of the heels muffled as they track across the rug towards the far wall, where she earlier noticed a door cut into the wood panelling. Now she can see almost all of him, she recognises the shoes as belonging to the man who opened the gates when she first arrived. She watches the back of his dark jacket as he takes the keys he has just removed from the desk drawer and unlocks the door. When he opens it, she sees it is a cupboard. Emboldened by the distance and the solid barrier of the man's shoulders, she raises her head above the level of the desk to get a better look, just in time to see the man flick on a light and reach into the deep recess to withdraw a gleaming, sizeable gun.

Iris sinks back down, feeling as if all the air has been sucked out of her. Through her narrow field of vision, she watches the man tuck the gun into the waistband of his trousers, and shut and lock the door. But she has already seen what the cupboard contains. Shelf upon shelf of densely packed weapons.

This is the first time Iris really understands that it could be real, the danger that pulses silently at Bruce Bonini's narrow throat, that he might actually be responsible for having people killed. That this isn't a plot from one of Hugh Hardman's films but something that happens in real life, is happening in *her* life. She tucks her hands under her arms to try to stop them from trembling as the black shoes once again approach the desk behind which she cowers.

Again there comes the sound of a drawer opening and closing. Then, to Iris's huge relief, the shoes head back towards the study door. *He is leaving!* The door opens then closes behind him, but the joy that floods through Iris's still-shaking limbs is short-lived as she hears a sickening clicking sound.

She is locked in.

On the other side of the door the footsteps fade into silence as the man makes his way back to the main lobby. But here in the study the rushing of Iris's blood is deafening in her own ears. Every instinct in her is telling her to stay where she is, curled up in a ball, and yet she knows she must try to get herself out. There will be another key somewhere in the room, she tells herself. There has to be. All she has to do is find the source of the first one.

Getting shakily to her feet she makes her way to the door, just in case she has made a mistake. But no, the door will not budge. Back in front of the desk, she gingerly tries the top drawer. Locked.

The bottom one slides open, but it contains only a stack

of ledgers. When she flicks open the top one, she sees the very first entry is labelled 'Raúl Herrera' and consists of a list of dates with amounts written next to them. Raúl's salary, is Iris's first guess, until she notices that all the amounts are different. Perhaps payments for extra jobs he is carrying out for Bruce? She has no time to speculate on what those jobs might be. With a man like Bruce.

The middle drawer contains various items of stationery. An elegant silver letter opener, a pair of steel scissors, their blades sharp and gleaming. A fountain pen with three pots of ink of different colours. All precisely ordered. No keys. The top drawer will not open. In a rising panic, she tries to remember if she'd heard the sound of a desk drawer being locked. Surely not. Now she is becoming desperate. How will she explain herself if Bruce comes in? What if no one arrives at all and she has to shout for help? She can think of nothing that would explain her presence in her host's private study.

She tries again, feeling around in the back corners of the middle drawer. Nothing. But as she withdraws her hand her knuckles brush against something on the underside of the drawer above. Closer inspection reveals a hook – and hanging from the hook, two keys. *Thank heavens.* Iris's heart surges with gratitude. She will never set a foot out of line again, she promises the god in whom she's not entirely sure she believes. Snatching both keys, she heads to the door, closing her eyes with relief when the second one unlocks it. Her first thought is to bolt, but first she must decide what to do with the key. Either she replaces it in the drawer and leaves the door unlocked, making it obvious that someone has been here, or she locks it from the outside and takes the key with her. Neither option is appealing. Still in an agony of indecision, she goes back to the desk to replace the other key, which she assumes must be the one the man used to open the gun cupboard. *Gun cupboard*. How ridiculous it sounds.

As she reaches into the drawer, craning her neck to see where the hook is, she spots something in the furthest reaches, a flash of colour hanging from the back of the locked top drawer, as if it has been forced out by whatever else is in there. She tugs tentatively and the thing comes out completely, revealing itself to be a woman's beautiful silk scarf decorated with flowers of pink and orange and yellow and giving off, when she holds it to her nose, the faintest whiff of perfume. As she opens it up, a slip of folded paper flutters to the floor. Bruce's name is scrawled across the outside and when she picks it up she sees it contains a brief message in the same messy hand:

Morning, sleepyhead! Gotta dash. Show yourself out. x

She tries to stuff the scarf and the note it was wrapped around back into the drawer through the same crack, but it will not go, and now comes the unmistakable sound of a man's voice along the passageway in the main hallway. Sweat trickling down her back, she scrambles to her feet and slams the drawer shut, cramming scarf and note into one of her deep dress pockets. Then she leaves the room, fumbling to lock the door behind her, which is where Bruce Bonini finds her, that overpowering leather-and-spice smell preceding his arrival.

'Can I help you, Miss Bailey?'

'I was just returning from the cloakroom and got a little disoriented. Your house is so palatial.'

Her back is to the door, the key folded in her right palm, slippery with sweat.

Bruce's flat, dark eyes rove unhurriedly over her face, as if trying to find a way into her head.

'It's that way.' He points in the direction from which he has just come and pulls back the corners of his dainty mouth into a smile that makes the fine hairs on Iris's arms stand on end.

As Iris crosses the lobby, her skin prickles, as if her host's gaze is a spider crawling on her back.

9

I RIS HAS NEVER been to a bridal shower, had not even heard of one until Nell invited her to Havana. Even after the term was explained she could not quite understand how it might fit in here, with this particular wedding, this particular bride. Who will be there, apart from Lana's family or Hugh's, or associates of the Boninis?

All the way to the venue, sandwiched stickily between Eugene and Joe in the back seat of Raúl's car, Iris picks over her ordeal in Bruce's study. The whole thing can't have lasted longer than ten minutes and yet it seemed as if time had stood still while she crouched behind that desk, and when she remembers the encounter with her host in the hallway outside, her skin feels both cold and clammy at the same time. Back in the safety of her room, she'd hidden the key in her case, then almost immediately taken it out again and tucked it inside one of her blue shoes under the bed. The scarf and note she'd shoved to the back of a drawer, but not before she'd raised the scarf to her nose once more to catch the lingering scent and tried to imagine Bruce doing the same. Was it Barbara's? Something about that scrawled 'show yourself out' told her it was not. Then she'd unfolded the page on which she'd typed out 'The quick brown fox jumps over the lazy dog' and stared at it for a good long time. A space before the letter e. The letter n just slightly misaligned with the others. This was definitely the same machine on which the anonymous note had been typed. So whoever wrote it was there in that house.

Bruce was the most obvious suspect, it being his study, and yet she could not imagine him sitting down, feeding paper into the machine. Typing the words *nell kills people*. And really, anyone could have got into that study, just as she had.

A couple of times when Iris glances up she locks eyes with Raúl, watching her in his rear-view mirror, and her throat feels dry.

Briefly, she toys with telling Joe and Eugene what happened, imagining the relief of sharing her fears. But can she really be certain they are to be trusted? She was trespassing, after all. Also, she worries whether she'd be able to relate the whole thing without her voice trembling or, God forbid, bursting into tears.

Iris's agitation is momentarily forgotten when they arrive at the Tropicana, situated in a lush park that appears like an oasis at the edge of the city. 'It's only the most famous nightclub in the world,' Joe tells her, shocked that she has never heard of it. 'All the big stars have played here. Josephine Baker? Nat King Cole? Carmen Miranda?'

'Oh, the fruit lady. Well, of course I know of *her*.' As soon as the words are out she regrets them. In her eagerness to prove to the arrogant photographer that she isn't completely ignorant, she has ended up sounding even more so.

The Tropicana is unlike any other building Iris has ever been in. Surrounded by what looks to be jungle and entered via an arched gateway, it has two enormous stages, one al fresco, almost appearing to be set into the jungle itself, with lines of tables radiating out from the circular stage like the rays of the sun, the other under a roof. But what a roof! Six vast concrete arches hold up sheets of glass so impossibly high it seems as if they are glazing the sky itself. On the ground, scores of formally set rectangular tables huddle in front of a wide stage. But what makes Iris really gasp are the enormous living palm trees that soar up towards the light. *Inside the roof.*

Eugene whistles admiringly. 'This place cost a bomb, and you can see why. Lucky that Prince Aly Khan and Rita Hayworth lost enough money here at the casino to pay for it all. I wonder there's no plaque to them. Can you imagine how it looks at night, when it's all lit up?'

Instead, it seems they will be treated to a far more sedate show than the famous night-time cabaret. The place isn't usually even open in the afternoons, but the owner is doing it as a favour to Bruce.

Iris is fast forming the opinion that Havana is a city that runs on favours.

They are shown to a small cluster of tables near the stage on which various musical instruments stand ready. The rest of the guests are here already and in their seats. Iris, Eugene and Joe are expected to mingle unobtrusively, sketching or taking photographs or, in Eugene's case, just chatting and being entertaining.

Champagne appears, and a modest band of musicians stroll on to the stage to polite applause. 'Good luck,' says

Eugene, heading off to corner the bride. Joe nods grimly and busies himself retrieving his photographic equipment from various cases, screwing in lenses, attaching flashes. He has even brought a black umbrella with a silver underside and a metallic sheet that rolls up.

Iris casts around in a panic. This is why she has been brought all this way. She must get busy. But every table seems to be a closed knot of bent heads deep in conversation and she sees no opening into which she might slip with her sketchpad. She knows she could go to sit with Nell, but since the arrival of the anonymous letter a strained note has crept into their nascent friendship. Not because Iris believes for one moment that there is any truth in those allegations but because she hasn't yet brought herself to mention it, and now that single sheet of paper sits like an invisible screen between the two of them. Iris's eyes alight on a friendly face. 'Come on over,' Connie beckons, and Iris gratefully goes to join her.

Connie is sitting with Meredith Summers and Barbara Bonini on a table set with a white linen cloth and crystal glasses. Iris still finds it strange that relations appear so cordial between Hugh Hardman's first wife and the family of his deceased second wife, but then Connie is such a friendly kind of person, and she and Hugh seemed to have enjoyed such a peculiarly civil divorce. And perhaps this is just what happens in sophisticated circles. Marriages are made and broken, and nobody makes a fuss about it.

While Iris settles herself down and takes out her pencils, Connie and Meredith continue a conversation they seem to have been in the middle of. 'It's an excellent school. It's produced three First Ladies, for heaven's sake. Yet you'd think I was sending her to Sing Sing, the way she carries on. I'm fond of her, don't misunderstand me. But my charity work leaves me so little free time. All those poor, destitute girls.'

Iris feels uncomfortable. They can only be talking about Faye Mickelson, who sits not even ten feet from their table, wearing a large brimmed hat to shield her sallow skin and a sleeveless jet-black dress under which her clavicle appears like a steel bar crossing between her narrow shoulders. Iris focuses her attention on Barbara Bonini, who is already on her third glass of champagne. First Iris sketches the outline of her subject, the round swell of her bosom emphasised by her low-cut dress, the texture of her red hair, which has been teased and set so that it rises in waves from her face and shows off the diamonds hanging from her earlobes.

Narrowing in on the face, Iris follows the line of the right eyelid, where it dips as if weighed down by the sheer volume of kohl, mascara and eyeshadow. The pencilled arches of her brows give her the appearance of being permanently alarmed. The outline of her lips has been painted slightly outside her natural mouth to make them seem fuller and the upper presses against the lower, as if there is a membrane joining them that cannot be breached. When Barbara finally summons the energy to raise her eyes, Iris notices that they seem clouded over, as if the grey-green is hidden behind a gauzy veil, and they don't focus on one particular thing but slide blankly from face to face, object to object, as if the whole lot were coated in oil.

'You're very young,' she says to Iris. It is a statement, not a question. 'I'm glad I'm not your age again.'

'Oh.' Iris does not know how to respond to this. 'Yes, well, I imagine there's a lot to be said for being wiser and more experienced.'

Barbara Bonini smiles without parting her lips, just the corners widening lazily, like a cat stretching.

'There is precisely nothing to be said for either of those things. Na-*da*. I'm just glad I don't have all those disappointments ahead of me, is all. Sometimes when I look back, it's just one after another after another. Like a row of dominoes. Ain't that right, you two?' She is appealing to Connie and Meredith, who halt in conversation as if a film has been frozen partway through the screening. 'Ain't it right that life's disappointments are like dominoes – once you turn twenty-one, down they all go, *clack, clack, clack, clack*?' Here Barbara helpfully flicks her hand open to demonstrate. 'One in front of the other, as far as the eye can see?'

'Well, my goodness, Barbara, aren't you a ray of sunshine? Would it kill you to be a little more encouraging to the poor girl?' Connie's kindly face is wreathed in smiles. 'I mean, for all you know, Iris here has a future ahead of her that is entirely roses and sunlight.'

But now that Barbara has come up with her dominoes analogy, she is not to be put off it.

'*Clack, clack, clack, clack,*' she says again, with that same flicking motion of her hand. 'Don't pretend it isn't so. When you were her age, you were married to your childhood sweetheart, all dewy-eyed with your two perfect children and your nice little starter home. And no clue that just ahead of you lay Jean Summers and divorce and all those arguments with Hugh about money and *clack, clack, clack, clack.*'

It is on this third repetition of the phrase that Iris realises just how drunk Barbara Bonini is.

'Don't be such an old sourpuss,' says Connie, and though her tone is light, her voice is clipped and her fingers twist the delicate silver cross around her neck. 'Hugh and I have a perfectly amicable relationship, because we've worked to make it that way.'

It's something Iris's mother says a lot, this need to 'work' at relationships. Iris feels privately that work takes up quite enough time as it is, without having to do more when you get home. Then she thinks of Peter, and how there are times she feels that in place of a conversation he is merely leaving spaces for her to say something before continuing with his monologue as if she hadn't spoken at all.

Barbara gets to her feet and lurches off in the direction of the bathroom, lugging her large handbag with her. Iris is glad her sketch is almost done and pleased with how the picture has turned out. There are Barbara's heavy lids, from under which her eyes gaze glassily out, and there is the lip-sticked mouth, and the diamonds glinting in her ears. Connie stares after her hostess, frowning in thought.

'She's a fine one to talk about arguments,' she says to Iris, her hand still worrying at her necklace. 'Do you know, one time on the *SallyAnn*, Barbara argued so ferociously with Jean they woke Nell up in her cabin clear at the other end of the boat?' Then she seems to recollect who she is talking to and her voice changes. 'But I expect all families bicker, don't they, dear? Pay me no mind.'

Iris is conscious she needs to move on. Already Eugene has covered three different tables, alighting first on one, then another, like a tiny, extraordinarily shaped bird. Joe, meanwhile, keeps himself apart, his camera forming a barrier between him and his subjects behind which his thoughts are impossible to read.

Excusing herself, Iris gathers up her things and once more casts around. The musicians behind her have launched into 'Quizás, Quizás, Quizás', which Iris recognises from the wireless. But here it has a different rhythm, more languid, heavier on the percussion. The singer is playing the maracas, flicking his wrist in a desultory way. He wears an emerald-green shirt entirely made from ruffles, like the plumage of an exotic bird, and tight, dark trousers. Behind him, a line of chorus girls wearing costumes in different rainbow colours with feathered tails, sequined leotards and extravagant head-dresses almost like sculptures shimmy and sashay under the multicoloured lights.

Nell sits nearby at the table with Faye Mickelson and two other women Iris does not recognise. Eugene is there also, mid-anecdote, the others gazing at him raptly as he speaks. It is a performance he gives, Iris sees now, the performance of being Eugene Stringer. How exhausting it must be.

Iris draws up a chair beside Nell. It's the first chance they've had to chat properly since the note arrived, and Iris hopes the American won't notice the new awkwardness between them. Nell asks her about her job in the typing pool and Iris finds herself telling her all about Mrs Latham and how the girls always think the clock behind her has stopped, so slowly do the hands move around, and the mushroom-faced draughtsmen, turning the quiet desperation of her days into amusing anecdotes that make Nell roar with laughter.

'How about you, Nell? Have you ever had a job?'

Nell makes a face. 'Only one that Pop got me, working for Jean, just menial stuff, you know. Answering fan mail, booking her travel. It wasn't exactly arduous, if you know what I'm saying.' She jerks her head in the direction of Faye, who is sitting directly opposite, and Iris understands her to mean that this is not the time for her to go into detail on what it was like having Jean Summers as a boss.

Iris flips over to a new page in her sketchbook to draw Faye. The girl has such an interesting face, its gauntness affording its strong features all the more prominence. She is all angles and dark shadows. Only in the eyes can one see any resemblance to her sister. That grey-blue which is like the early-morning sky on a washed-out summer's day back home.

'You are the sole bridesmaid, I understand,' says Iris when she catches Faye's eye. 'Exciting, but I imagine also quite a responsibility, making sure the bride arrives on time and no one trips over her dress.'

Faye smiles, and for a split second it is as if her face belongs to someone else entirely. She would be beautiful, Iris thinks with surprise, if she wasn't so terribly thin.

'I don't think Lana's dress has a train,' she says. It is the first time Iris has heard her voice properly. How quiet it is, as if the merest gust of wind could blow it away. 'It isn't to be a very conventional wedding.'

'I should think not when she's going to be Wife Number Three,' says Nell, who also seems to have partaken generously of the champagne on offer. 'And when the whole world thinks her husband is a horny old goat.'

Iris – who is drawing Faye's hands – notices how her long fingers dig suddenly into the starched white tablecloth.

'You shouldn't . . .' she begins. 'You should have more . . .' Her voice tails off to nothing.

'Oh, don't get in a tizz, Faye. Pop can do exactly what he pleases. It's all the same to me. He can marry Meredith, for all I care.' She gestures towards the neighbouring table. 'Or that waitress, or those dancers on the stage.'

They turn to look at the women in their colourful outfits, all uniformly smiling, as if their smiles themselves are part of their costumes. Now Nell sits back in her seat so that her breasts, barely contained by her strapless gown, are fully on display. Glancing up, Iris notices for the first time that Joe Garston has joined their table, silently training his lens first on one guest then another.

'I do hope you haven't been talking too much, Nellie,' says Connie, who has come up behind Nell and now plants a kiss on top of her daughter's head. 'We shall have to sew a zip in here, at this rate.' She runs a finger across Nell's vermilion-painted mouth.

'No, Mama,' Nell intones drolly, while rolling her eyes at Iris and making a throat-slitting motion with her hand.

'Are you looking forward to the wedding?' Iris asks Faye, trying to draw the girl out of herself.

Faye shrugs, her sharp little shoulders moving up and down like piano keys. 'I have been living with my grand-mother, but now that Lana is getting married to Hugh, we can all live in Manderley again.'

Faye lapses into silence, while all around them the con-versation glides seamlessly on: the music – Connie says she feels quite seasick with all this swaying and sashaying; the dancers' clothes – Nell declares she will get a costume made exactly the same to wear at her mother's fiftieth-birthday party to scandalise all the guests. 'What do you think, Mr Garston?' she asks, looking directly into the camera lens. 'Will it suit me?'

'I'm sure you'd look a picture, no matter what you wore,' he says, his face hidden behind his camera.

Now Nell and her mother are talking to the two other women at the table, who turn out to be Americans who live here in Havana and whose husbands are also in 'business', like Bruce. Iris studies their faces for signs that these two very ordinary-seeming women, with their tightly cinched waists and their white satin gloves which they wear despite the heat, might be gangsters' wives – some hardness around the features, perhaps – but finds none.

'Who are they?' she asks Joe, gesturing to a neighbouring table where sit two middle-aged women with glossy black hair and sour expressions. In between them is a beautiful young woman of about Iris's own age, with huge, dark eyes set into a narrow, high-cheekboned face and a slender throat adorned with a single string of white pearls.

'The wives of some Cuban bigshots Bonini is doing business with. Señoras Ferrer and Morales, if I remember right. I'd give them a swerve with your sketchpad, if I were you. I almost got my head bit off when I tried to take a photograph. I get the feeling they're none too keen to be associated with the gringo wedding. Husbands probably put the thumb screws on them to attend.'

'And the younger one?'

'Daughter, I believe.' Iris has to strain to hear, because Joe has abruptly turned his attention to fiddling with his camera lens. He is flustered, she realises. On account of the lovely Cuban girl. She is surprised at how much she minds.

Lana makes a little thank-you speech in her quiet, flat voice and as soon as she finishes Iris finds she cannot recall anything that was said. As with the portrait, the girl somehow manages to leave no impression of herself behind.

A few minutes later, when Iris excuses herself to go to the bathroom, she is surprised to find Meredith, straight-backed and stick thin in her velvet sheath dress, her bouffant hair so big it makes her head seem dangerously large for her bony neck, dabbing her eyes in the mirror.

'Are you all right, Mrs Summers?'

'Yes, perfectly. Thank you,' the older woman says stiffly. Then she pauses. 'Tell me, Iris, are you close to your family?'

Iris is taken aback. 'Oh, you know, we're just normal, I expect.'

'What I mean is, if you made a speech at your bridal shower, do you think you might mention your parents?'

Meredith's voice is bright and brittle, and Iris feels a groundswell of pity for her when it dawns on her that the bride-to-be did indeed neglect to include her grandmother in her speech.

'I imagine you might be surprised to know that Lana and I were once close, but her mother's death hit her very hard and I'm afraid she rather took it out on me.'

'I'm sorry,' says Iris, inadequately.

'That's partly why I came here to Havana,' says Meredith, in that same clipped voice. 'To make sure she wasn't marrying Hugh Hardman just to upset me. I thought I might be able to talk some sense into her. Only now I'm here, I hardly dare say a word, in case she shuts me out altogether.'

Meredith turns back to the mirror and pats the sides of her high, coiffured black hair.

'Let me give you some advice, Iris. Don't ever have children.'

Iris resumes her seat as the cabaret starts in earnest, feeling profoundly depressed by the exchange in the lavatories. But it isn't long before she forgets all about Meredith, so astonished is she by the spectacle of beautiful women in sequins and feathers descending from the tops of the trees around them and at the jugglers and acrobats on the stage, the colours, the ruffles, the rhythm, and the sheer dazzling exuberance of it all. It strikes her again how very unlikely it is that she, Iris Bailey, should find herself here, in this beautiful crystal-roofed space with this music that seems to get into one's very blood.

While her thoughts run in this vein, Iris's hands are working as if independently on a new sketch. She is pleased with this portrait. Faye Mickelson is a good model, naturally still and pensive, speaking only occasionally in her reed-thin voice. And all those hollows and planes which cast long shadows across her face and body translate well to the page. Iris is working on her arms, the long, graceful bones of them, the dainty nub of her wrist. But now she has seen something. Her hand stops mid-movement, pencil hovering over the page. Not wanting to draw attention to herself, she forces herself to continue sketching. The pencil scratches across the page, but Iris no longer sees what she is drawing or hears the rousing mamba booming out from the stage. Instead, her head is full of the silver lines crisscrossing the tender skin of Faye Mickelson's inner wrists.

*

It is a subdued party that climbs into Raúl's car at the end of the day, each lost in his or her own thoughts. Iris's already low spirits plummet through the floor when Raúl informs them they are making a social call on the way home to meet Bruce and Hugh at the house of the Ferrer family. They will have met Señora Ferrer at the bridal shower, he says, while Señor Ferrer works for the Cuban government. Raúl raises his hand above his head as if to indicate the highest level. Iris is slowly realising that Bruce's offer to host the wedding owes as much to self-interest as to generosity. From her short acquaintance with Havana, it strikes her as the kind of place where money and status matter. Parading a world-famous film director and a prominent writer around a city selling itself as the new mecca for hedonism and glamour is not going to harm Bruce's business reputation.

Despite her preoccupations, Iris remains acutely aware of Joe's physical presence in the back of the car, of the bare inch of space that separates his right arm from her left and the way she forgets to breathe when their thighs briefly connect as they go around a corner. They are driving back through the outskirts of the city, where the roads are wide and quiet and mercifully cooler at this mid-point between afternoon and evening. The big car turns left and Iris immediately notices a throng of people ahead, where an intersection is marked by a small tree-lined square.

Without warning, Raúl slams on the brakes and wrenches the steering wheel around to the left, executing an abrupt three-point turn in the road. 'Oh my,' says Eugene. 'This is exciting. Are we on the run, do you think?'

Joe says nothing, only stares grimly out of the back window towards, as Iris sees when she follows his gaze, a tree with a gnarled trunk that twists around itself and wide, spreading branches covered by a canopy of dense green leaves, from the bottom of which two feet in scuffed brown shoes are gently swinging.

As they pull away from the scene a woman in a red dress drops to her knees in the dust of the road and folds her chest over her lap like a box lid closing. Iris stifles the scream that is building in her throat. 'But what . . .'

'Rebel sympathiser, I expect,' says Joe curtly, with a barely perceptible nod towards Raúl, as if warning her not to say more. Iris glances over and meets Raúl's untroubled brown eyes in the rear-view mirror. He shrugs and says something in Spanish.

'This is Cuba,' Joe translates, his mouth set in a tight line. 'Human life here is cheap.'

To Iris, reeling from what she has just seen, it sounds like a threat.

The Ferrers' house stands on a corner, squat and fat, greedily taking up space in both directions. It is not a pretty house, built from large, greyish slabs of stone with balustrades around the balconies thick as a man's leg. But it is a house that commands respect. Perhaps that's why it is left unscreened from the road, the hedges trimmed low so as not to impede the view of the arched entrance or the colonnaded terrace that skirts the front.

When they arrive, there is a sleek, dark car parked in front and two of Bruce's men are ferrying boxes around the side of the house. Bruce, supervising impatiently, points to his watch as he sees Raúl drive up. The driver shrugs.

'The Ferrers love Italian wine, so I always bring a few

crates,' Bruce tells them when they get out of the car. His eyes, when he turns his attention to Iris, are dry beaks pecking at her clothes and skin.

Climbing the steps to the entrance, she steals another glance at the crates disappearing around the side of the house, noting how they are not uniform size, as one might expect if they were all full of wine bottles. Joe, too, has been staring, and when their eyes meet he raises his hand and, pointing his first two fingers to make a shooting gesture, his mouth forms a silent *pop*.

Guns? Iris's first thought is to laugh, but then she remembers the cupboard in Bruce's study, its shelves groaning with weapons, and the smile dies on her lips.

Inside, the house is dark, the shutters drawn, so that the furnishings, which are leafed in gold, shimmer in the gloom.

The Ferrer family is waiting to greet them in a vast drawing room dominated by ornate Italianate bronze statuettes displayed on squat plinths made from white marble threaded with gold. When Iris follows Joe and Eugene into the room, she finds them – Mrs Ferrer, whom she had glimpsed earlier at the bridal shower, and her husband and two youngish boys – grouped stiffly around a long glass table, looking for all the world as if they have been stuffed.

Even while introductions are being made, the Ferrers display little in the way of animation. *They despise us*, Iris realises suddenly, and feels heat rushing to her chest at being part of this circus of a wedding, which increasingly seems little more than a vehicle to advance Bruce's reputation and business interests here in Havana.

'I hope you do not mind the informal sitting room,' says Mr Ferrer politely. He has biscuit-coloured hair that blends almost seamlessly into his biscuit-coloured skin, and an elongated upper lip that he periodically scratches with the perfectly shaped nail of his little finger. 'It is so much more . . . cosy? Is that the correct word?'

While Bruce and Mr Ferrer retire to a card table at the back of the room, where they immediately start to confer in low voices, Hugh, Iris, Joe and Eugene are left to converse with Mrs Ferrer and the two boys, who have the studied fake smiles of people acting under duress. For a few agonising moments there is a silence. Then a look passes between Bruce and Hugh which Iris can't decipher but which makes Hugh's large nostrils flare, though he gives a perfunctory nod. After that his manner changes and he devotes himself to the Cuban woman, who is noticeably older than her husband, with thinning hair that has been sprayed in place to give the illusion of volume. Mrs Ferrer blinks nervously in the face of the famous director's energetic attention.

The older boy, meanwhile, keeps darting looks towards Eugene. 'He has read your book, Mr Stringer,' the woman says in a thick accent. 'It is an honour for him to meet you here in our house.' It is a sentence that contains a lot of h's, and each one must be spat out from the back of the throat like phlegm. From his position at the other table with Mr Ferrer, Bruce regularly glances over towards them, and again Iris feels the humiliation of their position here in Cuba, all of them nothing more than a calling card with which Bruce can oil the wheels of polite Cuban society. Why does Hugh put up with it?

Understanding that they are here to earn their keep, she takes out her sketchbook and starts drawing the Ferrer children at the table. The older has a soft, dark fuzz on his top lip that tugs at her heart and the younger has his father's thick fair hair, a tuft of which has escaped his mama's oiled comb and stands proud from the crown of his head. After the sketch is finished, she starts on Mrs Ferrer, generously giving her more hair and less bosom. She focuses on the dress, which is a stiff fabric that moves on its own, and the three loops of pearls around her neck. She notices how the woman's eyes dart anxiously to her husband and, whenever they do, there's a corresponding twitch in her cheek, as if she is clamping her teeth together hard and tight, and Iris bends her head to hide her pity. The sketches are received well, with the younger boy requesting to keep his and dragging out a promise from his mama that she will arrange for it to be taken to the framers the very next day.

Now, as Eugene politely engages the older Ferrer child in conversation about his book and Hugh goes into full charm throttle with his mama, Iris turns her pencil on Mr Ferrer, focusing on how he holds his cigarette, in between the first two fingers of his hand with his slight wrist angled sharply up, like a woman. There he goes again with that little fingernail, *scratch scratch scratch* on that upper lip. In contrast to his wife, his face is relaxed, pleasant almost. He does not look like a man who might inspire nervousness in his wife, or a man who, in conversation with Bruce Bonini, feels uncomfortable with the company he is keeping. Iris studies him carefully, looking for the giveaway.

When she was in art college, sketching the never-ending stream of life models who passed through the studio, she had learned to look for the different places where people hide their fears. Though all the models appeared on the surface to be relaxed and pliable, as they needed to be in order to do their job, and indeed most of them genuinely were, she could always tell the ones who were new to modelling, or who found the poses more stressful than they let on. She became expert at spotting the signs: a muscle tensed where it did not need to be, the pad of a finger pressing into a velvet cushion so it left a slight indentation.

Now she sees it. Under the table, one of Señor Ferrer's dainty feet, in its elegant shoe made of the softest leather, pulsing almost imperceptibly on the ball of the foot, a movement as slight but insistent as a heartbeat. As Iris gazes at it, she tries to dispel an image of another shoe, this one brown and scuffed and dangling beneath the branch of a tree.

Soon Iris is lost in her drawing and in the warm flush of pleasure that begins deep inside and spreads through her fingertips at seeing her subject take life on the page, knowing that she has him. The men are sitting side on to Iris, and a few times she is conscious of Bruce glancing sharply in her direction, but she is too engrossed to wonder why. The sketch is good. The man breathes on the page.

By the time they leave, Iris travelling back this time with Joe and Eugene in the car that was earlier unloading the crates of wine, her sketchbook is bulging with new drawings and she is feeling charged with renewed confidence.

Back at the house, Lana comes out to meet them. Iris observes her closely as Hugh gets out of the other car. She is in tennis whites again, her face scrubbed clean of make-up, and Iris's heart hurts with how young she looks, for all she is smiling broadly, as if delighted to be reunited with her fiancé. So intent is she on Lana that Iris doesn't notice Bruce until he is almost upon her.

'I would very much like to know what you were doing back there,' he says quietly, and though his tone is polite, it has a steel wire running through it.

'I was only . . .'

'Would you mind?' He is holding out his hand for her sketchbook. The others have stopped talking and turned to look. *What has she done?* Iris's mind races through the possibilities for transgression but finds none.

Bruce starts leafing through her drawings and Iris feels her face growing hot. It feels so invasive, some of the pictures just crude studies – a few lines to suggest shape and form, the zigzag of a soft pencil to show shading, and yet she has no reason to refuse. When he comes to the sketches of the Ferrer family, he slows down his leafing, stopping altogether at the portrait of Mr Ferrer.

'Wouldn't you say, Miss Bailey, that it's good manners to ask permission before drawing a person's picture?'

'I did. What I mean is, Mrs Ferrer and the children were quite amenable.'

'So you asked the wife but didn't think to ask the husband. Is that normal in England?'

'I didn't want to interrupt you.' Iris is mortified to realise her voice is rising dangerously, like a child defending itself from a scolding.

'Well, I think these are terrific drawings,' says Lana, taking the sketchbook from Bruce's hand and flicking through the pictures of the Ferrer family. 'You are clever, Iris. Would you mind if I kept them?'

Iris recognises the girl's clumsy attempt to rescue her and is grateful. 'Of course,' she says, ripping out the pages. 'It's your wedding.'

But following the others into the house with the ripe smell of Bruce's cologne seeping into her nostrils and down her throat, she can't help worrying that her perceived lapse in manners is yet another black mark against her.

How many black marks, she wonders, before a line is reached, and how will she know when she crosses it?

10

'YOU'RE A BIG GIRL. You must do what you want.'
Joe is leaning against the yellow wall of the guest
house – what is it with this man that he can never be
upright? – lighting up a cigarette that he has just removed
from behind his ear.

'I intend to.'

'Personally, I wouldn't trust him as far as I could kick
him, but if you want to take that risk, that's entirely up
to you.'

'Quite.'

Eugene, who has been listening to this bad-tempered
exchange, now weighs in.

'Well, I think it's a splendid idea. Or at least it would be
a splendid idea if you would just take me with you, Iris. I
take up next to no space, and I would so love to go out on
the town with you and Eddie-boy. A few Mojitos, and I'd
worm all the family secrets out of him. I'd find out if he
knows anything about that note, for a start.'

Iris makes a face. 'Of course he doesn't. Don't be absurd.'

'It's not absurd. Anyone in that house could have typed it.'

'Yes, but why would Eddie Hardman be sending anonymous warnings about his own sister?'

'Clearly, you've never had a sister.'

Iris bites the inside of her cheek. It's not Eugene's fault. He doesn't know about Wendy. Still, it hurts.

She wishes now she'd said no when Eddie Hardman blocked her way as she headed back to the guest house after that unsettling exchange with Bruce Bonini and asked her if she'd like him to show her around the city. 'As my guest, of course,' he'd said.

At the time she'd been touched by his tact. He must know she hadn't brought much money – Nell told her she wouldn't need to, and anyway, she has scant savings. All the same, it can be awkward, having to rely on a man to pay for you. Without warning, she thinks of Peter, and it occurs to her for the first time that she will have to ask him for money when they are married and she has to give up work.

'I have to escape my family, and you'd be doing me a huge favour, Miss Bailey,' Eddie had said, and Iris had found herself thinking, *Why not?* To spend an evening flirting with a handsome man, away from the tensions of the house and its sinister host. She is not married yet. Why shouldn't she?

'What have you got against Eddie?' she asks Joe.

She is sitting on the narrow green sofa, still dressed in the crêpe, which now smells of smoke and other people's perfume.

'I have nothing at all against Eddie Hardman. It's not his fault he's never had a job he didn't get through Daddy.'

'Ouch. Claws in!'

Joe glares at Eugene, then turns to her. 'But I should have thought it was obvious to you after what we saw earlier that

Havana is a dangerous place right now. The rebels have a lot of support here. Every day, ordinary people risk their lives trying to help them, smuggling weapons – whatever they can get hold of – or food or just warm clothes. It's freezing in those mountains. And the government is cracking down hard. Every night, there's more violence.'

'What kind of violence?' She instinctively drops her voice, speaking barely above a whisper, taking her cue from him.

'The rebels have taken to planting small bombs around the city, targeting mob-owned clubs and hotels. Do you not read any newspapers in England?'

His air of superiority infuriates her. 'With all of that going on, I'm surprised to find you here taking photographs of film stars and socialites rather than on the trail of bombers and revolutionaries. Though no one could blame you for choosing a *safer* kind of life.'

The widening of his eyes above the plume of cigarette smoke shows her blow has hit home, but it feels like a hollow victory.

An hour later, she is in the passenger seat of a sapphire-blue convertible car with a silk scarf knotted at her throat, just as she once saw Audrey Hepburn wearing in a magazine photograph. She is also wearing sunglasses with black frames that flick up at the outer corners and dark lenses. As she has so little call for them back home, she feels self-conscious and has to check an urge to keep touching them. She has on the green travelling dress, which she has washed out in her tiny bathroom and hung over the door, where it dried within minutes.

Determined to forget about the conversation with Eugene and Joe, she feels her spirits rise. For the first time in her life, she feels sophisticated. Glamorous, even. Here she is, passing under palm trees in this huge, gleaming car with a handsome man at the wheel while the sun bathes her skin in a golden glow. She thinks about London and Joyce and poor, hapless Pamela *clack-clack*ing on their typewriters under Mrs Latham's watchful eye, glancing up at the clock. *Oh, but surely the hands must have stopped moving.* Longing for home time. Wishing their lives away. For once, even thinking about her old art-school pals doesn't bring on the usual rush of jealousy. So what if they spent the day laughing together in the cafeteria about something Violet said or Eric's imitation of Mr Schroeder, their textiles tutor, or standing in a rare splash of English sunlight spilling through the windows of the main studio, lost in mixing up the exact paint shade for the soft flesh of an inner elbow? Still, they are not here. Driving with the top down through the streets of Havana, while this vibrant, unguessed-at world rushes past in a blur of colours. Lush, emerald trees, a house painted rose, or ochre, or lemon or a combination of them all. A fruit seller, his cart piled high with huge bunches of bananas, and green cricket-ball-sized fruits which Eddie tells her are guavas, insisting on buying one so she sees for herself the rich, pink flesh and tastes the strange, dense texture, thick like a pear, but far sweeter and lighter.

As they pull away from the side of the road, her tongue still tingles from the unfamiliar flavour. It surprises her how comfortable she feels with Eddie. He has such an easy manner, a wide smile with even white teeth. And so what if he got his job through his father? Plenty of people did.

Now that they have entered Havana proper, where there are modern hotels and office buildings flashier than any she has seen in London, the streets are thronged with people. Young women in gaily striped dresses, older widows head to toe in black. The men wear short sleeves and baggy trousers, and every time the car stops there are whistles and catcalls. 'Don't pay any attention. The Cubans are a primitive lot in so many ways once you get outside of the Country Club set. Head out of Havana and you'll get a shock – it's all shanty towns and wooden huts.' But Iris notices that the knuckles of Eddie's hands, which grip the steering wheel, have turned white.

They are in the old city, where crumbling houses painted in faded colours abut grand stone buildings, all pillars and steps. There are towering blocks of flats that block out the light, and cafés with tables that tumble out into the street. In its eclectic architecture, Havana reminds Iris of herself when she was packing her clothes before she came, trying on this outfit and then that one, changing her mind again and again, asking herself what places she might go, what impression she wishes to make, the clothes piling up on the bed in a mish-mash of styles and moods.

'So many parking meters,' she observes. 'You know there's talk of introducing them in London. People are up in arms.'

'Batista installed them. The Cubans detest them, of course, but they make him a fortune.'

'Where are we going now?' Iris dips her head as they pass an enormous modern building forming a distinctive V-shape so that she can see Eddie over the top of her sunglasses frame. She cannot get accustomed to how green everyone looks through the lenses, almost as if they aren't very well.

'First to the Malecón.'

'But isn't that a road?'

Eddie turns to her and, when he smiles, the setting sun turns his teeth pink.

They are sitting on the stone sea wall that lines the Malecón – Havana's famous coast road – while the swollen golden sun sinks towards the sea. Behind them, the grand buildings fronting the esplanade are streaked with pink and orange, and Eddie's face glows. For one strange, giddy moment Iris thinks she might cry. It is just so beautiful.

A man shuffles along the pavement towards them, startling Iris, who has turned towards the sea and the setting sun. He has his hand out and on his gaunt face is an expression of blank resignation, as if he expects rejection. There is a child behind him, holding on to the back of his worn cotton trousers. The boy wears sandals that are far too small and his narrow, filthy feet drag in the dust and Iris's heart hurts when she sees in his enormous brown eyes the same resignation as in the man's. A shadow flits over Eddie's burnished features.

'No,' he says, flapping a hand in the man's face.

The man doesn't even flinch. Just stands there with his long, grimy fingers reaching upwards.

'But couldn't we just . . .' Iris ventures.

'Go!'

Iris jumps at Eddie's loud exclamation, but the man carries on staring in silence at the two of them before finally moving off, the child trailing after.

'Sorry. It's just, if you give to one of them, they'll all be swarming around and it can get quite ugly. I was only thinking of you.'

'Thank you.'

'And now we should go for dinner.' Eddie sounds completely cheered, as if the scene with the man and the child didn't happen. 'And when we're done with dinner, we will drink our way around every bar in Havana.'

They haven't driven more than a couple of minutes back along the Malecón when Iris sees, to her right, a vast, pale building standing high up on a bluff, its twin towers lit up against the sky. She noticed it earlier when they had a tour around the city before the bridal shower, but up close it is far more imposing.

'The Hotel Nacional,' Eddie tells her as they pull up under a portico which houses the grand arched entrance. He tosses the car keys to the uniformed bellboy who rushes out to meet them.

Suddenly, Iris is not feeling so sophisticated. She has removed her sunglasses and untied her silk scarf, depositing both in her patent-leather handbag, and now she is left only with the sleeveless green dress that feels so provincial in the surroundings of the vast lobby lined with pillars holding up the arches that run the length of the room.

She follows Eddie into the dining room, where a waiter leads them to one of the circular tables laid with stiff white cloths. There is a pianist playing softly at one end in front of a stage cordoned off by a sweeping velvet curtain.

'How is it that you and Nell are so familiar with Havana?' Iris asks once they are seated in front of a dizzying array of glassware and silver cutlery.

'Pop and Bruce go back a long way. We've been coming out here for weekends and holidays for as long as I can remember. There are some beautiful beaches here, Iris, in a place called Varadero. There's talk of going there the day after tomorrow. You'll love it.'

A daytrip with the Hardmans? This is news to Iris, and not entirely welcome news at that.

'So you know all about the rebels, then? This Fidel Castro and his bombs.'

Eddie rolls his eyes as if bored. 'That's all internal Cuban politics, Iris. Nothing to do with you and me. Even if the Cuban government was overturned tomorrow – which it won't be, by the way, the military will never allow it – and Fidel Castro swept in and declared himself President, nothing would change for people like us. Havana runs on American dollars. No one would be fool enough to mess around with that. Don't you worry. Bruce and all the other American businessmen will be just fine.'

Instantly, Iris is back outside Bruce Bonini's closed study door with the key clasped in her fingers and that purloined scarf bulging in her pocket, her nerves knotted in her chest.

'You must be close to him. Bruce, I mean.' She tries to keep her voice neutral, but still she feels those deadened eyes crawling over her back.

'I guess so,' says Eddie. 'Though sometimes I do wonder if he and Pop actually like each other. Don't look so shocked, Iris. Bruce and Pop have a high old time together – or at least they used to when Bruce's brother was still alive and running the business, before Bruce got so serious. But they also like the things the other can give them. That's just how it is. My father has a romantic view of gang . . . of men like Bruce. That's why he dresses like John Wayne, for

chrissakes. He wants a world where men behave like men.'
Here Eddie deepens his voice in imitation of his father. 'And
when he's around Bruce, he gets to pretend to be an outlaw
without actually having to risk anything. And through Pop,
Bruce gets to mix with movie stars and writers and pretend
like he's cultured. You see, they both win.'

A glass of champagne has appeared by Iris's elbow and she
takes an appreciative sip. She had never had champagne
before coming to Cuba. Her parents drink wine on special
occasions and her mother sometimes asks for sherry at family
parties, although as far as Iris can see, takes little enjoyment
in it, grimacing each time she raises her glass to her lips. But
champagne is not something that features in their lives, apart
from as a shorthand for something else. *You'll be asking for
champagne next*, her father might say, after her mother sug-
gests they might venture further afield than Margate for their
next holiday or have fish twice a week instead of only on Fri-
days. Champagne is for people who dress for dinner and eat
crab on a whim and spend their summers on the French
Riviera.

Iris herself drinks wine if offered but, like espresso, only
to seem sophisticated as, privately, she believes it tastes worse
than vinegar. But champagne proves itself to be a revelation.
After only a few mouthfuls she feels brighter and wittier and
emboldened to probe more into Eddie's evidently complicated relationship with his father. It must have been hard,
she observes, to grow up in the shadow of someone so much
in the public eye. Luckily, Eddie, who has already drained
two glasses and is well into his third, does not need much
encouragement to expand.

'Pop could have kept out of the papers if he'd wanted.

He's the director, for chrissakes, not the star. But he thrives on that kinda razzamatazz. The cameras, the flashlights, being bundled in and out of cars. Attention. It's like oxygen to him. But only attention from people who don't know him. What do you make of that, Iris? You know, I never met anyone called Iris before – such a pretty name. With the rest of us – his wives and his kids – it was always conditional. Always on his terms. When Nell and I were little, he wanted our attention when it suited him, but then he wanted to forget about us for long periods of time, like we were a wireless he could switch off and on at will.'

How bitter he sounds, thinks Iris, taken aback.

'I'm sorry,' he says. 'Every man has his Achilles heel, and I guess my father is mine. Oh, don't look so unhappy, Iris. I love him. I just can't stand him sometimes.'

'So why is Lana marrying him?'

Eddie leans back in his chair and shrugs extravagantly. 'What you have to understand about Lana is that she worshipped Pop when she was a kid. Her mother was a bitch. Her and Faye's father was some country hick her mother ditched just as soon as her star started to rise. Then came a whole succession of powerful men she used to haul her way to the top. They weren't exactly the type of men you'd choose to tuck your daughters in at night, if you get my drift. A couple of drunks. A producer who later went to jail after he was found in a hotel room with two underage boys. Sorry, Iris. Anyway, the thing was, the old man was used to children and he was fun and charismatic. Lana and Faye were novelties to him, so he paid them a lot more attention than their own mother did, and a helluva lot more attention than he did to me and Nell by that stage.

You know, I do believe he was the first person in Lana's life who didn't expect her to look after them. No wonder the girls latched on to him like they had suckers on their fingertips.'

The champagne has made Iris light-headed and Eddie's words seem to pop like bubbles in her brain. *Bitch. Drunks. Underage.* When she tries to grab hold of them their meaning disappears into thin air.

'I think Lana and Faye convinced themselves they would stay with Pop after Jean died instead of being packed off to Meredith's. Faye took it particularly hard. But then, she isn't quite . . .'

'Isn't quite what?'

Iris is aware on some level that the conversation is inappropriate, that there is something dangerously unguarded about Eddie Hardman now that he has had a few drinks. But the champagne and the soft melody of the piano and the fact of being here in this grand room turn convention into vapour that drifts up to the high ceiling, where it mingles with the smoke of a hundred cigarettes and is lost.

'Faye Mickelson isn't quite normal. Even as a child she was always on the edge of things, if you know what I mean. Lurking around where she shouldn't be, snooping on things that were nothing to do with her. You know, before this week I hadn't seen her since . . . well, since Jean's funeral . . . but she hasn't changed. Still makes my skin crawl.'

'That's a bit strong.' Iris thinks about the young woman's hollowed cheeks, the silver tracks across her wrists.

'Is it? Do you know, one afternoon on that damned boat I came across her in Jean's cabin while all the others were up on deck, wearing her mother's dress and shoes, lipstick smeared over her mouth. And she saw me looking and asked me if I thought she was as pretty as her mother. She was still a child, for chrissakes. I told her I didn't think she should be in there, and do you know what she said? "Momma doesn't mind. And anyway, it'll all be mine sooner or later."'

'What did she mean?'

'You tell me. It made me feel kinda spooked, to tell you the truth, especially in view of . . . well, you know.'

Iris suppresses a shudder and casts around for a change of subject.

As she surveys her opulent surroundings her attention is snagged by a man sitting at a nearby table opposite a glamorous woman in a red satin off-the-shoulder dress.

'Is that . . . Johnny Weissmuller?'

Eddie doesn't even turn around. 'Probably. He practically lives here, you know, in this place.'

Iris gapes at the Tarzan actor. This hotel. This champagne. That famous physique that she grew up watching at the pictures on a Saturday morning. She looks around at all the well-fed, well-preserved faces, at the diamonds and the pearls, and remembers the boy they'd seen earlier out there on the sea front with his too-small shoes, the wooden huts she'd glimpsed along the unmade, flooded road.

'Does it ever seem strange to you,' she asks, 'that everyone here has so much, while all around there are people with nothing?'

Eddie drains his glass and frowns. 'What you have to understand, Iris, is that Cuba isn't like England. Outside Havana, there's no education, no civilisation to speak of. That's why American companies run the sugar and tobacco industries. Left to themselves, they'd all be still working their own little scraps of land, and Havana'd be some dead little Hicksville town where everything shuts at nine.'

Iris remembers Joe's comment about the gambling and the prostitution and finds herself wondering if the city's residents consider those a fair price to pay for being able to get a drink on a Sunday night.

'But surely Bruce and his associates . . . ?'

Eddie, whose eyes have narrowed suddenly, breaks in: 'Say, Iris, what's with all these questions? Is Bruce right about you?'

'What do you mean?'

Eddie giggles and gestures for more champagne. 'Bruce thinks you're a CIA spy.'

'Pardon?'

'Don't look so shocked, Iris. We've all told him he's crazy. He got some information that the government – our government, that is – has sent someone here to the wedding to nose around in his operations and, for some reason, he's convinced himself it's you, whereas anyone with a brain can see Joe Garston has CIA written all over him.'

Iris's head is spinning. This isn't real. Spies. Movie stars. None of it real.

'I don't understand. Why would . . .'

She remembers how Bruce found her outside his study, remembers the key hidden in her shoe. His anger when she'd sketched Señor Ferrer without his permission. A new bottle of champagne arrives at the table, and Eddie switches his attention to it, as if he has lost interest in what they are talking about.

'You mustn't get worked up about it, Iris. Half the people in this room have probably been on the CIA payroll at some time or other. They're recruiting anyone with a pulse. It's not a big deal.'

Not a big deal? Being accused of spying? But Eddie won't be drawn out further on the subject, and Iris forms the distinct opinion that he regrets having brought it up. And though there's a sick feeling in Iris's stomach, they return to talking of lighter things. Movies. Music. Now that Iris knows what Bruce suspects her of, she hesitates before she speaks, in case what she says might be misconstrued. Only later, after the food has come, a roast chicken cooked perfectly with lemon and garlic that Iris pretends to enjoy, and another bottle of champagne has appeared, as if by magic, does she risk bringing up his family again.

'How did Lana and your father find each other again after all those years?'

'Lana went to drama school in New York. You know she has ambitions to act? Well, you don't have to be a psychiatrist to work out where that comes from. Eight months ago she goes into class and finds the old man is the guest speaker. They go out for coffee for old times' sake, and before you know it, here we all are. In Havana. Acting like this is all completely normal.'

'So why *are* you here?'

The smile with which Eddie greets her very direct question is high on bitterness, low on warmth.

'My father can be very persuasive, Iris. Hell, I don't need to tell you – I saw you with him outside on the terrace last night. And let's not forget, he writes my pay-cheque.'

Dear Uncle Cyp

It doesn't surprise me at all about Dolly. You know the rumour about Fred was he only married her because she has those enormous feet and he could dress up in her shoes. Poor bitch. She would have her fairy tale, though, for all we all told her and told her.

As for my own marriage, I don't know what to tell you.

Oh, darling Cyp, what's a girl to do when she just can't make up her mind? The girls think the sun shines out of Hugh's hallowed ass, and I know if I leave him Mama will make her disapproval STRONGLY felt, in between salon appointments. And don't they say absence makes the heart grow fonder? Maybe when I get back from Spain and he wraps up his shoot in Arizona we'll take one look at each other and that old lust will return. There was a time when all that man had to do was look at me with those blue eyes and I swear I'd be as good as pregnant. Then one day you wake up and you think, Did he always make that noise when he ate, like a goddam cow chewing up the grass?

In the meantime, X is here, and even though we swore the last time we wouldn't do it again – guess what? (We did it again. And again. And again.) And the worst thing is, I don't think I even like him very much!

And no, I'm not going to tell you who it is, so don't even waste your breath. I love you dearly, Cyp, but I don't need to remind you of that old quote, 'Three people can keep a secret only if two of them are dead.'

Your Aunt Sap

PS. I have to take this to the mail myself as Molly just quit – just kidding – I fired her after I overheard her telling a caller I couldn't come to the phone as I was in the lavatory. IN THE LAV, CYP! Also, she always smelled vaguely of fried onions. So if you know anyone who wants to be my new assistant, send them my way. This morning, I had to make my own coffee. It tasted like liquid shit.

11

HER MOUTH IS lined with fur.

As she gradually regains consciousness, Iris discovers other disagreeable physical manifestations. For instance, she is burning up – her head, her arms, her legs even, all blazing with a sweaty heat that has her throwing off the sheet, as if it was made from molten metal. Her temples are being held in some sort of vice that is slowly compressing her skull and there is a nasty, sour taste on her tongue.

It is a mosquito that has woken her, a single high-pitched note that sounds as if something sharp is piercing through the cartilage of her ear.

She sits up and the room lurches viciously to the side, which is how she learns that she has failed to close both her mosquito net and the shutters. The room is dark but falls short of the pitch black of the previous night due to a sliver of moonlight. Her throat is parched. When the sick feeling goes away, she will get up and go downstairs to the little guest-house kitchen in search of water. Yes, water is the key.

And now she has put a picture of water in her head and it

is all she can think of. She knows she must not drink the water from the taps, but there must be some that has already been boiled and cooled. Or failing that, some lemonade or squeezed juice.

She scratches something on her arm and feels the swollen bump of a mosquito bite, and now that she has felt that first bump, she feels all the others – on her calf, her foot, her inner thigh. She curses the self that came crashing in here all those hours before and stripped off her clothes right down to her underwear and fell into bed without closing the net. What sort of state must she have been in?

She forces her mind back, remembering a drive through the dog-end of the night, couples in doorways – just a collection of hands and backs – music escaping from a basement bar into a hushed street, a man in a white vest leaning over a balcony, smoking, street dogs curled up on the pavements, their ribs like knives laid side by side in a cutlery tray. Transactions on street corners, eyes watching greedily as they drive past. Eddie, at the wheel, telling her about something so animatedly he doesn't see the parked car until they are almost upon it, swerving at the last minute so that they mount the opposite kerb, practically skimming the façade of the building on the other side. Iris remembers the wrought-iron grille of a doorway brushing her shoulder.

Then they must have arrived back here, though she has little memory of it. Did one of Bruce Bonini's men open the gates? She has a brief flash of a jacket worn over an undershirt, a face still bearing the imprint of a wrinkled sheet.

Now unease is prickling at her skin, under the itching of the mosquito bites. Instinctively, she knows she doesn't want to probe into the cause of it, wants to chase it from her mind, lock it out, pull down the shutters. But here it is, sliding in under the door, infecting her with the sickening knowledge that something bad happened last night.

Fragments come back unbidden. A casino, two women in diamonds and fur wraps, despite the heat outside, another ceaselessly feeding money from a silver clutch bag into a slot machine against the wall as if the world would end if she stopped, a man's braying laugh. Then bars. How many, she doesn't remember. They were looking for Ernest Hemingway, she remembers, the American writer. There were cocktails called Daiquiris that arrived in chilled triangular glasses, and two journalists, an American woman and a man from New Zealand, who'd asked lots of questions about the wedding that made a vein throb in Eddie's neck. Driving through the neon-lit streets, feeling the night hot and clammy on her skin and noticing for the first time the scantily dressed women, some of them not much older than children, leaning against buildings in the shadows, occasionally stepping out to approach a car or a group of men strolling by whose eyes travelled disinterestedly up and down the women's bodies.

Iris sees that her arm is bleeding where she scratched it and she tries to focus on that to stop the memory that is pushing insistently against the fragile membrane of her mind. But here it comes, tearing its way inside.

Eddie insisting on walking her back to her room. His arm heavy and hot around her shoulders. 'Let's go for a swim.' And his childish disappointment when she said no, just wanting her bed. 'I didn't have you down as such a square, Iris.' Her turning to him at the door of the guest house to say goodbye and that split second of clarity – *Oh, he's going to kiss me* – before his lips were on hers, his breath full of stale smoke and brandy, his tongue fat and wet like a rolled flannel.

Now they are on the sofa in the salon and Iris doesn't remember how she arrived here, only that she wishes she hadn't, but Eddie is on top of her and pressing down, so she is crushed into the unforgiving cushions. Surely she must have protested? Here comes another memory, words floating back through the lost hours. Eddie's voice in her ear. 'Ah, come on, Iris. Haven't we had fun? Haven't I been good to you?' And all the time his hand moving up her leg, under her dress. *The roll-on girdle.* Iris remembers feeling suffocated, as if all the air has been pressed out of her, trying to kick out with her legs but being held in place like a frog pinned out for dissection. Then closing her eyes as though – using an infant's reasoning – if she can't see what is happening, it cannot be real.

And then? What? Feeling suddenly so cold that bumps form on the exposed skin on her legs. At the same time realising she can breathe again, filling her lungs with air. Wriggling her legs to regain the feeling in them. Pulling down her dress. Opening her eyes to see Eddie with both his hands up, trying to prise off Joe Garston's arm, which is hooked around his neck. Or is it the voices that came first? Eddie shouting, 'Get your hands off me!' Joe muttering under his breath but managing to overpower the drunk interloper, who has undone his belt so that the ends flap uselessly around his thighs. Eugene appearing behind them wearing red silk pyjamas and looking like the gnome that Iris's Auntie Kathleen has in her garden by the pond, his eyes wide and strange without his glasses.

Now Eddie is gone – did someone throw him out? – and she is sitting up, assuring the others that she is perfectly fine.

'No damage done.' Had she really said that? Getting to her feet and bolting for the stairs, realising she is going to be sick. Did she make it to the toilet? She thinks she did. Hopes she did. She remembers standing in the shower for a very long time, not even caring that the water was cold. Coming out wrapped in a thin towel and hearing a gentle tapping on the door. Did this happen? Joe's voice soft as a whisper: 'Are you all right, Iris?' Her cursing the noisy pipes in this place that had told him she was still awake. Wanting to open the door and yet not wanting to at the same time. Leaning her forehead against the hard wood, fancying she could hear his breathing, as if he were doing the same on the other side, just inches away.

Falling asleep only to dream she is looking over the side of a boat, and there is Jean in the water, shouting to her. And she knows it is in her power to save her, if she can just figure out how. Panic building as Jean's desperation grows. After that, nothing, until just now. How many hours have passed? Surely only two or three at the most.

Shame washes over her, hot and treacle-sticky. She should never have agreed to go out with Eddie. Was she really so naïve she didn't think there'd be a price to pay for the stiff linen napkins and the crystal champagne flutes, for the big shiny car with the cream leather seats? Was she so full of hubris that she had imagined her own company was pay- ment enough – her sparkling wit, her stories about the typing pool, about Violet and Shirley and the art-school gang? She remembers her mother coming to find her in the garden once when she was about fifteen or sixteen and lying on a blanket on the lawn wearing a pair of shorts and a sleeveless top. 'I think it's time we talked about boys, Iris.' Sitting her- self down on the very edge of a stripy canvas deckchair so that the wooden bar must have been digging into her bottom. 'You're getting to the age when you're going to be interested in young men and they in you, which is completely natural. But what you must never forget, darling, is that it is a transaction. You have something very valuable that the boys will want, and it's your responsibility to make sure you get the best possible price for it. Do you see?'

It was an unusual display of maternal interest from her mother and at the time she had nodded in mute embarrassment, sure she understood perfectly. But now it's clear she hasn't understood at all. Not a thing. Sitting on her bed, amidst the ruin of her mosquito net, Iris groans at her own monumental foolishness. How will she face Eugene and Joe again? Or Eddie himself?

She has an urge to wrap herself up in the sheet and reassemble the mosquito net and never emerge from her bed again, but the need for a drink is overwhelming. She gets up and makes her way into her little bathroom, but at the sink she hesitates. If she drinks the water from the tap, she will be ill, and even though a part of her thinks that is no more than she deserves, she has no wish to become an embarrassment to Nell, who has been so kind.

Nell. The thought of seeing her new friend again after this mortifying incident with her brother fills Iris with dread.

Her reflection in the mirror over the sink comes as a shock. Her hair is wild around her pallid face, eyes ringed in black shadows. She walks back into the bedroom and picks up her hairbrush from her dressing table, then returns it. Really, what does it matter?

Easing open her bedroom door, she pads silently along the corridor, the tiles cool under her bare feet. At the top of the stairs she starts at the sight of the painting of Christ on the cross in the recess on the landing, illuminated where the dim silver light catches the glass. There is a pressure in her head, so she feels as if her brain has been taken out and replaced by a lump of lead, and her body is struggling with the effort of keeping it on top of her neck. Nausea sloshes around in the pit of her stomach. She will never drink again. Not ever.

Downstairs, she presses the light switch, but nothing happens so she feels her way along the short corridor to the kitchen. Again, she tries the switch without success. A power cut, maybe – Nell has warned her about these. Iris eases open the shutters on the kitchen window, which looks out on to a small, overgrown patch of garden. Such moonlight as there is allows her to see that on the top of the cooker stands a big pot of boiled and cooled water, covered with a lid so there can be no risk of mosquitos swimming around in there.

She drains the first glass of water in seconds, standing by the cooker. The second she drinks more slowly, looking out of the window without seeing as she gauges the effect of the water on her still-churning stomach. She pauses mid-swallow, her attention snagged by a movement out there in the semi-darkness. Is it some kind of animal? She'd asked Eddie earlier – such a pang of anxiety now when she thinks of him – whether she might encounter any monkeys while she was in Havana, and he'd laughed. Then, seeing her disappointment, he'd told her to look out for big rat-type things that live up in the trees. What had he called them? Hotties? Hooties? She wishes now she had done more research before coming here. But how? Like most of the people they know, her parents have a complete set of leather-bound volumes of the *Encyclopaedia Britannica* proudly displayed on a shelf in the living room, along with a Bible and assorted Agatha Christies and P. G. Wodehouses and *two* copies of the complete works of William Shakespeare – as if one wasn't more than enough – which each of her parents had acquired during their schooldays, both bearing a self-conscious fountain-pen signature on the flyleaf. And a stack of *Women's Weeklys*, organised chronologically, their pages marked with tiny pieces of paper wherever there is a recipe of which her mother particularly approves. But the encyclopaedia had proved unforthcoming on the subject of Cuba, beyond describing where it sat geographically (in the Caribbean Sea, ninety nautical miles off the coast of Florida) and its principal crops (sugar and tobacco).

Iris peers out at the trees, looking for a sighting of the enormous rodent, but there is no telltale rustling of leaves or swaying of branches. Instead, she sees a dark shadow over towards the back wall that changes shape in the dim light. She gasps. If it is an animal, it is a huge one. Are there bears in Cuba?

The shadow is growing, stretching itself upwards and revealing itself to be human. A person – man or woman, Iris cannot be sure – who has been crouching down in the foliage but has now stood up to their full height.

Instinctively, she steps back, suddenly feeling sober. She recalls what Joe was saying about Havana being a dangerous place. Backing into the corridor, she determines on waking her fellow housemates. But at the bottom of the stairs she falters. She can still see Eugene's expression of surprise as he stood, sleep-rumpled, at the door of the salon in those astonishing red pyjamas, still hear Joe muttering under his breath as he struggled with Eddie.

She pads softly back to the kitchen and, standing well to one side of the window, peers around the frame. Nothing. Where the dark shadow once was there is just empty space. She scans the rest of the garden but sees nothing untoward.

By now the sky has paled from inky black to the soft washed-out grey that presages the sunrise. In just a few hours, she is expected to be drawing Barbara Bonini. Isabella has arranged the portrait as a thank-you gift from the grateful soon-to-be newly-weds to their hosts and Iris is already dreading it. Quite apart from the question of how she will face Eddie if she encounters him over at the house, there is a glazed quality to the club owner's wife that she finds offputting and which she already knows will render her almost impossible to paint. First wilfully shut-off Lana and now the perpetually dazed hostess. So far, her subjects seem to have been handpicked to make her job as difficult as possible. Or maybe she just has no talent and this whole thing has been an almighty mistake from start to finish. Whichever the answer, Iris is sure she'll be far better equipped to deal with it if she goes back to bed and tries to sleep for another couple of hours instead of waking Eugene and Joe and having to deal with a lot of hoo-ha about a shadow she glimpsed through the darkness that isn't even there any longer and will probably turn out to be something and nothing. No. She will leave this until the morning – the morning proper – then toss it quite casually into the conversation in case there does turn out to be an obvious explanation. *The back hedge? But that's where the security guards go to smoke. I thought everyone knew that.*

Glass of water in hand, she feels her way back up to her room, closes the shutters against the encroaching dawn and, having disentangled the mosquito net, climbs inside it and falls gratefully back to sleep.

Never has she been more glad of her dark glasses. Despite the clear skies of the previous night, it has turned into a turgid sort of day, the heat thick, the sky overcast, clouds so low they dab at Iris's skin like sodden cotton balls as she sits awkwardly on the terrace of the guest house, drinking a cup of milkless, scalding coffee that has been brought to her by an unsmiling Joe Garston.

'So you don't intend to say anything at all?'

Even the black lenses can't protect Iris from the intensity of the photographer's disapproval. It is as if that late-night knock never happened, that softly voiced concern, the sense she'd had of him breathing through the door.

'He had had an awful lot to drink. So had I, so really, I'm sure I'm as much to blame as he is. He wasn't himself.'

This is the line she has decided upon. That alcohol led Eddie to take momentary leave of his senses. That she should not have put herself in that position. That it was high spirits that got out of hand. That it was her fault, is what she is essentially saying. And once she decided upon this line she felt so much relief that she has managed to convince herself that it is in fact what happened. But now here is Joe, brows knitted together, suggesting she should make some sort of complaint and spoil the wedding which Nell pulled so many strings to get her hired for and find herself labelled as one of those sorts of girls who lead men on and then cry foul play. Teases, Peter had called them. 'What I like about you, Iris, is that a man knows where he stands with you. You're not a tease.'

'One would have hoped that, if he wasn't himself, he would at least have the decency to be someone half civilised,' Eugene drawls from the chair opposite.

'If I hadn't come down to find out what all the noise was—' Joe begins.

'Then I should have pushed him away. I was doing just that when you arrived,' Iris replies quickly. She will not think about that crushing weight on top of her, that sense of being pinned in place. Instead she changes the subject.

'A most peculiar thing happened,' she begins, and is pleased with how it sounds. Not over-anxious.

She continues in this jaunty vein to tell them of the figure she saw from the kitchen window.

'I thought at first it was a bear,' she says. 'Then it stood straight up and I thought, Well, either this is a remarkably svelte bear, or it is in fact a human. So then I worried that it might be rebels planting bombs, as you said, Joe. But then it sort of disappeared.'

Her story, having started out so promisingly, has trailed off into anticlimax, her words as lacking in energy as she is herself. If only her head wasn't throbbing so. Joe says nothing, just stares at her as if she has said something too stupid to warrant a reply. Possibly it is this that prompts her to blurt out to them the story of how she'd got trapped in Bruce's study. A need to redeem herself, to make herself more than the foolish woman who had to be rescued. Or possibly it is her own thick head that has affected her judgement. But once she starts talking, she finds she cannot stop. She tells them about the typewriter, about hiding behind the desk – leaving out how her legs trembled and her mouth dried to sandpaper – about how Bruce had appeared just as she'd finished locking the study door.

Eugene is fascinated by the scarf and the folded note, Joe by the weapons store.

'What type of guns were they?'

Iris frowns. 'You know. Brown. Or maybe black. Sort of middle-sized.'

None of them notices Eddie Hardman arriving.

'Can I talk to you for a moment, please, Iris?'

What a different Eddie Hardman this is from the previous day. Shoulders bent, head down, childlike appeal in his pink-tinged eyes.

'You've got a nerve,' begins Joe, but Iris cuts him off by getting quickly to her feet – too quickly, her protesting stomach quickly informs her.

By now, Iris has fully convinced herself that her own newly constructed version of events is the truth. Eddie tried it on. No harm was done. She does not – *will* not – think of how his tongue probed her mouth like a giant sea slug, or how she felt like all the breath was being crushed from her. She will not make a fuss. Will not be a *tease*.

Ignoring Joe's glowering hostility, she gestures for Eddie to follow her and they go around the corner of the guest house to the overgrown garden at the back.

'Iris, I'm an idiot. I lose all sense when I drink like that. I can't even remember most of what happened, only that we were having a lovely time and then I ruined it by acting like a total brute. Can you forgive me?'

He seems sincere. Penitent. Her instinct, deep ingrained, is to put him out of his misery at once, for hasn't she decided she is as much at fault as he? Didn't she carry on drinking past the point she knew it was a bad idea? Didn't she let him inside the house? On this last, she isn't quite clear, but she supposes she must have, for, otherwise, how would he have got in? Still, she is stiff as she accepts his apology, which only makes him more abject.

'I will spend my entire life making it up to you,' he declares. Then he falls to his knees and starts shuffling towards her. 'From now on, wherever you go, I will follow like this, begging your forgiveness.'

She smiles in spite of herself. 'Don't be such an idiot.'

But after he has gone she feels dissatisfied and grubby. She is starting to see that Eddie is Hugh without the charisma. How frustrated he must feel that he can't inflict his will through charm alone, like his father. Her headache has almost gone, but in its place there is a dull, persistent ache of exhaustion and self-dislike. She wanders over to the back of the garden where she saw the shadowy figure earlier this morning. *Thought* she saw.

At the hedge she uses her foot to part the foliage this way and that. Does it look a bit *flattened*? She leans her head first one way and then the other, trying to see it from all angles before removing her foot and stepping away.

From here it is only a couple of yards to the back gate. A heavy wooden affair with a large metal bolt across the top and the bottom. Nothing out of the ordinary to see here.

Still, she shivers, despite the dense, swollen heat, and as she heads back to the terrace she can't shake off the feeling that someone is watching her.

12

BARBARA BONINI HAS now kept her waiting for forty minutes and Iris is fast losing the will to live. At first, she was relieved to find out from Isabella that her hostess wished to have her portrait painted inside the house, where it is at least cooler and she can sit at her easel in comfort. But the longer she waits, the more she feels an intruder. Someone who is somewhere she shouldn't be. On her way to the house earlier, she'd passed the swimming pool and been shocked to see Hugh Hardman stretched out on a lounger with his head in the lap of his first wife, the two of them quietly talking. It was nice, she'd told herself sternly, that they'd retained such a friendship, Hugh and Connie, in contrast to her mother's friend Betty, whose first husband can never be mentioned by name, only as 'you know who'. But still Iris hadn't been able to shake off her sense of being out of her depth here.

She has been shown into a grand living room, although Iris can't imagine a lot of living going on in this mausoleum of a room, where the floor is brown and cream marble, as are the towering marble columns that hold up the high ceiling. There are white chairs and sofas, but these have that look of being not much used, and a thick glass coffee table. Miniature palm trees in tall bronze pots line the walls, but rather than adding a homey feel to the room, these make it feel all the more like a vast hotel lobby, somewhere impersonal and public.

Iris has chosen a chair near the window in a spot where the light is good but not dazzling. She has set up her easel and arranged the armchair facing it, shifting it this way and that, until she is satisfied that it will show her subject to the best advantage.

But where *is* her subject?

Already the butler has been in twice, once to bring her some very welcome lemonade, which arrives on a golden tray in a crystal jug with a white muslin cloth over the top, and another time to inform her that Señora Bonini is on her way. Her eyes have been glued to the doorway ever since, as if she could will her hostess into being. Once, the doorbell sounded, a startlingly loud noise that made Iris jump in her seat, and a small man in a dark suit was ushered past and straight up the stairs. He carried a black leather bag that banged against his shins.

Footsteps herald a new arrival, but Iris's hopes of finally being able to get started are dashed when Nell bounces in, wearing tight white trousers that end just below the knee and a white gypsy-style top with embroidered flowers that skims her freckled shoulders.

'What are you doing, sitting here friendless and alone?'

Now that Nell is here, Iris acknowledges how much she has missed her. She has been largely avoiding her since finding the note – and last night's scene with Eddie has only made things worse. Nell is his sister, after all. Who knows what version of events he might have told her? But having her here in all her vivid warmth and energy makes something in Iris unfurl, something she hadn't even realised was furled in the first place.

She explains about her missing sitter and Nell makes a noise through her nose that is half snort and half exclamation and wholly dismissive.

'Barbara will be waiting for whatever shot her doctor just gave her to get her moving again. Last night she was so out of it I thought she'd actually been stuffed.'

'Out of it?'

'Oh, my good lord, Iris, you are just too precious for words. Surely you must have noticed by now how she just stares off into space as if she is receiving heavenly visitations, and how every now and then her eyes roll ever so slightly back into her head?'

Nell obligingly performs the actions she describes so that Iris can't help but smile, despite her hangover and her nervousness about running into Eddie again, and about Bruce's stolen scarf and key hidden back in her room and that bizarre thing Eddie said last night, which has only just come back to her, about her being a spy, and the whole sense she has this morning of being in a place she has no business being.

'The woman is like a walking drugstore. In the daytime it's uppers, and then from evening onwards it's just a long, blissful slide into oblivion.' Instantly it all falls into place and Iris could kick herself for not noticing before how much Barbara's glazed expression brings to mind her own mother. 'Mind you,' Nell continues, 'if I was married to Bruce Bonini, I'd need to be sedated the entire time too, especially after everything she's been through, poor bitch.'

Before Iris can ask her to expand, there's a sound of heels clicking on marble and Barbara Bonini floats into the room wearing a pale pink chiffon gown sprigged with roses that makes Iris want to cry when she sees it because, really, how is she to capture every one of those intricate, awkward little flowers, and a pair of enormous black glasses that sit on her face like a fly's eyes. Without apology, she settles herself down in the armchair Iris has prepared for her, gripping on to the arms as if she is at the dentist.

'I'll leave you two to it,' says Nell. As she passes Iris on her way out she rolls her eyes, though whether in exasperation or in another impression of Barbara's out-of-it-ness, Iris cannot be sure.

'Would you mind?'

Iris makes a gesture with her hands, and Barbara grudgingly removes her dark glasses. Without them, her face is pale and unfocused, like someone who has been woken up by the overhead light snapping suddenly on.

Iris starts sketching, but after sitting still for no more than three or four minutes, Barbara leans forward and rummages around in the large handbag she carries everywhere, eventually producing a small metal object which turns out to be a bell. Two or three fairly violent flicks of the wrist summon the butler, a tall man with a gleaming brown dome of a forehead, around which such black hair as he has left has been artfully arranged.

'Bring me a Mimosa,' Barbara says in a voice that is not so much a voice as a breath flavoured with words. Then she looks at Iris. 'Would you like one?'

Iris has no idea what a Mimosa might be, but the word sounds blessedly fresh and flowery and, besides, she really needs to strike up some kind of rapport with her sitter, or she'll end up with another lifeless portrait. 'Yes, please.'

A few minutes later the butler arrives back with two suspiciously champagne-looking glasses containing what looks to be orange juice, though something tells her that is not the whole story. Iris's liquor-poisoned stomach roils in protest.

Barbara Bonini is not a natural model. She sits stiffly upright, gazing grimly ahead, pausing only to gulp down her drink – which actually is delicious, now Iris has got over the fact that she is putting more alcohol into her system, having sworn off it for life only a couple of hours previously.

Iris studies her sitter's face. Handsome and yet hard, as if the features have been moulded from some heavy-grade plastic or Bakelite. Barbara's eyes have that same hooded look Iris observed when she sketched her the day before at the bridal shower, as if holding them open requires impossible reserves of strength. Iris remembers what the older woman had said about how disappointments were like rows of dominoes *clack-clack-clack*ing ahead as far as the eye could see and feels all at once profoundly depressed.

'You have a beautiful home, Mrs Bonini,' she says at length when the silence has gone on for longer than she can endure.

Her hostess looks around as if seeing the place for the first time – the pillars, the palms, the heavy curtains at the windows.

'Thank you,' she says eventually. 'Bruce flew an interior designer down here in a private plane. Put him up at the Nacional while the worst of it was being done. All that money, and it looks like Grand Central Station, only slightly less personal.'

Poissinal. Why hasn't Iris noticed before that Barbara's

accent is different to, say, Eddie's or Nell's? Harsher, as if her mouth is a grater the words have to pass through?

'You don't like it, then?'

Barbara shrugs. 'It's okay, I guess. Beats the apartment where I grew up. Ha! "Apartment" is too fine a word for it. Three rooms on the fourth floor of a tenement in Hell's Kitchen with a shared stove on the landing. You could fit that whole place into our front lobby.'

Despite her words, Barbara's voice is soft with nostalgia. But Hell's Kitchen? Iris rolls the alarming phrase around her head. Is it an actual place? she wonders. Or just a colourful expression?

While she is pondering, Barbara, who has now drained her Mimosa, rings the bell a second time and orders two more. When Iris protests that she hasn't yet finished her first, she is dismissed with a wave of the hand.

After the drinks arrive Barbara reluctantly resumes her position, but as Iris concentrates on her face she becomes aware that something very strange is happening to her hostess's features. Though she is still staring resolutely ahead, every now and then a small, almost imperceptible spasm passes over her, visible in a tensing around the neck and the jaw, a slight flaring of the nostrils.

'Are you feeling quite all right?' she asks eventually, wondering if perhaps the older woman might be suffering some sort of mini seizure, and here she is, just blithely drawing around her. 'Only you seem to be wincing, as if you're in pain.'

Barbara blinks at her. 'I'm exercising my downstairs.'

Now Iris really does wonder if the woman is quite all there. *Downstairs.* It makes no sense at all, unless she's talking about her ... *Oh.* Iris feels the blood rushing to her cheeks.

'Doc told me I gotta do it three times a day. Muscles like blancmange down there, apparently. That's what four babies will do to you.'

Four babies. Iris scours her memory for any mention of the Boninis having children, but can find none. But perhaps the children are all grown now. She inspects Barbara Bonini carefully. Mid to late forties, perhaps. It's quite possible, isn't it, that there is a whole brace of young Boninis walking around the streets of New York, or perhaps tucked away in boarding school. But now Barbara is continuing and, no, it seems there are no children in boarding school, no reverse-charges calls from phones in freezing dormitories or picking up of trunks and hockey sticks and PE kits from railway stations at the end of term.

'They all died, of course. One of them when she was a few hours old, the others while they were still inside, struggling towards the finishing line. But you have to push them out just the same, as if they were still living. Can you imagine that, Irene? Pushing out babies you know won't ever take a breath?'

Iris is too shocked to respond, certainly too shocked to correct her mistaken name. Four babies. All dead.

''Course that's all in the past now. Doctors pulled out my insides like turkey giblets. But still I gotta do the exercises. It's ironic, don't you think, Irene – four babies, and all I gotta show for it is a flabby fanny.'

Much to her dismay, Iris's eyes fill with tears, which she tries to hide by focusing on her drawing.

'I'm very sorry for your loss,' she says inadequately.

Barbara shrugs, as if losing interest in the whole conversation, and her face once more takes on its habitual vacant expression.

'Everybody's lost something, am I right?'

The session with Barbara is going surprisingly well. There's a kind of fire that gets into Iris's bloodstream when she knows her drawing is good, a burning, bubbling excitement that tells her she is doing what she was born to do. So she is annoyed when the mood is shattered by a loud knocking at the door, followed by the sound of raised voices.

The butler appears in the doorway, his face flushed. 'I'm sorry to disturb you, Señora Bonini. There is a man here to see Señor Bonini. When I said he wasn't home, he asked to speak to you. His name is Dwight Wilson.'

Barbara's face betrays no recognition.

'He says he used to captain Señor Hardman's boat.'

'Well, then, it's Mr Hardman he needs to talk to. Tell him to come back later.'

'I have told him, ma'am. I'm afraid he does not listen.'

A man appears in the doorway behind the butler, wearing an ill-fitting and very creased ivory suit into which he is sweating profusely. His shovel-shaped face is the deep puce of grapes on a vine after a long hot summer.

'Mrs Bonini? Do you remember me? How nice to see you again.' His voice is rushed, urgent, and he reaches into his pocket to take out a handkerchief with which to mop his face. The instant his hand emerges from his pocket, one of Bruce's men appears behind him, yanking his arm back.

'Hey, whaddaya doing? Geddof me. Mrs Bonini?'

Barbara appears frozen in her seat. 'My butler has already

told you. You need to talk to Mr Hardman, or my husband. I can't help you.'

The man behind Dwight Wilson jerks him backwards. 'You heard. Time to go.'

Now the captain's face darkens still further, although Iris wouldn't have thought it physiologically possible.

'You can't treat me like this. I know things. Tell Mr Hardman. He'll understand what I'm talking about.'

The end of this sentence is almost lost as the man is unceremoniously bundled out of the room, the butler trailing after him, leaving Iris stunned, pulse racing.

'Shall we resume?' she asks, when she is finally able to speak, realising that Barbara is not about to comment on what has just happened. But her sitter has lost interest in the portrait. Her eyes keep darting to her black bag. 'Or would you perhaps prefer to leave it for another time?'

'Yes. Another time.' Barbara's words are slurring into each other. 'That's right. That was kinda upsetting, you know? He was the skipper on the boat the night Jean . . . Well, it brings back memories. A thing like that.'

She gets to her feet, hugging her bag to her chest, and Iris has no option but to follow suit. But at the foot of the staircase Barbara hesitates, still agitated.

'It's all starting up again. First, they reopen the case. Now, he shows up. That skipper. I tell you something, Irene, she'd better get her story straight. That's all I gotta say on the subject.'

'Who? What story?'

'Lana. That's who.' Barbara is looking at Iris as if she has forgotten exactly who she is and why she is here. 'Everyone saw how she was on that boat. She wanted him, you know, even then. I can't blame the girl. Jean was a lousy mother. You couldn't blame her for fixating on the first guy who showed her any love, you know what I'm sayin'?'

Iris's head is spinning. Barbara can't seriously be suggesting Lana had anything to do with her mother's death. The girl couldn't have been much more than fifteen at the time. It's nonsense, of course, born out of whatever was in that doctor's black bag. And yet, might not this Dwight Wilson know something useful?

Iris knows that whatever happened to Jean Summers is none of her business, and yet the longer she spends here around the Hardman family, the more invested she feels in finding out the truth. That note – *nell kills people* – hadn't mentioned Jean by name, but to Iris the implication that Nell had something to do with her stepmother's death is all too clear. She doesn't believe it, of course, but still there's that niggling note of tension where, before, it had been so uncomplicated, had even appeared as if she and Nell could have become friends. Might Dwight Wilson be able to set her mind at rest?

Stepping out of the kitchen exit at the side of the house, she bumps right into Eugene. When she tells him about the scene that has just taken place his face takes on an urgency she hasn't seen before and she is surprised to see how seriously he is taking the commission he has made light of until now. 'Come on, let's see if we can catch him.'

Arriving out in front, Iris at first thinks they have lost the captain because the wide street appears completely deserted, all the residents safely walled up behind their giant gates. Then she spots him. Leaning against a stone wall further along the road, under the shade of a spreading, silver-barked tree.

Hands on the knees of his crumpled linen trousers, as if he has recently run a race.

'Captain Wilson?' Iris wonders how Eugene manages to sound so calm and unflustered, as if they just happened to be passing. Eugene introduces himself. 'I'm covering the Hardman wedding, and I couldn't help overhearing that nasty scene. I wanted to check up on you to make sure you were all right.'

Dwight Wilson stares at him through bloodshot eyes. 'Don't much know if it's any of your business how I am.'

Iris wants to go now. Wants to turn right around and head back into the house. But Eugene isn't finished yet.

'You're right, of course. It's just that – and I shouldn't really say this; I'm only an *employee* of the Hardmans, after all – but I was shocked at how you were treated just now and I thought that after all that *unpleasantness* you might be in need of something to calm your nerves. Personally, I always find a whiskey so *medicinal* on these sorts of occasions.'

Within ten minutes they are installed on the tiny outside terrace of a bar that overlooks the mouth of the estuary separating Miramar from the neighbouring district of Vedado, being served whiskey with elaborate courtesy by a waiter with liver spots on his hands and large, anxious eyes.

'He thinks we're spooks,' Wilson says as the waiter turns away. He has already drained his first glass while hers was still being poured. Not that she has the slightest intention of drinking it, but Eugene would insist on including her.

'Spooks?' she asks.

'Spies. CIA.'

Iris's stomach lurches. She has got through her entire life without once being accused of being a spy, and now it has happened twice within twenty-four hours. Perhaps Eddie is right and half the foreigners in this country are working for the CIA. Or perhaps there is, as Bruce suspects, one of them in the wedding party who is putting all the others at risk. She remembers what Eddie said about Joe Garston being the obvious candidate and her mouth goes dry.

When the captain is on his third whiskey he begins to thaw, lurching increasingly between lugubriousness and belligerence. His life, he informs them with no small degree of self-pity, unravelled quickly after Jean Summers' death five years ago. Hugh sold the yacht – too many memories – and no one wanted to hire a skipper with that kind of track record.

'But you were completely exonerated,' Eugene says obsequiously.

'Yeah, but you become tainted by association. People thought they could catch death just by brushing past me.'

Iris avoids looking too obviously at Dwight Wilson's creased, none-too-clean clothes. You might not be able to catch death from him, but it wouldn't surprise her if you could catch *something* you didn't want.

'I bummed around trying to find work and washed up in Mexico. A man can live pretty cheaply there. And no one asks too many questions.'

Another drink is poured from the bottle Eugene has ordered to the table. Iris, who hasn't touched hers, gazes out at a boat which is slowly chugging past on its way out to sea. To the right of her, along the length of the riverbank, she sees more boats, in a range of peeling colours, moored up alongside wooden shacks, while above, two of those wretched black vultures circle. The silence stretches on and it appears as if the captain has forgotten he was in the middle of speaking.

'Then you heard about the wedding,' prompts Eugene.

'The wedding?' Dwight seems confused. 'Oh yeah, Mr Hardman and the Summers girl. The old dog.'

He looks at Iris. 'Sorry, miss.' He doesn't seem particularly sorry. 'I got talking to a guy in a bar and turns out his brother is the pilot who flew the whole lot of them over from Miami, and I got to thinking about how the Hardmans and the Boninis get to carry on with their lives, while mine has been wrecked.'

'Through something completely out of your own hands,' says Eugene, refilling the captain's glass.

''Xactly. You know, I got something the police would be pretty interested in. I coulda gone to the papers with it and made a fortune telling my story, but I figured it wasn't mine to tell. That's how come I got to be so respected in the field, see, people knew I was discreet. I captained them all – Dean Martin, Marlene Dietrich. The things that went on!'

Dwight Wilson has a faraway look in his eye and Iris forms the impression it wouldn't take much to get him to expand on just what those things might have been, discretion be blowed.

'Does Mr Hardman know about this . . . whatever it is you have . . . that the police and papers would all be so interested in?' asks Eugene.

The captain sniffs. 'Yeah. I mentioned it to him. Not long after it happened.'

'And he paid you not to tell anyone?'

Dwight gives Eugene an injured look. 'No. He gave me something to show his gratitude that I'd kept it to myself.

That's a very different thing. But then, after the work stopped coming in, I wrote to him again. Mr Hardman. Asked him if he could put in a word for me with his pals. You know, he always told me I was like a brother to him. He has a way, doesn't he, of making a person feel important? Never got a response. Nada. Now that hurt me. I gotta say that.'

'After all the loyalty you showed him,' murmurs Eugene.

''Xactly. So when I heard he was just across the water here, getting hitched. To Jean's daughter, no less. Well.'

'You decided to come and remind him,' Eugene prompts, shooting Iris a meaningful look.

'Anyone would do the same,' she says hurriedly.

'And now that bitch won't even let me through the front door. Pardon, miss.'

'Frankly, they don't deserve your loyalty.' The bottle is three quarters empty after Eugene refills the captain's glass yet again. 'You know, if I was in your shoes, I might be tempted to show the world whatever it is you have. You don't owe the Hardmans anything. I could take a look myself, if you wanted me to.'

Iris can see that Eugene has gone too far. Dwight Wilson gazes at him through narrowed, bloodshot eyes.

'No need. I got plenty of other things I could say that they wouldn't want to get out. Like the fact Jean Summers insisted on separate cabins. Or the arguments the two of them had all through that voyage. Hardman accusing her of sleeping with everyone. Errol Flynn. Even his own son.'

'Eddie?'

'Maybe not sleeping with, but definitely leading him on. What was the word he used? *Flaunting.* She was flaunting herself in front of him. Gotta say, there's some truth in that. She used to wear these little bitty costumes. Left nothing to the imagination, if you get my drift. That boy didn't know where to look.'

'Mr Hardman should be more grateful for your integrity,' says Iris.

'They were at it again the night she went missing. I couldn't hear him, but I heard her all right. Telling him it was over and to leave her alone. You could tell she was trying to be quiet, but sound carries on a boat like that. She kept saying, "You don't scare me." But you wanna know something? She sounded terrified. And that's not even the worst of it.' Now the captain's tongue has been loosened and his feathers so completely ruffled it seems there is no holding him back. 'There was blood. The morning she went missing. A few drops on the deck itself, and a smear on the edge of the seating. I saw it when I got up just after dawn and assumed someone had a nosebleed or something. I went looking for Jimmy Palicki, the steward, to get something to clean it up, but by the time we got back up on deck it was gone.'

Eugene and Iris exchange a glance.

'The inquest said she hit her head when she fell, before she went in the water, but that wouldn't account for blood inside the boat,' says Eugene.

''Xactly. Now I'm not saying either of them did anything to her, Mr Hardman or the kid.' Dwight Wilson holds up his sausage-like fingers, as though the implications of what he is saying are nothing to do with him. 'I'm just telling you what I saw. One minute blood, the next no blood. That's gotta be worth something.'

13

'THANK YOU FOR coming, Iris. If I'm left to myself, I'll show up in something so unsuitable I'll be banished from the wedding, or else ridiculed in the newspapers, like at the premiere for Pop's last picture. Well, I had no *idea* that dress was so see-through, and the flash photography just made it all the worse.'

Nell and Iris are on their way into the centre of Havana to buy a dress for Nell to wear to the wedding, her mother having dismissed the one she brought with her as indecent. As Iris and her sketchbook are due afterwards at Bruce Bonini's club so that Iris can make a start on her drawing of Hugh, Iris has dressed up for her shopping expedition in a new yellow dress, one of the few things she bought specifically for this trip. She and her typing-pool ally Joyce had gone into town shopping on a Saturday, spending hours browsing the rails in Dickins & Jones on Regent Street. Iris is not a good shopper, her enthusiasm invariably waning after the second or third rail, but Joyce had applied herself to the task of buying a new dress with heroic determination. 'This one will look divine on you.' 'Oh, but this one will be just the thing for the evening.' The yellow had been an afterthought, snatched off the rail on the way to the fitting room, then wrapped in tissue and put in a box, Iris feeling a little sick as she handed over the money she'd painstakingly saved from her sketching gigs and watched the assistant load it into the cash chute to be whisked off to the cashier's department. And now Iris has thought of Joyce with her kind, open face, and a chasm of longing and homesickness opens up behind her ribs. What wouldn't she give to have her friend sitting here beside her? Not that Nell isn't the most generous of people, but since that strange note arrived Iris feels awkward, knowing she is hiding something from her. And now there's the conversation with Dwight Wilson, who has in his possession something Nell's father would pay money to keep from coming to light. Not to mention the thing with Eddie. Iris is determined not to allow what happened on that guest-house sofa to taint her relationship with his sister, but it casts a shadow nevertheless.

The taxi deposits them next to one of the open squares Havana seems to specialise in, lined, as they all are, with parking meters. There is another of those spreading trees with thick silver branches growing out of a monstrous grey, gnarled trunk. To her surprise, Nell is able to tell her the name. 'Ceiba. I flew here for a secret weekend last year with a trumpet player I was just crazy about. I thought we would have a high old time, but instead he spent the entire forty-eight hours lecturing me on the fauna and flora of Cuba from this almighty book he'd brought all the way from LA. Near enough bored me to death.' All around them, Havana bustles about its business. Lottery-ticket sellers with trays around their necks, a man pushing a cart piled high with pineapples.

They are heading for Havana's most famous department store, El Encanto, a grand building with a distinctive square-patterned façade that wraps around a busy corner. 'You know it means "The Enchantment" in English? Isn't that just divine?'

The store is indeed enchanting, selling some of the most exquisite things Iris has ever seen. Couture fashions from Paris – Dior, Chanel – lace dresses with tiny nipped-in waists and full tulle skirts, fitted woollen jackets with rabbit-fur collars. There's a department devoted only to embroidered linen napkins, and another to perfume, beautifully shaped bottles with tasselled satin atomisers arranged on shelves, the whole room heavy with scent. There are glass counters displaying gloves of the softest kid leather and silk scarves in every colour under the sun, and a whole room full of hats – little pillboxes that perch on top of your head; hats with wide, floppy brims that cover half the face; hats with veils, with bows, with feathers.

In her tight white trousers, her platinum hair shining under the strip lighting, Nell is a gleaming blade cutting through the froth and the lace and the big skirts with all the netting underneath, through the twinsets and the fascinators and the fans and the fawning saleswomen and the women with their flawless hair and make-up, as if they'd never set foot outside in that unforgiving heat.

'We need to get you a bathing suit, if we're going to Varadero tomorrow,' says Nell, picking up a wisp of fabric with so many different straps Iris finds it impossible to work out what goes where.

The reminder of their forthcoming daytrip to the beach gives Iris a twinge of apprehension. She has already questioned

Isabella as to whether it is appropriate for her to be tagging along on what is essentially a family outing, but it seems Bruce himself has asked that she join them. They will be visiting a hotel he has bought on the beach and he wants Iris to draw it for the cover of the new menus when the refurbishment is done. 'Don't worry, I already have a costume,' she says, more snappily than she intended.

In the women's fashion department, Nell riffles disdainfully through the rails of beautiful dresses as if they are old rags, while Iris, who grew up with the make-do-and-mend ethos of the war, watches on, transfixed. 'Why must everything be designed to make us all look a hundred and one years old?' Nell says, glaring at a garment with a Peter Pan collar and three-quarter-length sleeves. Finally, she finds something to her liking, a gold, shimmering floor-length gown cut low in the front and slashed to the thigh. When she parades around the sumptuous changing room in it, the sales assistants watch with eyes as wide as saucers.

Iris is surprised when Nell charges the dress to Bruce Bonini's account, but Nell brushes the matter off as if it is too dull to consider. 'Pop will square things with Bruce, I guess.'

How strange it would be, Iris thinks, to assume that money will always be there when you need it, as if it grows on a perennially flowering tree. And yet the more time she spends with this woman, the less convinced Iris is that Nell Hardman isn't a costume she dresses her real self up in, just like one of these glittering gowns. She remembers Nell's face when she told Iris about her father and Lana – how anxiety had changed the very shape of it, rinsing it of colour. Iris can still vividly recall how it felt out there on the terrace meeting Hugh, how he'd looked at her as if he had opened up a little door and was seeing into her very soul. Even Eddie had noticed. What was that he had said while they were at dinner, about her not needing to be told how persuasive Hugh is? If he was your father, a man like that, mightn't you feel you had to construct a persona to match up?

While they wait for the dress to be meticulously wrapped in tissue and ribbon, Nell talks about Connie and how she has given up pretending to be scandalised by her daughter. 'The truth is, she isn't terribly interested in me, Iris. Oh, she loves me, don't get me wrong, but women like Mama only ever really have room for one great passion in their life.'

Iris realises with a shock that she is talking about Hugh.

'I'm not saying she's still in love with him. But she is still consumed by him. What you have to remember is they were together since they were fourteen. He was her whole world. When she realised she couldn't be his wife any more, she had to find some other way of staying in his life, so she became his mother.' Iris remembers that tableau out by the swimming pool, Hugh's head in Connie's lap. 'Poor Mama. Her Church doesn't exactly believe in divorce. You know, I wouldn't be surprised if, deep down, she doesn't still consider herself married.'

It is a shock to emerge on to the noisy street after the cool of the store. They head towards a bench in the square in front, shaded from the glare of the sun, where they can sit and wait for Raúl. Next to them a man stands behind a knife-sharpening cart, shouting out to passers-by. A woman with two loaves of bread tucked under her arm stops to talk to him in a low, guttural voice. Noise is everywhere. The backfiring of car engines and the calls of the street vendors and of the people leaning out of upper windows to get the attention of their friends passing on the street. The piercing notes of a lone trumpeter in a white suit standing in the shade of a doorway, playing with a cloth cap at his feet. The shrieking of three schoolgirls gossiping under the tree. The crying of a toddler confronting his empty bowl outside the sundae parlour across the street.

'Say, isn't that Joe Garston over there?' Nell is sitting upright, craning to see over the roof of a powder-blue Chevrolet to the opposite pavement. 'My loins are stirring, so it has to be. Christ but that man is handsome. Who's the girl?'

Iris raises her head. Nell is right. There is the unmistakable figure of the photographer, deep in conversation with a young woman, slim and straight-backed, with glossy black hair. She wears a fitted skirt with a wide belt and a white sleeveless blouse, so that Joe's hand, which rests on her arm, is touching her bare skin. When the woman looks up and Iris gets a glimpse of her high cheekbones and fine, straight nose, there is a momentary tug of familiarity, but then she bows her head again and the moment is lost. In its place is a dull thud of disappointment in the pit of Iris's stomach as her gaze fixes on the point where their skins touch. *Idiot.* That will teach her to allow herself to indulge in schoolgirl fantasies. She swallows. Bites down on her back teeth. What does it matter, anyway? She will be gone from here in a couple of days and it will be as if none of these people ever existed. Back to Hemel Hempstead. And Peter.

'Well, isn't he a fast worker?' Nell's voice is throaty with admiration as she turns to smile at Iris, who forms the definite opinion that Joe Garston has just shot up in her friend's estimation.

They turn their attention back to the action across the road, but the spot where the photographer and his companion were standing just moments before is now empty, and only the ache in Iris's chest tells her they were ever there at all.

Raúl drops her off in front of a wide doorway with a portico held up by enormous marble pillars which suggest they have arrived at Bruce Bonini's club. They are in Vedado, so close to the Malecón Iris can feel the salt on her lips and hear the roar of the traffic on the busy coast road. The weather has thickened as they've been driving, the sky padded with grey felt, as if there might be a storm coming.

Inside, the air is cool. The lobby looks so similar to the Boninis' living room that Iris decides the same designer must be responsible for both. More marble, miniature palms in vast pots, a central fountain with a marble surround. A chandelier the size of a small car. A flight of stairs leads them to the first floor, where the lighting is dimmer and the marble is replaced by velvet and gilt. A coat-check girl in a strapless corset perches redundantly on a high stool, her elbows on the counter, her pretty face blank. Behind her the rails are largely empty, apart from the odd fur wrap, so incongruous, given the heat outside.

Iris follows the sound of laughter and the low hum of conversation and arrives at the door of a casino, compact but well stocked, with long roulette tables in the centre and slot machines around the edge and at the back two semi-circular blackjack tables, around one of which are grouped Hugh Hardman, Bruce Bonini and two other men, one of whom she recognises as Señor Ferrer. Eugene is also there, making notes in a spiral-bound notebook. Their host has been very insistent that Eugene's wedding reportage should include vignettes of Havana in all its hedonistic glory – 'background colour', he calls it – by which of course he means his own various business enterprises. This club, for example. There is a selection of glasses and ashtrays on the table, and in front of Hugh a huge pile of casino chips. The room is quiet, save for the piped sound of Vic Damone crooning softly about the street where you live, but then, Iris reminds herself, it is still daylight out there.

She takes in all these details slowly and carefully, to put off the moment where she must acknowledge the presence of Joe Garston, setting up his camera on the far side of the room. He can only have preceded her by a few minutes. She searches his face for any sign that he has come straight from a romantic rendezvous, but he remains as impassive as ever. Outrage bubbles up inside her, remembering how disapproving he'd seemed before her date with Eddie. And yet, not even twenty-four hours later, he is virtually canoodling with a woman in the street.

'Thank God you're here,' says Eugene, who has come over to greet her. 'There's so much testosterone blowing around that table I'm surprised I haven't grown a full beard already and invaded a small country. I know I suddenly have an overwhelming urge to hunt big game at the weekends.'

'Who's that with Bruce?'

'Well, obviously you've met Mr Ferrer.'

Iris remembers all too well Bruce's ill-concealed anger at her unsolicited sketch of the biscuit-coloured Cuban official, and how Joe had mimed a shooting gun as they'd watched the mystery crates disappearing around the side of the Ferrer house. 'He does something in government, and the little one with the fetching moustache is high up in the military police. Captain something or other. Diaz, I think. They're both friends of Bruce's.' He lowers his voice. 'The kind of friends you pay lots of money to and hope they don't kill you in your sleep.'

Iris glances over to the blackjack table and freezes when she sees Bruce himself staring right at her. Such black, black eyes. Anxiety grips her. Can he really suspect her of being a spy for the Americans? Has he discovered the key and scarf are missing? Does he know she was in his study, rifling through his desk? As she watches, he says something to the two Cubans and now the three of them are staring at her and she quickly looks away, her stomach roiling.

A small group of Americans enters. Two men, upper lips still beaded with sweat from the heat outside, and a round-faced woman of around sixty whose cantilevered bosom, swathed in some stiff, bejewelled fabric, precedes her into the room by quite some margin. The trio make their way towards the other blackjack table with a languidness akin to boredom, but when they catch sight of Hugh their demeanour visibly alters. The men straighten their backs, darting glances back and forth to the next table, while the woman pats her coiffured hair as if it is a beloved pet. Finally, after furious conferring, one of the men crosses to stand awkwardly at Hugh's shoulder, waiting for the director to finish his conversation and then finally turn his head as if only now becoming aware he has company. Iris catches the odd phrase – 'great admirers' is one, and 'such an honour' another. And now Hugh is raising himself up to his full height and following his new acquaintance to join the other two new arrivals, shaking hands with the man and grazing the woman's beringed knuckles with his lips until she is quite pink with delight. The man whose initial boldness procured this prize seeks to assert ownership by loudly naming one of Hugh's films as his favourite, whereupon Hugh launches into an anecdote that has his audience hanging on his every word, rapt. It is a gift, Iris thinks, to be able to make everyone you meet feel special. How might such a gift be used? And how might it be abused?

When Hugh has finished his story and regained his seat he beckons Iris over, and she wonders if he has been conscious of her presence all this time she has been hovering near the doorway, unsure of how to proceed.

'I can't imagine why anyone would want to see a picture of this old face,' he says, shaking back his hair and running a thumb and forefinger down the creases either side of his handsome nose. 'But Isabella has decreed it, and aren't we all too scared to say no to that woman? Let's go hide from these ghastly people in the bar upstairs. We'll find a nice dark booth where you can eviscerate me with your pencil and drip my guts across the page like Jackson Pollock.'

Bruce leans forward. An overpowering waft of cologne.

'That wasn't the deal,' he says under his breath. 'Visibility. That was the deal.' That little mouth of his hardly moves as he talks.

'I have been visible.' Hugh's voice, stripped of its habitual forceful intimacy, is cold as corroded metal. 'I have been charming.' He gestures to the Americans on the next table, who are still flushed from their brush with celebrity. 'And now I am going upstairs with this young lady to get my *fucking* wedding portrait done.'

As she follows him out of the room Iris isn't sure what has unnerved her more – the profanity so casually flung, or how Bruce was smiling as they left, as if it had all been light-hearted banter, and yet, glancing down, she'd noticed he was gripping his whiskey glass so tightly the tips of his perfectly manicured fingers were bloodless.

U-shaped booths lined with red velvet. Red velvet curtains on the windows and draped across the stage. Walls the colour of claret. Iris thinks the bar in Bruce's club must be a little like how it might feel to be inside a giant mouth. Their booth is in the section reserved for those who want only to drink and chat, while nearer the stage are tables for those preferring to watch the show, although being early still, there is no show, only a sultry woman in a figure-hugging red silk dress, singing into a microphone in such a heavy accent that it takes Iris several minutes to recognise the song as Frankie Laine's 'I Believe'. Only half of the tables are full, mostly of men, while at the bar sit five or six young women, all attractive and perfectly made up, not talking to one another, only gazing wearily ahead. When she studies the woman nearest to them Iris is astonished to discover that the intricate patterns of her 'stockings' are painted directly on to her bare leg. A waiter taps the shoulder of the youngest-looking of the women, plump-cheeked and adolescently awkward, and she obediently slips off her stool and follows him to a table where two middle-aged men in dinner jackets seem to be conducting some sort of business meeting, judging by the documents in front of them. As the girl approaches, the men's eyes slide down her as if they have weights on their lids.

*

'You know, I find you fascinating, Iris,' says Hugh, who has spread himself across the seat facing her. 'You have this surface fragility, but I also sense a steeliness running through you. Am I right, Iris?' It is something he does a lot, uses her name, and each time he does so his eyes find hers, shrinking the world down until it is just the two of them and she is trapped there with him until she feels short of breath.

'It's very attractive, that vulnerability of yours,' he goes on. 'No man can resist a damaged woman.'

'I assure you I'm not damaged,' says Iris, bending her burning face towards her sketchbook. A memory sears itself across her mind, herself this very morning standing in a cold shower after her date with Eddie, scrubbing at her skin. 'Well, perhaps just a little chipped.'

They begin the sitting. Hugh has a bottle of Scotch in front of him and drains it slowly. With each sip, each refill of his glass, he grows more loquacious, takes up more of the air in the booth, until Iris feels quite light-headed. The portrait itself comes together magically, as happens only rarely, she and her pencil seemingly just conduits for the energy that passes almost by osmosis from the subject on to the page. Here is Hugh's hair, of which he is so proud, sweeping back from his high, domed forehead, and here the hollow of his cheek, criss-crossed by the effects of the sun on his leathered skin. Here his huge hands moving through the air in demonstration of a point.

'You are a more straightforward subject than your fiancée.'

His face softens, and his eyes grow blurry. 'Oh, Lana. She's such a sweet girl. But yes, guarded. Always was. And who could blame her? What a start those girls had. I tried, of course. In my small way.'

He takes a long swig of his drink and his shoulders slump as if overcome by the tragedy of it all. But when he looks up again his eyes are dry and bright.

'Did Lana tell you about Manderley?'

'Manderley?'

'The ranch I bought for Jean. It's the most beautiful place, Iris. You would love it. This living, breathing structure hewn from wood and stone and pitted against a hostile, arid landscape – a triumph of humanity and hope. I cannot wait to see the old place again. I always felt alive there, do you know what I mean, Iris? Do you understand how some places can get into the very marrow of your bones until you don't know where you start and they end?'

Iris is taken aback by the difference between his fleeting, vague reference to his soon-to-be-wife and the passion with which he talks about the house.

'Yes, I've heard it's wonderful. Faye is so looking forward to living there again.'

Surprise wipes the easy smile from Hugh's face, making him look instantly a decade older, though he recovers quickly. 'Faye? Oh, I don't think so, Iris. You see, Faye isn't well. Emotionally, I mean. I'm sure you've noticed that, a clever girl like you. Even when her mother was still alive there was something not right about her. She was always following me around the house, hiding and listening. Everywhere I went, there she was. Jean was all in favour of sending her away then, but I persuaded her she was too young. Perhaps I must bear some of the blame.' He looks over at Iris, as if waiting for her to protest. 'And things have only got worse. Well, you must have seen her wrists. She needs specialist help, and we'll make sure we find her just the right kind of facility. I hear there's a clinic in San Francisco doing excellent work.'

Iris concentrates on creating the black shadows in the deep sockets of Hugh's eyes, pressing her pencil so hard against the paper that the tip of the lead breaks clean off. Meanwhile, her sitter's gaze wanders over to where the singer stands, accompanied by a pianist, in a pool of yellow light that turns her red dress into a flame and coats her skin in gold.

Later, when the bottle is almost drained and the portrait almost done and Hugh is stretched out practically horizontal on the red velvet seat, he turns the full force of his attention back to Iris.

'Aren't you the least bit scared of me, Miss Bailey? You must have heard the rumours, even all the way over there in England. It's always the husband. Isn't that what they say?'

'I don't know what you . . .'

'Oh, cut the crap, Iris. You're far too smart for that. There are some people who will always believe I killed my wife, even though the coroner was very clear Jean's death was an accident.'

'You think she fell, then.' Iris keeps her eyes trained on her paper.

Hugh nods sleepily. 'That, or she jumped. The truth is always more banal than fantasy, don't you think, Iris? The sad, tawdry fact is that my wife was having an affair on the set of her last picture.'

Iris is unsure how to react. She has already heard the infidelity rumour from Eugene, and then Dwight Wilson described how Hugh and Jean kept arguing about it, but the last thing she wants is for Hugh to know they've all been discussing it behind his back. She must have arranged her features into a convincing expression of surprise because Hugh nods.

'With that loser Flynn, most likely,' he continues. 'Lost in the whole romance of it all. Then she comes on the yacht and she's confronted with the reality of marriage and me, and the guilt got to her. She was a woman who felt things very strongly, you know, Iris.'

Abruptly, Hugh sits up straight and stares directly at her in that way he has that leaves her feeling skewered to her seat.

'You're real good at this, aren't you, Iris? Drawing out our secrets so that we bleed on to your page. You're like a priest, and here I am in the confessional.' He presses the large palms of his hands together as if in prayer.

As they leave the bar area, threading their way through the sparsely occupied tables in the centre of the room, past the young, plump-cheeked girl staring off into space while the two middle-aged businessmen talk to each other as if she isn't there, the singer launches into an up-tempo Spanish song, gyrating her hips and her feet in a complicated rhythm. Her dress has a split up to the thigh and her legs are long and muscular in her high-heeled red shoes. Hugh slows down then stops completely. The woman, sensing his scrutiny, looks over. Iris sees the exact moment their eyes meet. Blue eyes on brown. Something changes in the woman's face, as if she was only going through the motions before but now she comes to life. She tosses back her hair, licks her lips and, without tearing her gaze from his, she runs her hands up her body.

Iris pushes hotly ahead out of the door in her new yellow

dress that she'd thought so stylish when she watched it being wrapped in tissue by the sales assistant at Dickins & Jones but which now seems as dowdy as something her own mother would wear.

An hour or so later, after photographs have been taken to Bruce Bonini's satisfaction (the most beautiful waitresses rounded up to appear in the background, the impressive gold-framed mirror, the bar with 'Bonini's' picked out in neon above it) and Eugene made to repeat back facts about the club and other parts of Bruce's business empire, reading from his notes – facts that his host has suggested would make excellent copy, except that Iris gets the feeling Bruce's suggestions are more like demands – Iris and the two journalists are dismissed. The three of them stand on the pavement, looking in vain for a taxi. 'That little police chief said there'd been another explosion tonight,' says Eugene, overlooking the fact that Captain Diaz has several inches over him. 'Maybe all the taxi drivers have gone home.'

The sky has been heavy with swollen clouds the colour of granite, and as they start walking the rain starts. But this is not like English rain that begins with a gentle patter, building slowly and sensibly to a steady, rhythmic downpour before respectfully receding once again without any fuss. This rain comes out of nowhere and immediately is so hard and plentiful that Iris is soaked within seconds, the new yellow dress clinging to her back and shoulders and thighs. There is rain dripping from her eyelashes, from the end of her nose.

Joe, laden with his camera equipment, cannot even brush aside the hair which is hanging in sodden strands in his eyes, and Iris has to fight the urge to do it for him. Eugene, meanwhile, is a more bizarre sight than ever. He is wearing a white shirt which has been rendered see-through by the rain, and Iris's heart snags at the sight of his white vest over a childishly concave chest. Every few steps they must stop so that he can wipe his glasses, although there is soon not one single item of clothing dry enough to wipe them on.

Finally, success. A taxi driver who takes full advantage of their state to drive up his price to an extortionate level. 'Look,' he says sorrowfully, pointing to a small wet patch they have left on his leather upholstery. Then, apropos of nothing: 'I have six children.' Joe makes as if to leave in disgust, but Eugene stops him.

'If I go back out there, I'll dissolve clean away.' Impossible to refuse him, in his little white vest.

During the journey home, Iris is conscious of the hot, damp smell of her body and the dress which is plastered to her skin. The noise of the rain on the roof of the car is deafening, the view through the window obscured by sheets of relentlessly falling water. She tries to hold herself stiffly upright to avoid touching Joe, but each time the car turns a corner he seems to press closer to her – calves, thighs, the bare skin of their arms, everything touching. Finally, she feels his hand reaching for hers and her breath turns to dust in her lungs.

'Are you okay, Iris?' he asks softly. 'After what happened last night, with Eddie?'

Her eyes fill with tears and she is grateful for the darkness. For a moment she thinks about laying her head on Joe's shoulder, can almost feel the comfort of it, his warm, damp shirt against her cheek. Then she remembers what she saw earlier over the top of that car roof. Joe's head bent towards that woman's. Nell's admiring whistle: 'Well, isn't he a fast worker?' She refuses to be a trophy for such a man.

'Perfectly fine, thank you.' She moves her hand away and tries not to notice how her fingers still tingle from his touch long after he has shifted as far from her as he can get.

Arriving at the house, they dash from the taxi, only to find that by the time they reach the swimming pool the rain has stopped. They laugh awkwardly at each other in the sudden silence and Iris is glad of the darkness so no one can see how the sodden dress clings to her body. As they pass under the low-hanging branches that separate the guest house from the main one, the rainwater drips down the back of her neck and she shivers in the humid night air. There is a smell of damp earth and something sweet and pungent coming from a nearby bush.

Back in her room, Iris peels off the dress and the girdle and allows her damp skin to breathe freely. She has grown used, over the last two days, to the novelty of walking around naked. At home, the three-bar heater in her bedroom does so little to take the chill off the air that she is usually in a hurry to wriggle from one set of clothes into another. But in Cuba she has taken a quiet delight in her physical self. Only now, with the memory of Eddie Hardman still sticky on her skin, does she feel self-conscious.

She wanders over to her case, her bare feet spreading on the cool tiles. Then she stops quite still. When she was getting ready to go out earlier she had carefully extracted the yellow dress from its tissue wrapping then lovingly refolded the paper, running her fingers along the creases to make them neat and laying the ribbon on the top, almost as if she has another wrapped parcel to open. It is something she has always done. It is only eight years since clothes rationing ended, and Iris has vivid memories of how, as a child, her uniform was always either too big: *plenty of growing room*; or too short and tight: *it'll do another year*. She remembers scratchy wool jumpers with the elbows reinforced with mismatching patches and an ugly dress she'd been so delighted to grow out of, only for her mother to refashion it into a skirt. Iris had never been so glad to see the end of anything as that pink ration book. Even now, new clothes are enough of a rarity for the unpacking of them to be a ceremonial event. The unpicking of the ribbon, the preservation of the paper. Everything done in a particular way.

Except now, it isn't.

The paper is there where she left it at the top of her case. Neatly folded. But not the way she would fold it. And true, the ribbon is still laid across the top, but not as she would have done it, not so that it looks from a distance as if it had never been opened, as if she might once again get to savour the sheer joy of uncovering something new and unworn, something that contains in its folds and seams and tucks a myriad tender hopes and dreams.

She must be mistaken. Even so, Iris feels suddenly exposed in her nakedness and, after checking to make sure the scarf and key are still where she hid them, she reaches through the mosquito net to snatch up the sheet from the bed to wrap around herself.

14

DOWNSTAIRS AGAIN, WEARING blissfully dry clothes, Iris finds the guest house silent and dark. Unable to shake off that sense of unease she'd felt standing in her room surveying her case, she decides to head towards the main house in search of company. She gets as far as the swimming pool before second thoughts set in. They are so exhausting, these Hardmans, with their shifting dynamics and murky family history and the way they turn first this side to her and then that, never showing quite the same face from one time to the next so that she cannot get her bearings. And though she'd felt close to Eugene and Joe back there in the taxi, all of them linked by their rain-sodden clothes and their outsider status, what does she really know of them, after all? She has not forgotten what Eddie said in the restaurant of the Nacional – that if some-one in the wedding party really is working for the CIA, it will turn out to be Joe.

Next to the swimming pool, the backs of the recliners form hunched shadows in the dim light coming from lamps at either end. Iris makes her way towards the nearest one.

The cushion will be soaking, but she can take it off and stretch out on the wooden base, watching the stars.

She is already lying down, having laid the cushion on the ground next to the chair, when a rustling and a creaking noise alert her to the fact she is not alone out here. Her heart stops. Two recliners along, a large cocoon of blankets changes shape in the dark.

Iris shoots upright with a sharp intake of breath.

'I'm sorry. I didn't mean to startle you.' The voice is as insubstantial as smoke, as if the air itself has just breathed loudly.

'Faye? Are you all right?'

The bundle of blankets shifts and a face emerges, ghostly pale in the dim light.

'Yes. Thank you. I like these moments when the rain stops and the earth seems, I don't know, washed clean, I guess. Don't you?'

'It certainly makes a jolly nice change from the wretched heat.'

'Is it really always foggy in England, Iris? I heard you can't see your hand in front of your face. I have to say I kinda like the idea that you can hide from your own self like that.'

'We do have other kinds of weather as well. Sometimes it's even warm enough not to wear a coat, though naturally, one draws the line at taking off one's cardigan.'

'Are you joking, Iris?'

Faye Mickelson sounds like a child and Iris regrets her levity, particularly when she remembers what Hugh told her about Faye's disturbed emotional state.

'You must come to visit. Then you would find out for yourself.'

'I'm not really one for travel. I would never even have come this far if not for Lana. I wish they would have just got married in California, instead of having to come all the way out here, where the sun is so fierce, for all I try to cover up, and my clothes stick to me and there are so many bugs my skin itches all the time. But I couldn't not be here. Since Mommy died, there haven't been so many happy times. But that's all gonna change now I'll be living with Lana and Hugh back at Manderley and everything will be like it was.'

Pity stoppers up Iris's throat. Not only does the girl have no clue about the fate Hugh has lined up for her, but she seems determined to rewrite history, painting a rosy picture of how things were when Jean Summers was alive.

'I'm sure you must miss your mother terribly.' Iris chooses her words carefully. 'Though from what Lana has told me, life with her wasn't always without its challenges.'

Faye grows agitated, her voice higher pitched. 'You mustn't listen to Lana. Mommy was beautiful, inside and out. That's why people were so jealous of her.'

'Well, I'm sure that's not . . . ?'

'They *were*. Everyone was. Connie, for one. She never forgave Mommy for taking Hugh away. You know she was always calling him up, pretending Eddie or Nell were having problems so he'd have to go over there. One time she even showed up at the door. It was just me at home with the housekeeper. I was really young at the time, but I remember this lady standing there, all red in the face and calling Mommy a whore, and of course I had no idea what that meant, and saying Hugh had made a terrible mistake. "I give it five years," she kept saying. And five years later she was dead. Don't you think that's spooky, Iris?'

The conversation has passed beyond Iris's control, and she is conscious of Faye's raised voice and the way she is rubbing incessantly at the scars on her wrist. When Nell appears, looming from the shadows, it's all Iris can do not to jump up and hug her she is so relieved.

'So this is where the party is happening. I've been sent to fetch you, Iris. Apparently, there are actual Cubans here. A whole family of them. Brucie is trying to buy some real estate – another nightclub or hotel – from the father, who is some big-shot tobacco boss. Or maybe it's sugar. Anyways, he invited them over so he could sweet-talk them, only he must have forgotten and he's still out with Pop, and Barbara is tight as a tick so Isabella has stepped in to try to avert a diplomatic incident by pimping out your services. You're to draw the daughter. There, I knew you'd be thrilled. Although, to be fair, they're not exactly jumping up and down with excitement either.'

Iris groans. She is starting to despise the so-called talent that has brought her here. How cheap it appears when wheeled out as a favour or a gift, and now as a sop to mollify one of Bruce Bonini's disgruntled business contacts.

Nell leads the way to the house. Outside on the terrace, Eugene and Joe are in conversation with Connie and Meredith, all four of them clutching glasses filled with some kind of milky-looking cocktail. As Iris approaches, Eugene says something that makes the other three roar with laughter and Iris wishes more than anything that she could draw up one of those heavy wrought-iron chairs and join them. But no, she must follow Nell inside, not looking to see if Joe's eyes are on her but feeling them all the same.

The visitors are sitting stony-faced in the downstairs salon where earlier Iris had sketched Barbara Bonini. Her hostess is also there, along with Lana and Isabella, who leaps to her feet the second Iris appears in the doorway and grasps Iris's hands, as if trying to save herself from drowning.

'And here is the genius herself. Oh my *Gad*, you will not believe the talent of this woman. She will make you look like film stars. Believe.'

The Cuban family, straight-backed in their seats, do not smile or bend in the slightest in the face of the party planner's charm onslaught.

'These are the Morrises,' says Barbara, sweeping her arm around in the visitors' general direction.

'We are the Morales,' corrects the father, who is pristine in a bone-coloured suit with a starched white handkerchief in the breast pocket and an open white shirt topped by a patterned silk cravat. Iris notices he holds himself so upright that his jacket does not touch the chair-back, as if he is making a point that he is not about to make himself at home here. Either that, or he does not trust the cleanliness of the furnishings in this spotless house.

His wife is black-haired and handsome, wearing a midnight-blue gown in a stiff fabric that doesn't so much cover as encase her, and the clusters of diamonds at her throat and earlobes sparkle in the light from the overhead chandelier. When Iris is introduced she does a strange movement with her mouth, as if she is exercising her lips rather than smiling. Iris is sure she recognises her from the table next to them at the bridal shower.

'And now *Eerees* will draw your most beautiful daughter, Luisa. Oh my *Gad*, such a face she has, it will be like a dream for her to draw it.'

Iris nods in agreement. 'Oh yes. Definitely.' She turns her smile towards the girl, sitting poised on one of the Boninis' uniquely uncomfortable chairs, and gives a start of surprise. It is her. The woman whose glossy black hair, bent so close to Joe Garston's, had so unmoored her earlier in the day. Up close, she is exquisitely beautiful, around Iris's own age, with hair cut like Elizabeth Taylor's and a tiny waist. So that is why she seemed familiar, because she'd been at the Tropicana the previous day.

Clearly, Nell recognises her, too, because she gives Iris a raised-eyebrowed *Well, this is a turn-up* glance before excusing herself to rejoin the others on the terrace.

Isabella has summoned someone to bring Iris's art equipment, set aside in a cupboard since this morning's session with Barbara. Iris begins tentatively and is relieved when Luisa, stiff at first, visibly softens to the rhythm of her pencil strokes. They exchange a few pleasantries about the bridal shower and Iris compliments her on her impeccable English. 'Well, I will hope this to be the case,' says Señor Morales, whose own grasp of the language is less impressive than his daughter's. 'The money cost of that school.'

'I expect you have some American friends you can practise on,' Iris tells Luisa softly, keeping her eyes on her paper in case some hint of Joe Garston should reveal itself in them. 'There are so many Americans in Havana.'

If she was hoping for some sign that she has hit a nerve,

she is disappointed. Luisa's face remains impassive. 'I'm afraid my father wouldn't approve of that.'

'Have you visited the yacht club, Miss Bailey?' Señora Morales asks, pivoting her diamonds towards Iris. When Iris shakes her head, she looks astounded, as if it is simply not conceivable to be in Havana and not have experienced the yacht club.

'We have parties there, and balls,' says Luisa, 'and Mama likes to eat there on a Sunday. Well, I should say that is not entirely true, as no one really likes to eat there. The meat tastes like the tyres of a car, but she likes to be seen to eat there.'

Señora Morales exclaims in Spanish and pretends to look cross.

'And you're not worried by the rebels in the mountains, this Fidel Castro?' Iris asks, her eyes still on her picture, which is going well. The change in the atmosphere is tangible. A tightening of the air. When she looks up she realises from the closed expressions on the older Moraleses and the surprise of the younger one that she has said the wrong thing.

'The rebels are nothing,' says Señor Morales in a clipped voice. 'They will be defeated. But this is not a subject for conversation.'

'Oh, I am sorry.'

'We should leave,' he says, half rising. 'Mr Bonini is not coming.'

'No,' says Barbara, coming suddenly to life, as if realising for the first time that this scrupulously polite Cuban would not be here in her house if he wasn't important in some way to her husband's business-expansion plans. 'You're gonna wait for your daughter's portrait, aintchya?'

But Señor Morales is not for turning. 'Miss Bailey seems to be reaching the end of her charming picture.'

Now Barbara becomes desperate. 'Wait. Listen.' She rises unsteadily to her feet. Iris notices as she passes that she has something crusted under one nostril and feels embarrassed on her behalf. Unaware, Barbara makes her way to the record player, which sits inside a wooden cabinet. Riffling impatiently through the records in the compartment underneath, she stops with an exclamation of triumph. 'Here. You must stay. Listen.'

She opens the lid of the record player and extracts a record from its sleeve. The Morales family, arrested in their various stages of departure, take on the appearance of a tableau vivant while Barbara fumbles with the needle. There is an alarming scratching noise and then a burst of music so loud Iris jumps in her seat. Finally, Barbara manages to adjust the level down to only mildly deafening. It is Cuban music, a mambo Iris believes it is called, all wooden sticks and shakers and conga drums.

To Iris's embarrassment, Barbara begins to dance. She is wearing a tight dusty-pink dress that restricts the movement of her legs and seems to be struggling to balance, but still she gamely swings her hips and puts one hand under the opposite elbow and waggles her finger.

'I love the Cuban music,' she says, shimmying up to the Moraleses, who appear to be frozen in shock.

'Come, let's dance.' She is holding a hand out to Luisa, while still wiggling around the room on her high white heels. 'I know you Cuban women are such terrific dancers. You have it in your blood. Not like us Americans, with our damn flat feet. Come on, forget Bruce. Let's have our own party.'

Luisa Morales does not reach out. Does not take Barbara's outstretched hand. 'I don't like to dance,' she says.

Now Barbara cuts a lonely figure, swaying in the middle of the room. Iris wants to go to her to take her arm, guide her back to her seat, but it is not her place.

'It is time for us to go,' Señor Morales shouts over the top of the music.

'You must come to the wedding,' Barbara shouts back in desperation, just as Isabella turns the record-player volume down further.

Now Lana, who until now has been sitting on the other side of the room with a faraway look, as if she is not here with these people but somewhere else entirely, glances over, her attention fully engaged. With all eyes on her, Barbara, still gamely gyrating to the now barely audible music, must repeat her offer. No matter that Lana is glaring at her so, and Luisa Morales, gathering up her white gloves, is raising her eyebrow at her mama as if to say, *These people.*

'Will you come?' Barbara repeats, desperate. 'You can talk to Bruce then.'

Señor Morales nods once. So curt a gesture he might just as well be tossing his hair from his eyes (if hair he had).

After they have gone Lana turns on Barbara, and her face is quite transformed by animation.

'What gives you the right?' she asks. Her voice is low and tremulous.

'I beg your pardon?'

Barbara has abandoned her dancing and is standing by the closed French doors, lighting a cigarette.

'This is my wedding. Why is everyone trying to take it out of my hands?'

'Honey, this ain't your wedding,' says Barbara. 'What in God's name gave you that idea? This is Hugh's wedding, and Bruce's. It's just another goddam production to them. You know what I'm saying? All you gotta do is show up and look pretty. The sooner you realise that, the better. Don't be like your ma. She thought she was the one calling the shots, and look where that got her.'

Now Lana is on her feet. 'What do you mean?'

But Barbara has turned up the music again and is in the middle of the floor with her eyes closed, while her hips swing from side to side and her feet, in those perilously high heels, pick out a rhythm that is entirely her own.

To my poor (hungry) Uncle Cyp

I'm afraid even a hunger strike won't persuade me to tell you the name. I haven't forgotten that the last person who let you in on a secret read all about it in the Cholly Knickerbocker column the very next week. So you'd best start eating again before you waste clear away.

There's nothing to tell, anyway. X and I are about as mismatched as can be. We've only met up a few times and, to be quite frank, the last time was really only because I was afraid of what might happen if I said no. The truth is, he's not a very nice man, Cyp, as I'm discovering. Sometimes I wonder if I only got with him to get back at Hugh. What is wrong with me that I only ever seem to choose men I trust to be capable of treating me badly? Why can't I choose someone like you, Cyp, who'll make me laugh and be nice to me? Well, aside from the fact that I'd have to grow a dick, which might be tricky. But yes, I'll be careful, especially since Hugh basically forced Nell on me as my new assistant – for which read spy. Honestly, Cyp, I don't know how it happened. No sooner had he found out Molly was gone than Nell was at my door with that friendly smile of hers that only a hardened killer could say no to. So now I've Hugh's daughter reporting back to him on everything I do. I'm practically a nun.

Oh but, Cyppie, don't you sometimes feel like it's all such a terrible waste? Sometimes I look at my life, the savage pleasure Hugh and I get from hurting each other, the momentary thrill of knowing that a man is in love with me or that a picture I made has grossed millions of dollars, all those fleeting feelings that turn to nothing within seconds, like when you hold a diamond up to the light and find it's paste after all, and I think, what's the point of it all?

Mama bought a gift for Faye last week, a mechanical toy which was far too young for her – Mama has no concept of children aging because she is so determined never to do the same herself. Anyways, when we got it out of the box it didn't work. Everything looked so pretty and shiny but there was a tiny bit inside that was broken. If you shook it, you could hear it rattling around. That's how I am. My life looks so perfect and yet there's this tiny broken part that means the whole thing can't work – for all the studio send their hair stylists and their make-up artists and the girl who picks out my clothes that I have to pretend to have thrown on any time a photographer catches me unawares. For all that *Variety* called me the Girl with the Thousand-Watt Smile. (Oh, puh-lease.)

Mustn't get maudlin!

So, guess what Hugh is planning for his forty-fifth birthday party? This will make you laugh. Four days on the *SallyAnn* in the Gulf of Mexico with family and friends. And guess how I found out? By reading it in the *Post*! Can you imagine, Cyp, me and Hugh on a boat together for four whole days with no escape? And Eddie barely bothering to cover up the bulge in his pants, not to mention Nell and Lana and Faye. All those adolescent-girl hormones in one small space – it'll be a miracle if we don't all break out in acne instantly. You know, every time I'm away from the girls, like now, I miss them madly and I vow to myself that I'll spend time with them properly, listening to them like a real mom should (i.e. not like Mama). But then I see them again, and Lana is so lumpy and serious and Faye gives me the heebies with all her creeping around and inside of ten minutes I'm looking at the clock and wondering how soon I can leave.

And God help us if the 'friends' he's invited are the Boninis. Last time I saw Barbara I kissed her on the cheek, and I swear I was high for a week! There's another reason for not wanting them there that I can't tell you about, but believe me when I say it will be an A-grade disaster if the Boninis are on board.

Wasn't it Hem himself who said that life breaks everyone in the end? I have a nasty feeling this boat trip will break me.

Your sad Aunt Sap

15

DOES ANYONE REALLY enjoy playing cards? Iris would very much like to know. It seems to her as if the best that can be said of cards is that they are a way of making time pass. Much like staring off into space or flicking through a magazine one has read before. She is thinking this as she considers her hand and waits for Eugene, who is on her left, to play his turn.

It is half an hour since the Cubans' departure, but the strained atmosphere they left behind them persists. Barbara disappeared upstairs soon after they went and was gone so long Iris assumed she'd gone to bed, but then she reappeared full of new energy, her eyes wide and strangely bright.

'Cards?' she'd said. 'What are we, a hundred years old? Come on, let's shake things up around here.'

Then she'd done a wiggle that left Iris fearful of a repeat of the mambo episode. When no one got up to join her, she'd sat down as far from Lana as possible. They are outside on the terrace, around the long glass table. The air is humid as ever.

'Rummy!' shrieks Connie from the top of the table. 'I win. Oh my! I never win.'

'That's a lie,' observes Meredith, next to her. 'You win all the time because you're the only one who cares about winning.'

'Now, Meredith. How can you say such a thing? I don't give a hoot who wins, and you know it. I'm not at all that sort of person. Although I will admit I'm something of a fiend for canasta. Has anyone played it? Oh my, it's just the most marvellous game. Let me explain the rules . . .'

From around the side of the house comes the sound of car doors slamming and men's voices raised. Someone is singing 'I Believe' in a tremulous baritone. There's laughter, then Bruce and Hugh appear around the corner, accompanied by Eddie.

'What is this? A ladies' bridge club?' Hugh's vast presence fills the back terrace.

Lana gets up and steps wordlessly into his embrace. Seeing them together, Iris is struck by how completely the slight young woman is subsumed into her fiancé's commanding frame. Eddie stands behind his father's shoulder, his expression closed off. Only when his eyes lock on to Iris's does his demeanour change. 'Here you are,' he says, hurrying over. 'The evening has been so dull without you.'

Eddie looks so rueful Iris urges herself to soften. He has clearly put last night's episode behind him, this morning's apology wiping the slate clean, and it would be churlish, wouldn't it, not to do the same?

The newly returned men are in high spirits, holding glasses full to the brim in their hands. 'How about that guy with the wig?' Bruce and Hugh are remembering a man they met at the blackjack table, accompanied by a woman in a gold lamé dress whose one job had been to stand behind him and mop his face every now and then with a linen handkerchief.

'Every time she mopped, it was a fresh one,' Bruce continues. 'Her bag was full of the goddam things.'

It is a curious thing, but even while Bruce is bantering with Hugh he gives the impression of playing the part of a man bantering with his friend. While Hugh is evidently and exuberantly drunk, Bruce's inebriation seems somehow knowing.

Now Lana is telling Hugh and Bruce about the Moraleses' visit, and suddenly the mood shifts.

'Why did he come tonight?' asks Bruce in a dangerously soft voice. 'I sent Raúl with a message telling him arrangements had changed.'

Now he turns to Barbara, who is sitting at the end of the table, nursing a Mojito.

'And you couldn't keep them here? It was too much to ask, that you entertain this important man until I get back?'

Barbara flaps her hand. 'I tried already. The whole family were like they were stuffed – am I right, Lana? I'd have had more luck trying to entertain this table. I even tried to put some of *their* kind of music on, to make them feel at home. Didn't I do that, Irene?' She is squinting down the table in Iris's direction. 'Didn't I play Cuban music for them? I even got up to dance. All Cubans love dancing, don't they? That's what I said to myself, I said, "Barbara, what do all Cubans like? Dancing, that's what!" So don't you tell me I didn't try.'

'I'm interested that you're buying more real estate in Havana, Mr Bonini,' interjects Eugene, and Iris gets the feeling he is trying to puncture the swelling balloon of tension around the table. 'Aren't you worried about the rebels?'

Bruce turns to regard the diminutive journalist. A few seconds pass. It's funny, Iris thinks, that when Hugh Hardman looks at you, it is like he is opening a secret door and climbing right inside you, while Bruce's black eyes seem to suck the very marrow out of your bones. Eventually, he speaks: 'Business is business is business. The whole world over. Idealism don't talk, your pretty words in the newspapers don't talk. You know what talks, Mr Stringer? Money. American dollars. I like this government. I hope they stay in power for the next fifty years. But if Castro and the Argentine, that whassisname – Guevara – rode into town tomorrow, everything would carry on just the same, because the Cuban government will always want our business. Myself and Meyer will go on buying real estate and making nice with whoever is in charge, and they'll go on taking our money and leaving us alone.'

'Meyer?'

'Meyer Lansky. Owns a big slice of this city. He'll be at the wedding.'

Iris's eyes move to Lana, still standing pinned to Hugh's side with his arm around her shoulder, and she sees a strange, hard look pass over the girl's face. How must it be, she thinks, to have what should be the best day of your life taken over so completely that it is as if you are merely ornamental to it? Lana has no parents to back her up, only Meredith, who seems to view her charge with the same detachment as a valuable painting she's been tasked with looking after and is only too happy to hand over to someone else for safekeeping.

Now the men are here, there is no question of more cards. Instead, drinks are made and the group leaves the table for the comfort of the padded armchairs and sofas. The butler busies himself lighting candles which smell sharply of lemon and which he leaves burning on low tables and along the wall dividing the terrace from the garden. 'To ward off the mosquitoes,' explains Eddie, who has positioned himself so close to Iris on the sofa that when she raises her glass to her lips her arm brushes his. She does not ask herself how she feels about his proximity. She already feels an impostor here. She mustn't make a fuss, mustn't mind about Joe, who is sitting opposite but who, ever since Eddie sat down, looks through her as if she isn't there.

Nell pulls a chair up to Joe until her knees are practically touching his. She is wearing a kimono belted at the waist.

'Hope you don't mind me sitting here. I'm being eaten alive down there by bugs. Look at this.' She leans in towards Joe and pulls the kimono aside to reveal two livid red bumps on her creamy skin. 'That's why I'm covered up like a god-dam nun.'

'Hardly,' says Eugene under his breath.

'You prefer women to be more subtle?' Iris asks in a low, teasing voice.

'Princess, I don't prefer women at all.'

Oh! 'I didn't know.'

'That makes one of you.' Her confusion must show on her face, because he smiles. 'Relax, Princess. It's purely a theoretical issue in any case, as neither sex looks twice at me, so I'm spared the thrill of being considered a criminal.'

'I'm sure that's not so.' But Iris cannot look at him because she knows, as he does too, that looks are currency. And if you can't have looks, you'd better have money, but despite his early success, she isn't sure Eugene has much of that left either.

So intent is Iris on Eugene that she hasn't been paying attention to what is happening elsewhere, but now she becomes aware of raised voices to her right.

'I'm only saying it's tradition for the bride's family to have final say over the guest list.'

Meredith is standing, all big hair and tiny body, leaning against a pillar, holding the cigarette holder which is so much a part of her it seems almost to be an extra finger, in her right hand. She is addressing herself to Hugh, who looks for once too drunk and tired to shrug on the mantle of his charm.

'Invite who you damn well like, Meredith. But remember, a wedding is a calling card. Lana wants to be an actress, so she has to learn to manipulate her public image. Just as I do. Everything is show, Meredith. Even Jean knew that.'

'Leave Jean out of this.'

'Why? She was Lana's mother. She was my wife. And God knows she wasn't easy. I earned the right to talk about her.' Hugh's high spirits have visibly nose-dived.

'By trying to direct her life as if it was one of your movies?'

'Meredith!' Connie, sitting fanning herself on a rocking chair, looks up sharply. Without her usual smile, her face seems hard and unfamiliar.

'What? I'm sick of us all walking around on thin ice around him. As if it's normal for a man to be marrying his own stepdaughter.'

This is when Iris realises that Meredith, too, is drunk. There are angry red blotches on her bony chest and she leans on the pillar as if it is holding her up. Iris's muscles tense. She is unused to confrontation. In her house, there are no arguments, just silent battles of will and the endless undercurrent of her mother's unhappiness. But no raised voices, no accusations. She does not know how to interpret what is happening here. Has no idea how far it might go.

'You don't need to speak for me, Meredith.' This is Lana now, stepping out physically from her fiancé's protective arm to challenge her grandmother. 'I'm quite capable of fighting my own battles. And I'm a very different person to my mother.'

'That's what I'm afraid of,' says Meredith, ignoring the warning looks from Connie and Faye, who is curled up in a chair to Connie's right. 'At least your mother was old enough and tough enough to hold her own.'

'Spit it out, Meredith.' Hugh, having previously appeared almost not to be bothered, now turns the full force of his personality on his former mother-in-law. 'What are you implying?'

Finally, Meredith seems to realise she has gone too far. She swallows then takes in a huge lungful of smoke as if to steady herself. But still Hugh waits for an answer, the cords of his neck standing tight and proud against his sun-toughened skin.

'I'm not implying anything.' Her eyes slide off to the right, her frail body slumps. Hugh, however, isn't finished. He advances towards Meredith, smiling in a way that ties a knot in Iris's stomach.

'I'm curious as to what you think I should have done. Put up with her screwing some other guy right under my nose?'

'You never had any proof of that, and you know it.'

By now Hugh is just inches away from his soon-to-be grandmother-in-law. Or is she still his mother-in-law? Iris isn't sure. Even from where she sits at the other end of the terrace, she feels the waves of heat coming off him, along with the alcohol fumes, and feels afraid suddenly at what he might do, a man like this.

'Didn't I?'

'Didn't you what?' asks Meredith, placing one of her skeletal hands flat against her breastbone.

'Didn't I have proof? Would it surprise you to know that your daughter was six weeks pregnant when she died?'

There's an audible gasp from somewhere to Iris's left.

'The coroner told me in confidence, as it wasn't a matter of public interest. And frankly, none of the rest of you had shown the slightest interest in his report.'

'We didn't want . . .' says Meredith, at the exact same moment as Lana says, 'It was too painful.'

Hugh nods. As if they've only confirmed what he was saying. 'As most of you know,' Hugh continues, playing now to his audience, 'I'd been away shooting in Arizona for two months before that birthday trip and Jean had been living it up on the Costa Brava. We only met up for the first time the day we set sail. You do the math, Meredith.'

For a moment or two all of them are frozen, their expressions masks moulded to their skulls. Then paralysis gives way to a murmur of sound. 'What the . . .' Eddie bursts out, but Iris doesn't hear the rest of what he says, so focused is she on Connie, who is directly in her line of sight, her face ashen, dry lips parted in surprise, eyes locked on her daughter, who stares, wide-eyed, straight back at her.

16

IRIS HAS NOT slept well. All night she has been thinking about the revelations outside on the terrace, something niggling away in the back of her mind, though when she tries to grasp it, it slithers out of reach. Her eyes are puffy and feel glued together by tiredness and her limbs are heavy and clumsy, her skin dotted with the raised red bumps of mosquito bites. She has scratched one on her arm so vigorously during the night that it now oozes something clear and unpleasant. In the bathroom mirror she sees she has another bite in the centre of her forehead. Well, isn't this just turning out to be her day? She was hoping to wear the yellow dress again, but it hangs so limp and forlorn over the back of the chair after the previous evening's soaking that she has not the heart to put it on.

Once again in the green travelling dress, she opens her door then hesitates on the threshold, remembering that conviction she'd had of someone having been in her room. On impulse, she dashes back inside and rips out a page from her smallest sketchbook, stacked up with the others on the dressing table. Tearing off a corner, she folds it in half and steps out into the corridor, inserting the tiny fragment of folded paper into the crack of the door near to the floor as she closes it behind her.

Outside, she stands on the terrace of the guest house rubbing her arms to stop herself scratching the bites. It doesn't work. The sun isn't long risen and the temperature is still mild, the air fresh on her skin. The sky is a pale, delicate rose-gold and there is still moisture on the flat, green leaves of the banana trees. Iris loves this time of day, when everything is new and all things seem possible.

The small white buds of the night-flowering jasmine haven't yet completely closed and their sweet fragrance still scents the soft early-morning air. At the base of one of the wooden posts that form the frame of the terrace roof the jasmine becomes entangled with a second plant, this one with larger, yellow, bell-shaped blooms. There is an insect there the size of a big bumblebee, but it doesn't look like any bee Iris has seen before. It is moving its wings too fast for her to get a good look at it, but she catches a flash of scarlet and iridescent blue-green. She tries to step forward to investigate further, only to find herself held back by two hands which have seized her firmly around the tops of her arms.

'Don't move,' says Joe Garston's voice in her ear. He is standing so close his breath is hot on her neck and she fancies she can feel his heart beating through the back of her dress. 'That's the bee hummingbird, the smallest bird in the world. You only find them in Cuba. Look how fast his wings have to beat to keep him up in the air while he tries to get to the flower.'

'Him? How are you so sure your bird is a male?'

'Because of his red head and those turquoise feathers. The females are a much drabber species altogether.'

It is the most exquisite creature Iris has ever seen. Tiny, with those vivid colours, suspended in the air by force of will and that blur of furiously flapping wings.

For a few moments they stand and watch. Iris is conscious of Joe's hands still on her shoulders, his fingers warm against her skin and the whole length of his body so close behind her so that if she stepped back just an inch she would be pressed up against him with no space between them. The smell of him: soap and smoke and something else that gets into her nose and mouth until it is carried around in her bloodstream and into the beating heart of her.

If only, she thinks. *If only I could capture this moment in a bottle and stopper up the top, and take it home with me like an exquisite perfume that I could dab on my wrists whenever life gets dull and gloomy.* When she came home from another day at Underwood & Sturrock, or another firm just like it, and her mother was downstairs stewing beef and resentment; or in that impossible-to-imagine future with Peter describing his latest canvas at length over a supper prepared by her, she could open up the bottle and be transported back to this moment, with this man, watching a creature smaller than her thumb, a precious jewel with beating wings that keep it pinned implausibly in mid-air.

She hears Joe swallow behind her. Feels the gap between them narrowing. Closes her eyes because it is suddenly too much.

You're engaged. The words come to her in her mother's voice and she takes a step forward, startling the tiny creature, which moves off to other flowers, other admirers.

'Tell me how you started taking photographs.' It is all Iris can think of to say as she tears herself away from him, dropping down on to the nearest terrace chair so that he won't notice how unsteady her legs are. And perhaps the sight of the tiny hummingbird has mellowed him, because instead of closing down the conversation, as he has done before when she asked about himself, he sits down on a chair close by and tells her how he won his first camera from a drunken English officer in a game of poker when he was posted to Bremen after the war, to help enforce the American Zone of Occupation. The next morning, he'd felt bad and offered to return it, but the man had told him he didn't want it.

'He said he hadn't touched it in months – years, even. It sickened him, in fact. He was hungover and I put it down to that until I found one of the newspaper guys, a former official war photographer, who helped me develop the film that was in the camera and saw it was all photographs of prisoners-of-war taken just after they were liberated. The things that were on those photographs, Iris. The things that man must have seen.' His voice is hoarse, as if it is breaking upon the hard impossibility of the images he describes. 'I was too young to see active combat in the war, but those pictures changed something in me. I can't properly explain, but I felt a responsibility once I saw them, to bear witness.'

'Witness?'

'To the worst things human beings can do to each other. After that, I started taking pictures wherever I could, and when I left the army I got a job with the Associated Press, who packed me off to Korea to photograph the craziness over there.'

'And now you're taking pictures of ritzy weddings.'

He glances over sharply. 'There comes a time when you just have to say, "Enough."'

'I imagine one must need an escape from the horror of it all.'

'I needed an escape from me. The truth is, I was scared all the time, and though I think I got kinda addicted to my own fear, it's an exhausting way to live. Also . . .' He stops to take a cigarette from the pack in his pocket and light it. Iris has never been a smoker, but she sees how smoking can be a kind of punctuation for some people, a pause in the conversation to take stock and consider.

'Also?'

'Someone died, Iris. Because of me.'

Shoulders hunched. Head bent over his cigarette, which he holds between his thumb and third finger, the lit tip facing into his palm. Anwar had been his interpreter in Egypt the year before, when Joe had gone to cover the Suez Crisis. Older than Joe, married with a young son, the two had formed a strong bond, with naturally cautious Anwar curbing some of Joe's more foolhardy plans. They'd argued about going to the so-called Hedgehog region, a series of defensively important ridges. Their usual guide was sick and his replacement was untested. Anwar wanted to wait, but Joe was impatient to catch up with a contact who was travelling with the invading Israeli forces. The guide misjudged their route and they found themselves slap-bang in the middle of the fighting. Anwar was shot through the head just a couple of feet behind Joe.

'He wouldn't have been there if it wasn't for me. Suez wasn't even our war, Iris. There wasn't a pressing reason for me to be there in the first place. It was just ego. Me wanting to prove something to myself.'

Iris had been a young child during the war, sheltered from the worst of it. Since then, such conflicts as she has experienced have been so trivial as to be inconsequential – arguments with her parents (her mother) about some perceived infringement of her rights, glowering at Mrs Latham across the typing-pool desks. One time while she was at art school, she and Shirley had come across the after-math of an automobile accident. It was a freezing-cold day, with ice on the roads, and a car coming down Crouch Hill hadn't been able to stop and had crashed into a bus passing on the main road. She can still remember her total paralysis as she gazed in horror at the two injured men who'd been pulled from the wreckage. Shirley had been far quicker to respond, taking her cardigan off to make a pillow for one of the men's head. Afterwards, Iris had been so ashamed at her inaction, and for a long time afterwards she'd invented scenarios in her head where she'd known exactly what to do, had administered first aid, had at least held their hands until the ambulance arrived.

She understands now how heavy Joe's heart must be, with all the things he has seen. No wonder he can be moody and prickly. No wonder he always seems so on edge.

'So you've given up war reporting?'

'I thought I had. I came here so sure I could do this. Take pretty pictures. Bank the money.'

'And?'

Iris has been leaning towards Joe as he speaks, closing the physical distance between them as if his unexpected open-ness has broken some invisible barrier that was keeping them apart. For a moment they pause, just inches from each other, time suspended, just as the hummingbird was suspended in the air. Then he reaches for her and pulls her roughly towards him, and who can tell whose mouth finds whose, whose lips part first.

When Peter kisses her Iris hears a commentary in her head, as if she is watching the two of them from the outside. *Now his tongue is in my mouth. Now his hand is on my breast. My fingers are stroking the back of his head.* But with Joe there are no words, there is no thought, there is only feeling, as everything inside her dissolves into the hard heat of him.

'Where are you two? What am I missing?'

Eugene's high-pitched voice from the hallway breaks the spell. Joe jumps to his feet and thrusts his hands in his pockets, leaving Iris with her face tilted towards thin air, feeling cold and confused.

'Nothing,' they reply in unison.

The next twenty minutes pass in a blur of jumbled emotions. Only as they make their way to the main house some time later, where they have been asked to gather in readiness for the day's trip to the beach, does Iris feel her thoughts settle and her spirits rise, in spite of her initial misgivings at having to spend an uninterrupted day with this complicated family. Like most British children of her age and class, she grew up on a diet of yearly holidays by the sea. The Isle of Wight, Cornwall, Bournemouth. Two weeks crammed with her parents into adjoining rooms in a B&B, all chintz bedspreads and pink suites in the shared bathrooms, the toilet paper discreetly stored under a white, lace-frilled cover, or sometimes a flat rented through an advertisement in *The*

Lady, with a partial sea view and a neatly typed, yellowing list of instructions in a kitchen drawer. To Iris, the beach symbolises freedom from school, sand in her shoes. Her mother for once relaxed, almost happy.

She'd felt bad for snapping at Nell over the swimsuits in El Encanto yesterday, especially after her new friend apologised to her later on, assuming she was upset about being tasked with drawing an image of the hotel to be used on menus and brochures: 'You'll think I got you here under false pretenses, telling you it's for a wedding when actually you're just working for Bruce.' But Iris was hardly in a position to object, and actually she finds she is glad to be getting away from this house. She hasn't forgotten that someone here used Bruce Bonini's typewriter to send her the note about Nell. And she is conscious of the key she took from Bruce's study, and the scarf with its accompanying note, hidden in her room. At least on the beach she will know Bruce is right there with them and not rifling through her things.

Regrouped in front of the house, Eddie appears in front of her dressed all in white, with ivory-coloured linen trousers. His blond hair gleams in the morning sun and his skin has a golden glow that speaks of long summers in beach houses and winters on the ski slopes.

'Iris, you'll drive with me, won't you? We'll have the top down and sing along to the radio and frighten the natives.'

He has such a wide, pleasant smile, yet there is something behind it she sees now that she did not before, an assumption of acquiescence. It is a statement phrased as a question.

'I don't know . . .' she says feebly, which Eddie seems to

210

take as encouragement, stepping closer and putting an arm around her as if to steer her to his car. 'That is to say . . .'

'Eddie, my darling, you are to take Faye. She promises she will vomit if she is not in the open air at all times.' Isabella has swooped in, in an outfit as red and bold as the head of the bee hummingbird. 'Iris and Eugene and Joe will go by taxi. All is arranged.' Eddie doesn't look best pleased, but he does what he is told.

Watching his retreating back, Iris wishes she'd been firmer in her refusal, shaken off his arm, made it clear she didn't want him to touch her. She glances at Joe and he looks away coldly, as if their kiss and that moment earlier when they watched the little hummingbird and the world held its breath had never happened. His mouth on hers, that sense of things dissolving inside her.

The taxi is another cavernous American car, painted canary yellow. The driver is a tiny Cuban man who can hardly see over the steering wheel and speaks no English whatsoever. Joe slides into the front seat next to him as if he can't bear to be near her.

'Last night was a peach, wasn't it?' says Eugene, the minute they drive off. 'The pregnancy bombshell? Bet Hugh is sore at himself this morning for letting it out of the bag.'

'Why do you think he never said anything before?' asks Iris.

'Because it makes him look guilty as sin. It means he had a clear motive for killing Jean. Jealous husband. Big blow-out drunken argument with his wife. She taunts him that she's pregnant. He knows it can't be his. *Splash.* Over she goes.'

There is a new, hard note in Eugene's voice that Iris can't place and doesn't much like.

'But he said it was the coroner who told him she was pregnant.'

'Well, he would say that. If he admits he knew before she went overboard, he might as well get "I did it" tattooed across his head. You heard what Dwight Wilson said. They were sleeping separately. They argued the night she died. You've spent time with him, Iris. Can you honestly tell me there isn't any part of you that might consider him capable of it?'

Iris is quiet. She cannot believe they are talking here about murder. As if they are discussing the weather or the scenery.

'If we really do think there's a possibility Hugh killed his wife, we should do something, shouldn't we? I mean, how can we let him go ahead and marry Lana if there's even the slightest chance he did something to her mother?'

This time, it is Joe who cuts in. 'Look, even if Hardman did push Jean off the boat in the middle of a drunken row, it doesn't mean to say he meant to do it. Maybe there was a struggle and she fell in. Maybe she was walking away and she slipped. There's nothing to say he'd do the same to another woman.'

'And you'd take that chance?'

'I'm just saying that maybe we should all mind our own business. What is the point in raking all of this up again? If you ask me, it's much more likely to be Eddie. We know his character.' Iris stares fixedly at the back of the seat in front, knowing full well what he means by that. 'And we know he had good reason to resent Jean.'

'I think someone was in my room,' Iris says, needing to change the subject.

'Eddie Hardman?' Joe's voice is sharp.

'No, not him. And I have no proof. It's just a feeling I had when I got in yesterday evening of things being disturbed.'

'You see,' says Eugene. 'Someone is looking for something, or knows something. We have to investigate before they murder us in our beds.'

'Shut up, will you?' says Joe irritably.

'But what would they be looking for in my room?'

Iris tries not to think about the scarf and note in the back of the drawer or the key hidden in her blue shoe. She certainly can't risk bringing up the spying thing, not until she is sure the real CIA agent isn't either of them.

'Did they take anything?' Joe wants to know, peering around the seat in front of her.

'No, nothing was gone.'

They lapse into silence. Iris gazes out of her window at the scenery. They are out of the city now, following the coast road out to the east, past small fishing villages and narrow sandy beaches strewn with branches and seaweed. They have been travelling parallel to a railway, and now they pass a distinctive green locomotive train, inching slowly along the wooden track. 'Hershey Train,' the driver tells them, and makes a walking movement with his fingers to mimic the little train's speed.

An hour passes. Two. Iris doesn't need to be told that today will be scorching. Back home at this time of day, the art-school gang would be sitting down to lunch in the cafeteria, gossiping about a particular tutor or student, or else arguing some point of politics or philosophy simply for the pleasure of the argument itself. For once, Iris does not wish herself back there, in her paint-dappled overalls and the flat, rubber-soled shoes that her mother forbade her to wear at home so that her bag was always weighed down with an extra pair of leather pumps that she changed into around the corner from her house. Or sitting somewhere with Peter, with his arm across her like the iron bar strapped over her lap on the funfair ride.

She does not want to be the person she is in England.

Here in Cuba, where the colours sing and the heat burns and there are tiny, perfectly formed birds that dazzle in the sunlight, and Hardmans who live as they please and go where they like in the knowledge there is nowhere in the world their money won't admit them, and a dark-haired man who holds himself open a crack then slams himself shut again without explanation, kissing her one minute and ignoring her the next, here she sees for the first time how confined her life has been.

They pass a young woman, Iris's own age, walking by the roadside pushing an old-fashioned pram into which are crammed a toddler and a younger child. *There are other lives outside mine*, Iris thinks. Might it be possible to *choose* a different life to the one set out for her? The thought feels dangerous.

They arrive at a bridge crossing the mouth of a wide river, where it meets the sea. 'Varadero,' says the driver. Iris has already learned their destination is a spit of land fringed by white sand beaches at the tip of which Bruce has acquired a large hotel that he intends to turn into a casino and nightclub to rival the Tropicana. Everywhere there are signs of development. Hulking cranes, piles of rubble encroaching on to pristine beaches, half-built constructions.

*

Three hours after setting off, they pull into a sweeping drive-way that deposits them outside a white palace surrounded by palms, though the car park to the side still resembles a building site, all loose stones and sand and potholes.

Inside, it is cool and tiled in terracotta. 'Bruce hasn't had a chance to marble the joint yet,' whispers Eugene in Iris's ear.

A few moments later Barbara and Bruce and Hugh and Lana arrive, having been driven by Raúl, who leans against the side of the car and winks at Iris.

Eddie pulls up with Faye, who leans her head on her arm over the passenger door as if sleeping. The atmosphere between them is thick, as if it has been a long time since anyone spoke.

Another taxi approaches, mint green, its chrome bumper glinting in the white heat of the day. The driver jumps out, almost before the car has stopped moving, to open the back door for Nell, who is resplendent in a strapless yellow polka-dot dress cinched in at the waist with a white belt. Her platinum-blonde hair is held back from her face by a yellow polka-dot scarf, her lips painted brilliant red, and when she smiles at the man it is as dazzling as if the sun itself has come out to shine only on him. After her emerge Connie and Meredith, the latter in outsized black glasses that all but obscure her face. Iris wonders how she slept last night after the revelations of Jean's pregnancy and the incontrovertible proof that her daughter had been having an affair before she died.

Bruce shows them all around his new acquisition with the offhand air of one to whom ownership is second nature. He and Hugh are alike in this, thinks Iris, although Hugh's ownership is of people rather than property.

The hotel is grand but has seen better days. The papered wall in the lobby has blistered with damp and a stale smell of boiled vegetables hangs over the restaurant, with its bank of windows looking out on to the private white-sand beach and then the sea.

'Just needs a little imagination,' says Bruce.

'And a million bucks,' adds Barbara.

Iris has brought with her the only swimsuit she owns. It is blue and white, ruched at the hips and cut low across the thighs. When she bought it two summers ago for a family holiday in Dorset, she had thought it modern and daring, but here in Cuba she feels overdressed. Her body is so pale compared to the others' and mottled with angry mosquito bites. She has not bought a kaftan or tunic to wear to the beach, would not even have heard of such an item, so she pulls on the green dress over the costume and carries a towel, as well as a bag containing her sketchbook and pencils.

The women change upstairs in the presidential suite. The bathroom door opens and Barbara emerges in a green, diaphanous kaftan draped over a plunging costume and high-heeled mules, her red hair covered by a huge, floppy-brimmed hat.

'Are we ready for some fun?' she says gaily.

She seems to have forgotten to blend in some powder which is clumped around her nose, but no one bothers to tell her.

17

Two rows of umbrellas are set out on the beach, each with a pair of chairs underneath. Hugh is lounging in the front row, wearing an open shirt that reveals a broad chest covered in whorls of hair, most of which are coarse and grey. Iris watches as Lana approaches the seat next to him, only to find a pair of sunglasses and a pack of cigarettes already there.

'Sweetheart, Bruce and I have a little business to discuss. You don't mind, do you?'

'No, of course not.' Lana moves away and Iris feels an ache of sympathy.

Iris makes her way to the furthest umbrella, from where she will have the best view of the hotel, in order to start her drawing. Next to her are Connie and Meredith, with Faye sitting behind them, as ever tightly wrapped up, this time in a thin cotton sheet, her face hidden from the sun behind large sunglasses and a wide-brimmed hat.

Iris unzips her green dress and tries to wriggle out of it as unobtrusively as she can before turning the chair around and hopping on quickly with her sketchbook open. She looks beyond her own pale legs at the rectangular building, and sighs.

'I feel just awful about this, Iris,' says Nell, coming to sit beside her. 'You came to draw wedding portraits, not to design merchandise for a goddam hotel.'

'Don't worry, Nell. I prefer to be useful, don't you?'

'Honey, you're talking to a woman who has made a life's work out of being utterly without point or purpose.'

'Nonsense.'

'It's quite true, I'm afraid. My mother's life's purpose is my father – and will stay that way, no matter how many other women he marries. What's mine? Men?'

'There must be other things you are interested in.'

Nell shakes her head. 'The only job I've ever had was as Jean's assistant and, even though Pop foisted me on Jean, I was so clueless I think she felt sorry for me by the end. Before that, I had thought at one time I might be an actress. My school drama coach was keen for me to try. Pop said, "Of course you should act, Nellie, if that's what makes you happy – as long as you're fine playing the blonde whose body is chopped into pieces and tossed in the dumpster."'

She gives a mirthless bark of laughter and then falls silent. Then: 'Iris? Did something happen between you and Eddie the other night?'

Iris stiffens. *His rolled tongue in her mouth, her pelvis cracking under his weight.*

Nell groans softly. 'He tried it on, didn't he? I knew it. Iris, I'm so sorry. He can be such a brute. I hope you gave him hell.'

'I didn't . . . Joe had to ask him to leave in the end.'

'Men.' Nell sounds bitter. 'They're all so terribly predictable.'

Iris tries to lose herself in her sketch, but the building is all horizontal lines and dull dimensions. She has no doubts she can produce a decent draught drawing – she ought to have picked up *something* at Underwood & Sturrock – but it won't be anything special. Since she was young, her ability to draw was always the one thing that set her apart, the only thing she excelled at. She has always been confident that, given a pad of paper and a pencil, she can create something good and true. And yet, since she arrived in Cuba, what has she achieved? A pretty-enough portrait of Lana that still fails to convey the essence of the girl, a few quick sketches at the bridal shower. Yes, she was pleased with the pictures of Barbara and Hugh, but still she feels she needs to do more to earn her place here.

Raúl is sitting on the hotel terrace. Iris is surprised to see him so comfortable there, his long legs up on an empty chair. There is a lack of formality between employer and staff that surprises her, particularly given Bruce Bonini's quiet but iron-clad authority. But then, what does she know, either about class distinctions in this strange country or about the Boninis? Raúl catches her looking at him and raises two fingers to his temple in salute and Iris hurriedly looks away.

The next time she looks, Raúl has got leisurely to his feet and is ambling across the beach. He has on his usual crisp white shirt and dark trousers and tie but, despite the blinding heat, he manages to look cool and fresh.

As he passes behind Barbara's chair she turns and says something to him, picking up her empty glass and waving it around. He stops still, as if considering her request, then shakes his head with a smile and moves off.

Barbara freezes, her hand still in mid-air. Then she lies back and pulls her sunglasses over her eyes, but not before Iris has seen the look of burning humiliation on her face.

To Iris's left, Connie is determinedly flicking through a copy of *Ladies' Home Journal*. She has black visors clipped on to her normal glasses which she flips down over the lenses, even though she is fully in the shade. She looks so perfectly unruffled that Iris wonders if she might have imagined the look that passed between her and Nell the night before, after Hugh dropped his bombshell.

Lana claims the chair in the row behind Iris, next to her sister, Faye. They are silent as the bride-to-be rolls out her towel and lays it over the chair cushion, before untying the bow at the front of her beach cover-up and lying back. She is wearing a white one-piece swimsuit and her glossy blonde hair falls around her shoulders. *She ought to be happy*, Iris thinks. *She ought to be horsing around on the sand with some light-hearted boy who thinks she's the most beautiful thing in the world.*

She remembers the afternoon they'd seen Lana and Eddie out on the tennis court. The way Lana's skirt had flown up as she sailed over the net, how she'd snorted with laughter as Eddie pretended to cower on the floor.

'Poor Iris, put to work even on the beach,' says a voice.

Eddie has pulled up a seat next to her and stretched himself out. She averts her eyes from where his thighs emerge from a pair of tight, waist-high trunks.

'I don't mind. It's what I'm here for, after all.'

'Come on, Iris. Why are you so buttoned up? You're not still sore about the other night, are you? I said sorry, didn't I?'

Iris doesn't reply, but she can feel the flush crawling over her skin, making her bites itch. There is a note of petulance in Eddie's voice, as if she is acting unreasonably. Is she? So he *tried it on*, as Nell put it. He wouldn't be the first man to do that. At art school, there was a handful of occasions where boys she had no interest in had overstepped the mark, fingers creeping up inside her skirt while they sat squashed into a booth in the refectory, a peck on the cheek that had somehow turned into something else, a tongue probing at her closed lips, trying to find a way in. She'd always been able to see it off with a friendly shove. Has her sense of humour evaporated in the Havana heat?

'I don't trust that Joe Garston.' Eddie has been staring at the photographer, who is crouched on the sand, taking photographs of Hugh and Bruce. 'I don't buy his hardened-war-photographer story for a minute. I've been making some calls about him, actually. Turns out he didn't have the stomach for battle, ran away and gave up the first moment things got heated.'

As if he can sense them looking, Joe glances over from behind his camera. His gaze is so hard and ungiving Iris has to look away.

Iris casts around for Eugene and sees him chatting to Barbara Bonini. He is still fully dressed, in long trousers and long-sleeved shirt, with a straw hat over his large, domed forehead. The two of them have a table set up in between their chairs on which sit two enormous glass globes holding an opaque pink cocktail.

'I don't know why Pop invited that poison dwarf Stringer either,' says Eddie moodily, following her line of sight and frowning. 'He is always nosing around. He's supposed to be here to cover a wedding. But now he has hold of this new

221

pregnancy angle proving what a total *slut* Jean was, it's all going to start up again. All those reporters, all those headlines.'

'It's not exactly a normal wedding, though, is it?' says Iris, trying not to show her shock at the word he just used for his dead stepmother.

'Because Pop can't keep his pecker in his pants and Lana doesn't know her own mind?'

'If that's really what you think, why are you even here?'

Eddie drums his fingers on the side of his chair. 'They're my family, Iris. Both of them.' He sounds childish, suddenly. Lost. 'How would it look if I didn't come?'

Iris's drawing is taking a lifeless sort of shape. She puts it aside and gazes out at the ocean, wondering if her need to cool down can overcome her dread of everyone watching her in her matronly swimsuit.

'I'll go in if you do,' says Connie, on the other side of her to Eddie.

'It is very tempting.'

'Come on. Fortune favours the brave. Isn't that right, Iris?'

They get to their feet and Iris has to stop herself reaching a hand around to tug down the lower edge of her costume so that it more adequately covers her bottom. But as they venture across the burning sand the only thing she can think about is the pain in the soles of her feet and the need to get to the water as soon as possible.

Paddling in the shallows, Iris is amazed to find she can see so clearly through the water, see how her toes dig into the fine shingle and the fragments of white shell nestling in the sand. So different from the sea back home, which seems always to be a murky swirl of silt and seaweed.

Connie is uncharacteristically subdued, gazing out to the horizon.

'Are you feeling quite all right?' Iris asks eventually.

'Oh yes, bless your heart for asking. It's not always easy, trying to keep the peace in a family like ours, but I'm a tough old nut.'

'Still, it must have come as a shock, the revelations from last night.' Iris is hesitant, not wanting to appear as if she is probing for gossip.

Connie shoots her a sharp look. Iris remembers what Nell has told her about her mother not believing in divorce and making Hugh her life's work, married or not. Connie's crucifix necklace, glinting on her freckled chest, is a reminder that, though economic necessity might have prompted her to sign the divorce papers, in the eyes of her Church, she and Hugh are still married. Iris still struggles to imagine Connie and Hugh ever being together, but she knows they were really just children when they first met, different people in a different time. Who knows what vagaries of youth brought them together and then kept them there for so long?

'It just saddens me, that's all.'

Connie has on a swimsuit with a voluminous skirt that flaps around her thighs and a tightly corseted bodice to hold everything in place. It is clear where Nell gets her voluptuousness from. The sun burnishes her fair hair, and as a swell of water hits her and she lets out a brief peal of laughter, Iris has a glimpse of the girl who once captured the young Hugh's heart. She shudders. Like most young people, Iris believes secretly that age is something that happens to others. It seems so utterly impossible that her smooth skin will one day crease like chamois leather or that her strong bones will turn treacherous and brittle. Or that she will stop feeling as if everyone else operates according to a code she has yet to crack and wondering if there will ever come a day when, like Connie, she will comfortably inhabit the world, sure of how it works and her place in it.

'I still care for Hugh,' Connie continues. 'It breaks my heart to think what he must have gone through, keeping a thing like that secret all this time out of loyalty for *that woman's* reputation.'

18

'WELL? HAVE YOU found anything out?'

'Nothing about Jean, but plenty about how the family view me and writers in general,' replies Eugene.

'What do you mean?'

'Let me see. Barbara doesn't read anything that won't fit on a drugstore label, Meredith tried to read one of my books but says, frankly, if she wants to experience unpleasant rich people behaving badly, she'll just go to the Golf Club social again.'

'Ouch.'

'Yeah, this morning has done wonders for my self-esteem.'

'And you really haven't learned anything new?'

'Only that Bruce never wanted me here. He doesn't like "my sort", his wife told me. Though she was at pains to point out that "my sort" is her very favourite sort. She can't be doing with "regular men", she says.'

'Well, that's nice,' says Iris uncertainly. 'Or is it?'

They are sitting outside, under the hotel awning, eating a lunch of cold chicken and hot puffs – pastry stuffed with meat and jam. Iris had been relieved to learn that lunch, in the hotel's deserted dining room, would be 'family only' and that afterwards they would have an hour to digest under the umbrellas, before heading home again. Already she has had enough of this beach, of these people. This too-hot day, this too-fraught family.

'I think we've been sidelined because I ask too many questions,' says Eugene, who is flicking through a copy of *Havana Life*. 'I expect Hugh regrets dropping his bombshell last night in front of me.'

It is on the tip of Iris's tongue to say that it's more likely because their host believes one of them to be a spy, but again she holds back.

Joe, who has been standing on the shoreline taking photographs of the hotel, wanders over, and though Iris affects total disinterest, her treacherous heart pitches from side to side in her chest like the deck of a ferry she once took to the Isle of Wight. He seems tense, and Iris notices how tired he looks, with dark smudges of shadow under his eyes. Can they really have kissed just hours ago, she and this quasi-stranger?

'Not eating with your boyfriend today?' he asks her coldly.

'I can hardly be rude to him, can I? Not when his father is paying for me to be here.'

There is a momentary stand-off, then Joe changes the subject, returning again to her suspicion that someone was in her room. She tells him about the tissue paper and the ribbon. She is half expecting to be mocked, but instead he looks thoughtful.

'I'm sure there's nothing to worry about, but still, you

must be careful, Iris,' he says, and something in her stomach turns to liquid when he says her name. 'Cuba is not like England. Here, no one is held accountable.'

There comes a snort of disgust from Eugene. 'Hemingway,' he mutters, jabbing his finger down on a double-page spread in the newspaper. 'Rambling on about Spain again. You'd think he took on Franco single-handedly.'

'Oh!'

Both men look up at Iris's exclamation.

'It's just that something has been bothering me ever since last night, and now I've remembered. When I read the newspaper cutting about Jean Summers' inquest, it said that traces of anti-malarial medicine had been found in Jean's bloodstream. But last night Hugh said she'd been filming in the Costa Brava. My friend Joyce went there recently on holiday with her family and was told there was no malaria in northern Spain. Don't you think that's odd?'

To her disappointment, neither Eugene nor Joe seems particularly interested.

'Jean was a drama queen,' Eugene says dreamily. 'At least, I imagine so. Wouldn't it be just like her to insist on medication, even if none were needed?'

Their conversation is halted by the reappearance of the family, who emerge from the hotel more animated than when they went in and, in the case of some of the women, sporting a complete change of outfit.

Seeing Iris with Joe and Eugene on the terrace, Nell makes a beeline for them. She is wearing yet another bikini, this one bubblegum-pink satin, with tight shorts that come up just beneath her tummy button and a halterneck top.

She has thrown a loose, gauzy white wrap over the whole thing.

Iris tries to imagine going home with such a costume in her suitcase, imagines wearing it on the beach with her parents, or with Peter. Imagines herself telling them, 'I'll wear what I damn well please.'

'You two don't know how lucky you are to have missed that lunch. I thought it would never end. Pop and Bruce got into an argument about the best way to crack a crab. They kept making the kitchen bring them more and more so they could demonstrate their technique. It was like crab genocide in there.'

Watching Joe relight the cigar he was smoking earlier, her face lights up. 'Oh, I love a cigar. Do you mind?'

She has pulled up a chair next to the photographer and Iris feels a sharp tug behind her ribcage. They look so right together, Joe with his dark good looks and Nell shining like the sun. Nell takes a long drag on the cigar, holding the smoke in her mouth. Joe smiles at her, and Iris looks away.

She goes inside, keen to escape the heat and to have a go at detangling her hair. The presidential suite is deserted, the living room strewn still with discarded clothes. Nell's polka-dot dress tossed over the back of a chair. A pair of green, backless, high-heeled shoes. Iris heads into the bedroom at the back where she left her own things neatly folded, and gazes in dismay into the full-length mirror on the wardrobe door. Her hair is stiff with salt and frizzy at the ends and the tip of her nose is red from the sun.

She wanders out through the French windows on to the

shaded balcony. From here she has a view over the beach. Her gaze is drawn as if by a magnet to the lean, dark figure of Joe Garston. How quickly he has become the fixed point around which everything else revolves.

As she tracks Joe's progress across the sand she becomes aware of women's voices wafting along the balcony from the next doorway, which leads into the presidential suite living room. Curious, Iris edges closer to the sound.

'I had no more idea than you did.' It is unmistakably Connie's voice, although shriller than Iris has heard it before. 'She told you it was Hugh's. Didn't you tell me she said you and Eddie wouldn't inherit a cent once it was born?'

'She was such a bitch. God rest her black soul.'

'Now, Nellie.'

'But what I don't understand is . . .'

Iris has just enough time between registering that Nell's voice is getting louder and Nell herself stepping out on to the balcony to retreat to the far end.

'Oh.' Nell frowns at her. 'Iris, you gave me a shock. I had no idea there was anyone else here.'

'I came up to try to salvage my hair,' Iris says, hoping that the other woman can't hear her heart thundering in her chest. 'And then I thought I heard someone calling my name on the beach so I came out here to take a look.'

Even to her own ears, her explanation rings with the tinny sound of untruth.

Nell carries on regarding her, for once unsmiling, and yet again Iris notices how much of Nell's attractiveness is channelled through the force of her exuberant personality. Connie breezes out behind her daughter, her voice calm as ever. 'Come with me, dear. We'll have those tangles sorted lickety-split.'

She hooks her arm through Iris's and leads her back through the suite. Only Nell remains, watching thoughtfully.

An hour later they are all regrouped outside the hotel. Standing on the edge of the crystal water, wearing the green dress over her costume, Iris tries to focus on her surroundings, the undulating sand that ripples away on both sides as far as the eye can see, the wild grass that grows at the back of the beach, seemingly out of the sand itself, the way the colour of the sea changes the further she looks, from turquoise in front of her to deep navy blue at the back, specked with the occasional white of a cresting wave. It is like something from a painting, but still a threadworm of dread wriggles in the lining of her stomach. There is no getting away from it. Nell and Connie sounded *guilty* back there on the balcony. She can't stop thinking of that anonymous note. *don't trust nell. she kills people.* Of course she knows it is only trouble-making. And yet.

Iris wills herself to focus on something else. She gazes back at the hotel, still part surrounded by scaffolding and rubble, and imagines how different the scene would have looked twenty or thirty years ago, before it was built. Joe has told her that this whole area was bought up in the 1920s by a wealthy American businessman called Dupont who has been steadily selling off individual slices of it ever since.

For the first time in her life, it occurs to her how absurd it is for an individual to lay claim to land that has stood untouched for millions of years – land that exists in a country that isn't even his own. For all he might have given back to the region, as Joe explained, the drinking-water plant, the school, she cannot stop thinking of the arrogance of it all. To parcel up all this beauty and sell it off to the highest bidders. What gives him the right?

She looks down through the crystal-clear water at her bare toes digging into the pale, fine sand. This sand, that has been here for millions of years, is private. How peculiar.

'If it gets any hotter, I swear I'll melt. This goddam country.'

Barbara Bonini is wearing a diaphanous garment which she drops to reveal a swimming costume so tightly ruched and wrapped and boned that it moves quite independently of her. For a moment she stands next to Iris, swaying as if caught in a breeze, although the day is completely still. She reaches out and grabs on to Iris's arm, her grip surprisingly firm.

'Current is stronger than you'd think, ain't it?'

There is no current.

'I gotta cool off, or I swear I'm just gonna flat out blow up. You had the change, Irene? Whaddami talking about, you're only a baby. Well, let me tell you it's another one of nature's little jokes on women. First, you get a whole lot of parts that don't even work, and then you gotta go through hell getting shot of them.'

Barbara's eyes are covered by her sunglasses, so Iris can't tell if they are focused, but her speech is slurred and her waxy skin is covered in a sheen of perspiration.

Letting go of her arm, Barbara wades unsteadily ahead into the deeper water. Iris has a moment of misgiving, seeing how the older woman stumbles and frowns down at the seabed as if, rather than a smooth sheet of sand, it is strewn with hidden obstacles one might trip on. Should she go with her? But Barbara has already righted herself and is pressing on. Iris herself is in a strange mood, feeling suddenly very alone and unsure whom she can trust. Is there really a spy here, among these people? Worse, is there someone capable of murdering Jean Summers yet still passing themselves off as a normal human being? This is what most scares her, that there might not be anything to mark this person out. She has sketched most of the wedding party. Wouldn't she have been able to sense if there was something that dark under the surface of one of them? Wouldn't it spill out on to the page?

Ahead of her, Barbara finally stops her faltering progress and flops heavily into the water. She swims in an aimless circle, her dark glasses giving her the look of a bug-eyed sea creature.

Iris's thoughts return to Connie and Nell. So they knew Jean was pregnant but had believed the baby to be Hugh's. Why hadn't they spoken up last night when Hugh dropped his bombshell? Why had they feigned surprise, like the rest of them? And what did it mean that they'd believed Nell and Eddie to have been on the point of being disinherited?

'Hey! Hey! You should geddin' here!' Barbara is shouting to Joe, stood on the beach talking to Nell, who lies stretched out on a towel at his feet, but her voice cannot cut through the turgid air.

Iris's eyes linger on the American photographer, until she forces herself to think instead about Peter. Her fiancé. She deliberately focuses on the early days in their relationship, how thrilling it had been to find out he was interested in her, how she'd hardly slept for excitement the night after their first date. She makes herself think about the tops of his arms, and how she'd stare at them across the cafeteria in the days before they met and imagine them wrapped around her. She thinks about how he'd stepped in to defend her to her parents and make it possible for her to come here. He must love her, then. Surely? These feelings for Joe are all tied up in the whole strange experience of being so far from home, she tells herself, in a country so full of heat, where music pulses through the very pavements and morals seem to burn away in the sun.

So deciding, she looks up, surprised to see how much further out Barbara Bonini is now. Well, good; perhaps a swim will sober her up a little. Except she doesn't seem to be swimming, more like floating. A chill creeps through Iris's body, overtaking her legs, her arms, her liver and kidneys. She is moving before she is even conscious of formulating the thought, but she is not a particularly strong swimmer and rapidly she feels her legs growing sluggish under the weight of her dress.

Approaching the dark shape of Barbara in the water, Iris's heart quickens. Is she moving? She tries to swim faster, but that blasted dress is holding her back. When she finally draws close enough to get a proper look, she is at first relieved to see that Barbara is on her back rather than face down, but panic sets in as she searches in vain for signs of breathing.

By the time Iris reaches her, Barbara's skin is turning grey, although Iris thinks she sees faint movement in her chest. She tries to hook her arm around the older woman's head, only for Barbara to slip beneath the surface of the water. Grabbing her under her arms, Iris tries to swim, but she is exhausted now, her dress pulling her down. All of a sudden, she feels fingers gripping the arm that is wrapped around Barbara's body and a blow lands on the side of her head, pushing her under and filling her nose and mouth with salty water. Barbara has come around and is thrashing her limbs in a blind frenzy. Iris fights her way to the surface and spits out the water, only to be submerged once again by Barbara using her head to get purchase.

Now Iris is truly afraid. She tries to wrestle the older woman aside, but Barbara is bigger and desperation makes her strong. Iris feels her lungs burning, the pressure in her chest building as if she is about to burst.

Just as she feels she can't hold her breath any longer but must open her mouth and take a big gulp of seawater, the weight on top of her lifts abruptly and she goes shooting to the surface.

'Are you all right?'

Joe Garston is attempting to tread water beside her while fielding a still-flailing Barbara Bonini. Iris can't speak but nods her assent. He hesitates for a moment as if unsure but then starts striking out towards the shore, dragging the suddenly docile Barbara behind him.

Several long moments later Iris staggers out of the water. Barbara is already laid out on the sand, with Joe sitting bent over her, his back heaving as he coughs.

Now there is a fussing and a gathering of bare legs around them. There are arms coming down towards Barbara, turning her on her side, bashing her on the back. Now there are gasps and admonishments and conflicting instructions on what to do. 'Breathe air into her mouth,' insists Hugh. 'No, sit her up so that the water comes out,' says Connie. Bruce drops to his haunches next to his wife and for a moment Iris thinks he has come to offer comfort, but instead he berates her, quietly, under his breath: What did she think she was doing? All that liquor washing around her system, plus whatever is in those pills that quack of a doctor gives her, it's a miracle she isn't being washed up in Miami right this second.

Even through the rushing in Iris's ears she registers the coldness in Bruce's voice. His wife nearly died and he has not one tender word for her.

A towel appears around her shoulders. 'A hero needs a cape,' says Eugene. He is looking from her to Joe, a hand on each of their shoulders. And now Joe looks at her and she finds herself feeling breathless all over again.

'Are you sure you're okay, Iris?'

His voice is raspy, as if the coughing has stripped his throat raw, but the concern in it contrasts so starkly with the way Bruce Bonini has just spoken to his wife that Iris feels hot tears come to her eyes and has to look down at the sand.

Bruce stands up to summon Raúl from the shade at the back of the beach. Barbara moans and tries to raise herself up. 'I need a brandy,' she slurs, her eyes unfocused. 'So cold.'

When Raúl comes into view Bruce gestures towards his wife, prone on the ground. 'Take her inside,' he says. But when Raúl bends into Barbara's line of vision she shoots upright.

'Geddim outta here!' she shrieks, flailing around with her arm. 'I coulda died out there, and you dare to send your bastard son to pick me up. Geddim away from me.'

Raúl glances at Bruce and then straightens up, turning

back towards the hotel with an expression that looks to Iris very much like a smirk.

She puts her head in her hands, but still she senses the reverberations of shock in the air around them. The silent echo of Barbara's words.

Bastard son.

19

EVEN ALL THESE hours on, and having had a very nearly hot shower in her room and changed into her dry trousers and white blouse and even draped a cardigan over her shoulders, Iris does not quite feel warm. The chill in her bones is made sharper by the unpleasant conviction that, once again, someone has been in her room. The tiny scrap of paper she tucked in near the bottom of the crack of the door earlier was lying on the floor of the corridor when she came rushing indoors, almost the last of their party to arrive, having somehow agreed to accompany Barbara, who had at the last minute decided she was still in too much shock to travel and insisted on repairing to the hotel bar for one more shot of whiskey.

Sitting on her bed, Iris turns the scrap round and round in her hands as if it might somehow reveal its secrets. It is possible, she supposes, it could have dropped out of its own accord. It is very small, and a strong draught might have dislodged it. Except that there is no draught in that stuffy corridor. Iris has been stalling on checking that the stolen scarf and key are still in their hiding places, but now she forces herself to her feet. The scarf is there in the drawer where she left it, still wrapped around that scrawled note, but when she plunges her hand into the blue shoe under her bed, searching for the key, her fingers close around empty air.

She bites back a flare of panic. It's the wrong shoe. But when she searches the other one and finds it, too, empty, she has to face the truth. The key to Bruce's study is gone.

Downstairs on the terrace, she finds Eugene. He looks up at her expectantly. 'Well?'

'Well what?'

He widens his eyes. 'Our hostess's outburst. Wasn't it delicious?'

'I suppose it does explain a lot.' The arrogant tilt of the chauffeur's head, the way he stayed leaning against the wall as one approached and only straightened up slowly right at the last minute. And . . . 'Oh.'

'Oh what?' Eugene is instantly on the alert.

'I've just remembered. When I went to look for the type-writer and ended up in Bruce's office there was a ledger in the bottom drawer of his desk with pages of payments to Raúl.'

'And you didn't think to tell me?'

'I thought it must be for doing jobs. I had no idea it could be some sort of *allowance*. Anyway. I have more pressing concerns.'

'What concerns?' Joe has appeared in the doorway, wearing a dazed expression, as if that scene out at sea, dragging Barbara's resisting body to shore, has depleted him. He yawns and stretches, his shirt riding up to show a patch of tanned skin.

Iris tells them about the missing key. She tries to be calm, but her voice wobbles dangerously.

'Iris,' begins Joe, at the exact same moment that Eugene says, 'Oh, you poor thing.' And then amid the resulting confusion there sounds a distant rumble of thunder from the direction of the swimming pool. No, not thunder, a loud groan, because here comes another. And now Isabella comes staggering through the trees, her hand held to her forehead in an attitude of high drama.

'Oh, mother of *Gad*, I am having a heart attack. Here, feel.' She grabs Joe's hand and holds it to her heaving bosom, this evening encased in a sleeveless emerald-green blouse which she wears over a pair of straining capri pants. Iris can't help smiling at the look of mild alarm on the photographer's face.

'Can you feel how it is jumping? Like it wants to jump right out of my body into that plant there? Today I have worked like a dog.' *Dag*. 'No. What am I saying?' She holds up her own hand and gives it a hard slap. 'No one would treat a dog like *dees*. But tell me. All of you creative geniuses. What do you think of my efforts? Isn't it the most beautiful thing you ever saw? Or is it terrible? Awful. The guests will be insulted to be here. You can tell me the truth. No, I *een-seest* on it.'

Fulsome assurances follow that the house and garden are utterly transformed. And indeed, it is so. When they arrived back from their day at the seaside, Iris had been jolted out of her post-drama trance by the spectacle of the lawn, which had been fashioned into a replica of the set of Hugh's first hit film, *Beach Belles*, with brightly coloured umbrellas and bamboo cabanas. Overhead, strings of coloured lights are threaded through the trees. The terrace has been converted into a beach bar, with a jukebox and mismatched wooden tables in contrasting bright colours and a bamboo counter, piled high with pineapples and coconuts in front of shelves stacked with every drink under the sun.

Despite it being late and the party weary to their very bones, there is to be yet another outing tonight. This time to the Biltmore Yacht and Country Club just along the coast, at the very edges of Miramar. Iris tries to duck out of it, but Isabella says Nell has asked for her particularly. Iris is relieved at this confirmation of friendship. She hasn't forgotten Nell's unsmiling face out there on the balcony.

So it is that Iris finds herself, some forty-five minutes later, being driven around a circular lawn complete with central flag post, then pulling up in front of the colonnaded entrance of a low, red-roofed building.

Upstairs, they enter into a bar, and Iris immediately notices how well dressed the women are. Diamonds, pearls, fox furs, bare shoulders, long necks that crane around to see who is coming through the door then slide over her and Eugene and Joe, as if they are made from the same marble as the floor.

The Hardmans and Boninis, or a representative sample of them at least, are already installed at a table at the back of the room. As Iris threads her way across the floor she notices that the windows at the back overlook a private white-sand beach and, to the right, a large swimming pool. Both sea and pool are empty at this stage of the evening, when the sun is a low, golden orb puddling into the vast, dark sea. On a terrace down below, men in black jackets stand smoking cigars with their backs to a staircase that leads down on to the sand, as if this view – the palm-fronded beach umbrellas against an orange-streaked sky – was not even worth looking at.

This is the first place Iris has been where most of the other guests appear to be Cuban. The air is thick with cigar smoke and Spanish words that, to Iris's ears, rise and fall in a melodic cadence to match the classical music that plays discreetly in the background. These people glitter and sparkle under the crystal lights, the women with their diamond rings and necklaces, the men with their brilliantined hair. There do not seem to be many Americans, and Iris wonders if you have to be a member to come here and, if so, how Bruce Bonini has managed to get them in. But all is revealed when she sees the Morales family also seated around the table, though at a distance from their guests, as if keeping themselves as separate as they can.

'How did Bruce win over Señor Morales?' she whispers to Eugene.

'Morales is hedging his bets,' he replies. 'They all are. Better to sell their assets now, while the Americans will still pay top dollar for them, than risk Castro and his pals coming in and seizing them.'

'Could he do that? Castro, I mean.'

'Who knows? At the moment, he is only talking about ending corruption and restoring the constitution so that the poor wretches working in the fields might get to eat once in a while, but plenty worry he'll go a whole lot further. Why take the chance?'

'I feel like something they just found clinging to the underneath of their lettuce leaf.'

'Well, don't take it to heart. Word is they turned away the president himself on account of the shade of his skin not being exactly to their taste.'

At the table, Nell pulls Iris down into an empty seat next to her. 'I'm so glad you're here, Iris. You're the only thing making this whole wedding endurable.'

'The only thing?' Iris looks meaningfully at Joe, who is remonstrating with the maître d', who appears to be attempting to relieve him of his camera.

'I'm not gonna deny he's easy on the eye, but Joe Garston isn't interested in me, honey. Girls like me, we only get guys who lack imagination, who want everything laid out there in the open, with no hidden surprises.'

It is one of those moments when Iris finds herself experiencing several conflicting emotions all at once. Sympathy for Nell, relief that the awkwardness of that moment out on the balcony seems to be forgotten, affection towards her for plucking her from her life and showing her something different. But at the same time, she can't forget what she overheard earlier, nor the words typed in that note. Nell grew up surrounded by actors. Could this be a role she is playing – the straight-talking friend? And if so, why?

Across the table, a pale and listless Lana Mickelson rests her head on her fiancé's shoulder. It's a curious thing that the more Iris studies Lana, the more insubstantial the girl appears, as if Iris has sketched the outline of her but forgotten to fill it in. Iris finds herself willing Hugh to put his arm around his bride-to-be and give her the comfort she seems to be seeking. But the director is relating an anecdote to Luisa Morales and acts as if he has not noticed. Glancing around the table, Iris receives an unpleasant jolt when she finds herself locking eyes with a man she recognises from Bruce's club as the chief of military police, Captain Diaz. He smiles at her, the tight line of his mouth exactly parallel with that straight strip of moustache.

Coming back from the powder room some time later, she is intercepted by Hugh. 'You were tremendous back there, rescuing poor old Barbara. So brave.' To Iris's consternation, his eyes appear to film over with tears. 'I could kick myself for not realising she was in trouble. When I think of what could have happened to you . . .' He reaches out one of his big hands and, keeping his gaze fixed on hers, his fingers stroke rhythmically up and down her arm, rooting her to the spot.

'There you are, Iris. I've been looking all over.'

Eugene appears at Hugh's elbow and Iris gratefully excuses herself, but not before she has noted the shadow of annoyance that flitted over Hugh's face at being interrupted.

Neither she nor Eugene can face going back to the table. It has become all too clear that their presence here in Havana, and Joe's, too, is as much about raising Bruce Bonini's business profile as about Lana and Hugh's wedding, and they resent being turned into walking advertisements for him. Instead, they make their way downstairs to the raised terrace. There's a breeze coming off the sea and Iris enjoys the novelty of feeling almost cool.

'I keep thinking about Barbara,' says Iris. 'Married all these years to that man. All those lost babies. And all the time knowing he's fathered a son with someone else.'

'Not just fathered – he's also given him a job and has him living above the garage, so she has to see him every day and be reminded. That's inhuman. No wonder Barbara's blood-stream is almost one hundred per cent cocaine and barbiturates.'

'Cocaine?' Iris stares at him, incredulous. But then her attention is snagged by the sight of a familiar figure arriving on the sands just below them. Even before he has properly come into view, the knot in her stomach announces his identity.

'You've fallen quite hard for him, haven't you?' Eugene has followed her gaze to where Joe stands in the shadow of the building, lighting up a cigar.

Iris opens her mouth to protest, but Eugene places a small finger gently across it and gives her a sad smile.

'I can't blame you in the slightest. He is the most debonair of men.'

There is something in his tone that catches in Iris's throat, and now she sees what really has been staring her in the face all this time.

'You, too?'

'Oh, Princess, don't look so concerned. I'm always falling in love with unsuitable people. In actual fact, that's my only criterion for love – the more unsuitable the better – it means I'm always broken-hearted, which is the ideal condition for a writer to create his best work. And now, who is this?'

Joe has been joined by someone else, who is all but obscured by the dark shadow where the steps meet the wall and the two seem to be holding an intense conversation, which ends abruptly when a man on the terrace, who is as wide as he is tall, lets out a bellow of a laugh that booms out towards the sea, startling Joe's companion into a hasty departure. But not before Iris has seen, with a savage twisting of her stomach, a flash of a bare calf and a glimpse of a high-heeled satin shoe that she recognises as belonging to Luisa Morales.

'What if Hugh did something to Jean?' Iris has turned around in a decisive manner so that her back is now to the beach and Joe Garston.

'Because she'd told him she was pregnant and he knew it wasn't his?'

'Or maybe he knew she was leaving him and he didn't want to lose her.'

'I think he'd shed more tears over losing his precious house.'

'I feel worried for Lana.'

Now that she's said it, she realises it is true. Though she has struggled to bond with Lana, it doesn't prevent Iris feeling sorry for the girl. It can't have been easy, growing up in the shadow of a mother feted around the world for being the most beautiful film star of her day. Or to be lumbered with caring for an emotionally needy younger sister. How might a girl caught between two such high-maintenance personalities learn to suppress her own feelings?

'Me, too,' says Eugene softly. 'If Jean Summers was no match for Hugh, what chance does little Lana have?'

'Pardon, Señor.' A black-jacketed maître d' has appeared at Hugh's shoulder, where he sits at the table, chatting to Iris. 'There is a man outside who wishes to speak to you.'

Hugh looks irritated. 'Who is it?'

'He said he was Mr Wilson, Señor. Mr Dwight Wilson.'

Hugh's face tightens as if setting hard. 'Will you excuse me?'

Iris is both relieved to see him go and, as before, a little

245

bereft. He is such a big presence, Hugh Hardman, that his absence leaves a hole. Mostly, though, she is curious. Over the last couple of eventful days she has almost forgotten about Dwight Wilson. Now she wonders how Hugh will deal with him turning up here at this place where he might have assumed to hold court? To her surprise, she finds herself feeling sorry for the skipper, the depths he has been brought to. Hugh disappears through the door. Making a sudden decision, Iris gets up to follow.

When she reaches the top of the divided staircase in the entrance hall, she stops. Downstairs, Hugh crosses the lobby between the two grand pillars and exits through the front doors. Iris cannot very well follow without alerting the attention of the uniformed doorman. She wanders back into the corridor in search of a vantage point. There is a door further along that leads into a deserted library with soaring ceilings and, on closer investigation, an arched doorway giving out on to a balcony.

She steps outside, heart jumping painfully at the loud creaking of the glass door's hinges.

From the balcony, she is able to observe Hugh Hardman remonstrating with an even more dissolute-looking Dwight Wilson just beyond the ring of parked cars. Though she can't hear what they are saying, it is clear that whatever the captain is after, he is not about to get it. Iris remembers what he'd said about having something Hugh had paid him not to make public. If he is trying his luck again, he is getting very short shrift.

She is hidden in the dark shadows to the side of the balcony and so intent on the figures out there in the driveway that she doesn't notice she is not alone until she feels the heat of someone standing close – too close – behind her.

'I wonder what you're doing here, Iris Bailey. Seems to me, you're either spying on my father or you're sweet on him. Which is it?'

Eddie braces his arms on either side of Iris, penning her into place, while he presses himself against her back until she is pushed right up against the balustrade. His breath is rum-soaked and she can feel the hardness of him through the thin fabric of her dress. 'Let me alone,' she tries to say, but the solid bulk of him turns the words to dust.

'I followed you from the bar. You're such a tease, Iris. What has my father got that I don't?'

She feels as if every part of her is frozen in place. Down below, Hugh has turned away from Dwight Wilson and is striding back towards the club doors. The seaman's shoulders slump and, though Iris knows what he is and what he has done, still there is something about the disdainful way with which Hugh turns his back on him, as if he is beneath consideration, that sparks something back into life that has been briefly overpowered by the pressure of Eddie's groin pressing against her, his hand on her hip. A flare of outrage.

'Stop!' At first it is little more than a croak. She tries again: 'Stop!' This time she is loud enough that Hugh, about to pass under the balcony, glances upwards, and Eddie, whether because of the shock of Iris finding her voice, or of locking eyes with his father, releases his grip on her. She quickly slides under his arm and escapes into the corridor, heading the opposite way from the bar, towards the back terrace, from where she follows the back stairs down on to the sand and stands leaning against the cool of the building, with her arms wrapped around herself to stop herself trembling.

She can still feel the hardness of him imprinted into her back. Why didn't she scream straight away? What is wrong with her? Only after she is calm enough that her breathing is almost under control does the next question come. How will she have to pay for this?

Unable to face rejoining the others, Iris heads around the side of the clubhouse in search of Dwight Wilson. She catches up with him along the driveway, his suit in a worse state of disrepair even than the last time they saw him. She wonders if he has been drinking solidly since then. When he opens his mouth to speak, it's all Iris can do not to turn away from his yeasty breath.

'He called me a louse. Me. All the things I could have said, if I wasn't a man of discretion. That's why the stars all vied to hire me . . .'

'Yes, you said before. Marlene Dietrich, Dean Martin.'

'He thinks I was bluffing. About the note. I told him I destroyed it, you see.'

Iris understands immediately that it is this note with which he was blackmailing Hugh. 'After he paid you what you asked for.'

'S'right. But I have it. Safe and sound.' He starts patting his pockets. 'I wasn't pulling a fast one. I just realised it was worth more, see, than he gave me. I undersold it.'

'So what's on this note?'

Dwight stops patting and his bleary eyes take on a cunning look. 'How much is it worth to you?'

'Oh, for heaven's sake.'

Iris has had enough. All at once, the whole business

sickens her. All so sordid. But as she turns to go the skipper crumples.

'No, wait. Please. I'm sorry. I wasn't always like this. I had a reputation. I had a job. Integrity.'

She sees that it is important to him that she understands he is more than the man she sees here. The sharp jab of pity takes her by surprise. 'Were you the only one affected like this, Captain Wilson? How about the other crew member? How has he fared?'

She wants to hear that someone has escaped unharmed, but Dwight Wilson doesn't know where he is.

'I didn't know Jimmy Palicki, never met him before that voyage. Never saw him again after. But you can always ask Mrs Hardman. She'll know.'

'Mrs Hardman died off that boat, or don't you even remember that?'

'Not that Mrs Hardman. The first one. Palicki was the son of a friend of hers, or a neighbour. Or a cousin. It don't matter anyhow, all that matters is she recommended him for the job.'

On the way back to the table, Iris turns this new information over in her mind. On one hand, it's not surprising that Connie might try to help out a friend by finding their son a job on Hugh's yacht. She was on excellent terms with her former husband, after all, and both her children had found work through him. Why not her friends', too? But on the other, doesn't it mean she had someone on board the *Sally-Ann* who was in her debt? How far might someone be prepared to go to repay it?

Back in the bar, Iris avoids Eddie and Hugh. Instead she

focuses on the shallow planes of Lana's face, the broad cheekbones, the eyes that are similar enough to her mother's that the likeness is there but which, by dint of being just a fraction narrower, just that tiny bit less blue, somehow miss being beautiful, and her heart tears softly. What chance does this quiet, still girl have against men like the Hardmans? For the first time in this whole surreal week, it is starting to really hit home to her what is at stake here. These might be Hollywood people, but this is not a movie. These are real lives.

And what if one of those lives is at risk? The police wouldn't have reopened their investigation into Jean Summers' death unless there was strong evidence it wasn't an accident. Is it too much of a stretch to believe that, if someone killed Jean and got away with it, they might do the same again?

She leans across the table. 'Are you nervous about tomorrow?'

Lana looks startled, as if she had forgotten she was getting married until Iris reminded her.

'I'm sure Isabella and Meredith have everything in hand.'

That unnatural calm of hers.

'But aren't . . .'

Iris's question is cut short by a scene that is erupting at the far end of the table, where the chief of the military police, Captain Diaz, has come over to confer with Señor Morales. The Cuban businessman stands up so abruptly his chair crashes backwards to the floor. He says something sharply in Spanish to his wife and her hands fly up to her mouth in shock. The two of them rush from the bar. All around, there is a groundswell of noise from the other guests as one leans towards the other, the snouts of their fox furs nuzzling one another, hands over their faces, murmuring behind their satin gloves and diamond rings.

'What's happening?' Iris asks Eugene, whose pale eyes bulge behind his lenses with the thrill of scandal. He shrugs. 'Times like this I wish I'd learned Spanish at school instead of Latin. What even is the point of Latin?'

Iris looks back to Lana and sees Hugh standing behind her, one hand on her shoulder.

'What's happened, darling?' Lana asks him, and to Iris's ears the girl's voice stumbles over the endearment as if she is forcing herself.

'It seems the Morales girl has just been found in a compromising position with our very own official wedding photographer. Now things will get interesting.'

'You know, Princess, it might not be what it appeared.'

'How so?'

'Well, supposing one of them spilled something and they went looking for something to mop up with. You know, one of those cleaning things?'

'And one of those *things* happened to be stored under Luisa Morales's dress?'

Eugene does not have an easy answer for this.

'Sorry,' he concedes. Iris can't help being touched by her companion's clumsy attempts to make her feel better. But nothing can rid her of this humiliation and grief, this cheese wire around her heart. That she should have been so taken in by Joe. That she should have allowed herself to feel something for him. Kissed him as she had, feeling her body respond to his touch.

In the back of the taxi misery settles over Iris. Her eyes feel hot and itchy. Then fury takes over. At all of them: Eddie, of course, but also Joe, Hugh, Peter, even Mr Sturrock and Mr Underwood. At their assumption that she is the blank canvas on which they can paint their own self-portraits according to their own designs. But mostly, she is furious with herself for allowing it to happen, for becoming engaged to Peter seemingly without her consent, for Eddie pressing himself into her back and Hugh's fingers stroking her arm, for her mute acceptance of Mr Sturrock's eight, for the fantasy she has constructed around Joe Garston since he stepped behind her to watch the hummingbird on the terrace, as if even her daydreams have to be pegged to a man's impulses and desires.

Iris hadn't realised until the scene back there at the Biltmore how little regard the highest echelons of Cuban society held for the Americans, nor how strict an eye they kept on their daughters. It was the maître d' who had found them, the same one who earlier had tussled with Joe over his camera. The two of them, Joe and Luisa, had been discovered in a clinch with their clothes dishevelled and Joe's hand busy under Luisa's dress, or at least that's what Hugh later reported. Which in itself was bad enough, but made considerably worse by the fact that a close, elderly relative of Julio Lobo, the sugar supremo, and practically Cuban royalty, witnessed the whole thing, having spotted young Luisa Morales slipping through a door she had no business going through just moments after the tall, dark American.

That's when her parents had been informed. Iris had

followed Eugene to find out what the furore was about and watched from the stairs as Señor Morales, white-lipped with anger, ushered his wife and an ashen-faced Luisa out through the front lobby, summoning his driver with just a raised finger, the black car pulling up directly outside the door before the silent threesome were swallowed up into its vast interior.

Joe Garston was immediately ejected from the club, and then they were all informed, via a word in Bruce's ear from the maître d', that as the member who'd invited them was no longer on the premises club rules dictated they all had to leave. Bruce had acquiesced politely enough, but Iris could see a vein at his temple that she hadn't noticed before, raised like a worm under the skin.

Outside, while they waited for their cars, Joe had approached from the shadows, where he'd been leaning against the wall, smoking. His mouth was set into a grim line and he had a look in his eyes which, in a different man, she might have mistaken for appeal. As he drew near, she turned abruptly towards Lana, who had observed the whole eviction with her usual detachment.

'I do hope this hasn't upset you,' Iris said, angling her back to the photographer.

Lana shrugged. 'It's really nothing to do with me.'

When she said it Iris had the strangest notion that she could have been talking about the whole thing – the wedding, the guests, this whole strange week. All of it nothing to do with her.

A car pulled up and Lana climbed inside. Before Iris could follow her, Hugh leaned out of the passenger side and beckoned to Joe. 'Casanova. A word.' She could just make out the dark, still shape of Bruce Bonini sitting in the back.

So here she is, sitting with Eugene, in the back of a different car, which has no air conditioning, so the windows are open to the night. As they wait at the end of the club's driveway to turn left into the main road, a figure appears by her window, making her jump clear out of her skin. Dwight Wilson leans in to press something into her hand.

'Take this,' he says. 'I don't want it. Integrity. Tell Hardman he hasn't taken that from me. Tell him.'

It is a folded piece of paper that, Iris sees when she smooths it out as the taxi pulls away, is embossed with something at the top – a name or address – and contains random figures and some handwriting that neither she nor Eugene can make out in the dark.

She refolds it and stares out of the window. The air seems thick with petrol fumes and there's a smell coming off the sea that might be rotting seaweed or discarded fish from the morning's catch. She swallows, but there's a lump of something raw and solid in her throat, and she makes a gulping noise and turns her face to the outside so that the acrid smell gets in her nose and her mouth until she feels she must surely suffocate from it.

Only gradually does she become aware of a steadying warmth spreading up from her left hand, through her arm and across her body, soothing her ragged heart. When she looks dumbly down, she sees that Eugene has taken her hand. He squeezes it softly, giving her a small, sweet smile, before turning his face to the front, as if out of delicacy for her feelings. Iris looks away, out of the window, and now the tears that have built up behind her eyes spill over, rolling down her face, where the hot wind dries them almost instantly to her cheeks. She feels hollow, as if she isn't a real person but a desiccated skin with nothing inside. Only the solidity of Eugene's hand in hers keeps her from being blown out into that black, noxious-smelling night sky.

20

IRIS RUBS HER salt-streaked face as she follows Eugene around the side of the house. Her feet drag, and the thought of going back to the guest house, where she runs the risk of an encounter with Joe Garston, is unendurable, so she is relieved when they round the corner to find herself immediately summoned by Connie, who, despite the lateness of the hour, is sitting with Meredith on the terrace-cum-beach bar.

She hurries over, settling herself down when Connie pats the wooden barrel next to her. Meredith is nearby, leaning over a gaily painted table playing solitaire, the ridge of her spine like a fistful of knuckles.

'My dear, what in heaven's name has gone on? Bruce just arrived back with a face that could curdle milk, and then our nice photographer walked straight past without a word, even though we both called out, didn't we, Meredith? What did we miss?'

Iris tells the story and tries to gird her voice when she mentions the courting couple in the cleaning cupboard, his hand under her dress.

'Will the Moraleses still be coming to the wedding?' Meredith's mind is on guest lists and canapés.

'It's Nellie I worry for. I think she had a soft spot for Mr Garston. Who knew he'd turn out to be such a *heel*.'

'Your daughter will be heartbroken for precisely as long as it takes to apply a new coat of lipstick,' says Meredith, turning back to her cards, and now Iris sees that it's not solitaire in front of her after all but a series of photographs laid out carefully on the low table.

'Meredith has been going through some photographs of Lana when she was little. She thought it would be nice for Lana to see them on the eve of her wedding.'

As she hunches over the photographs, Meredith's narrow, pointed shoulder blades protrude from her bony back like a bat's folded wings.

Iris puts her hand out towards the nearest photo. 'May I?'

The colours on the photograph are washed out, as if it has been left out on a windowsill. It shows two young girls around twelve and seven. The older girl is plump and awkward in a dress that strains across the tummy and little white gloves that look to be digging into her wrists. Iris recognises Lana from her impassive gaze at the camera but, otherwise, she would never have known her. Her little sister has Faye's long neck and arms, though her skin has yet to acquire that sallow tinge. Iris's heart aches at the sight of her shyly hopeful expression. What would that little girl think of the future life has made for her? What would either of them think?

'They were darling girls, really,' says Meredith, in a mellower tone than Iris has yet heard from her. 'So eager to please. And then here's their beautiful mama.'

She has picked up another photograph that shows a young Jean Summers, before the peroxide and the fame.

Just another pretty girl in a floral dress sitting back on her elbows on a beach with her bare legs straight out in front of her and the wind ruffling her light brown hair and her smile as dazzling as the sun. What kind of a chance did she stand? Iris thinks. With looks like that, in a world like this?

As they've been sitting there, Iris has been aware of the low murmur of men's voices coming through the open doors to the salon, but now the volume starts to build. Iris clearly hears Hugh's unmistakable voice saying something about Joe Garston. Now Bruce Bonini's soft, clipped vowels cut across the night air.

'Yeah? Well, I want him gone. That stunt of his could have cost me the Morales deal.'

Hugh says something that sounds like a joke, but when Bruce replies, his voice is dangerously quiet. 'Fuck you. You think this is funny? Just remember who's bankrolling this wedding of yours, who's paying to build bamboo huts in the garden and fly a girl over from England to do a few scribbles.'

Iris feels a hot rush of humiliation, that word, 'scribbles', getting straight into the exposed nerve of her deepest insecurity. Her discomfort only increases when Bruce adds: 'If that's even who she really is.'

Iris glances at Connie, who looks flushed. Meredith, meanwhile, appears to be affecting selective deafness, though Iris is sure both women are listening just as intently as she is.

'What do you think your new bride would say if she knew just how much debt she was marrying into?' Bruce continues. 'You think she'd still look at you with those gooey eyes if she knew her husband hadn't paid for a single fucking bloom in that bouquet she'll be carrying?'

Now Hugh gets angry. 'Don't pretend you're doing this out of the goodness of your heart and not to prove to Batista and his buddies that you can attract Hollywood's finest to this godforsaken island. This whole wedding is a public-relations coup for you.'

Bruce's reply is drowned out by the startling sound of Elvis Presley singing 'Hound Dog' at volume. Iris's head whips around to see Connie leaning over the jukebox. Meredith, who has been taking ever deeper drags on her cigarette so that her thin cheeks appear entirely perforated, has her hand pressed to her chest. Bruce appears at the French windows, silhouetted against the light from the salon chandeliers, puffing on one of his cigars.

'Ladies,' he says curtly, and withdraws back into the house, closing the doors behind him.

'Did you know?' Meredith glares at Connie across the table once the song has finished.

'Know what, dear?'

'About the debts. Did you know he had no money? Oh, what am I asking? Of course you must have known. He still pays for everything you have, doesn't he?'

Even in the dim light Iris sees Connie's face darken.

'Now, Meredith. My financial arrangements are none of your concern. And Hugh's financial arrangements are none of my concern either.'

'Well, let's think about this, shall we? He hasn't had a box-office hit since my daughter died. Is that why he's marrying Lana? For Jean's estate? For Manderley?'

'You're being ridiculous, Meredith. Hugh isn't broke.

That's just sour grapes from Bruce because he's sore about his business deal. You mustn't pay it any mind. Honestly, all this *fuss*. What must our guest artist be thinking of us?'

Meredith frowns at Iris, as if only just remembering she is here. 'I just don't want to think of Lana—'

'Don't pay it another thought. That's only Bruce blowing off steam.'

From her position next to Connie, Iris wills Meredith to protest further. She looks down at that softly lumpen girl in the photograph in her too-small dress. Someone needs to fight for her, surely, to protect her?

'They're my responsibility is all I'm saying. Jean's girls. I have to look out for them.'

'Well, of *course* you do. They've been lucky to have you. Now why don't you show us some more of those photographs? How old would the girls have been in this one? Doesn't Faye look pretty enough to eat? That's Manderley in the background, isn't it?'

She has picked up a photograph from the table that shows the adolescent Lana and Faye with their mother in the driveway of a striking-looking house made of glass and cedarwood and stone. The house is surrounded by enormous cacti of the type Iris has only ever seen in movies which twist and gnarl up into the sky with spines that protrude like the bristles on a hairbrush.

Lana, still plump, with a shallow, doughy face and wearing a pair of blue jeans that do little for her and a man's checked flannel shirt, stands awkwardly beside a large Woodie-style station-wagon car with her arm around her younger sister, who is more recognisable as the Faye of today. Wearing a thick jumper despite the sun from which her wrists emerge shockingly thin, Faye presents a determinedly unsmiling face to the camera. Iris supposes it is Hugh behind the camera. From the ages of the two girls, she would guess the picture was taken pretty close to the date of Jean's death.

'You can just see Lana starting to lose that puppy fat in this one,' says Connie. 'Who would have believed there was a swan inside all that padding?'

'She wouldn't have lost it at all if I hadn't put her on a diet just as soon as she came to live with me,' Meredith says. 'Out went all that garbage Jean had been feeding her. Just good plain food. And some of those wonder diet pills my doctor prescribes. Maybe you'd like me to pass a few your way, Connie?'

Connie laughs. 'I'm perfectly happy the way I am, thank you.' But as Iris watches she presses one thumbnail so hard into the soft skin of the opposite inside wrist that it leaves a perfect crescent-shaped dent. What does it cost her, Iris wonders, this iron self-control?

Meredith starts to list the various foods she cuts out in order to retain her twig-thin figure. 'Bread, of course. Butter and cream, well, it goes without saying . . .' But here, Iris, who has turned back to the photograph, loses track because her whole focus is trained on the figure on the other side of the car from the two sisters. The wavy blonde hair is recognisable from a thousand magazine covers and a hundred cinema trips; the face, which wears a long-suffering expression as if impatient for the picture to be taken, is almost as familiar to Iris as her own. And yet it is not how Jean Summers looks or what she is doing but rather what she is *wearing* that makes Iris's whole body feel tight, as if all the air has been sucked right out of it.

'And you're quite sure?'

'Quite. Yes. Absolutely.'

'It's the same scarf that was in Bruce's desk drawer.'

'Without a doubt. It has quite an unusual pattern, you see, as if it's been handmade, using a silkscreen.'

'And you think that means . . .'

'Yes. Well, it would make sense, wouldn't it? Particularly as there was that intimate note with it. "Morning, sleepyhead! Gotta dash. Show yourself out." With a kiss at the end.'

Eugene is quiet. Digesting. Then: 'Oh my. Poor Barbara. Can you imagine?'

He takes his glasses off and wipes them on the hem of his shirt.

Poor Barbara indeed, thinks Iris. Of course, there might be a perfectly blameless reason why Bruce keeps Jean Summers' scent-soaked scarf in his desk drawer, but all Iris's instincts tell her that there was something between them. She remembers how when she'd first seen the scarf she'd imagined him pressing it to his nose and felt as if she'd intruded on something unbearably intimate. And if, as that photograph suggested, Jean had been in the habit of wearing that particular scarf around the time of the ill-fated boat trip, wouldn't it stand to reason that Bruce was the man Jean was seeing before her death? And if that was the case, wouldn't it make sense that the baby Jean was carrying when she was fished out of the water was his?

What would that do to a woman who had lost four babies

of her own? Raúl must have been humiliation enough, but this? Right under her nose?

'Would it be provocation enough, do you think?'

Iris doesn't have to ask what Eugene means; it's been playing through her own mind ever since she saw the photograph. How desperate would a woman be who had discovered her husband was in love with one of the most beautiful women in the world and might be about to leave her? How far might she go to make sure that didn't happen? Connie has already told them Barbara and Jean argued so fiercely on board the *SallyAnn* that they woke Nell up clear the other end of the yacht.

'Why Bruce, though?' Iris wants to know. 'Jean could have had anyone. Why would she have chosen him?'

'He's an attractive man. Don't look at me like that. Those eyes. And more than that, he's an attractive man with power. That's a lethal combination. Literally, in Jean's case.'

The two of them are sitting outside on the guest-house terrace, which has escaped Isabella's ministrations and remains blessedly beach-theme-free. Eugene has mixed them both what he jokingly called a Mojito but is actually just neat rum with a squeeze of lime and some random herbs he has plucked from the flowerbed in front, and the two glasses sit on the table between them.

As Iris leans forward to take a sip, a rustling in her pocket reminds her of the paper Dwight Wilson stuffed into her hand as she was leaving the club earlier, and she spreads it on the table where they can read it with the help of Eugene's flashlight. The first shock is that the embossed type at the top spells out 'Jean Summers' with an address underneath starting with 'Manderley'. Somehow, seeing her name there in black and white makes everything that much more real. Underneath the address there are three random letters – 'Cyp' – and at the bottom a series of equally random numbers. But it is the handwritten message that brings Iris's hand to her mouth.

> *Hugh is going to go crazy*
> *enough to kill me*

'The writing is the same,' she says, 'as the note that was with the scarf.' She runs to her room to fetch the slip of paper she'd found in Bruce's desk drawer. When the two pages are laid next to each other, there can be no doubt the same writer was responsible for both.

'This proves that Bruce was having an affair with Jean, and clearly she was scared stiff of what Hugh would do when he found out.' She glances at Eugene, who is staring at the two notes with a stricken look in his eyes.

'If Wilson took this from Jean's cabin after she died, it's pretty damning, don't you think?' Iris asks. 'For Hugh, I mean.'

Eugene nods, but it is as if his attention is elsewhere. Iris grows frustrated with his continued silence.

'What do you think those letters mean?' she asks.

He shrugs.

'Well, what about the numbers?'

Eugene seems to snap to attention. 'Looks to me like she could maybe have been working out how much she'd need to get away from him.'

'But she had money of her own.'

'The numbers are not exactly the main issue here, I'd say.'

Iris has to agree. The handwriting, round and messy as a child's, leaves her shaken. Her eye follows the lines of it, the loops of the l's, the careful dots of the i's, as if she is watching Jean's fingers create it, and somehow it brings her to life. This screen icon who in the end was just a woman who got things wrong and wrote badly. And was apparently terrified of her husband.

'It doesn't prove anything, though,' Iris says. 'We don't know when she wrote this, or even if it was really her who wrote it at all.'

'Oh, it was her,' says Eugene emphatically. When Iris glances over questioningly, he adds: 'It has to be.'

Iris and Eugene slump dejectedly back in their seats to finish their drinks, each lost in his or her thoughts. Which is where Joe Garston finds them when he comes sloping from the direction of the main house some ten minutes later.

'Tell me all,' says Eugene, springing back to attention. 'Did Papa Morales run you out of town? Will there be a duel? Shall I hold your coat?'

Leaning against the post with the vine curving around it, Joe shrugs, his hands deep in his pockets. His eyes dart to Iris as if trying to gauge her mood and she pretends not to notice.

'I don't expect I'll be welcomed back to the yacht club any time soon, put it that way.'

'Looks like you could use a drink. I'll fix you one now.' Iris feels a flare of panic as Eugene disappears into the house and she is left alone with Joe.

'Yes, I think I'll go too.' She gets to her feet, only to find his hand reaching out to circle her wrist.

'I just wanted to say—' He breaks off when he sees how she glares at his fingers on her arm. Stepping back, he raises his hands in the air as if to show he means no harm.

'It isn't what you think, Iris. With Luisa. What I mean is, it didn't mean anything.' He glances at her only in snatches, unable to fully meet her eyes.

Her anger blooms. Does he really not see how this makes it worse rather than better? That whatever his feelings for her, Iris, they are so negligible they can be thrown away on something of no importance whatsoever.

'No need to explain anything to me,' she says. 'As you know, I'm very happily engaged.'

She is savagely pleased by the surprise on his face. Picking up her glass, she heads indoors, but suddenly he is there again in her path. She feels his hand, touching her waist this time, his hot palm burning through the fabric of the yellow dress.

'Please,' he says, his brown eyes willing her to look up, but she does not.

'Big day tomorrow,' she says, pulling away. 'Must get some sleep.'

Only once out of sight does she lean her head against the wall of the hallway and weep.

Iris is looking forward to getting to her room, where she can be alone, but when she arrives at the end of the upstairs landing she hesitates, struck by the conviction that someone is inside. The events of this evening have pushed the disappearance of Bruce's key from her mind, but now it comes back to her with full force.

She strains to listen through the heavy door. Did that

creaking come from inside the room or is it just the water pipes outside? For a moment she considers going back downstairs to find Eugene, but the thought of having to face Joe again stops her. She puts her hand on the door knob and presses her ear to the wood. Cautiously, she nudges the door open, freezing when, in the dim light from the table lamp, she sees a figure on her bed.

'Don't scream, Iris, for pity's sake.'

Nell is hunched over, her arms wrapped around herself, make-up smudged and smeared. On her lap is the anonymous letter that was slid under Iris's door three days before, the one she had tucked safely away in her case.

'I came to talk to you about what happened at the club. I wanted to make sure you were all right. I know you're soft on Joe Garston.'

'I'm not anything of the . . .'

'Oh, please. Anyhow, I didn't want to get drawn into a conversation with my mother and Meredith, so I was fixing to wait for you here. Then, when you were taking so long, I got bored and was looking for a piece of paper to write you a note. Only . . .'

'. . . you found that instead.'

Iris sits down next to Nell on the bed.

'It came the night after I arrived.'

'And you didn't think you should tell me?'

'I didn't want to upset you. And . . .'

'And you thought it was true.'

'No. I didn't. Not for a minute . . .' The lie sticks in her throat.

'Someone here really hates me.'

Nell's voice is slow and thick. Iris wonders how much she

has had to drink, and how long she has been sitting here in the near-dark, her mind racing.

'And you have no idea who could have sent it?'

Nell shakes her head and wipes away a tear. Iris notices for the first time that her friend has her father's big hands, and it makes her seem oddly vulnerable.

'I told you they've reopened the investigation into Jean's death, and I know I'll be top of their suspect list, and oh, Iris, I just can't bear it. Why can't it all just go away? Haven't my family suffered enough?'

'Why, though?'

'Because of everything we've—'

'Not the bit about your family. I mean, why would you be top of the suspect list?'

Nell gets to her feet and walks to the window. 'I'm just that sort of person. I'm too loud. I make enemies. Well, you read the note.'

Iris wonders why Nell still has her back to her.

'I'm sure if the police have a suspect list, you wouldn't even be on it, Nell. Unless there's anything you're not—'

'You will help me, though, Iris, won't you?' Nell turns round, and Iris sees that fresh tears have left black tracks of caked mascara down her cheeks. 'You'll help me clear my name? Jean was a bitch, but I didn't hurt her. I wouldn't. No matter what this lousy note says.'

Dear Cyp

Can you hear that noise that sounds like someone hollering down a deep, deep well? Listen? That's me after two days on this wretched boat. Oh, Cyp, I am such a fool. Remember X? Oh, who am I kidding? I know you've already guessed it's Bruce Bonini. You're the smartest man I ever met. As well as the kindest. Anyway, Bruce left me a little present, if you know what I'm saying. What's more, I think he did it deliberately. 'I say, Cyp, what do you call a woman who relies on the pull-it-out method?' 'I don't know, Sap, what do you call her?' 'Pregnant.' Boom boom tish. Like I told you before, he's not a very nice mam. In fact, to tell you the God's honest truth, he scares me a little. You know how greedy I am, Cyp, always wanting more, but this time I really bit off more than I could chew.

The only one who knows about the baby is Nell. I told you she's Hugh's spy-in-the-camp, and she heard me in the john in the morning, getting reacquainted with my breakfast. Of course, she thinks it's Hugh's. But Hugh will work it out, for all he can't conceive of anyone having a life outside of him. I think Mama suspects, too, though she hasn't said anything. Did I tell you Meredith is here on the boat? She sorta invited herself, although Hugh's face when he found out she was coming was almost worth having to put up with her watching me eat for four days. Lord knows I love her, but I don't think that woman has had solid food in her mouth since 1945 – unless Benzedrines count – so she stares at other people's like she could suck it up through her eyeballs.

Hugh and I do nothing but drink and fight and drink and fight in a never-ending circle like a bicycle wheel going round and round all the live-long day. I feel wrung out with it all. Empty. If a great hand was to squeeze me hard around the middle, all that would come out would be the tiniest trickle of regret. Sometimes I hang over the side of the boat and look at the sea and think, 'Why not?' Oh, don't fret, when I think of the girls I remember why not. And most of the time I'm just fine. No one would guess there was a single cloud on my horizon. I always was a better actress than the bastard critics give me credit for.

I can't tell you how much I wish you were here, Cyp. Though, once I'd introduced you to my messed-up family, you'd probably drop me like a stone. What I wouldn't give to be back in New York with you, drinking Martinis in our booth in Bemelmans, bitching about Vidal, or whoever your arch-enemy is today. Do you know, I think you're the only person in my life who never wanted anything from me, apart from my company?

Hell, they're all shouting for me up on deck and I'm still only halfway through putting on my war paint ready to go ashore for dinner. I'll mail this from there.

Onwards and upwards!

Your Aunt Sap

PS. Do you believe in God, Cyp? I'm quite certain that you don't, as you don't believe in much of anything. But if you do, even just a little bit, please pray for me. I am so very far from home.

21

IN HER STICKY bed, Iris throws the cover off, then snatches it back up again when she hears a mosquito whine. She positions herself on her front so that her cheek becomes creased from a fold in the sheet underneath her, then on her side, until her shoulder twinges in protest. And now on her back, from where her eyes become transfixed by the glint of the brass fitting on the ceiling fan as it groans its slow rotation.

She jumps at the sound of the shutters creaking, sure that whoever took the key from her shoe has returned. Footsteps on the stairs send her springing from her bed, her heartbeat slowing only once she hears the sound of Eugene's door closing down the hall.

Her thoughts tumble around in her head in sympathy with the blades of the fan. Nell, Joe. Luisa. Barbara, Eddie. She pictures Jean sitting at the dressing table in her cabin, committing her fears to paper, in case anything should happen to her. What would Hugh have gone crazy about? Was he on the verge of finding out it was his own best friend she was having an affair with? If anyone killed Jean, it surely has to have been Hugh. Then, just moments later, she sees, in the fever heat of the night, how Barbara Bonini, half crazed by her own private sadnesses, might have flown at Jean Summers in a momentary loss of self-control on learning she was pregnant with her husband's child. Perhaps she heard Hugh and Jean arguing about it on deck and came up to confront Jean, finding her staggering around the deck, drunk. A burst of anger, an impulsive push.

But there is something Nell hasn't told her. Iris is sure of it. And someone here clearly thinks she is guilty. Or wants Iris to think she is guilty.

She comes back to Hugh. Hugh, who – Jean wrote – might kill her. Who, having found out on board the *SallyAnn* that his wife was pregnant by another man – despite his pantomime of being shocked by the coroner's bombshell – made sure she could never leave him. She remembers how Dwight Wilson heard Jean saying, 'You don't scare me,' on the night she died, but how he'd said she sounded terrified.

While all of these alarming scenarios are percolating in her brain, her heart is doing something else entirely, tightening incrementally, as if wrapped in wet gauze that is slowly drying. She is glad, she tells herself, she has discovered what Joe Garston is truly like before anything has really happened between them. A kiss means nothing. Not in these kinds of circles.

Thus Iris's thoughts and feelings roil on throughout the long, airless night as she watches the light between the cracks in the shutters subtly change. She must have slept, finally, because she wakes with a jolt to find the whole room bathed in a yolky light from just these narrow gaps in the wood.

Just one more day. That's all she has to endure. As soon as the wedding guests leave she will be going back to the airport and then home. To Peter. She is lucky, she tells herself again, to have a man who is crazy enough about her to want to marry her.

So why does she feel like she has swallowed a large, jagged rock?

Iris is nervous about today's wedding. Not just because of Joe or Eddie or the tensions in the family but because she so wants to be a success. She knows how expensive it was to get her here. The knowledge that Bruce Bonini paid for her fare is ice in her veins. She must do a good job so that he won't blame Nell for insisting on hiring her. But so much depends on her connection with her subjects. How can she hope to capture a likeness if everyone here is hiding something? Havana and its visitors, it seems to her, are like the jasmine on the vine outside, only ever showing themselves in the dark.

The next moment she is reminding herself that there ought not to be a wedding at all. She can't prove that Hugh Hardman killed his last wife, but there is plenty that points in that direction. What will Lana's life be like, married to a man like that? The girl has no family to warn her or protect her – she hardly speaks to her grandmother, and her sister is in no position to offer support. Can Iris stand by and let it happen?

She is not the only one to have slept badly. Downstairs on the terrace, having reluctantly hauled herself out of bed, she finds Eugene with his head bent over a letter that he quickly crams into his billfold as she approaches.

'Look at my eyes,' he says, removing his glasses and pulling down his eyelids to reveal livid pink flesh. 'That's what a night of existential dread will do for you, Iris. Do you know, it's been seven years since I wrote anything that people actually wanted to read. The editors don't call any more. That snake Vidal is getting the commissions that ought by all divine right to be mine, even though they have to shake out his copy when they take it out of the envelope to get rid of all the coils of dead skin.'

'You'll be able to write about this, though, won't you? The wedding?'

Eugene, head in hand, raises a little finger, as if this is all the suggestion merits.

'A society wedding,' he says into his soft palm. 'Please kill me now.'

'So why are you here? You must have known how it would be.'

'To find out what happened to Jean.'

Iris looks over sharply. It makes sense for Eugene to want to get to the bottom of the case so that he can write the definitive exposé about it. Book, even. There is a vogue in America at the moment for literary works based on true-crime subjects. Yet she has sensed before a hesitation in him that she cannot quite understand. Now there is this – the way he says 'Jean' with an almost proprietorial softness.

Eugene heads into the house in search of aspirin for his throbbing head, and Iris sits alone. It is her last morning in Cuba. The last time she will drink her coffee watching the sun paint pin-sharp black shadows across the grass, breathing in the final lingering notes of the night-blooming jasmine. The last time the banana leaves will whisper like silk at the faintest wisp of a breeze. The last time she will look up and see the rich emerald-green of the trees stamped against a blue sky that seems to go on in all directions without end.

She thinks about Hemel Hempstead and how low the sky is there, always pressing down, grey and damp, like the sponge pad into which Mrs Latham dips her forefinger when she is turning pages or sealing envelopes, and how it is broken up by clouds and chimney stacks and telephone wires so that it is never one vast expanse but small mismatched pockets sewn together like an old-fashioned quilt grown grubby with use. She thinks of how her mother's features seem to fade year on year and how sometimes when they say goodbye, Peter makes a clicking noise with his tongue in the back of his mouth and winks at the same time, as if he is copying Humphrey Bogart.

Thinking about home makes her throat close up, so she compels herself back into the here and the now. Her eyes, searching for something to focus on, fall upon Eugene's billfold, made of worn, shiny leather, lying there on the table. There's a corner of a page sticking out, and Iris remembers how he had hastily crammed the letter into his wallet when she arrived. She will not snoop. Wouldn't dream of taking it out when it is so clearly private. Even so, she cannot resist lifting up the tip of the corner with her finger. To her disappointment, there are only three words visible, written in a rounded, messy handwriting that seems oddly familiar: 'Dear Uncle Cyp.'

Cyp? Isn't that what was written at the top of Jean's note?

Hearing footsteps approaching, she withdraws her finger so that the writing is once more hidden. But it is not Eugene who comes into view but Joe, looking as if he has aged ten years. His normally olive skin is the colour of underwear gone grey and there are violet shadows under his eyes.

Iris is horribly aware of that unshifting rock at the base of her stomach.

Joe takes a seat at the little round table. Just as she is preparing to leave, he reaches out and places his hand lightly over hers where it rests on the glass top. She is too surprised to react, can only gaze down at his knuckles, white as pearls under his skin. She notes how small her own hand looks under his and looks at the points at which their two skins touch and feels her flesh to be on fire. More than anything in the world, she longs to shift her chair next to his so she can rest her cheek on his shoulder. She imagines how that might feel, the warmth of him, the smell.

Then she remembers the double sting of hurt and humiliation of Luisa, and how Peter is waiting for her back in England, and about Eddie and the things men do to get what they want and she stands up abruptly, ripping her hand away from his. They look at each other, each waiting for the other to speak. The moment stretches as they hold each other's eyes. But now someone is coming along the path from the main house, footsteps snapping the tension out on the terrace.

Here, emerging through the trees, is Lana.

The bride-to-be wears a dress of white satin that dips in the front, but not too low. It has short sleeves that puff up from the shoulder and then in again at the bicep, and a satin bow that ties at the back. It is the kind of dress a young girl might wear to a First Communion, but it is not a dress to make one gasp. Not a dress to wrap in tissue and pass on to a daughter in the hope it brings her happiness.

Iris's heart feels tight. Lana should be radiant, and yet she looks ill at ease and uncomfortable, the dress cutting her off at all the wrong places, the widest part of her arms and calves.

'You look lovely,' she lies because, really, what else can she say? In her head she sees another white dress, the one Lana was wearing to play tennis with Eddie. She sees the girl soaring over the net, her white skirt flying.

Lana and Iris are now sitting by the swimming pool in a wooden shelter with a gaily striped canopy overhead and a bamboo bar with an array of drinks arranged behind it. They occupy a bamboo booth, facing each other across a table made from fruit crates. Iris has fetched the portrait of Lana from her room and it is spread out in front of them, and Lana is telling her how much she loves it.

'I was worried I hadn't quite captured the essence of you,' Iris says.

Lana gives her strange half-smile. 'Perhaps that's exactly why I love it so. You know, I think you're so brave, Iris.'

'Me?' Iris can't help laughing.

'Look at you. You're not so much older than me. And yet here you are, all alone, thousands of miles from home, with this strange family. Holding your own. I do admire you so.'

Iris doesn't know how to respond. Back in England, she might have recognised herself in Lana's description, foolishly mistaking stubbornness for courage and dissatisfaction for adventurousness. Only, here in Cuba, under this remorseless sun, with all these undercurrents she cannot fathom, where the thick night air is pierced by the sound of bombs and bodies swing from trees, and women wearing dead foxes around their necks lose fortunes on roulette while girls who are little more than children stand on street corners and lean into open car windows, where one man can pin her down on a sofa and another can make her feel like the most special woman in the world and yet just hours later be fondling someone else, only here does she realise how little she really knows about anything, and what a dangerous position that puts her in.

She looks more closely at Lana. Sees the raised pink line on her inside arm where she has scratched the skin with her fingernail, sees how those wisps of baby hair around her face are damp with sweat.

'Are you scared, Lana? Is that why you brought this up?'

Lana shrugs, her puffed sleeves rising and falling. 'Isn't everyone scared on their wedding day?'

'Well, yes, of course, but . . .' Iris breaks off. It isn't her place to say anything to Lana. The note from Jean, assuming it was indeed from Jean, that 'Hugh is going to go crazy enough to kill me,' doesn't prove anything. Yet Iris's mouth, as if operating under a different system to the rest of her body, continues voicing the words she knows she ought not to say.

'What I mean is, are you scared you might be making a mistake?'

Now the words are out there in the space between them, hovering low over that portrait of a reclining Lana who is keeping goodness knows what secrets.

'I don't know.' Lana's grey-blue eyes meet Iris's. 'You can't imagine what it was like with Mommy when we were young, never knowing which Mommy she'd be – the loving, happy one who got me to practise her lines with her while she cooked us pancakes, or the one who told us we'd ruined her life or who sat on the sofa and drank until she peed herself and told me she was so glad I was there to clean her up. Then, when she got together with Hugh, everything changed. He was the first person who really seemed like he wanted to take care of *me*. I was tired of looking after everyone else.

'You know she accused me of being in love with him one time? A ten-year-old child, as I was when they met. She told me it was embarrassing how I acted around him. She was drunk, but even so. After Mommy died and Hugh didn't adopt us like Faye and I hoped, I still had fantasies that he would come and take me away from Meredith.'

'But Meredith isn't a bad person.'

A shadow flits over Lana's face. 'There are things about Meredith you don't know.'

Iris doesn't know what she is talking about, but she shivers nonetheless.

'Meredith didn't have the first idea how to cope with two grieving girls. Faye stopped eating and started trying to hurt herself. You've seen her wrists. She was in and out of hospital. And I felt hollowed out.'

'And meeting Hugh again made you feel more solid?'

'When he came to give that talk at college, I wasn't expecting to feel anything. It had been five years, and I'd grown up in the meantime. But it felt like something clicked into place. Like, finally, someone had come for me.' She falls silent. Then: 'How do you know, Iris, whether or not it's love? You're engaged to be married. You must know.'

Iris doesn't want to think of Peter, but Lana insists. 'Please, Iris, tell me how it feels, to be in love.'

Iris can think only of Joe Garston and how her hand burned at his touch earlier and her body seemed to melt into his when they kissed that early morning of the bee hummingbird.

'Lana, I'm no expert. But I think it's something one just knows, and if you're having to ask . . .'

'. . . Then I probably don't?' Iris is shocked by the younger woman's matter-of-factness. 'I don't know if that's true, though. I've loved him almost ever since I can remember. It's just . . .' Lana breaks off to trace the line of her own face in the portrait with her finger.

'Just what, Lana?'

'Just that I sometimes feel like I'm disappearing when I'm around him. Like a balloon that has a tiny hole in it and the air is going out bit by bit.'

'You don't have to go through with it, you know? It's not too late to call it off.'

Lana eyes her steadily. 'But what about all the money he's spent?'

Iris takes a deep breath. 'It isn't Hugh who's paid for the wedding.'

'Pardon?'

'It's not my place to say this, but Hugh is in debt. Lots of debt. I overheard him talking to Bruce last night. Bruce is the one who has laid out all the money for today. Not just from the goodness of his heart either. It makes his business look good and shows he can attract glamorous stars to Cuba, makes him look like an attractive partner for the Cuban government.'

Lana absorbs this new information. 'Hugh is broke?' she asks finally.

Iris nods, wishing she was not having this conversation. And yet, how could she stand by and not say anything?

'So you think he's marrying me for money?'

The question is so direct Iris is taken by surprise.

'No. I mean, that might be part of it but I'm sure that's not the only thing.'

'He's always wanted to get Manderley back. I remember him telephoning Meredith after Jean died and he'd just found out about the new will. I could hear him shouting down the line.'

'Lana, I'm sure it's not just about the money or the house.'

But Lana is getting to her feet. 'I want to thank you,' she says with a dignity that skewers Iris's heart. 'I know it can't have been easy to say these things, and I'm very grateful.'

And she is gone, across the lawn, weaving around a hot-pink beach umbrella. The hem of her white dress flutters at her calves as she walks, as if proffering surrender.

Still seated in the cabana, Iris swings between self-congratulation (Lana deserved to be told the truth) and fear (if Lana calls off the wedding and Bruce loses face in front of the people he is trying to impress, how might he react?).

The missing key weighs heavily on Iris. The knowledge that someone was in her room, discovering what she stole from Bruce, makes her skin crawl. How much more precarious will her position be if Bruce discovers she has also told Lana about Hugh's debts and persuaded her to cancel the wedding?

So deep in thought is she that when she looks up and sees Bruce himself standing in the doorway of the cabana, wearing his wedding dress-suit, Iris wonders for a brief, wild moment if her own thoughts have conjured him.

'I don't think we've had a chance to properly get to know one another, have we, Miss Bailey?'

Unable to meet his eyes, Iris finds her gaze alighting on his perfectly shaped black brows. The smell of him. That sticky, invasive scent of leather and spice.

'Only, it's a funny thing. Someone was in my private office.' His fine brows are raised. Her blood is roaring in her ears.

'Tell me. Who do you work for, Miss Bailey?'

Surprise makes Iris forget to look away and a splinter of fear travels through her as she finds his black eyes studying her reaction.

'I . . . That is . . . Mr Sturrock and Mr Underwood.'

'I see. And who would Mr Sturrock and Mr Underwood work for?'

'I don't understand.'

'Don't you?'

Outside by the pool Iris hears people moving around, clinking glasses. The catering staff Isabella has hired.

'I should go,' she says, moving towards the exit, trying not to run.

Bruce steps back to let her pass. 'You take care now,' he says softly.

22

BY THE TIME Iris gets back to her room her heart has just about stopped slamming against her ribs and she is already playing down what just happened. So Bruce sought her out? So what? He is paying for her to be here. He is entitled. And his strange question about who she works for could have been idle curiosity. She won't think too hard about what he said about someone being in his study. He was just testing her reaction. He has no proof. Directly after the wedding, this very night, she will go to the airport and back to her real life. She has only to get through the next few hours.

She takes down the dress that has been hanging in the wardrobe on a padded coat hanger ever since she arrived. It had appeared one afternoon in her Hemel Hempstead bedroom after she'd returned from work. Her mother was still hardly speaking to her and yet there, spread across the bed, was this froth of palest pink satin and net and tulle. There had been satin shoes to match, with pointed toes and pencil-thin heels. It was not what Iris herself would have chosen – a little too virginal and fussy – yet it was easily the nicest dress she'd ever owned, and, when she tried it on, she knew instantly that it suited her.

An olive branch! She'd practically flown out of her room in search of her mother, tracking her down to the garden, where she was grimly cutting sprigs of rosemary for the joint that sat in a roasting tin in the kitchen, pink and glistening under its tight strings. 'I won't have those people looking down on us,' was all her mother would say. Afterwards, more than her disappointment that the dress was not after all a peace offering, it was that 'us' that had rankled most with Iris, as if she was nothing but an extension of her parents.

Yet isn't that just what she'll be if she marries Peter? An extension of someone else?

Iris has another girdle to wear with the dress, a full-body, strapless thing with garter snaps in front and back for the stockings she has also laid out on the bed. But when she looks at them and imagines how the nylon of the stockings will feel against her skin, the way the girdle will encase her middle until everything feels damp and clammy and she herself feels like nothing so much as sausage meat in its casing, something hardens inside her. Iris has never been in favour of the kind of upholstered underwear her friends go in for. She remembers her art-school friend Violet wearing a padded bullet bra under her sweater at a party and someone knocking into her so that one of the tips inverted in on itself and she had to rush to the lavatory to manipulate it back into shape.

Lana's words come back to her, about thinking her brave, and though Iris knows Lana would not have said that if she had seen how she jumped at the slightest noise in the night, still she draws strength from the notion and she pulls on the dress over her normal, high-waisted knickers, zipping it up at the back without any bra whatsoever. At first she tells herself she is just testing out how it feels, that she will go back and put the girdle on, will not go all but naked to a wedding. Eddie lurks around the edges of her mind. The weight of him. How his thick tongue had filled her mouth until she thought she would gag, and how last night he had pressed himself against her as if he had the right. She does not want to do anything that could be misconstrued. Won't the rigid underwear provide an extra layer of protection? She reaches for the girdle. And stops.

Isn't this always what she ends up doing? Changing her behaviour to accommodate someone else's? Can't she, just for once, follow her own course according to her own desires? She only has a few hours left in which to be herself, here in Havana where there is no Peter, no typing pool, no grief-diminished mother. She bundles the girdle and stockings back into her case.

At the door of her room she hesitates, thinking she hears someone outside, but when she steps into the corridor no one is there. She makes her way, in her unfamiliar heels, to the top of the stairs and stands listening for signs that Joe might be in the salon or on the terrace. The cool, dark house breathes around her.

It happens as if in a film, as if to someone else. One minute she is there on the lip of the narrow wooden staircase and the next the air is knocked from her lungs and her flimsy heels have given way so she tumbles forward, conscious only of the tiled floor of the hallway coming up to meet her and of a dark shape brushing past her as she falls.

*

'Someone definitely pushed me.'

Outside, she is seated with her leg up on a chair and Eugene is pressing a wet towel to the bleeding gash in her knee while Joe paces the perimeter of the terrace, pausing occasionally to look at her before resuming his pacing.

'But wouldn't we have seen them, Princess?'

Joe and Eugene had been approaching from the main house along the tree-screened path when they heard Iris scream.

'Not if they hid around the side of the house until you'd gone in.'

'Why?' asks Joe yet again. 'Why would someone do that?'

'Because she's getting too close to the truth about what happened to Jean Summers?' says Eugene.

'Or the truth about Bruce Bonini,' says Iris, before filling them in on the strange exchange she had with their host in the bamboo cabana. When she gets to the part about him asking who she is working for, and the implication that she is reporting back to the CIA, she studies their faces carefully, looking for a trace of panic or guilt, but finds none. Only a bark of surprise from Eugene. 'No offence, Princess. But you? A spy?'

Joe has stopped his pacing and glares with an ever-deepening scowl and Iris feels a spark of anger ignite inside her. How dare he judge her? How dare any of them? She puts her hand to her elbow, which is throbbing painfully. Now that the shock of the fall has worn off, fury is taking over. She is so sick of being in thrall to the moods of men. Eddie, Hugh, Bruce, Joe, even Eugene. Is this how Jean felt? she wonders. Is that why she changed her will without telling her husband? Is that why she was punished?

'At least the blood is all on the inside of your dress, Princess. There were a few drops on your shoes, but I've managed to dab those off.'

'Perhaps you shouldn't go to the party,' says Joe.

'After I've flown all this way? Don't be silly.' Iris doesn't tell him she isn't sure there will be a party, or a wedding. She was right to tell Lana the truth, she tells herself. And yet, dear God, the consequences.

Some time later, the trio make their way along the path to the main house. Iris is half expecting Isabella to intercept them to explain that the wedding is cancelled, but there is no sign. Instead, Faye comes picking her way across the lawn, dressed in a floral gown that accentuates the sharp blades of her collarbone and shoulders. Iris's eyes travel to her wrists, which are hidden underneath a pair of white gloves. The girl's shrunken face bears a wide-eyed expression of alarm, and Iris's muscles tense. This is it. The announcement that Lana has called the whole thing off, that the day is ruined.

'Are you all right, Iris?' Her soft, halting voice. 'You're white as a sheet.'

Iris starts. 'I'm fine, thank you, Faye, but . . . how is your sister?'

'Oh, you know, Lana doesn't give much away.'

'And she's here?'

''Course not. She's gone off with Hugh to sign the wedding papers and when she comes back she'll be Mrs Hardman. Just like Mommy.'

23

'MY *DARLINK.*' ISABELLA's orange silk crushes up against Iris's pink satin. Then she sees Iris's arm and she steps back with her hand on her chest. 'Oh my *Gad*, what has happened to you?'

'I . . . fell.'

'And yet still you are beautiful like a picture. Life is *nat* fair. But now the guests are arriving. It is time to adopt the position!'

Iris is ushered into the house, where a corner of the entrance hallway has been converted into a mini art studio with an easel and a chair boasting intricate gold-leafed ironwork and upholstered in ivory silk on which her sitters can pose in comfort. All around are arranged her pencils and pens and charcoals, the small, cigarette-sized rolls of paper she uses for blending, the tissue she sometimes needs for creating lighter shades and a stack of thick, luxurious drawing paper cut to various sizes.

Already guests are arriving, the men in black jackets, the women in dresses that swish and whisper as they walk, stiff silks and soft velvets and lace that just about rescues décolletages from tipping into vulgarity. There are elaborate hairdos that tower upwards, curls piled upon curls, and others that are so much sprayed as to render them entirely incapable of independent movement. There is a perfume that smells of early-morning grass and another that to Iris has the sickly scent of flowers that have been left to over-ripen in their vase. There are men with moustaches and men with cigars and one man whose face has a most unnatural look, as if the skin has been pinned back behind his ears.

Iris feels herself becoming caught up in it all. There is something about a wedding that encourages a suspension of reality, the venue and guests becoming their own little world within a world.

A crowd has built up by the door and there comes a hush, where even the silks stop their whispering. Iris sees a man threading his way through the knot of guests, who fall back to let him pass. There is no disguising the famous blue eyes, that mischievous smile. As if to prove it, here comes his wife, and she is easily the most beautiful woman Iris has ever seen, with black hair that sweeps back off her face in waves and wide-set green eyes.

While old blue eyes seems at ease, greeting the crowd as if he knows them, shaking hands, waving to people at the back, his lady is in no mood for niceties. As soon as they make it through the scrum of people she drops her husband's hand as if it is hot to the touch. 'Get your hands off me, you fucking bastard,' she hisses as they pass by where Iris sits.

'Five bucks says that marriage doesn't last the day,' says Nell, who has appeared by Iris's side. 'I heard she's been spending more time with Hemingway than her own husband. Since she swam naked in his pool, he won't let his staff change the water.'

Nell is wearing the shimmering gold dress they bought together. She has a coating of powder on her face that glitters where it catches the light and her lips are the red of the fresh scab on Iris's knee. There is little trace of the distraught woman from the previous night. Iris is starting to realise that Nell uses her risqué wardrobe and bold make-up as a protective lacquer, just like the spray that holds the women guests' hair so stiffly in place.

'But then what marriages *do* last, when it comes to it?' Nell tucks Iris's arm in hers as she speaks. 'So maybe the problem isn't with the people in the marriage, maybe it's with marriage itself. What do you say, Iris?'

'My parents are still married.'

'Happily?'

'Enough. I mean, no one is happy all the time, are they?'

A shout goes up from the doorway, a man whistles and a woman lets out a theatrical cheer. Hugh and Lana come through the door, he carrying her in his arms, as if he has bought her in some market. They are married. After everything Iris told Lana. Iris remembers those two lines of childish scrawl – *Hugh is going to go crazy enough to kill me* – and shudders.

'Oh, Lana,' says Nell softly, echoing Iris's thoughts. 'What have you done?'

Eddie appears next to Nell in a crisp white shirt and black tie, and Iris's nerve endings tie themselves into tight knots one after the other. He has caught the sun and his eyes look startlingly blue against his bronzed skin. Yet all Iris can see are the thick arms that he used to hold her down.

Her hand goes to the graze on her elbow. She remembers how Dwight Wilson had told them Eddie had as good a reason as anyone else for having a grudge against Jean, who'd known the boy had a crush on her and had – what was the word he'd used – *flaunted* herself around him. Might he not now hold a similar grudge against Iris herself? Might it have been him waiting for her upstairs in that shadowy recess on the guest-house landing?

'What in God's name is Lana wearing? Nellie, couldn't you have kitted her out? Something like Iris has on? Although Iris could wear a mail sack and it would still look like a million dollars.'

Eddie means her to be flattered but Iris feels only a prickling revulsion.

Isabella sweeps over in a swirl of orange dress and white hair and heaving bosom. Her be-ringed hands clasp the shoulders of a slender young man who wears a dark suit and an expression of quiet alarm at finding himself thus propelled through this glittering crowd.

'Behold your first rat.'

'I beg your pardon,' says the young man, revealing himself to be not a man at all but a young woman dressed up like a man. 'I think she might mean guinea pig,' says Iris helpfully. And so it begins, an endless procession of guests, some with faces so familiar she finds herself scrutinising them as she draws, mentally listing all the films she might have seen them in. Was it that one about the woman who suspects her husband is trying to kill her, or that other one about rich oil-mining families in Texas?

There are guests who want to talk – about the wedding, the salaciousness of it, about Cuba, Havana, this house, how foreign it all is. Though rarely do they ever talk about her or ask her how she came to be here. There are guests who prefer to sit in silence, treating the business of being drawn with the utmost solemnity, striking a pose from which they are careful not to deviate. All of them with their own fears and desires and doubts and opinions. All needing to be silently assessed, gently probed to discover what it is they want from her, from this. How it is they wish to be seen.

Iris falls gratefully into the trance-like state she assumes when she draws where nothing else exists except the pencil in her hand and the person in the chair, where she translates to paper not just the visible lines of them but also the spirit of them, the way this man's face lightens when he talks about his newborn son, this young girl's giggle behind her hand. So much of drawing, she has found, is forgetting one is drawing at all, otherwise the brain sees only what it expects to see, rather than the textures and shadows and flesh and blood that bring a person to life.

While she works, the others appear to her in snippets in the periphery of her vision. Barbara laughs too loudly and too long over something said by someone – could that be Hemingway himself, barrel-chested and booming, taking up all the air in the room? Connie is everywhere, scooping up anyone who looks lost or ill at ease, introducing guests to one another, a pudgy hand on an arm, always a ready compliment: 'I do declare I saw your last movie five times, I loved it so much', 'Isn't that the most darling dress, but then you do have the figure for it.' Iris can see now how she would have been an asset to Hugh, remembering names, facilitating conversations. Her very ordinariness is a gift in itself. There is nothing to measure oneself against and find oneself wanting. More than that, Connie reflects back to people their very best, idealised selves, honing in on the thing of which they are most privately proud and dropping it into the conversation like liquid gold. It is a talent – making people feel better about themselves – in some ways not dissimilar to what Iris tries to achieve in her portraits. In her brief glimpses Iris notices that Connie looks more stylish today, wearing a simple sheath dress in place of her usual fussy tucks and bows.

Meredith, she sees less of. A couple of glimpses across the vast hallway – her stiff black dome of hair, a flash of a silver cigarette holder. Once, Iris looks up and sees the older woman standing alone by the front door, staring into the distance with a look on her face as if her heart is breaking.

Bruce appears from time to time, huddled in corners with other men who puff on cigars and pretend to laugh when, intermittently, they are joined by wives or outsiders and pleasantries are called for, only to close ranks again once alone, their black-jacketed backs forming a circle of crows from the centre of which a plume of smoke rises as through the top of a wigwam. Captain Diaz, the military police chief is there, the black line of his moustache cutting like a scar through his upper lip. One time, Iris glances over and finds Bruce staring right back at her and a bolt of cold dread roots her to the spot so that even after he has looked away there are raised goosebumps on her skin that take an age to disappear.

There are some days where Iris can pick up a pencil and all her movements feel unnatural and stiff and everything that emerges on to the page looks like a picture and not like a person living and breathing there on the paper. But today is not one of those days and, as word spreads and guests show off their likenesses, the cluster of people around Iris's corner of the entrance lobby grows steadily.

When she has been drawing for well over an hour, Iris looks up from her easel to find that her next sitter is Luisa Morales, wearing a pair of large dark glasses and a blue silk dress.

'Perhaps we can finish the drawing from earlier,' says Luisa, sinking into the cushioned armchair.

'I'm afraid we would need to start a new one. The glasses. The hair.'

'Yes, of course.'

Their conversation is stilted.

'Perhaps I could move the chair nearer to you so that you can see more easily?'

Iris is just about to explain that's not how she works, when she realises that Luisa is trying to move out of the range of hearing of the people standing behind her.

'As you wish.'

Luisa pulls her chair up close, and Iris notices that the young woman's hands are shaking, though she tries her best to hide it by clasping them together. Despite everything, she feels a warm swell of compassion.

Iris begins drawing in bold strokes. Though she works in silence, still she feels the force of her subject's energy trained upon her like a torch.

'I was hoping,' Luisa says, leaning in, 'that you might deliver a message for me. To Joe.'

Instantly, Iris's compassion vanishes. So this is why she has come here. To ask Iris to be her go-between.

'My father is watching me all the time.'

Iris glances up and, sure enough, she sees Señor Morales standing just inside the door to the main salon, looking directly at her.

Iris's instinct is to refuse. Then she glances again at Luisa's trembling hands. And nods, so slightly and curtly she might just as well not have bothered.

Some thirty minutes later she takes advantage of a break in the queue of people waiting for portraits to seek out Joe. She finds him in the formal dining room where Iris was first introduced to the family. He is taking photographs of Lana and Hugh, who have just cut the cake and are posing for the camera in a variety of theatrical attitudes, using the knife as a prop. It is the first time Iris has seen them have fun together, and she feels cheered – until Hugh bends his new bride's head back and mimes slicing the blade of the knife across her throat.

Iris approaches Joe, cursing her uncomfortable heels. His face lights up when he sees her, but the smile falters at her expression.

'I have a message from your . . .' she stops herself saying 'girlfriend', realising how childish it will sound, 'from Luisa. She says, "Eight o'clock, around the side."'

For a second or two Joe's face retains that same arrested-in-the-act-of-smiling expression. Then he nods. His eyes are on hers and he seems nervous as he reaches out for her. 'Iris, you must know how much I . . .'

'I really must go now.' Her voice is bright and brittle as she pulls away. 'There's so much still to be done. I can't quite believe we're leaving tonight.'

It is as if he is a stranger she has encountered at the buffet table and must now engage in polite conversation. She sees his hurt and is glad. Let him be offended. Did he think she would still be panting after him, like a little lap dog, after everything he's done?

Iris wanders out to the garden through the grand double doors at the far end of the main hallway. Just beyond the pool is a specially constructed stage on which a band is playing a selection of tunes from Hollywood musicals. In front of the stage a few couples are dancing to Louis Armstrong's 'Calypso' from *High Society*. All around the lawn there are guests arranged in various poses and clusters. The celebrity couple have holed up in one of the bamboo cabanas, from which the sound of raised voices can clearly be heard. Under a garish yellow umbrella, a plain middle-aged man in a rather crumpled suit and thick grey socks sits on an upturned crate, looking glum.

'Graham Greene,' hisses a voice in her ear. 'He's one of yours. Great writer. Congenitally miserable, of course, but that's an occupational requirement.'

Eugene still has that over-animated look, as if he has been up all night drinking strong coffee and has passed beyond tiredness into a state of waking mania.

They watch Barbara, dressed all in black, being escorted inside by a small man in a dark suit.

'Isn't that her doctor?'

'Must be time to charge her batteries again.'

'You know, I can see that all the evidence points to Hugh having done something to Jean, but I can't help thinking Barbara knows more than she's letting on. Connie said Nell heard her and Jean arguing furiously on that boat. And heaven knows she had reason enough to hate her.'

'You think *Barbara* killed Jean?' Eugene's eyebrows sail northwards. 'Even after Dwight Wilson's note?'

'No. Or at least not deliberately. I would just like the chance to ask her why they were arguing, or to show her the scarf and that note that was with it and see her reaction. I'm sure I'd be able to tell instantly if there'd been some kind of altercation that ended up with Jean going in the water. And then Nell would be in the clear and I wouldn't have to worry about Lana being in danger and . . . What?'

'I didn't say anything.'

'No, really. Why are you looking at me like that?'

'Nothing. Except that we have the scarf, and we know where Barbara will be for the next half-hour or so.'

'You can't seriously be suggesting . . .'

'I'm not suggesting anything, except . . . We're leaving tonight, Princess, so it's now or never. What harm could it do?' It's as if Eugene has shifted into a new gear. His pale eyes burn with vigour behind the lenses. Iris is surprised to find him so riled up about the work he usually disparages. 'If the doctor has just been, Barbara will be so out of it we could ask her the combination to her safe and she'd give it to us. We just go get the scarf and the note, and head on upstairs and have a little conversation with our hostess. I'll tell her I need more information for my piece.'

Iris stares at him. 'You know you're actually crazy, don't you? If you think for a minute I'd go along with something like that . . .'

Five minutes later, she and Eugene are creeping up the back stairs of the house. Though it was his idea, now that they are executing it he is hanging back as if having second thoughts. They have decided that if they are challenged, she will say Iris is looking for one of her sitters, to finish off a drawing.

But they are not challenged. The stairs go up three storeys but Eugene stops on the first-floor landing, a wide, impersonal space dominated by a white plinth on which is displayed a monstrous bronze statue of a kneeling woman, her head hanging low as if embarrassed, hair sweeping the floor.

'How will we know which room is hers?' Iris whispers, gazing forlornly down the endless corridor.

'It has to be the room in the central turret, the one that has the grand balcony,' Eugene hisses back. 'Bruce would insist on it, don't you think?'

They make their way past heavy, dark-framed oil paintings of landscapes and fruit bowls and a succession of identical walnut doors on both sides. In contrast to the activity downstairs, up here the air is thick and muffled and surprisingly cool. It is also very dark, with only a series of glass wall lamps lighting the way.

Iris's mouth is dry as they arrive at the middle section where the corridor opens out into a circular shape. Towards the back there is a large arched window, set into the curved wall, which would doubtless let in a stream of light if it wasn't for the impenetrable shutters, while to the front a grand double doorway, also arched, presents an uninviting façade. The two of them stop and exchange nervous glances.

Eugene steps tentatively forward towards the closed doors, but almost immediately there comes the sound of a man's voice from just inside the room and, to her horror, Iris sees the handle turning. Eugene's eyes widen in dismay, and Iris just has time to yank him away, dragging him backwards into the narrower part of the corridor, where there is a small corner section that is partially hidden from view. There is nowhere else to hide. If the person coming out of the bedroom turns this way, they will certainly be discovered. She rehearses the excuse about the missing sitter again in her head and hears how ridiculous it sounds.

She and Eugene stand pressed to the wall, barely breathing, listening to the door creak open and then click closed again and the sound of footsteps approaching. Are they coming this way? Iris squeezes her eyes closed and stands rigid with panic. Then she peers around the corner and could weep with relief to see the doctor's back retreating along the corridor towards the main staircase. Eugene collapses theatrically against the wall. 'We should leave,' Iris mouths, jerking her thumb in the direction they have just come from. Eugene shakes his head and she sees that the zealous light from earlier is back in his eyes.

Before she can talk him out of it, he is knocking on the polished door. A faint voice comes back: 'Whaddaya forget now? I paid the cheque, didn't I?' Iris takes a deep breath and follows Eugene into the room.

Barbara, wearing a bead-encrusted black dress, is splayed out on the biggest bed Iris has ever seen. There are black satin sheets monogrammed in gold. Vast swathes of black-and-white fabric loop around the picture windows that lead out on to the huge balcony, tied off with extravagant bows of material. What Iris notices most of all is the cold. The temperature in the room is so much lower than out in the corridor that, to Iris, standing on the threshold, it is as if Barbara is lying in a gigantic refrigerator. The air-conditioning machine responsible for these polar conditions is in the corner and makes a noise like a plane about to take off, but these details seem not to register with Barbara, who gazes at her visitors with a glassy impassivity from the vantage point of her many pillows.

'May we come in?' Eugene asks in a voice several pitches higher than usual. 'I just have a few teeny-tiny questions for my piece and I wanted to make sure I caught you and, well, isn't this just the most divine room? You do have the most exquisite taste.'

Barbara smiles beatifically and flaps her hand for them to come in.

'As long as you don't mind the temperature,' she slurs. 'Bruce says it's colder than the morgue in here, but I gotta tell you, any warmer and I'd be sweating so much you'd have to swim over here.' She peers at Iris. 'Did I ask you already if you've had the change, Irene?'

Eugene raises an eyebrow at Iris, who shakes her head.

They move forward to stand awkwardly by the bed. Their hostess is so clearly out of her rational mind with whatever the doctor just gave her it seems to Iris it would be underhand to take advantage of her condition by pressing her for answers, and yet Eugene is right. It is now or never.

'Mrs Bonini? May I call you Barbara? It's only that I feel so at home with you. It's a gift some people have. That easy intimacy.'

Eugene is talking too much. Barbara's eyes are losing focus.

'We just wondered whether you might recognise this scarf.'

From her bag, Iris produces the scarf she inadvertently stole from Bruce's desk drawer. Barbara Bonini raises her head an inch off the pillow and reaches out to take the scarf from Iris. She surveys it for a moment or two then drops her head back again.

'Not mine. Not my colours.'

'We think it belonged to Jean,' Eugene says. 'Jean Summers.'

They are scanning her face for signs of a reaction, but there is none. In fact, Barbara's eyelids are drooping, her fingers still wound around the scarf.

'It was in your husband's desk drawer,' Iris says, desperate. 'With this note.' She holds up the scrap of paper – 'Morning, sleepyhead' in Jean's terrible scrawl.

But Barbara's eyes are closed and she seems hardly to register what they say.

'Sure, sure,' she says – *showa, showa* – nodding as much as her stack of pillows will allow. 'Anyways, I wanna thank you both for dropping in. Did you bring anything to drink, by any chance? I'm a little dry.'

At the bottom of the back stairs, Iris and Eugene pause before they part company.

'I really thought there was a chance . . .' says Iris.

'Me too.'

'You'd better give me the scarf back now, for safe-keeping.'

'I haven't got it. I thought you picked it up.'

Iris pictures it, wound around Barbara's fingers. They stare at each other, the implications sinking in. The scarf there. In Bruce Bonini's bedroom.

'We have to go back,' says Iris. But as she turns Barbara's doctor reappears behind her.

'Excuse me, please.' He pushes past her up the stairs, pre-sumably to rejoin his patient.

'Look, even if Bruce does see it and works out where it came from, we'll be on our way to the airport by then,' says

Eugene. 'He might not even recognise it. We're only assuming he kept it for sentimental reasons. Maybe he put it in the drawer years ago and just forgot it was there.'

Iris nods, biting the inside of her lip hard enough to taste the metal of blood.

'I've been looking for you.' Eddie, tall and broad and entitled, blocks her path. Having parted from Eugene, she has taken the servants' corridor that runs past the kitchen so she can get back to her makeshift studio in the lobby without being seen. Apart from her and Eddie, there is no one else around. 'Where are you off to? Come drink with me.'

He is swaying and his eyes have that unfocused look Iris remembers from the night of their date. A tremor runs from the pit of her stomach up through her body and down her arms and legs.

'I'm afraid I have to work.' She wants to raise her voice to summon someone else – a lost guest, misjudging the way to the bathroom, or a waitress scurrying in to collect another tray of drinks. Yet just like on the balcony of the Biltmore Club, something holds her back, some deep-rooted conditioning against making a fuss. 'It is why I'm here, after all. I don't think your father would be too impressed if I took the rest of the day off.'

Eddie advances until he is just inches away from her. 'There, you see, my father has bought you and now I claim you for my own. I'll square it with him. Come on, Iris, stop playing games with me.'

He has his hands on her now, those big, meaty baseball player hands of his, one on each shoulder, and is propelling her backwards through a doorway. Before Iris has a chance to react she finds herself in some sort of cupboard. Linen, she realises, as her eyes wildly scan the shelves in the dim light. Tablecloths and napkins. Surely, then, a cupboard that will be in constant use on an occasion like today? Or perhaps not, since all the tables are done up to look like beach bars. Thus run her thoughts while she tries not to admit what is happening here, now that Eddie has her pinioned against the back wall, the corner of the shelf digging into her back, his hand yanking at the strap of her dress, trying to force the bodice down. She remembers how readily she'd abandoned that stiffly upholstered bra, how she'd stood there in her bedroom, that thrill of liberation. Is this the price one pays, then, for the novelty of putting oneself first? Is this how it is?

Anger erupts.

'Stop it!' She says it out loud. Not just in her head. Eddie doesn't let go of her, though he does pause.

'Stop it! Stop it! Stop it!'

She has found her voice. And now it is found, it will not be silenced. '*Stop it!*' What was a cry becomes a scream, and still it goes on.

'*Stop! Stop! Stop!*'

She feels as if every tissue of her is scalding, her very bones on fire.

'What are you doing? You're crazy. You want everyone to hear?' Eddie is furious, but there is a new note in his voice that wasn't there before. Fear. Of her, and her sudden unpredictability. The knowledge makes Iris's bones and sinews tingle. When Eddie relaxes his hold, she brings up her knee as hard as she can into his groin.

Eddie lets out a yell of pain and, as his hands drop from

her shoulders in order to cradle the damaged part of him, she pushes past and out through the door.

Hurrying along the passageway, she waits for guilt to descend. She has made a scene. She has not played by the rules. She has hurt someone, for goodness' sake. But it doesn't come.

Breathlessly installing herself back behind her easel, Iris has no time to reflect on what has just passed because already there is a small queue of guests waiting. She concentrates her energies on these, coaxing from them what she needs to guide her pencils across the paper, concentrating not on their obvious features but on the spaces between them and the way different parts relate to one another. All the time, something is surging through her veins, vibrating through the fingers that hold the pencil. Something unfamiliar that makes her shoulders flare and her heart swell. As she works, she prods this new feeling. Finally, it comes to her, what it is, this heat that radiates from the base of her stomach out into every part of her until her body thrums with it.

Power.

24

'IT IS A MARVEL. You are a marvel. Everyone sings your praises. I say, "Enough already or I will have to *keel* her." '

Isabella is sitting in the cushioned armchair, with her legs splayed and her head thrown back, her arms hanging loosely over the sides. In her orange dress she looks like an exotic bloom, dropped from a plant, whose petals are already wilting. How exhausting it must be, not only to be responsible for all of this but to be constantly on show, constantly performing. Iris understands completely why Isabella is so much in demand – that her clients are not only buying her imagination and her flair and her contacts but Isabella herself. How must it feel to have made a product of oneself? What must it cost to make a living from giving pieces of yourself away? And yet Isabella manages to stay so generous and unfailingly kind.

It is that hour of a wedding where the champagne and the canapés – the tiny crab-paste pastries and quail's eggs and oysters and delicate discs of fried plantain – begin to take their toll, the guests slowing and slurring and slumping. For the first time in hours, there is no one waiting to see Iris, which is how Isabella has ended up in the chair. Out in the garden, the band has stopped playing and the singer is saying something into his microphone. A murmur goes round and the remaining guests in the house start drifting towards the back doors.

'Speeches starting,' says Isabella. 'I should go.' She stirs herself reluctantly.

'Do you worry about Lana?' Iris checks that they cannot be overheard before asking. 'What I mean is, did you ever consider not taking the job, when you found out who they were to each other, she and Mr Hardman?'

Isabella, whose eyes are shut, doesn't react, and for a moment Iris wonders if she has fallen asleep.

'Darlink, I have lived approximately five hundred thousand years and I have learned only one thing, and that is never to judge. You know, relationships are like those gigantic blocks of ice in the sea. What we see on the surface is so small a part, so how can we even guess what happens underneath? People are like that, too. Never think you know, Iris. As soon as you think you know, you become closed up like this.' She mimes snapping her fist shut.

'Yes, but doesn't it bother you that he might be marrying her just to get her money and the house he gave to Jean? Or so he can have someone to control or so he can feel young again? Or that Lana is marrying him because he was the only one who was nice to her when she was a child, or because she's somehow in competition with her own mother?'

'You see!' Isabella sits up, beaming.

'What?'

'Sometimes two people get married and it is impossible to think of one reason, not even one, why they are doing it.

But you have just given me six. Doesn't that make you feel better?'

Iris watches Isabella head out in the direction of the back, where the sun is now low in the sky. A big cheer has just gone up and Iris sees how the wedding planner draws her shoulders back and imagines her animating her face in the same way Iris would have done if she'd been drawing her. Iris contemplates going to join her but catches sight of Eddie standing on the terrace just outside and changes her mind. Instead, she wanders out through the front door, where the driveway is full of cars whose drivers slouch on the grass under the trees. They stare at Iris with open curiosity. Feeling self-conscious in her pink dress and scratched arm and the shoes that have already made the back of one heel bleed, she makes her way around to the side out of sight, where there are three vans loading and unloading boxes of catering equipment. Iris watches as two men take from the back of one the most enormous bottle of champagne she has ever seen and stagger with it along the path that leads to the side kitchen entrance to the house.

The van nearest the gate is small and dented along the side and is parked under the lowest-hanging tree, its back doors open. In the gathering dusk, Iris makes out a woman, with a silk scarf hiding her hair and wearing sunglasses despite the gloom, lifting something into the boot. Only her blue dress helps Iris recognise her as Luisa Morales. The woman jumps when Iris walks over.

'Please,' she says, and Iris is shocked at the fear constricting her voice. 'Leave me alone.'

'But what . . . ?'

'Go back inside. And do not tell anyone you saw me here.'

A man comes out of the side door of the house, carrying a large box. He rudely avoids Iris's eyes and hisses something at Luisa in Spanish.

'Please, Iris. Go now.'

She sounds desperate, and Iris moves away, only to turn back after a few steps when Luisa calls her name.

'I want to tell you, Iris, there is nothing between Joe Garston and me. He loves you, I think. Now please, please, go.'

Iris does as she is instructed. *Loves*. As she walks off, it is as if her legs are moving entirely without input from her brain. She heads back in through the front door of the house, conscious of a warmth crawling over her stomach and chest and face. *Loves*. Unthinkable. Preposterous.

She heads out to the back of the house in a daze, snatching up a sketchbook on the way, feeling it important to have a prop to counteract the fluttering in her chest. Eddie has disappeared, and Bruce Bonini is making a best man's speech from the stage in front of a magnificent orange-and-pink sky. He is talking about how he met Hugh a quarter of a century before, and how he became like a brother to him after his own brother died. It is the first chink of vulnerability Bruce has shown since she arrived and Iris is surprised to find herself almost feeling sorry for him. Hugh and he had bonded, Bruce is saying, through their ambition to succeed and a weakness for Cuban cigars. Iris tries to imagine Bruce and Hugh as young men, stripped of the authority they have now, but it is impossible. Bruce recalls a road trip the two of them took to Mexico. Iris works backwards in her head and decides Connie would have been pregnant with Nell at the time, home alone with a two-year-old while her husband drank tequila and played poker as if he didn't have a care in the world.

Iris stops listening to what Bruce is saying, returning to the scene with Luisa a few moments before. She looks around for Joe and is half relieved, half disappointed not to see him. Glancing at her watch, she sees it's just after eight. He will be with *her*, then. But she is in that van, with the man with the boxes. Nothing makes sense.

Loves. The word has taken residence in Iris's brain and will not shift.

Iris doesn't register immediately that there has been a shift in the atmosphere of the gathering. Bruce has stopped talking and a hush has fallen over the crowd, into which a lone woman's voice is shouting from just behind Iris. The voice is rough, as if there are small stones in the woman's throat.

'I said, do ya recognise this?'

Barbara Bonini comes staggering unsteadily past Iris's shoulder, heading through the crowd, which parts as she passes. Iris sees with shock that, in contrast to her sober black dress, her hostess has a gaily patterned silk scarf around her neck. *Oh no. Surely she can't be about to . . . Not here . . . Not now . . .* Iris casts around wildly until she locates Eugene in the crowd. He is staring at Barbara, also slack-mouthed. Then he looks over and his eyes meet Iris's. He shakes his head, as if to say, *No, me neither.*

Barbara has reached the stage and Iris wonders whether she intends to climb up there and, if so, how she will achieve it. The stage is not high, but Barbara is, and she has enough problems just walking in a line. Iris feels as if her lungs have ceased working, her breath turned to ash. Her mind is still frustratingly muddied, but she knows fundamentally that whatever is about to happen is to do with her and Eugene and the things they said to Barbara up there in that bedroom with black satin sheets and the curtains tied in flamboyant bows at the windows. She scans across the crowd until she sees Lana standing in the front with Hugh, his arm around her shoulders, both of them wearing matching expressions of surprise. They look easy with each other and Iris is reminded of her conversation with Isabella about how there is so much unguessable hidden under the surface of a relationship.

Somehow Barbara has made it up on to the stage, where she teeters on her high heels, proffering the scarf that used to be Jean's to her husband, from whose drawer Iris liberated it.

'Look familiar to ya?' The microphone picks up her voice, thick and slurry, with extra feedback on that last word.

Bruce says something in a low voice, but there is no mistaking the anger that throbs under every syllable, and Iris becomes aware of movement on both sides of her. Men in suits with dark glasses, Bruce's 'associates', stirring into life.

'Whassamatta? Cat got ya tongue? Lemme jog your memory. This scarf was Jean's. You remember Jean? The broad who was married to your best friend, who you were screwing behind his back and who you got pregnant before she conveniently fell offa the side of the boat.'

It is awful. Unbearable. Iris takes out her sketchbook and begins drawing, unable to face what is happening head on. Art has always been her escape in stressful situations, a buffer between her and the world.

Iris's pencil takes in Hugh, who stands as still as if he has been freeze-framed in one of his own movies. The men in suits begin to move forward, and Bruce reaches for his wife, but it is all too late because, in one bound, Hugh has released himself from his stupor and landed on the stage, his long legs bringing him within inches of Barbara's still-swaying form. He snatches the scarf from her hand and, in a gesture Iris finds almost shockingly intimate, presses it to his nose and inhales so deeply she can hear it all the way from the back.

'Is it true? Hell, I don't even have to ask. It's written all over your goddam face.'

A gasp goes up from the assembled guests as Hugh brings back his arm and drives his fist into the right cheek of the man who is paying for his wedding.

The men in suits are running, Bruce's nose is exploding in a crack of gristle and a flume of blood. Barbara has been struck accidentally with the back swing of Hugh's elbow, collapsing on to the stage floor. Iris's pencil scratches furiously across the paper. She cannot watch. Lana, on the contrary, is rooted to the spot, observing everything, as if this is a play being staged for her entertainment.

'Oh my word, what have we done?' Eugene sounds thrilled as he joins her, and Iris, who is only now recovering the power of thought, feels for the first time irritated with him. These are real people – the Boninis, the Hardmans. This is Lana's wedding day, which she will remember for the rest of her life. Really, what *have* they done?

Iris and Eugene stare at each other across a wooden barrel.

'Barbara had no idea,' says Iris.

'Which leaves us with Hugh.'

Iris's thoughts go to Lana, in her misguided dress, and her chest feels tight.

'I'm not convinced,' she says. 'Did you see his face when Barbara said that thing about Bruce . . .' Iris cannot say the word 'screwing' out loud, '. . . about him having an affair with Jean? He looked as if someone had taken a very big straw and sucked all the air out of him.'

Then who? The police would not have reopened the investigation into Jean's death unless they thought someone had harmed her. Nell comes, unbidden, into Iris's mind, her face closed up with whatever it is she is holding back.

Luisa Morales emerges through the open French doors that lead from the house, her dark glasses on the top of her head, looking cool and beautiful and nothing like the nervous woman in the van who'd begged Iris not to say anything. Moments later, Joe also comes strolling around the side passageway of the house, hands thrust determinedly into pockets.

It's a good job Iris feels nothing at all, she tells herself, ignoring the stabbing jolt of pain behind her ribs.

Behind them, by the makeshift stage, Isabella has led Barbara away. No doubt the doctor has been recalled with his magic black bag. Bruce is being treated by the men in suits and Iris is horrified to notice one of them has used Jean's scarf to staunch the bleeding from his boss's nose. Until now, Jean has been an abstract figure in Iris's mind – the two-dimensional woman gazing out from the front of a magazine or a film poster. This is the first time she truly feels the loss of her, all that vitality channelled into a vividly coloured scarf now soaked with blood. Something of this must be going through Eugene's mind because he strides over and snatches it from the man's hand, leaving him too surprised to react. When he reappears, his eyes are blurry behind his spectacles.

'Are you all right, Iris?' Joe materialises next to her, and yet again Iris imagines how it would feel to lean her head on his shoulder, where his white shirt sticks to the skin underneath. She forces herself to picture him with Luisa, doing whatever it was they were doing out there in the shadows, and angles her body away from him.

'Perfectly fine, thank you.'

The wedding party is breaking up, guests herded away by Bruce's besuited men. Iris thinks anxiously of Isabella and Meredith. All the money spent. And it ends like this, in blood and scandal.

The family starts to drift over. Iris scrambles to her feet to give Lana and Faye some privacy, only for Lana to ask her to please stay. 'While there are still guests here who want to stare at me as if I am some exhibit in a zoo, it would be so nice to have people around me who are – well, not friends; I know that – but at least not strangers either.'

What can she do but sit back down, feeling awkward and sorry for this girl with her badly chosen dress and her unreadable expression? Faye looks even more insubstantial than usual, inhabiting her chair like a ghost.

Connie and Meredith approach, the former with her arm firmly looped through the arm of the latter, as if she might otherwise take flight. Connie's face has been wiped clear of her usual smile, giving her a sunken expression that makes her seem at once ten years older. In contrast, Meredith seems overly animated, her widely stretched eyes darting from one face to the next.

Eugene stands at the makeshift bar, mixing cocktails as Eddie and Nell arrive. Eddie glowers at Joe and Eugene and refuses to look at Iris at all. 'Surely it's time for you three to just fuck off?'

'Enough, Eddie,' says Connie, and she is not smiling.

'I invited them to stay,' says Lana, staring levelly at Eddie. Iris understands, with a fizzing of hope, that it is a challenge. Lana's marriage has given her status here in this family, which she lacked before.

'You're such a bore sometimes, Eddie,' says Nell, detaching herself from him in order to squeeze in next to Iris, who is only relieved that her brother cannot now take that place.

'If no one else will say it, I will,' says Eddie, looking around to make sure they are not overheard. 'Today proves that Bruce Bonini did something to Jean. She was pregnant with his baby – don't say I didn't warn you all that she was the type – and told him she wouldn't leave Dad and he lost his temper.'

While Lana and Faye exclaim, Iris exchanges glances with Eugene. She is no fan of Bruce, but doesn't the 'Hugh is going to go crazy enough to kill me' message Dwight Wilson handed Iris through the car window last night point to Hugh being the primary suspect? Aren't they morally obliged to produce it? Clearly Eugene agrees, because he coughs and says: 'We should probably let you all know that there's a note.'

His huge eyes cast around behind those round glasses to see the effect of his words, and Iris briefly wonders if he is driven as much by curiosity to observe their reactions as by thoughts of justice or truth.

The provenance of the note must now be explained and the note itself produced.

'It's definitely Jean's writing,' says Meredith, pale even for her.

Lana picks it up, and Iris could cry when she sees how the worn piece of paper shakes in the girl's hand, that damning 'Hugh is going to go crazy enough to kill me' so clearly legible in her mother's careless scrawl.

For a moment it all hangs there in the heavy night air. The implications of it. The reverberations from it. Those childlike penned loops form a tourniquet around Iris's heart, so heaven knows what effect they must be having on Jean's daughter.

The silence is broken by a shout from inside the house, followed by a cacophony of voices. Bruce emerges, blood still caked on his face, crashing through the doors from the salon, the raised worm of outrage once again throbbing under the skin of his forehead. To Iris's horror, he heads straight for her. She focuses on his nose, normally so delicately formed, now splayed across his face.

'Who are you working for? I'll ask you again.' There are no niceties.

'I told you. Mr Sturrock—'

'And Mr Underwood. What kinda idiot do you think I am, Miss Bailey?'

'I don't know what—'

'The CIA don't have no jurisdiction here. You got no protection. I got every right to sell whatever I damn choose to whomever I damn choose. I know you were in my room. I know you stole my key. So where the hell are they?'

His voice is so quiet, but tight, as if there is a far louder voice inside straining to burst free, the broadening of his accent the only overt giveaway that there is something very wrong. She sees the toll it takes, this self-control, in the set of his jaw and the white line around his pressed lips.

Now Iris understands. The storeroom full of weapons. The key stolen from her room.

Her thoughts fly to the memory of Luisa Morales in her black glasses, her terror at being seen in the van outside, the man loading boxes into the back, her urgent need to see Joe. Now it falls into place. She remembers how Joe had sat up straighter when she talked about what she'd seen in Bruce's study. Was it he who took the key from her room? Her eyes swing towards him, just as Nell squares up to Bruce.

'What are you saying? There's clearly been some mistake. Iris doesn't work for . . .'

'Ask her where she was during the speeches.'

'You're being ridiculous.'

Only the darkening of his skin gives him away. Such an iron grip he has on himself.

'Ask her.'

'I was here, watching.' She remembers something. 'I was sketching the whole time.' She fetches her sketchbook.

Connie snatches the book from her and begins to leaf through. 'Well, now Bruce, it's all here. Barbara with that scarf. And here's Hugh, kinda blurry, so he must have been moving quickly and . . . Oh my, he really did hit you hard.'

'And I guess you wouldn't know either,' Bruce continues, as if Connie hasn't spoken, his gaze still fixed on Iris, 'how the American government comes to know I'm financing this wedding? I just had a call from my guys back in California to say they've been sniffing around, asking questions about where the money is coming from.'

Iris shakes her head slowly.

'This is ridiculous,' Nell interjects. 'I met Iris in London. She was working as a secretary and sketching at parties. She's never even been out of England before. I doubt you could find anyone less likely to work for the CIA.'

For the first time, Iris sees a glimmer of what could be doubt in Bruce's dark eyes.

'Then you won't object to me searching your room.'

She objects very much. Is on the point of retorting that she knows very well he has searched it before, looking for the key – the same key that Joe Garston stole. And while she's at it, she could ask him if he didn't send someone that very morning to wait for her outside it, to scare her into backing off. That brush of a sleeve as she fell down the narrow stairs. Her fingers go to her arm and she picks at the fresh scab.

'Not at all.'

The whole scene with Bruce cannot have lasted more than a few minutes, but Iris feels, watching him walk off in the direction of the guest house with two of his men, as if she has run the longest race of her life. Joe, who has been looking stricken throughout this exchange, clears his throat as if he is about to speak, but she silences him with a slight shake of the head. Whatever it is he is about to say about Luisa Morales and Bruce's depleted weapons store can wait. She does not want to hear his explanations or apologies here. Not now. Not in front of these people.

She notices Hugh has joined them. It is something novel, the idea of Hugh Hardman slipping unobserved into a gathering, not expecting the assembly to automatically reshape itself with himself at the centre of it.

'He really oughta sack whoever has been feeding him this baloney,' says Nell. 'The idea that one of us is sending back information to the CIA. As if any of us had the first idea Bruce was paying for the whole shebang.' Her voice tails off when she sees how intently Iris is staring at Lana.

'What?' she asks, looking from one to the other. 'What am I missing?'

Suddenly, Hugh has Lana by the hand and is pulling her urgently away, gesturing with his other hand, knuckles grazed red and raw, for Iris to follow. She hears Eddie behind. 'Will someone tell me what the hell is going on?'

The swimming-pool area is still teeming with uniformed staff bustling around collecting champagne flutes and highball glasses, so instead Hugh leads them around to the other side of the house, where Iris has never been before and where there is a fenced-off area criss-crossed with washing lines, some already laden with the white tablecloths from the dining-room buffet.

'Explain,' he says to Lana, dropping her hand.

'I don't know what you . . .' Lana begins, stopping when Hugh steps in front of her and grabs the tops of her arms so she cannot look away.

'This morning you come to me quizzing me about Bruce financing the wedding, and now suddenly the government is on his case, asking where the money is coming from. Coincidence? I don't think so. So explain,' he says again.

Lana closes her eyes. Sighs. Then glances behind her, as if checking they cannot be overheard.

'The CIA came to see me around a year ago while I was in drama school. They wanted a way to get to Bruce, and they knew how close the two of you are.'

'So they already knew your college had invited me to talk there?'

Lana shakes her head. 'It was my suggestion that the college invite you. I was on the Events Committee. They didn't know in college who my mother was. I always used my father's name, Mickelson. That's the way I wanted it. The two men who came to see me were very sweet. Paternal, you know. They talked a lot about duty and how important it is for us to keep control over what happens here in Cuba, it being so close and all. At first, they just wanted me to see if I could rebuild a relationship with you, as a stepdaughter I mean, and get myself invited down here to Havana to report back on Bruce. Then when things went . . . the way they did . . . well, it was even better.'

'You mean when you pretended to fall in love with me?'

Lana looks flushed, yet there is something vaguely triumphant about her. Hugh, meanwhile, seems diminished. He drops his arms and his tall, broad frame curves over itself in a C shape. He looks, for once, like a man well into middle age.

'But why, Lana?' Iris wants to know. She'd guessed, as soon as Bruce accused her of telling the CIA that he was bankrolling the wedding, that the real leak had come from Lana. The girl must have phoned directly after their talk this morning. 'Jean left you well off, didn't she? Why did you agree?'

'Revenge,' says Hugh bitterly. 'That's the only reason. You never forgave me for not taking you and Faye on when Jean died.'

'There was an element of that, to start with. Grandma didn't have the first clue how to cope with two grieving girls. We thought you loved us.' She gazes at him levelly, until it is Hugh who looks away. 'And I guess I felt important for the first time in my life. Those men came to *me*. It didn't really seem like such a big deal. Come here. Report back on how Bruce does business. They have so many other people here in Havana. I was just a small cog.'

'But the marriage, Lana,' Iris bursts out. 'Why did you go through with it? Surely they must have offered to get you out?'

Lana nods, and Iris notices how her eyes slide away from Hugh to a point on the floor. 'Something changed,' she says softly. 'The anger went. And one day I realised I was looking forward to seeing Hugh. Spending time with him.'

'And so he gets what he wanted all along – Manderley.' Iris knows she shouldn't say it, but she is so angry suddenly. That Lana, for all she thought she was acting for herself, has once again allowed herself to be manipulated. That Hugh will, as always, come out on top.

'Not exactly.'

From the corner of her eye, Iris notices Hugh's head, bowed up until now, shoot sharply up at Lana's reply.

'I know you think me naïve, Iris, but I am not entirely idiotic. I have made over Manderley and the bulk of Mommy's estate to Faye.'

There is a smile playing around the corners of Lana's

mouth, and Iris feels a twinge of optimism. She sneaks a look at Hugh. For all he appears shell-shocked, there is a look in his eyes that Iris hasn't seen before, certainly not in relation to his new bride. It is only as she withdraws to rejoin the others, leaving the newly-weds to themselves, that she manages to identify it: admiration.

25

IRIS RESUMES HER seat, ignoring the sea of questioning glances. 'You'll have to ask your father,' she says, when Eddie demands to know what they've been talking about. She will not look at anyone. Will not give Lana away.

'You could ask him about *that* while you're at it,' says Joe, indicating Jean's note, which lies on the table. Joe's voice is light and even, but there is no doubting the hostility that flows between him and Eddie Hardman.

'What's that supposed to mean?'

'I should have thought it was self-explanatory.' Joe picks the note up and reads: 'Hugh is going to go crazy enough to kill me.'

'What's that? Why will I go crazy?'

Hugh and Lana stand on the threshold of the terrace, their heads framed by the Havana night.

'What are you reading from?' Hugh asks, holding out his hand. Joe hesitates before handing over the creased paper.

'But this is Jean's handwriting,' says Hugh, frowning. Then his face hardens as realisation dawns. 'A present from Dwight Wilson, I presume.' He drops Lana's hand, which Iris hadn't even noticed he was holding. Takes a deep breath.

'I know how bad this looks,' he says, not addressing anyone in particular. 'I'm not even going to try to convince you that I don't know what the hell Jean was talking about. But that's the God's honest truth.'

Lana says nothing, only fixes her new husband with that steady grey gaze. The tension is unendurable.

'Aw, for chrissakes, it's not what it seems, okay?'

Everyone swings to face Nell, who is standing in the shadows against the wall of the house, her gold dress shimmering in the gloom. She holds her long necklace in her hand, running the ends through her fingers, and Iris realises it is the first time she has ever seen her look properly nervous.

'Care to tell us how exactly you know this?' asks Meredith.

'Because I was with Jean when she wrote that note. I went in to see her about a week before we went on the boat. I'd only just started working as her assistant, after Pop practically begged her to find me a job, but it wasn't going so well. You know how she could be.' She looks around, as if for endorsement. 'So she called me to the house in Beverly Hills. Pop was away. Even for Jean, she was a mess. She told me she was pregnant and she didn't want it. She asked me to get her some pills to make it go away. She said she couldn't do it herself in case it got back to Pop or anyone from the studio. 'Course, I said no. I'm not some drugs whore. But then she said if she had the baby, Hugh would have another heir and Eddie and I would be written out of his will. How was I to know she'd already changed her will and Pop was broke? I'll say one thing, she was a damn sight better actress than I ever thought.'

'You must have known it couldn't be mine,' says Hugh. 'I'd been away two months by then.'

'She told me she'd flown to Arizona for a weekend to surprise you,' said Nell.

'And they say romance is dead,' Eddie sneers.

'So I got the pills, pretended they were for me,' Nell goes on, as if her brother hasn't spoken. 'The doc said they're usually used for malaria. Nasty things. Give you blurred vision and weird thoughts. Nausea. Gut ache. You know the kinda thing. And right after we got on the boat I took them to her. She was sitting in her cabin and she had that notebook open and a pen in her hand. She'd been in the middle of writing to someone – maybe Cyp is a nickname.' Iris's eyes swivel to Eugene, as thoughts shuffle around inside her head like a deck of cards. That letter crammed into his billfold. *Dear Uncle Cyp.* A suspicion takes form in her mind that would explain what Eugene is doing here, a man of his reputation reporting on a wedding. He knew her. Jean. He knew her well enough that she gave him a nickname and wrote her letters. But there is no time to dwell on this startling new information, because Nell is still talking:

'So she'd already written that line at the top to this Cyp person – *Hugh is going to go crazy* – but when I gave her the instructions that the quack doctor gave me, she just wrote them down on the same page: you know how lazy she was. Dosages, you know. That's what all the numbers are. Then I tried to warn her what he'd said about overdosing, how much would be fatal.'

'*Enough to kill me*,' says Eugene, who is staring at the note, unaware of Iris's scrutiny. 'So the second line doesn't actually have anything to do with the line above it?'

'I thought the game was up when Barbara found the pills in Jean's cabin one afternoon with my name on the label. You should have heard the two of them rowing when Jean wouldn't let her take any. She thought Jean was keeping the good stuff for herself.'

'So where is the bottle now?'

'Jimmy Palicki picked it up,' says Nell. 'He was worried it might look bad for me, my name being on the bottle and all, so he brought it to Mama. Showed up one night out of the blue. You know she got him the job in the first place. He's a neighbourhood kid. So then I had to explain it all to Mama.'

'Which did *not* sit well with me, as you can imagine,' says Connie, her fingers fluttering around the little cross she wears around her neck. 'I don't know what Jean was *thinking*, getting Nellie involved in something like that.'

'Did Jimmy Palicki tell you anything else?' Lana asks Connie, inscrutable as ever.

'I don't know what you mean.'

'Only that it's quite the coincidence that the investigation into what happened to Mommy is reopened again right when Hugh and I announce we're getting married. Almost like someone wanted to stop the wedding going ahead. Everyone knows the most likely reason for them to do that is that Palicki finally came forward and told the police something new.'

'Oh, for heaven's sake. As if I'm likely to implicate my own daughter in something like this.'

'No,' says Lana, 'but what if he had some other new information?'

'I've never heard anything more ridiculous. Why on earth would I want to stop the wedding?'

Lana says nothing, just returns Connie's gaze coolly and levelly until the older woman looks away, her face pink and mottled.

'Perhaps he told them about the blood on the deck,' muses Eugene.

'What blood?' comes the chorus of voices.

Iris looks over sharply. Did it slip out accidentally? Eugene, looking like nothing so much as an overgrown schoolboy in a too-grown-up suit, is giving nothing away.

'I looked everywhere for that bottle.'

For a moment they all look at one another, unsure where this new voice has come from, then Iris realises it is Faye who has spoken. Faye, who so rarely speaks in company, who has listened to everything curled up in a chair, scratching at her arm with a piece of bamboo that had been woven in to create the bar.

'You knew about the pills?' asks Lana.

'I knew Mommy was taking something that was making her ill, and I saw *her* name on the label.' Faye nods her head towards Nell. 'I thought she was trying to kill her. Mommy could hardly walk straight after she'd taken one of those. I used to follow her around the deck sometimes, to make sure she didn't wobble off. Until she screamed at me to leave her alone.'

All of it said in that breathy voice that is more air than words. 'After she died, I tried to find the bottle to prove it was Nell, but it had gone. And when I told the police, they didn't listen. I was only just thirteen and already with a psychiatric file as thick as your arm.'

'Is that why you wrote me that note, Faye?' asks Iris slowly. '*Nell kills people.*'

The girl nods. 'I wanted to protect you.'

'From me?' Nell is shaking her platinum curls, as if she's never heard anything so preposterous. 'Charming, I'm sure.'

'Well, someone did kill her,' says Faye defensively. 'Otherwise, the police wouldn't be asking all their questions again. Someone made those bruises on her wrists. Those marks on her poor head. If it wasn't Nell, who was it?'

'Me. It was me.'

Meredith's voice cracks, although she remains sitting ramrod straight, that bouffant hair like a hard black halo around her face.

'Except I didn't kill her. She did it herself. You know my Jean, no one ever could get her to do something she didn't want to do. Now, can that be an end to it?'

But of course it cannot be, because they are all watching Meredith with their lips parted and their eyes wide, and Iris is thinking, as no doubt they all are, *Well, this is odd*, and only after that initial detached surprise does the emotional backlash arrive. The exclamations and the questions and the building clamour, and here is Meredith, finally stripped back and laid bare, without even her silver cigarette holder to hide behind.

'She came to see me.' Resigned now. Monotonal. 'That night. After everyone had gone to bed.'

'Meredith, you don't have to say anything more.' Lana's voice is terse.

'I want to say more. I've been wanting to say it for five years. Christ, but she was in a state. Oh, my sweet God, was she in a state. She'd had a fight with him. Bruce. She was shaking all over. She was terrified of that man, by the end.

That's why she could never have his baby. She'd told him again that it was over between them, but he threatened to expose her to the press. I don't believe he cared a hoot about her. It was all about keeping control.'

Iris struggles to keep up. So when Dwight Wilson overheard Jean saying, 'It's over,' the night she died, she'd been talking to Bruce, not Hugh?

'Jean was a fighter. Well, you all know that. But that night, she was broken. I hadn't seen her like that in years. She felt so alone. I think that was the thing.'

'She had friends, though, who loved her. This Cyp,' Eugene bursts out. Meredith glances over in surprise.

'I could tell right away she'd taken something bad,' she continues. 'She was slurring her words and she said she felt sick and, finally, I got her to admit she'd taken those pills. To bring on the miscarriage. I knew she was in a bad way, but you've got to believe me, if I'd known she was dying, I'd have got help. Instead, I took her out on to the deck, to get some air, you know. I thought that might revive her. And, at first, it seemed to. I sat on the seat and she lay curled up with her head in my lap and she was calmer. She went to sleep. I was stroking her hair. It was like she was a child again. I thought maybe this was it, all our differences were behind us. I was happy, you know. Can you believe it? So then, after a while, I was getting cold, but I didn't want to move her, and I guess we must have both dozed, but then I woke up and could feel something warm and wet in my lap, and when I looked down I saw Jean had vomited and I knew instantly that she was . . . well, she was dead.'

Meredith has taken off the high-heeled shoes she has been wearing for the wedding, and Iris sees how she is tapping one of her surprisingly long, bony feet on the floor, softly but persistently.

'Mommy was with you when she died?' Faye asks, her eyes huge in her thin face.

'That doesn't make any sense,' says Eddie. 'What about the marks and bruising on her wrists? Those cuts on her head? Who are you covering up for, Meredith?'

'Oh, grow up, Eddie. I'm not covering for anyone. When I realised Jean was dead, I went into shock. She was my only child. I loved her. Even when I didn't like her. Lord knows how long I stayed, cradling her head in my lap. Then I got to think about Lana and Faye. It's a crime, don't forget, what Jean tried to do. I thought how terrible it was going to be when it came out that their mother had died trying to get rid of her own baby. Then I thought of how much they adored Hugh and how dreadful it would be when it came out that the baby wasn't even his. I worried they'd be left destitute. Jean never told me she'd changed her will, so I was thinking about how Hugh would be entitled to all of it and how her girls would be left without a cent, as well as without a mother. I panicked.'

'Oh my God.' Here is Faye, realisation dawning on her just seconds before Iris herself cottons on to what Meredith has done. 'You pushed her over the side, didn't you?'

Meredith lets out a strangled sound at her granddaughter's blunt words.

'You have to understand how it was, Faye. I wasn't thinking straight. I wanted to protect you and your sister. God knows, I haven't always been a model grandmother, but I've always, always, had your best interests at heart. When I stood up, Jean fell on to the floor. I tried to lift her back up on to the bench, but she was too heavy, so I picked her up by the wrists and dragged her along the deck to where the steps were – remember? – that led up to the sun deck? And I somehow managed to pull her up those one at a time.'

Iris, whose initial shock has gradually given way to a profound pity, tries not to imagine how Jean's gleaming blonde head might have bumped on every step, how the blood would have formed itself into dark bruises under the pale skin of her wrists. Tries not to picture how a sixty-something woman might break as she sent her own daughter into that terrible, black sea.

'I talked to her the whole time,' Meredith says, and there's a pleading note in her voice. When Iris looks up and sees how her tightly stretched cheeks are slick with tears, she feels something caving inside her. 'I told her she was loved. It's important you girls know that, your mother knew she was loved.'

'She wasn't dead, though.' There is nothing triumphant about Hugh's rebuttal. If anything, he sounds defeated. Flat. 'Didn't you read the coroner's report?'

'None of us read it,' says Lana. 'Not the details of it. It would have been too upsetting.'

Meredith says nothing, standing so still that, if it wasn't for the lone teardrop descending slowly on her face, she might be a statue, made from the very marble of which the Boninis have made such good use.

'There was seawater in her lungs,' says Eddie, watching Meredith closely for her reaction. 'And traces of foam in her mouth, which means she died from drowning.'

'That isn't possible,' says Meredith, and it is as if every tiny bone in her bolstered face gives way at once.

'Oh, I'm afraid it is,' says Eddie. 'Your daughter was still alive when you threw her overboard.'

The soft, rhythmic thud of a moth's wings beating against a lantern's paper casing breaks the silence that follows Eddie's remark. Then Hugh does something surprising. He walks over to the table where Lana has seated herself on the outskirts of the group and crouches down so he is on her level. Then he reaches out to touch her face.

'Are you all right, darling?' The full force of his blue-eyed Hughness is trained on her.

Iris expects Lana to crumble. But instead she gets to her feet. 'The thing is, I knew.'

'What?'

'Oh, not about Jean being alive when she went over, but all the rest of it. I knew. Does that surprise you, Hugh? Just how many secrets I've kept from you?'

Finally, Lana's face is alive, and Iris wishes more than anything that she could draw her now, with all of her on display.

'I saw the blood on Meredith's shoes the morning after, when we were all searching for Jean, and on the deck. I washed it off. I didn't know what else to do. I didn't want anything bad to happen to Meredith. I thought she'd snapped. Mom could do that to people. I thought they'd argued, the two of them. Tussled. And Jean had gone over. I knew she'd been drinking heavily. Afterwards, I put it out of my mind. I kept away from Meredith as much as I could and tried to tell myself it never happened.

'It's what I've always had to do – build compartments inside my mind so I can shut away my own feelings and get

331

on with looking after everyone else. Jean. Faye. Meredith. You. But, you know, I'm sick of holding myself in check. Sick of going along with things I don't want.'

'Like this wedding,' says Hugh quietly.

The air hisses with the collective intake of breath.

Still crouched on the floor in front of his new bride, Hugh looks bewildered. Iris senses the power shifting between them in this dark Cuban night.

'You're right,' says Lana eventually. 'I didn't want this wedding. But I want you. I *choose* you.'

26

THEY ARE GATHERED outside on the driveway. The house behind them is sporadically lit up, but the guests are long departed and the trees that screen the house from the road in front loom dark against the inky sky.

No one speaks. In fact, surprisingly few words have been exchanged in the last hour while they have packed up their things and made their final checks of their rooms, looking under beds and in drawers, making sure nothing has been left behind. It is as if the evening's revelations have shocked the words from their mouths and wiped their minds clear of thought. Only the needles of fear pressing into the base of Iris's spine and the cigarette butts on the floor of her room left by Bruce's men remind her that this is all real. The guns. The CIA, the rebels. All of it real.

The night air is still warm, but for once not uncomfortably so as Iris closes her eyes and breathes Havana in for the last time. The stillness of this night in this place, combined with the sense of life throbbing around the edges, the awareness that all around them the heartbeat of this city pulses on in the rhythm of the music and the dancing in the clubs and the catcalls of the men who lean up against the buildings or sprawl on the wall of the Malecón, the clicking of the women's heels on the city streets, the howling of the thin cats that roam the narrow alleyways of the old town. She breathes in also the change that is coming, the awareness of which is present in every atom, in every particle of that volatile city. And she breathes in the last of its smells – eucalyptus, plantains frying, petrol, cigar smoke, women's perfume so strong it remains in a room long after the woman herself has left it.

This is what she will remember, she tells herself. Not Bruce Bonini, or the cold dread that he is not yet finished with her.

A door opens somewhere in the back of the house and closes again with a slam, and now there comes a sense of something approaching, some energy or force that cannot be denied.

'I cannot *believe* that you are all leaving me, you genius people. No, I will not let you go, I will *throw* myself in front of the taxi to stop you.'

Isabella is doing a good job at imitating herself, but still there is a tinny note to her voice that Iris has never heard there before, as if she, too, has been hollowed out by what has happened here today.

'I'm so sorry, Isabella,' she says, finding her own voice. 'You worked so hard to make this wedding perfect, and then it was ruined.'

Isabella gapes at her. 'Are you joking me, darling? It was not ruined. It was the best of weddings. You cannot buy the kind of publicity it will get. That's good for Bruce, good for Hugh. Definitely good for me. And for all of you, too. People will talk about this wedding for years and pretend they were here. It was fabulous.'

But still there is a new brittleness about Isabella, as if someone has taken a fine sandpaper to the surface of her.

'Pop and Lana have gone on their honeymoon.' Iris hasn't even noticed Nell standing in the shadows behind Isabella. Something has happened to her. Normally, Nell shines so, but tonight she all but disappears into the gloom of the garden. 'Can you believe they actually left, after everything that's gone on?'

Iris finds she can believe it. There is something about the joint enterprise of Hugh and Lana that seems not to allow for too much introspection, some barrier the two of them seem able to construct around themselves.

'Did she and Meredith talk, at least, before they left?' asks Eugene, the lights from the house glinting off his glasses.

'Yes, they talked. Faye, too. It was strained, but then their relationship has never been easy. But there were hugs at the end of it, so that has to be a good thing, right?'

'What will happen to Meredith?' Joe has been so silent up until now, standing off on his own on the outskirts of the group, that his voice comes as a shock. Iris has been determinedly not thinking about him and how, in just a few hours' time, she will say goodbye and never see him again. She has definitely been avoiding thinking about Peter, who will be waiting to meet her from the train station when she arrives back in England the day after tomorrow, following a brief stopover in New York and then further refuelling stops in Newfoundland and Ireland. She had tried to dissuade him from coming, only to capitulate reluctantly when he complained, 'You'll have been gone over a week by then. Anyone would think you weren't looking forward to seeing me.'

'I don't know,' Nell says. 'I guess it kinda depends on y'all.'

Iris doesn't need to look to know she is addressing Eugene directly. The reporter doesn't reply, but as he shifts uneasily from foot to foot the light catches his face and Iris sees how troubled he looks. She remembers the letter she'd glimpsed. *Dear Uncle Cyp*. Whatever Eugene's connection with Jean, she has a feeling he won't be seeking to make money out of her death.

'But surely someone will . . . Eddie will . . .' says Iris.

'Eddie will do what he's told. I know you think him a bully, Iris, and Christ knows, you have the right, but at heart he's just a lost little boy who can't figure out how to make his daddy love him. Once you know that about Eddie, you can keep him in line.'

A sudden blinding light comes from the front door, which has been flung open to reveal Barbara Bonini standing unsteadily in the doorway in her black dress and heels.

'You gotta get outta here. My husband is on the phone to that weaselly police-chief friend of his. Sounds like they're on the way over.'

Iris's stomach twists like a helix. Brown shoes swinging from the bottom branches of the tree.

'The bastard taxi is late,' says Isabella.

'Raúl will take us.'

Barbara shouts to Raúl, who has been observing them this whole time from a distance. Iris thinks he will not respond, will ignore her, as he did on the beach, and continue his leaning and listening and smoking. But finally, he straightens. Saunters slowly over.

'You gotta drive to the airport straight away.' Raúl looks at her, impassive. 'There will be four passengers.'

'But there are only three . . .' Iris falls silent as she notices the luggage in the doorway, including Barbara's precious black medicine bag.

'Like I say, there will be four of us,' Barbara repeats. And now it seems Raúl understands and there is a softening of his expression as he nods just once and begins loading Barbara's bags into the car. They are not so dissimilar, it occurs to Iris, both of them manipulated by Bruce. Barbara has decided to join their flight to New York, she tells them. She's going home to Hell's Kitchen. No one asks if she will be coming back again.

Engulfed by Isabella, Iris inhales her exotic scent, glad she is not saying goodbye for ever. Isabella is orchestrating a big party in Wiltshire in a couple of months' time and has invited Iris to draw there, for all she calls it *thees Weeltshire*, as if suspicious as to whether such a place exists. Nell is harder to leave, even though Iris is aware of the clock ticking down and the others waiting in the car, and she has one eye on the gate, half expecting to see the chrome bumper of Captain Diaz's sleek black car glinting in the moonlight.

'I'm so sorry for how things turned out, but so happy I met you,' Nell says in Iris's ear.

Iris's heart is too heavy for her to speak.

As she turns to get into the car a beam of dazzling light blinds her. She stands blinking, only recognising the smell of Bruce Bonini's cologne when it is too late to move. With the torch light angled away from him, Bruce's eyes are black holes in the pale moon of his face.

'Your friends can go, but I'm afraid you must stay, Miss Bailey.'

'But why? I haven't done anything.'

Iris's voice is shrill. From the corner of her eye, she sees a struggle going on in the back of the car. Joe trying to get out and Eugene blocking his way.

'Some very valuable things have been stolen from me. Things that were already promised to some very important people. And you were the only person who knew where they were and how to unlock the door. Please don't pretend you weren't in my office that day I saw you. The key disappeared right after you left.'

A muffled shout comes from the back of the car: Joe's voice. 'Let go of me.' In the darkness where one of Bruce's men stands, Iris hears a metallic click. The moonlight reflects off steel, sickly white. Iris finds she cannot breathe, cannot swallow. She will be left here. And she will die. Human life here is cheap, Raúl said. She is a nobody. Why should her life be worth any more than the unseen man with the scuffed brown shoes hanging from the tree?

'Ledder go.'

Barbara has got out of the front seat of the car and is facing her husband, who barely glances in her direction.

'You go,' he says quietly. 'Visit your mother.'

'I will, but she comes too. Don't forget, sweetheart, I been with you from the beginning. I know things. I know plenty. I know you been supplying those boys in the mountains with the same weapons they've been using against your friends in power. You think Batista and his pals are gonna take kindly to that?'

Bruce's face is unreadable in the semi-light.

'I know you,' Barbara repeats. 'I know what your father used to do to you and your brother when you were a kid. Everyone in the neighbourhood knew it.'

Havana holds its breath in the breezeless air. Then Barbara says in a low voice, 'Geddin the car, Irene.'

Iris looks at Bruce. For a moment, she wavers, unsure her legs will hold her. Then she stumbles forward towards the open back seat and hands reach out to pull her inside.

Barbara climbs back into the passenger seat. Still, Bruce does not move.

'Drive,' Barbara tells Raúl. He sits as if he hasn't heard, looking ahead.

Now Bruce comes to life and starts towards the car. He gestures at Raúl, flicking his hand to tell him to get out. And maybe it is this that does it, this casual flick, or maybe it was Raúl's intention the whole time to snap on the engine and throw the car into gear and roar out of the gate just as Bruce's fingertips touch the door handle.

Iris's last view of her host is that small mouth opened in a circle of surprise just about the size of the barrel of a gun.

As they drive they check behind to see if the police are following them, and even when they pull up outside the airport Iris has a moment of blind fear, wondering if there will be an ambush, Captain Diaz appearing through the knots of suited businessmen and women with shopping bags. But as they get out of the car there is no sign.

Though they have talked about it in the car, Iris is still struggling to understand the scene back there on the driveway, between Barbara and Bruce. Can Bruce really be selling weapons to both the rebels and the government?

Surely one has to pick a side in a country like this? But Joe had explained that even the CIA were making deals with both sides up until recently, and, as he pointed out, Bruce is a businessman. The rebels, despite being camped out in the mountains, have money behind them, courtesy of Batista's predecessor, who is currently in exile in Miami, and using funds he creamed off from the Cuban treasury to bankroll an opposition he hopes will restore him to power. In the absence of any internal moral framework, Bruce will sell to the highest bidder.

Iris's heart is pounding as they walk through the glass doors of the terminal. Once, a child screams behind her and she stops stock still with her hand on her chest, waiting for the tap on her shoulder, the sight of Captain Diaz's pencil moustache. Only once they get through the Cubana Airlines check-in desk does she dare to breathe normally.

'Can I talk to you a moment, Iris?' Joe grips her arm, holding her back while the other two walk on. Iris allows herself to be led off to the side.

Joe lets go of her arm. Leans against the wall of the terminal. Lights a cigarette with hands that won't stop shaking.

'I'm so sorry I put you in danger, Iris. You've gotta believe me, I never imagined Bonini would think you had anything to do with it.'

He stops. Breathes heavily.

'I thought I was resigned to weddings and fashion shoots. I told myself I was better off. At least I couldn't get anyone else killed, taking pictures of dresses and flowers. But since I arrived here and saw how things are, I had this notion to go to the mountains and find Castro, to photograph this revolution that's coming. You must have felt it, Iris, the energy in the air here? Don't you want to be part of it? Then, when you told me about Bonini's hidden cache of weapons . . .'

'. . . You thought it was the perfect bargaining chip to get Castro to agree.'

Joe nods.

'And Luisa Morales?'

'Is probably the bravest person I ever met. She works secretly for the Rebel Army. Can you imagine the courage it takes to go against your family and everything and everyone you know? To risk going to prison, or something much worse, because your conscience tells you it's the right thing to do?' His admiration is a knife pressing against Iris's ribs. Then he sighs. 'But there was never anything between us.' His eyes, locked on to Iris's, are soft and pleading, and when Iris asks him about what happened in that cupboard at the yacht club, she finds her own voice unsteady.

'I went to tell her to call the operation off. When I saw how frightened you were that someone had been in your room, I couldn't bear it.'

'But she persuaded you otherwise.'

'She told me how things are. You know how most Cuban children don't go to school, Iris? And their parents labour in poverty their whole lives because foreign corporations own all the land. What kind of life is that? Luisa and I were talking in the corridor and we heard someone coming and panicked. Then, when we realised we were about to be caught, it's all I could think of doing. I couldn't look at you afterwards. I wanted so badly to tell you the truth.' He sounds so sincere, his voice breaking at the edges, and she feels that hard rock she's been carrying around in the pit of her stomach crumbling into dust.

'I hope you at least got what you wanted out of it,' she says, trying to sound in control of herself, as if her head isn't a churning mess of thoughts and emotions.

She is gratified to see he at least looks shamefaced.

'I think so. I've been told to go back home and wait for Castro's people to contact us.'

'Us?'

'Eugene is coming with me, to do the words. I think we'll make a pretty good team.'

Iris is glad about this, at least. That Eugene will get his chance to make a difference. She starts to move away, but Joe reaches for her again.

'The truth is, Iris, ever since I first saw you, I haven't been able to stop thinking about you. Even through all the madness with meeting up with Luisa and organising the weapon heist, if I closed my eyes for a second, all I could see was you. But at the same time I knew if I tried to get close to you I'd be putting you in danger just by association.'

They regard each other in silence, until the long drawn-out moment is broken by a woman's voice crackling over a loud speaker, announcing the boarding of their flight to New York, and Eugene coming to find them.

On board the aeroplane, Iris looks for Joe, aware that these will be the last hours they can spend together and conscious of all the things they have not said, of Peter sitting like a boulder between them. Instead, Barbara pulls her down into the seat next to hers.

'I can't believe I've actually done it,' she says, opening her handbag and withdrawing a handful of pills, which she washes down with a whiskey from a passing stewardess. 'I've finally left him. And after all that, it was that easy. Get in the car, buy a ticket. *Bam, bam, bam.*' She clicks her fingers in time with her *bam*s. Iris thinks of Bruce, with his little mouth and his wealth and the unsmiling men he surrounds himself with. She does not believe it will be so easy.

'Where will you go?'

'Back to my parents' apartment. Go dancing with my sisters in the evenings. Help out in my father's hardware store.'

Iris nods, though she cannot imagine it. Still, she hopes it might be true that Barbara could find a life away from that house, that husband. Rediscover the person she was before the money and the marriage turned her into someone else. She turns around, looking for Joe and Eugene, but the air in the cabin is thick with cigarette smoke and she can't see beyond the row behind. Miraculously, she sleeps, the tensions of the day and of the days before dissolving into a tiredness that is absorbed into her very bones. And when she awakes, they are landing in Idlewild Airport.

'How long before your flight home?' asks Barbara, her voice thick with sleep and whatever was in those pink pills she took.

'Six hours. Maybe seven.'

'Poor you. It's a crummy old airport. You can't even get a decent drink.'

When she is finally reunited with Joe, his bloodshot eyes suggest he hasn't shared the luxury of sleep. His grip on her arm is tight.

'Don't go back to England,' he urges her, holding her back before she can enter the baggage hall with the others. 'Don't go back to your fiancé. Surely, if nothing else, this week has taught you what can happen if you marry the wrong person.'

'What makes you think Peter is the wrong person?' She opts for anger, because it is safer than grief.

'Because I'm the right person.'

Iris is silenced.

He runs a hand through his hair. 'Hell, Iris, I can't hardly think straight. All I know is I can't bear to leave you here. Stay with me. Marry me, if that's what it takes.'

Marry? Suddenly, Iris feels as if she cannot breathe. She remembers the kiss back there on the guest-house terrace, that sense she'd had of dissolving into the heat of him. But that isn't real, is it? Peter is real. Her parents. Not Havana, which already seems to her like something she dreamt. Not this man with his blunt, ink-smudged fingers and his way of standing so close to her it takes all her willpower not to reach out and trace the tear-shaped groove between his nose and upper lip.

'Don't be silly. I have my whole life in England.' Now that life comes to her in a series of images, like a slide show in her mind. Her bedroom back in Hemel Hempstead, the typing pool, Peter in his suit, with his hair slicked down. Still she persists: 'And what would I do here in America? Wait for you at home on my own while you go off around the world taking photographs?'

She pictures herself sitting by the door of a cramped New York flat, waiting to hear the key in the lock, jumping up to make sure her hair looks right and the dinner is perfect. And part of her would be prepared to put up with that, because behind the tiny galley kitchen there will be a bedroom where she can be alone with this man who makes her heart feel as if it is too full, simply too big to stay constrained in her chest. Then she thinks of her mother and how her whole day is pegged upon the fixed points of her father's departure for work and his return home, and she feels as if she is suffocating.

'There you are,' says Eugene, his eyes flicking from one to the other. 'Barbara is in the line for the cases. She sent me to fetch you. I think lines are quite the novelty for her. She's not quite sure how it works.'

But no one moves. With Joe's hand still pressing on her arm, Iris finally brings her gaze up to meet his.

'Are you ready, Iris?' asks Eugene gently.

She considers for a moment. Blinks. Nods. 'Ready,' she says.

Epilogue

THE ROOM IS tiny, dominated by the window, with its malfunctioning, termite-infested sash. The weak winter sun filtering through the glass reveals how badly it requires a clean. The furnishings are basic and the metal frame of the narrow bed sags in the middle under a faded eiderdown with pale pink roses. In the top-right corner above the window, a patch of black mould grows bigger every day.

To Iris, it is the most beautiful room she has ever slept in.

Outside, the wail of a police siren rises above the city noise that has become so much part and parcel of Iris's life that it no longer registers – the cry of the hot-dog vendor on the opposite corner, the hooting of car horns by the busy intersection, the screaming of the Benedettis' baby in the upstairs apartment, the clunking of the building's antiquated pipes, the myriad different sounds that make up a November afternoon in Brooklyn.

She sits in bed with her sketchbook open on her lap and the eiderdown pulled up over her legs. Despite the gurgling, clanking cast-iron radiator, the room still feels cold and damp. She resumes her sketch, an illustration to accompany a fashion feature on 'the new shape' which will go into the

February 1958 issue of *McCall's* magazine. To Iris, the new shape, which is fitted in the bodice, with a scooped neck and a skirt that flares from a slightly higher waist than before, is so similar to the old shape as to not warrant a second glance. But work is work and she cannot afford to turn it down, even though it involves drawing from photographs, which she detests. Tiny steps, she keeps telling herself.

Now comes a new sound – the *click click click* of a key turning in the front door, the upstairs baby's crying momentarily amplified as the door opens to the corridor outside, before closing again with a welcome thud. Iris puts down her pencils, raises her eyes to the door expectantly, waiting for his soft knock. The door edges open and here he is, her thoughts instantly calming at the sight of his face, which has become so dear to her.

'Oh my,' says Eugene, flopping down on to the end of her bed. 'You will not believe what just happened.'

He tells her about his day, and she laughs and eventually drifts off a little, because his days are always so eventful and so comical and, after all, today's drama is not a million miles away from yesterday's. She is thinking about Joe, who will be back from Vietnam tomorrow, or the day after that. Though the region is superficially peaceful after the upheavals of the past years, Joe believes there is a big conflict brewing between the US-supported South and the Soviet-backed North. Iris hopes to God he is wrong.

Eugene tells her about the play he is working on. The main character is a naïve young British girl set loose in Manhattan. He denies it has anything to do with her. They have never talked properly about his relationship with Jean Summers. Iris can't bring up the 'Dear Uncle Cyp' letter without admitting to snooping, and Eugene doesn't mention it. The fact he hasn't tried to write anything to cash in on the case tells her all she needs to know. Well, that and the framed photograph on the living-room wall of an elderly couple who Iris mistook at first for Eugene's grandparents, before he explained that they were a comedy act from years ago calling themselves Uncle Cyp and Aunt Sap. She'd almost asked him then, about Jean, but he'd had such a sad look on his face that she hadn't pressed it. He will tell her when he's ready.

Hanging alongside that photograph is a much larger one that shows Eugene next to a handsome giant of a man in army fatigues with a beard and cigar. The man, Castro, has his arm around Eugene's narrow shoulders and the two of them are laughing together. The photograph, taken by Joe Garston, accompanied Eugene's now iconic and award-winning feature 'Five Days with Fidel'. He says he has scratched that itch now and can go back to writing scandal and froth, but sometimes she walks in and finds him gazing at that photograph with a strange, serious look on his face. More so since news came of Luisa Morales' arrest, while trying to smuggle a deconstructed and de-activated Second World War machine gun into Havana from Miami in her shopping bags. She hasn't been heard from since.

When Iris thinks back to that strange week in Havana, it takes on the intense surreality of a fevered dream, though if she closes her eyes, she can feel the spray of the seawater over the Malecón and hear the men's whistles and the bootblack's shouts and the sound of a lone trumpet player in a white suit leaning against a wall at sunset, and feel the damp heat coming off the pavements after a downpour that burned itself out before it really began.

She hears from Nell regularly. Well, regular for Nell, which means nothing for weeks and then seven or eight letters and calls all at once. Lana and Hugh are still married, although they spend long periods apart. Faye surprised everyone by moving to Paris, where she is finally growing physically stronger. Meredith battles her demons in her own way. Nell thinks she has had another face lift, though she would never admit it. 'Her only available emotion now is surprise.' She is ill, Nell says, though she won't admit that either. She came to stay with Nell and Connie and her coughing fits kept everyone awake. Not that Nell will be living with her mother for long. She met a man on her flight back from Havana to New Orleans and they are getting married in June. She thinks he is some kind of diplomat. Though he could be a spy. She doesn't really care. She rarely mentions Eddie, and Iris never asks. He is still working for his father is all she knows. Hasn't managed to persuade anyone with money to invest in him making his own films. It's not exactly punishment for the wrongs he did her, and almost certainly to other women, too, because she knows by now that men like that have a pattern of behaviour and lack the tools to deviate from it, but it will have to do. Meanwhile, the police investigation into Jean's death has gone quiet, in the absence of any new leads.

Iris and Joe once bumped into Barbara Bonini stumbling out of the 21 Club on 52nd Street with a man who was not Bruce but might just as well have been. Same immaculate dark suit, same heavy silver cufflinks, same paper-cut smile. 'Bruce mustn't know you saw me with Lenny,' Barbara said, taking them aside. 'He'd kill me.' When she saw Iris's expression, she'd said, 'What can I say? I tried to change my life, but my sisters don't go out dancing now they've got the kiddies, and my old friends' husbands told them not to talk to me, and after two weeks at my folks' place I just about died from boredom. Until Lenny came along.'

Eugene goes into the kitchen to fix them both a Martini. Some days, Iris worries she's overstayed her welcome, but he assures her he likes having her around. 'New York can be so lonely,' he says. At first, she had laughed. After all, Eugene knows everyone and regularly has invitations to four or five different glittering events in the same evening. But the longer she is here, the more she understands how it is possible to feel on the edge of things, even when there you are right slap bang in the middle. Besides, no one was using her neglected little room before she came. It's the one room in the apartment that Eugene hadn't got around to sprucing up with the money he got from his first book. In fact, he was only using it to store his mildewed boxes of research, so she doesn't feel too much of an imposition.

Iris's eyes travel with satisfaction around her little kingdom, coming to rest on the little chest of drawers in the corner, on top of which lies a pale blue aerogramme letter, the paper so wafer thin its corners rise up in the draught from the broken sash, revealing the address written in her mother's blue, sloping writing. At least her parents are talking to her again: she must count that as a positive thing, even if the words are stilted and her mother chose to take up half the letter telling her about Peter's whirlwind marriage to a girl only just out of school. He'd invited Iris's parents, told them he didn't hold Iris's behaviour against them and in fact felt sorry for them, being 'abandoned' by their only child. Iris fears for his young bride, remembering the weight of his arm like an iron bar across her shoulders.

Iris leans back against the rickety headboard and closes her eyes to breathe it all in, the sounds and smells of New York, the unfamiliar feeling of being in exactly the place she is meant to be at this precise moment in time, the gentle but persistent vibration in the air that is her future coming towards her, throbbing with energy and possibility.

Then she sits back up, picks up her pencil and begins to draw.

Cyp

This is the second time I've started writing to you. I scribbled over the first note because I'm a damn fool. Say, wouldn't it be a fine thing if we could do the same with our lives – just start over whenever we mess up? Clean page? Only thing is, I'd be forever on page one, forever starting, never maturing, if you know what I mean.

I'm sorry about yesterday's note. Your Auntie Sap was feeling sorry for herself and needed to give herself an almighty slap.

Oh, to hell with it, though, Cyp. To hell with them all. This morning, it rained like you wouldn't believe. Outta the blue, the heavens opened up. You should have seen them all running for shelter, like when you lift up a pot in the garden and all the bugs scurry to get outta the light. (Except Barbara. You know, I think if you dropped an atomic bomb, it would still take a half-hour to get that woman moving.) Not me. I stood on the deck in that Dior silk gown I wore to the premiere of *A Different Dawn* and I threw out my arms and turned my face to the sky and opened my mouth as wide as it would go and I drank in the world, Cyp. All of it. All the shitty bits, and the bits that make you sick and tired to the very marrow of your bones, and the unexpected bits that make you feel you have electricity running through your veins, and the bits that make you wanna dance and never stop. I drank the whole fucking world, Cyp. And you know what? I still want more.

I'm sending this ashore with Jimmy, the steward, because it's Hugh's birthday today and we're having a special lobster feast on board the boat. You know, sometimes, like yesterday, I'm all boo-hoo about my life, and then I think about being a lobster plunged into boiling water and cooked alive so that we can tear it apart and pick at its flesh, and I think, fuck it, life is precious. Even when it's shit, it's precious just the same.

And here endeth my sermon.

Your Sap

Acknowledgements

There was a moment, sitting on the stone wall of the Malecón in Havana, watching the sun set over a molten sea, where I thought, 'Life really doesn't get much better than this.' I don't think I'll ever get over how lucky I am to do a job that allows me moments like that, so there are some huge, heart-felt thank-yous to be made.

First, as ever, to my brilliant agent Felicity Blunt, who read and re-read this manuscript until Havana was imprinted on her eyeballs, and then, when she couldn't read it one more time, gave it to Lisa Babalis, whose last-minute insight made it a better book. And to my American agent Deborah Schneider, who found such a lovely home at Atria for my first two outings as Rachel Rhys.

Transworld has always been the most generous of publishers and I'm so grateful to everyone there for allowing me to continue to write, which is the only thing I've ever been able to – or wanted to – do. Particular thanks go to editor Jane Lawson and publicist Alison Barrow. There's nothing these two don't know about books and I learn something new from them with every fresh publication. Thanks also to Sarah Day and Kate Samano, and to Richard Ogle for the stunning cover which transports me back to Cuba every time I look at it. A big debt of gratitude also to the sales team, who get my books into the shops and into the eyeline of more readers.

There's a character called Theresa Manuel who features indirectly in the Prologue as the wife of Antonio Manuel, the fisherman who discovers Jean's body. Theresa actually deserves a whole book to herself, according to her husband Darren, who won the bidding for a character name in the auction for CLIC Sargent – the amazing charity that supports young people with cancer and their families. Darren wrote of his wife that she is 'as beautiful to see as she is in spirit', and when I pictured Antonio out there on the still water, I imagined him thinking of his own Theresa in just such a loving way – well, once he'd got over his petty grievances.

I've long dreamed of visiting Cuba and I was utterly intoxicated by it (once I'd got over my fear of being asked to dance). My trip was vastly improved by the companionship of Roma Cartwright, who asked all the questions I was too polite to, and whose increasingly desperate attempt to buy eggs for breakfast remains one of my fondest memories. There can be few places in the world facing such hardship with such indomitable spirit and such reserves of creativity and heart and hope, so a huge thank-you goes to all the Cubans we met who made our stay so joyful and so memorable, the owners of the casas where we stayed, in particular Ana Iris, and trumpet virtuoso Julio Padron, for helping us better understand the rhythm of this magical island.

I read lots of books about Cuba before embarking on my own, and anyone who is interested in the region (or just in great literature) should do themselves a favour and read *Our*

Woman in Havana by Sarah Rainsford, *Next Year in Havana* by Chanel Cleeton and *Telex from Cuba* by Rachel Kushner. And, of course, *Our Man in Havana* by Graham Greene. There's also a ground-breaking film called *Soy Cuba* which was made shortly after the period when *Island of Secrets* is set. Its breathtaking opening sequence perfectly illustrates the contrasts and contradictions of this unique place at this particular time.

I'm lucky enough to be surrounded by supportive friends and family and I'm grateful to each and every one, even if their support didn't quite stretch to sitting through all my hundreds of Cuba photographs. (One day, I'll work out how to load them on to a slideshow and ply everyone with daiquiris and nail the door shut so there can be no escape.) My writer friends are a lifeline – literally – and I still can't believe I get to hang out with them all.

I've had so much support from bloggers and reviewers over the ten years I've been writing fiction and I never take it for granted. Nor do I ever forget that it's readers who keep the book world afloat. So to everyone who has bought my books or borrowed them from the library or reviewed them, I'm raising a large Havana Club mojito to you all. And if you want to see my slideshow, you only have to ask.

By the way:
I love connecting with readers. Sign up to my newsletter on www.tammycohen.co.uk. Or get in touch via Twitter (@MsTamarCohen), Facebook (www.facebook.com/MsTamarCohen) or Instagram (tammycohenwriter).

A DANGEROUS CROSSING
Rachel Rhys

England, September 1939
Lily Shepherd boards a cruise liner for a new life in Australia and is immediately plunged into a world of cocktails, jazz and glamorous friends. But as the sun beats down, poisonous secrets begin to surface. Suddenly Lily finds herself trapped in a ship with nowhere to go . . .

Australia, six weeks later
As the cruise liner docks, a beautiful young woman is escorted on to dry land in handcuffs. Two passengers are dead, war is declared, and Lily Shepherd's life is changed forever.

What has she done?

'An exquisite story of love, murder, adventure and dark secrets' LISA JEWELL

'Gripping and ripe with danger' *Sunday Express*

'An utter treat . . . a glorious mix of proper old-school glamour and a plot full of class war, politics and sexual tension . . . A masterful storyteller' VERONICA HENRY

A FATAL INHERITANCE
Rachel Rhys

London, 1948: Eve Forrester is trapped in a loveless marriage, in a gloomy suburb.

Out of the blue, she receives a solicitor's letter. A wealthy stranger has left her a mystery inheritance and she must travel to the French Riviera to claim it.

Eve discovers that her legacy is an enchanting villa on the sea, and suddenly life could not be more glamorous. But as she mingles with film-stars and writers, angry rivals to her fortune begin to emerge.

Alone in paradise, Eve must unlock the story behind her surprise bequest – before it's too late.

'A glorious read' MARIAN KEYES

'I completely lost myself in Rhys's lovingly evoked 1940s French Riviera and was gripped by the slow-burn mystery' LISA JEWELL

'Perfect summer reading' CLARE MACKINTOSH